VALIDE

BARBARA CHASE-RIBOUD

WILLIAM MORROW AND COMPANY, INC.
NEW YORK

Printed in the United States of America

Contents

The Characters in the Novel

The Empresses
Catherine II, the Great, Empress of all the Russias
Mihrishah, Valide, mother of Selim III
Naksh-i-dil, Valide, mother of Mahmud II

The Emperors
Sultan Abdulhamid I
Sultan Selim III, Abdulhamid's nephew
Sultan Mustafa IV, Abdulhamid's son
Sultan Mahmud II, Abdulhamid's son by Naksh-i-dil
Napoleon Bonaparte, the Sultan El Kabir

The Sultanas
Fatima Sultane, daughter of the Grand Vizier Halil Hamid
Hadidge Sultane, sister of Selim III
Esma Sultane, sister of Mahmud and Mustafa IV

The Favorites
Ali Efendi, favorite of Naksh-i-dil
Ishak Bey, favorite of Selim III
Dr. Lorenzo, favorite of Hadidge Sultane
Simon Zorich, favorite of Catherine II

The Eunuchs
The Black Eunuch, the Kizlar Aga Edris
Hitabetullah, slave of Naksh-i-dil
Geronimo Delleda, a Jesuit

The Admirals
Reis Hamidou ⎫
Hasan Gazi, Captain Pasha ⎬ the Ottoman Fleet
Huseyin Pasha Kuchuk ⎭
John Paul Jones ⎫
I. V. Hannibal ⎬ the Russian Fleet
Captain Decatur, the American Fleet

Many Turkish words and titles such as Vâlide and Nakş-i-dil have been Anglicized, some phonetically, some, like Vâlide, by eliminating unfamiliar accents. I have done this for the comfort of the English reader in full knowledge of the contradictions it imposes.

—B.C.R.

Author's Note

In homage to the stupendous lives of the real characters who pass through this novel and who have never had the right to a biography of their own.

—B.C.R.

No dwellinge house but a house of pleasure, and lykewyse a house of slaughter.
—THOMAS DALLAM, supplier
of musical instruments to
the Harem of Topkapi, 1599

Harem

1. Carriage Entrance
2. Wardrobe Room
3. Divan Room (Kubbe Alti)
4. Eunuchs' Guardroom
5. Shawl Gate
6. Passage Leading to the Screen Gate
7. Conservatory of Selim III
8. Screen Gate
9. Halberdiers' Quarters
10. Sultan's Mounting Block
11. Black Eunuchs' Mosque
12. Black Eunuchs' Baths
13. Black Eunuchs' Courtyard
14. Apartment of the Munhasip (Chief Reader)
15. Apartment of the Treasurer (Black Eunuch)
16. Quarante Courtyard
17. Black Eunuchs' Quarters
18. Black Eunuchs' Lavatories
19. Princes' School
20. Apartment of the Chief of the Black Eunuchs
21. Main Entrance to the Harem
22. Second Eunuchs' Guardroom
23. Corridor Used as a Pantry for the Royal Kitchens (situated on the right of the second enclosure)
24. Favorites' Courtyard
25. Favorites' Apartments
26. Sleeping Quarters of the Odalisques
27. Staircase Leading to the Upper Floor of the Odalisques' Building
28. Odalisques' Baths
29. Side Kitchen
30. Storeroom
31. Washhouse
32. Odalisques' Lavatories
33. Staircase Leading to the Harem's Infirmary
34. Infirmary
35. Infirmary Courtyard
36. Sleeping Quarters of the Wetnurses, etc.
37. Gate of Death
38. Sultane Valide's Courtyard
39. Throne Gate
39a. Sultan's Mounting Block
40. Corridor of the Sultane Valide's Apartments
41. Ground Floor of her Apartments
42. Valide's Bedchamber

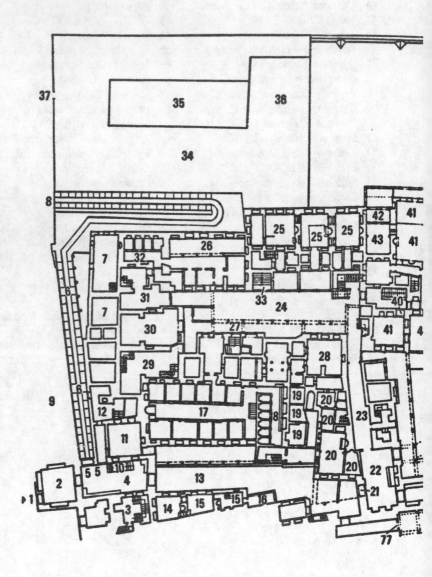

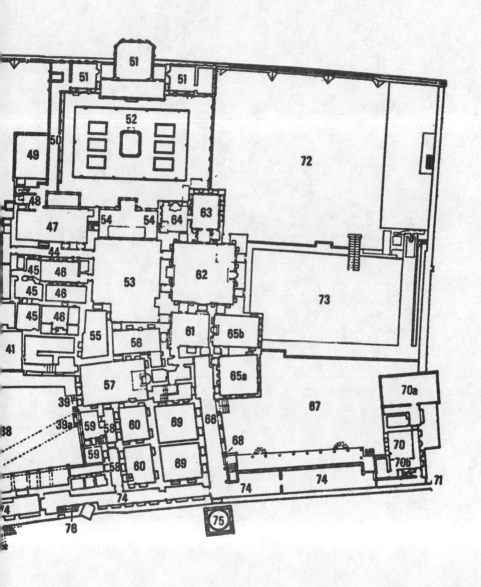

PROLOGUE

VALIDE SULTANE
·1814·

• PROLOGUE •

THE VALIDE SULTANE 1814

Constantinople, August 15, 1817

The Sultane Valide is dead. I've seen her placed in her crypt or mausoleum which she had been building for two years and that the Padishah intends to complete. I saw the coffin leave the palace. Two pages transported it in one of the Sultan's covered caïques which traversed the Bosphorus. Her palace was next to that of the Grand-Seigneur, near Bechick-Tash. Many important persons of rank waited on the other shore to take charge of the coffin, as is the custom. One vies for the honor of carrying, after his death, the person whom one has respected in life, or at least to touch him, which is easy for ordinary Turks. But this time the sepulcher was closed and deposited in the center of her crypt which is an immense salon painted in green arabesques. In general, the tombs of Sultans and Sultanes are buildings where the living would be very well housed. His Highness sent the shawl to cover the sarcophagus.

It is said that the deceased Sultane was French, of American origin, and that she was born in Nantes; it is added that when she was barely two years old, her parents embarked with her for America and were captured by corsairs and transported to Algiers where they perished. The little girl was bought by a slave merchant who calculated that a beauty of such a tender age would one day repay him commensurate with the upbringing he would provide. He was not mistaken in his perseverance, for at fourteen she was a resplendent beauty sold to the Dey of Algiers to be included in the tribute he owed to the Grand-Seigneur. She was sent to Sultan Abdulhamid, who found her comely and elevated her to the rank of Kadine, that is to say, he married her. She gave him Mahmud, the reigning Sultan. Mahmud has always had the greatest respect for his mother. It is said that she surpassed in comeliness and amiability the Circassians or Georgians which is not surprising since she was French. The Grand-Seigneur took upon himself all the annual charities of the Valide. For example, the midpoint of Ramadan is celebrated and cakes are distributed called Baclava. It is a flaky pastry, a trifle too rich but nevertheless quite exquisite. One would not believe that this philanthropy on the part of the Valide is a matter of 200,000 francs. All the Janissaries, that is to say the entire city of Constantinople, would receive their plate of Baclava as all the men of Constantinople are Janissaries.

The Sultane died of a malignant fever. Her son expelled her doctor as is the practice in this country: if the patient succumbs, one does away with the man who has given only useless succor. It doesn't seem to me that this tradition renders the Turkish doctor any more successful or more expert than ours. We have done what we could to distract the Grand-Seigneur, who, since this fatal event, is plunged, it is said, into a profound sorrow. The incognito promenades proposed to him are the sort of dissipation he prefers above all others.

The Turks never wear mourning: the color black is for them as blue or green is in Europe. In general grief doesn't leave lingering consequences on these people who love lightly; who acknowledge less than we affliction and regret. The habit of accepting everything as a blessing from heaven renders them almost insensible to suffering we would find unbearably cruel.

The Sultane Valide openly favored, second only to her son, Ali Efendi: the Sultan continues to lavish upon him his devotion. "It is in memory of my mother," he has said, "that he deserves my beneficence." Certainly there is a French soul in such touching goodness.

—Letter LXXXVII, Lettres du Bosphore,
La Comtesse de La Ferte-Meun, Constantinople,
August 15, 1817 (published anonymously, Paris, 1820).

Constantinople, June 26, 1814

The Valide Sultane touched her forehead to the woven silken threads of her prayer rug for the last time as the wooden drums and the cry of "Yanghinvar," "Fire," rang out. The sound struck her temples like the blow of a saber. No, God, she thought, not again—never again. But the warning drums struck in cadence, and she could imagine, even from the silence and shadow of her sanctuary, the clamor of the Seymens and Janissaries rushing to the scene, and the screams and lamentations of the owners of the burning houses. But it was only that, she thought, and nothing more. Only another of the innumerable Istanbul fires. . . . The Valide sat back upon her heels and picked up the tespi lying in splendor beside her. There were ninety-nine large and perfectly matched pearls. The tespi was famous even in Europe.

She let a pearl drop between her thumb and forefinger. "O God, Nothing But What You Are," she whispered. "O All-Merciful," as another pearl dropped between thumb and forefinger; "O Most Merciful Lord; O Pious; O Saint of Saints; O Savior; O Protector; O August; O Defender; O Absolute; O Loftiness; O Supremacy; O Molder; O Grace; O Chastiser; O Subsidizer; O Purveyor; O Lover of Victory; O Sapient; O Immensity; O Omnipresent; O Annihilator of the Arrogant; O Magnifier; O Dispenser of Honor; O Sower; O Penetrator; O Auditor; O Judge; O Witness; O Justice; O Gracious; O Superb; O Salvation; O Irresistible; O Consolation; O Solace; O High and Mighty; O Maximum; O Guardian; O Nurturer; O Avenger of Insults to Himself; O Munificent; O Scrutinizer; O Question; O Answer; O Tremendous; O Doctor; O Lover; O Author; O Inventor; O Truth; O Perpetual; O Strong; O Landlord; O Cum Laude; O Rejoicer; O Deliverer; O Resurrector; O Life; O Creator; O Exterminator; O Gloriosissimo; O Unique; O First; O Last; O Immortal; O Beloved; O Kismet Maker; O Cure; O Cause; O Effect; O Beginning; O End; O Visible; O Invisible; O Almighty; O Omnipotent; O Perfection; O Good; O Virtue; O Nobility; O Seducer of Repentance; O Castigator; O Sublimer; O Remittor; O Conductor; O Endowed of Majesty; O Omniscient; O Pleasure and Orgasm; O Prolific; O Obstructor; O Humbler; O Humiliator; O Forbearer; O Light; O Guide; O Opus; O Accountant; O Miraculous; O Autocrat; O Eternal . . ."

The last pearl fell, the weight of the tespi an unbearable fatigue for the Empress. Fire and war. Would there never be an end to it? She rose to her feet and flung her turban across the room, her luxurious hair falling down to her knees in a river of red-gold streaked with gray.

The Queen Mother turned her head slowly, stretching an opulent neck marked by an ancient thread-thin scar which circled it from ear to ear. As Valide she was the sworn enemy of her God, her race. She was, in a way, the sworn enemy of all women: a slave who was the supreme ruler of slaves. How ironic that the Grand-Seigneur, the Sultan, Absolute Ruler of the Ottoman Empire, was, by law, the son of a slave woman. A slave woman who possessed power, accompanied by the sacred words: *Our Lady.* A royal cortege trailed behind her. Bodyguards presented arms as she advanced between a double row of prostrated subjects who beseeched the mother of the Sultan to intercede for them in the name of her son. The messages from the postulants, embellished with bakshish, passed through the hands of the Black Eunuch, who delivered them respectfully, raising them to his forehead and kissing them tenderly, as the etiquette of the court required. The Valide was responsible for the administration and discipline of the harem. Every request, every question, no matter from what quarter, was submitted to her; from the annual budget of the Eski Serai to a pass for a Kadine to spend a day in the country. Every inhabitant of the harem down to the last slave owed her total obedience. No one sat in her presence. One stood, arms crossed over the chest, one's answers and questions punctuated by "Yes Our Lady" or "No Our Lady."

The Valide's power was great. The Ottomans accepted that a Sultan could have many wives, but he could have only one Empress. Thus the mother of the Sultan occupied the unique place of honor that nothing could alter save death. She was entrusted with the most intimate and private possessions of her son—his women. From slave, she had become master, from prisoner to jailer, from property to absolute despot. She had survived poison, intrigue, revolt, insurrection, surgery, childbirth, massacre and assassination. For she had been taught by the master of survival, the black slave.

The Sultana looked down at her pearls. No medium had yet been devised, she thought, for the translation of life into language. Nor could any words recall the dazzling fluidity of days, single yet fixed in sequence, that had fallen like the shaft of a tremendous waterfall into time.

The Valide knew that women like her, of the islands called America, were thought to be dissipated by an enervating climate as sweet as it was treacherous, but were, on the contrary, able to confront mortal shocks with a vitality and a resistance that matched the violence of the tropics. They were a race that prospered on devastation, thought the Valide Sultane. Was it the tropical sun which made them forget so easily, yet burned into them, an undying lust for vengeance?

A few hours ago, Mahmud had placed a dispatch in her hands. She had looked up at him pleadingly, hoping that there had been some error, some mistake . . . It was not possible. . . . Mahmud shook his head, the white cone of his turban waving in the air like a negating forefinger. Joséphine Bonaparte was dead. On May 29, 1814, the reputed Empress of all the French, had died, so far from the islands of America where she had been born. The Valide's last tenuous tie with the Occident, her last allegiance with her destiny, was gone. Now there were only the vast steppes of Anatolia, she thought, the ramparts of Cairo, the desert winds of Arabia, the lead domes of Istanbul. And when her time came, she thought, there would be no cross to look upon, only the cross-turned-crescent and the shawl of the Prophet's daughter Fatima.

The prophecy had become more real to her than the power she possessed. She was the only one left alive. . . .

The dispatch slipped from her hand. It fell face up, and fluttered across the marble floor like the petals of a flower, skimming over the veined blue and white expanse as if to the gentle music of the fountain that stood in the center of the room. The Valide rose to a considerable height for a woman. She closed her eyes. The fretted light from above played on a face long removed from the frantic strivings of the outside world.

The Queen of All Moslem Women looked confusedly around her apartments, at the gleaming brocades that cascaded like water from the walls, breaking the gleaming onyx and veined marble. The rich silk carpets were piled two and three thick over the immense sitting room that was as long and as wide as a cathedral. The room was tiled with large floral designs, and the high ceiling was painted and gilded. At both ends were podiums, which constituted long sofas. They, too, were covered with silk carpets, gold-embroidered, fringed silk brocades, and a double row of cushions stamped in gold thread on satin. The tiles were framed with strips of cedar held with silver nails, and the vaulted ceiling was a fresco of woven cedar strips. In the center of the room a marble fountain gave the air its freshness and serenity, and the soft music of cascading water that fell from one basin to another was the only sound in the silence.

To the left were her baths, attached to those of her son, Mahmud, which linked the Selamlik, the men's quarters of the palace, with the harem. Between them was the "Golden Road," the narrow, exquisitely tiled alleyway along which the chosen favorite was led from the harem to the Sultan's rooms.

From this place she ruled her domain, the harem and, through her beloved and only son, Mahmud, the entire Empire of the Ottomans. With the French defeated, the Russians exhausted, Europe at war, she could survey serenely the most vast empire in the world.

Eight centuries had built the mightiest empire the world had ever known. It stretched from Greece, Albania, the Balkans and the Caucasus, down the valleys of the Tigris and the Euphrates, to Persia and the Persian Gulf, and across Syria to the Red Sea, Egypt and Algiers to Gibraltar. But the greatest jewel, that which Napoleon had so desperately craved, had always been and would always be, by name, Constantinople to those who coveted it and Istanbul to those who possessed it.

The Queen Mother rose from her couch. Her court dress was of a richness and elaborateness so surprising that she never failed to smile. Her dullimano was of purple cloth, fitted and embroidered on either side from top to bottom with a line of perfect pearls the size of an ordinary button. This coat, lined with ermine, had long sleeves and cuffs turned back at the bottom. Attached at the waist were two tassels of smaller pearls flanked by large diamonds. Under her coat, but fully visible, her drawers of thin rose-colored damask brocaded with silver flowers, reached to her shoes, concealing her legs. Over them she wore a smock of fine white silk gauze, edged with embroidery, closed across her breast by a large diamond in the form of a lozenge, but the shape and color of her fine bosom were quite visible. Her fitted waistcoat of white and gold damask had very long sleeves that fell back and were trimmed with gold fringe and pearl buttons. Over this she wore a girdle, the width of four fingers and completely studded with diamonds.

The Valide wore three necklaces that fell to her knees: one was of large pearls, at the end of which hung an emerald the size of a large country egg; the second was composed of two hundred of the most beautifully matched emeralds; and the third was made of diamonds, a thousand of them, the size of peas and of perfect roundness. But it was her earrings that eclipsed all the rest. These were two pear-shaped diamonds, the size of walnuts. On her head she wore a talpock draped with four strings of pearls, the whitest and most perfect in existence. These were attached by two roses sculpted from a single large ruby surrounded by twenty pure diamonds. Her hair, which she wore Turkish style, flowed loosely over her shoulders and down her back, and diamond-headed pins attached by silver chains were scattered among the red strands.

She wore a wide diamond bracelet on her right wrist, and on five fingers, five solitaire diamond rings. No Queens in Europe she knew possessed half of her jewels. And under her velvet slippers encrusted with rosettes of pearls, gold cord and precious stones lay the palace treasury. But more than any treasure, thought the Queen Mother, more than life itself, the jewel, the treasure of her existence, was Mahmud. How could she even think of the prophecy when she had her son? She had willed him a great ruler, greater than her old enemy Catherine II, greater than their new enemy Bonaparte. A Sultan with whom the whole world would have to reckon; who would change the face of Asia, reform his medieval empire, make history. They had indeed changed the course of history in Russia and Europe; now, they must make their own. Mahmud ruled forty million souls and one eighth of the surface of the world. Mahmud was *Allah's Shadow on Earth.* . . .

"Tatch-ul-Mestourat, Valide Sultane, Diadem of the Veiled Heads, Queen of Queens, Modest Lady, your escort is waiting. . . ."

A familiar, peculiar half-tenor voice interrupted the Valide's reverie. She turned and then flushed as if the Chief Black Eunuch could read her thoughts. He had always had the knack of silence, and now as his shadow fell upon her, she looked up into the expressionless dark eyes that had watched her for twenty-five years. He had seen everything with those eyes: tears and terror, pride, passion, happiness, abysmal grief, yet no eyes were as sad as his, she thought.

How innocent the Sultans were, she thought, to imagine that the choice of the blackest and most ferocious-looking eunuchs was an extra guarantee against infidelities. To her the Kizlar Aga had never been repulsive, or terrifying, or exotic. He had always been the most beautiful of men. He always reminded her of her American slave Big Alphonse, except that Alphonse had been bigger, blacker and uglier than the Black Eunuch would ever be. How could a Sultan have imagined that for her black skin held either mystery or fear. It had been her only link with home. She had pressed against black skin, touched and smelled it, before she ever knew white skin existed. The fact that the Kizlar Aga was awesomely dressed in a sapphire-blue silk pelisse embroidered with pearls and silver thread and lined in sable, the long sleeves nearly reaching the floor, and in a turban which added another two feet to his already imposing height, only made their third-of-a-century masquerade more pathetic.

"Has Mahmud made his choice of Kadine for his bed tonight, Kizlar Aga?"

"My Queen, it is always Besma Kadine. The Sultan wants no other wife."

"But Besma is pregnant. It is a good excuse and well nigh time that he occupies himself with his other wives, at least until the birth. His wives are becoming impossible. They claim their conjugal rights as Kadines. Mahmud is perfectly free to compromise the Laws of his Harem, but he must do so by firman, not by negligence or caprice. . . . And you and I know he cannot. He cannot budge even his little finger, change even the most antiquated of protocols, without a protest from an Ulema, or the Grand Vizier, or the Aga of the Janissaries, or *somebody!* He must bide his time."

No one knew the etiquette of the harem better than the Valide.

"One day," she continued, "he will have one wife, if that is what he desires . . . one day. . . . But for the moment, he has four wives and they demand no-bet-geçesi, to sleep with the Sultan! Tell Ismahish Ikbal Mahmud will visit her tonight. I'll speak with Mahmud myself. And make sure his robes are full of silver and a nice present. It is bad enough that he neglects his favorites and leaves them to intrigue all day."

The Valide glanced up at the Chief Black Eunuch. In this world of silences and glances, their exchange spoke volumes. *Yes, I know that Besma, the slave girl Mahmud found in a public bath on one of his incognito excursions into Istanbul, has his heart. But the rules must be obeyed. We have no choice. Mahmud had wanted to spare his brother as well, and we tried, didn't we, friend?*

There was no look so profound, not even the look of love, thought the Kizlar Aga, as complicity in assassination. Never a word had passed between them. There had been only silence and one glance. The Valide had removed the diamond ring from her left hand and had dropped it into the gold sash around the Black Eunuch's waist. The way in which empires rose and fell, thought the Chief Black Eunuch, observing his mistress, was exactly the way souls were saved or damned. The mechanism was the same. The fault might be a grain of sand or a holy war. The fault might be forgivable, irresponsible, or even admirable, but only the consequences counted in the end.

Aloud he said: "Our Lady, perhaps Third Kadine Shapir Kadine would be better tonight. She is less likely to complain if the Sultan falls asleep instead of plowing the fields."

"You are right, Edris-Ibn-Munquidh Aga. Shapir is safer. And less likely to protest if an abortion is necessary. She already has a Princess. Let it be recorded thus."

The Chief Black Eunuch looked directly into the eyes of the Tatch-ul-Mestourat, which he rarely did. Another command given and obeyed if necessary. For this was how he ruled, by obedience. This was his power.

"So it shall be Shapir tonight, Diadem of the Veiled Heads?"

"Yes, it shall be Shapir. The handkerchief shall be sent. Is there something else, Kizlar Aga?"

"And you will speak of Ali Efendi's message to Sultan Mahmud?"

"Yes, yes, of course." The Valide's heart stopped. "It was *I* you must know who was behind the screen at the reunion of the *Divan* yesterday, remember."

Her eyes had gone slate gray. Ali Efendi's name on the lips of anyone, except perhaps this towering man before her, would make her start with fright and love. *That the Blessings of Allah be upon him.*

She was old, thought the Valide. Old. She knew a thousand ways to please a man and she had used them all.

The Chief Black Eunuch bowed and began to back out of the room. The Valide lowered her veil and followed him almost as if she were being pulled by invisible silken cords. Her walk had remained the gliding artificial one which she had learned as a child. She had never learned the strange tiptoe dancing steps of the Turkish women, just as she had never lost her foreign accent.

The Valide was tall for a woman, straight and strongly built; the years and years of sedentary existence had put flesh on a body that once had been slim; flesh that had been burnished to the translucent whiteness of porcelain by unceasing hours in the harem baths. But her most splendid and arresting feature was her eyes, which could be a harsh tropical green or a pale flint-hard emerald, the slate gray of the sky before a storm or the turquoise waters of the Archipelago. They were eyes that had a hint of fanaticism about them, and her whole body, despite its resplendent fittings, gave off a hard, almost military air. The face was pale under the fiery red rouge, its perfect oval accentuated by the strange, wide-spaced eyes, darkened eyebrows and wide mouth. Her flesh seemed to be part of her very soul, all forged into one elaborate and polished armor. The long hands were never still, nor were the upturned eyes. But the mouth was formed as if made for silence, its straight, firm line fashioned to be kept shut. The Valide moved as if she were old, although she was a woman in the prime of life.

She glanced up at the Chief Black Eunuch as she passed. Under the high white cone of his turban, she knew his curly hair to be grizzled with age, the only indication, she thought, of his sixty odd years. . . . He, too, had been a man in the prime of life when she had first gazed upon him . . . if a eunuch could be said to *have* a prime of life.

Outside, white eunuchs waited in the courtyard to escort her on her daily visit to Mahmud after prayers. It was the moment of the day she cherished. She would ride out to greet him, traveling through the vast tree-shaded gardens of the palace. Four guards carried the four-sided silk pavilion under which she rode on horseback. The four silken sheets hid her from all eyes, her mount led by an armed white eunuch. The cry of *"Var Halvette"* would precede her, the harsh sound flinging itself out upon the emptiness like the screech of a falcon.

Under the transparent silver gauze of her veil, the Valide's face caught the last rays of the deepening sunlight. The eyes that had made a Sultan weep looked out beyond the dark full cedars and the lean black cypresses onto the Marmara and the Bosphorus toward the Mediterranean, and beyond, to the Atlantic, America, home.

She lifted her head. She had to face the real world from the graffiti on the harem walls to the eternal rebellion in Moldavia. The Tatch-ul-Mestourat passed in front of the Black Eunuch. She had been taught survival on a slave plantation, patience in the harem of God, a convent. But she had prevailed in the convent of man, the harem.

The Kizlar Aga gazed after her. Thirty-four years. Black Eunuch and White Slave.

Of all the women he had ruled, loved, detested, punished and obeyed, thought the Chief Black Eunuch, the Valide, who had passed so close to him his robes would carry her perfume all day, was the only one whose essence had escaped him. Sometimes, he thought that the Valide possessed under her drawers that which he had lost forever. For how, the Chief Black Eunuch asked himself, could a man hope to capture women's hearts if his faithful eunuchs had not begun by subjugating their minds . . . ?

BOOK I

THE *ARGUS*
·1781·

• CHAPTER ONE •

THE *ARGUS* 1781

One speaks of the nature, in ignorance of the manner,
How can one speak of navigation?
War, Commerce and piracy,
Are all one and the same.

—GOETHE, *Faust*

It was in the nature of the open and endless sea that nothing was ever sighted upon it without itself being seen, thought the Captain of the *Argus*. The ship's bell struck the alarm, and with a dry tremor of fear and anticipation, he spotted three Algerian corsairs cruising on the horizon. The *Argus* had weathered the Strait of Gibraltar, and the ship with its small group of passengers and its cargo of sugar was making for Zantes. There was nothing to do now, thought the Captain, but make full sail and double back toward the Provençal coast. The wind was more favorable than not, and they might be able to make the coast of Spain and the Cap of Los Palos between Almería and Alicante without being overtaken.

The three pirate ships decided to give chase. The Captain hardly heard himself shout the warning: "Pirates ahead! All hands on deck!"

The warning splintered the calm of the ship like an exploding cannonball. Frenzied sailors raced to their posts, falling out of their hammocks, scrambling up the masts, massing on the prow, unfurling the hatched-down ropes, cursing and shouting. Fear swept over the half-naked men like the midafternoon sun that bore down upon them this twenty-ninth of June, 1781.

"By Mary, Mother of Jesus," shouted Captain de Chaumareys, "they are going to have to catch us to take us." The ten-cannon frigate strained and groaned and doubled back upon itself, turning toward the open sea by force of the lateen sails that the Captain prayed would hold in face of the strong winds threatening to break in two both the lateen yard and the mast. But de Chaumareys knew he had to hazard everything. It was a matter of freedom.

"Oh, God, Captain," wailed his Second Mate, Rafanni, an Italian from Nice returning home after six years in the islands of America. "The passengers are trying to get on deck. Mr. Delaye wants to know what the hell's going on."

"Tell those godforsaken passengers to remain below in their cabins, Mr. Rafanni. Try to calm them down. Assure them there is no immediate danger. We are going to outrun those circumcised, heathen sons of bitches!"

The *Argus* was holding. The ship was advancing at a speed that made them seem as if they were being carried on air rather than water. The three pirate ships bore down on them with full sails.

Rafanni saw it happen first.

"Look, they're done for."

The two men watched the miracle. The masts of two of the three ships broke in the wind like straws, and the third corsair was lowering its sail in fear of the same misfortune.

"We've escaped!" The three corsairs disappeared beyond the horizon. Captain de Chaumareys gave the order to lower the mainsail and replace it with the square sail so that the strain on the mast would be lessened. They were out of danger. Or so he thought.

It was four o'clock in the afternoon and de Chaumareys was just about to go below to consult his charts when, giving a cursory glance toward the horizon, he saw to his disbelief . . . another ship, as if they were destined to meet every corsair vessel on the coast of Barbary, for it was bearing down upon them, flagless. The *Argus* fled toward the Lagoon of Mar Menor. It raced toward the darkness as if into the arms of a lover. Night closed in on them, as warm and silken as a cashmere shawl, the ship settled into the blackness, and the Algerian corsair was lost to view.

Captain de Chaumareys went below to calm his passengers and decide what to do. After nine weeks at sea, he knew his passengers and his crew like a book. He had in fact a talent for reading both men and women, indispensable for the commander of a vessel who had to make split-second decisions, however arbitrary, and enforce them through sheer will, cunning and, if necessary, violence. He knew what to expect at the Captain's table tonight. There would be outraged silence from Dr. Manguelas, barely concealed rage from the Abbot de Tullenville, repressed tears from Madame the Countess de Trezin de Cangey. The only calm and welcome eyes he would meet tonight at dinner would be the green ones of the convent schoolgirl and the black eyes of her slave. Nothing could disturb the stony-faced indifference to fate that that black female had. . . .

The Captain and his pilot stayed up all night with their maps. They were not in the least out of danger, as they had guaranteed their worried passengers. They had merely assured them of a good night's sleep. The *Argus* would change routes, the pilot decided. The ship would weather Cap Nao the same night and make for the island of Ibiza. At nightfall on the second day they arrived at Palma, but even with favorable winds they couldn't risk landing without light. The *Argus* kept sailing all night. At about two in the morning, the pilot, Lyon, shook the Captain awake.

A change of wind had taken them off course, miles away from where they wanted to go . . . the coast of Corsica was in sight. They could try for Ajaccio. By four in the morning, Ajaccio was in sight, and by sunup the watch on the point had sighted, with a shout of despair, another pair of Algerian corsairs. For once in his life, Captain de Chaumareys made a singular mistake of judgment. Instead of fleeing toward the open sea, he turned his ship toward land. If he couldn't save the ship, he could at least save himself, his crew, his passengers.

As was their custom, the two pirate ships bore straight down upon them. The smaller of the two ships, best able to maneuver, advanced within firing distance of its twelve cannons.

De Chaumareys raised the red flag and ordered a cannon volley fired without ammunition. This piece of bravura, which made the pirates think that he was going to defend himself, forced them to lower their mainsail and take counsel. The empty volley meant that de Chaumareys was not going to fight, but it didn't mean he was not going to run. The Captain ordered the large sail lowered. The smaller of the two pirate ships was so close that it was within musket range. The two ships began to exchange shots. De Chaumareys could hear screams from below as an Algerian musket shot whistled past his ear. As a last resort, they raised sails and veered around as much as they could to be able to sail close to the wind and to gain on the two enemy ships. Just as it seemed that this execution would have an effect, one of the crew missed a maneuver. The sail gave way and de Chaumareys, despite the efforts of the crew, saw his advantage disappear in a few instants.

At this point, thought the Captain, there was nothing to do except change into a clean shirt, preferably a new one, since the shirt on one's back and the breeches on one's ass were the only things the pirates left you with when you fell into their hands as captives and as slaves.

Lasseau, one of his crew who had already been captured once, approached him shouting over the din of musket fire.

"Captain, they'll not broadside you if you surrender." But his eyes spoke volumes about slavery in Algiers. Perhaps they would all be ransomed by the French Consul and perhaps not. Captain de Chaumareys made one of those decisions that had more to do with the indescribable pain of losing one's freedom to act rather than the bravura of dying to preserve it. Before he realized what he had done, the terrible sound of his ship's own cannons, loaded this time, struck his ear as the cries and screams of the Algerian corsair, surprised at being attacked, rent the air. The second ship was almost board to board; the Algerians had begun to lash the two ships together as the Algerian ensign was raised.

The men topside were hacking away at the wreck of the mast on the deck as the Algerians sprang from the shrouds and were upon the ship, pouring over the bows, leaping and vaulting like cats. In a moment, the deck of the *Argus* was swarming with soldiers armed with sabers. Musket shots whistled through the air, and in the distance the inhabitants of Tabarque heard the boom of the cannons and saw three miniature ships on the horizon surrounded by puffs of smoke.

Just as Captain de Chaumareys was about to call for quarter, something so evil happened that those who survived the day would never cease to wonder at it. The *Argus* fired a broadside at the second corsair at the same instant that the corsair fired upon the *Argus,* and one of the pirate cannonballs met one from the *Argus.* The cannonball from the *Argus* split into two pieces, half of which flew back and killed the Captain. To the men on board, it seemed an omen to lay down arms. They would be slaves, but who knew? Alive they at least could be ransomed. Dead, like Captain de Chaumareys, their souls might be free but their miserable bodies would cease to love, to procreate and to grow old.

The soldiers began to strip the sailors and break open the cases. Several of the Algerians were wounded. The Captain lay in a pool of blood.

The Reis Barmaksis, who had remained on his own ship, the *Oukil el*

Harj, now joined his partner, the Reis Memmou, on the deck of the *Argus.* Barmaksis, who was known as Mano Morta, "Dead-Hand," because of his mutilated left hand, beckoned the stripped pilot before him. The pilot, Lyon, had witnessed the soldiers dividing the clothes of the crew, and he began to speak in Arabic to plead for compassion for the men who without their shirts, bound and lashed to the deck, would all have unbearable sunburns by nightfall. The tone of voice of Reis Barmaksis made Lyon regret the liberty he had taken.

"You son of shit. You are not in my presence for two minutes and you dare to open your bloody mouth!" The Reis's saber flashed in the sun, opening a long gash on Lyon's shoulder. The pain, the harshness of Barmaksis's voice and the horrible gaze he fixed upon Lyon made the pilot drop to his knees with a groan. Yet, he had heard an almost imperceptible European accent in the Reis's Arabic, and recognized him for who he was: Mano Morta, the Venetian renegade. The second Reis spoke:

"I want to see your passengers."

And turning to the slightly wounded blond, blue-eyed boy at his side, he ordered him to fetch the passengers.

"This is your first prize, Hamidou. Have the honor to go below and take the Christian captives."

The pilot intervened again, this time at the risk of his life or at least a saber slash across his face. He addressed Dead-Hand:

"Excellence, Mano Morta, allow me, as the Captain of this ship now, to conduct the passengers. There are women amongst them who may not have the force or the presence of mind to follow orders."

Reis Memmou nodded silently. Women were precious bounty. It was stupid to risk an accident.

Reis Memmou was quite satisfied. This capture would bring their total for the year to sixteen ships and the sum of 457,313 francs. Of the ships, two had been slavers out of Nantes which had brought enormous bounty when sold back to their respective Nantian companies, Michel & Grou and Exaudy & Liprot. As was his habit, Memmou delivered captured slave ships with their human cargo intact except when there were Moslems amongst the captives. These he freed according to the dictates of the Koran. For according to Allah, no Moslem had the right to enslave another Moslem. Slaving was now at its height and at its most lucrative. The islands of America was its biggest client, and Nantes, that city of angelic beauty, was its capital. The trading companies sent out their slavers armed, and several times their ships had given

Reis Memmou battle. When slavers had the temerity to do this, he personally sold the crews and captains into slavery in Algiers and ransomed the rest of the cargo, minus the Moslems, back to the Nantes businessmen the ships belonged to.

Memmou had heard that the Nantians had begged the famous American Captain John Paul Jones to clear the Mediterranean of the Algerian Reis. What did they think? That the Americans were too good to pay a yearly ransom to Algiers just like everyone else for the safety of their ships? First, thought the Reis with contempt, the Americans had better get themselves a *fleet* before their Captains began talking about *clearing* the seas.

The two Reis nodded silently. The pilot, Lyon, went below and ushered the passengers into the presence of the Algerians. One by one they arrived on deck, blinking in the sunlight, disheveled and terrified. The Commissar Delaye fainted from fright. As the last two passengers emerged into the sunlight, the Reis Barmaksis and the Reis Memmou, along with every man on deck, fell silent. The young boy, who would one day be the richest, most famous and most hunted of the Barbary pirates, caught his breath. He had never in all his fourteen years seen anything so beautiful.

The fifteen-year-old Creole, on her way from her convent in the islands of America, and her nineteen-year-old slave, Angélique-Aimée Céleste, dropped to their knees before the men. Slave and mistress began to pray, their rosaries in hand, the Creole's gleaming beads fastened with her father's Cross of Merit hypnotizing the astonished young boy Hamidou and subduing the rest of the crew.

The white girl's green eyes blazed with hatred. It was the first time she had ever seen heathens and infidels and her whole perfectly formed body revolted against the sight, the smell, the maleness of them. She felt herself violated even without their greedy, curious, ignorant eyes upon her. She who had kept herself even from impure thoughts in hopes of serving the glory of God had now fallen further from salvation than her worst nightmares, her worst imaginings. She had come face to face with the famous *fate worse than death.* . . .

Mary, Mother of God, help us. Protect your servants of the True Faith, in this, our hour of trial. Let us not show fear, nor stray from the path of the righteous. But grant us, oh, Lord, that we shall live to serve you. As God is our Master and our Savior and Jesus Christ is the Son of God. In the Name of the Father, the Son and the Holy Ghost. Amen.

CHAPTER TWO

THE WHITE SLAVE 1781

The history of every people demonstrates that in order to render slavery useful, it must be rendered at least bearable; that force never prevents the soul's revolt; that it is in the interest of the master that the slave wants to live; and that one can expect nothing more of him, once he no longer fears death.

—CITIZEN LOUIS FRANK,
Doctor of the "Armée d'Orient"

Algiers was a natural fortress: a towering formation of dazzling whitewashed buildings dominating a snug harbor which offered a safe hideout for both the men and ships of every nation of the world. The white cubes of the Kasbah piled up the hillside, nestling under the cannons of the Ottomans and the green flag of Islam. In the labyrinths of the Medina, where overhanging eaves left only a slit of vivid blue sky, all races congregated: Spanish, Italian, Berber, English, Greek and Arab. But more than a third of the population of Algiers was slave.

In the year of the Haigera 1210, there were 1,586 Christian slaves: 882 Spanish, 51 Dutch, 44 Greeks, 16 Sardinians, 64 Genovese, 32 Livornese, 8 from Palma, 168 Portuguese, 3 Maltese, 9 Tabarkians, 4 Flemish, 246 French, 167 Neapolitans, 48 Austrians, 44 Sicilians, 20 Corsicans, 1 Rumanian, 55 Piedmontese, 5 Prussians and 16 Americans.

The harbor activity was intense. The azure waters of the bay thronged with commercial ships from every nation. The slave trade from the Guinean coast passed through Algiers, clogging the waterway with a constant stream of black slaves.

Reis Memmou led his tired, terrified Christians along the uneven cobbled alleys, slimy with filth and crawling with rats that fattened on the refuse slung into the streets under the hot sun. Entrails glowed red on butchers' stalls in the bazaars beside bouquets of red carnations. Hamidou trotted silently alongside the Christian girl and her slave, speechlessly. He was desperate to be of service, teeming with plans for freeing his beloved. But how? To take her where? He couldn't even tell her he loved her. He didn't speak a word of French. If he had had the power of languages, he thought, he could try to convince her to convert to Islam and, by becoming a renegade, free herself. Desperation was making him itch and his feverish eyes darted from the left to the right as if the answer to his dilemma might be walking beside him.

At the arrival of the Reis's ship, the crowds assembled along the waterfront and the streets to demonstrate their admiration for the corsairs who brought new revenue and to gawk at the new slaves. The weary captives wound their way through the terrifying, agitated crowd, which harassed and spat on them, their strange guttural screams adding to the dread of slavery each of the Christians felt. They were being led straight to the Dey's palace, a fortress located deep within the Kasbah, ruled by the Pasha Baba Mohammed Ibn-Osman, who had come to power in 1765 and had reigned for sixteen years. His Reis adored him, and for Hamidou, he was simply Allah on earth. In effect, Baba Mohammed was a worthy successor to Barbarossa, the Greek renegade who had captured Algiers for the Turks more than two hundred years ago and who lay in a splendid gray granite tomb in Istanbul that was engraved with the words "Dead Is the Captain of the Sea." It was now Baba Mohammed who was the terror of the Mediterranean. As master of the Barbary pirates, he defended his men against all comers, and his raiding expeditions against infidels went unavenged. The tributes he extracted from the European nations were the highest possible.

"Oh, Lord, have mercy on us. What will become of us?" whispered the Creole to her slave.

"Courage, Mistress. Perhaps we will be ransomed, or at least you, Mistress. It seems that is what they do with Europeans. One of the sailors explained to me last night. They send for the French Consul and he negotiates a ransom according to their needs and your rank."

"Do you really believe that, Angélique? Then why are there so many Christian slaves in Algiers?"

"Only poor slaves like me, Mistress, not Grands Blancs."

"But these people make slaves of whites! What will become of us?"

"Slaves don't have futures," replied Angélique.

The young woman glanced sideways at her slave. The rancor and bitterness of her last words sent a chill down her spine. Angélique, her lovely, sweet, calm, docile Angélique, was alive with hatred for her. The Grande Blanche's lips began to move in prayer. She prayed for Angélique's soul. She prayed that her slave would be freed from the sin of hatred. As if in answer, Angélique's lips began to move also and they found themselves once again in devoted accord.

Hamidou glanced back at the plodding line of prisoners, some of whom were uttering soft groans. The pilot of the *Argus* was suffering from his wounds and the sailors were stripped to the waist with only their smallclothes to cover them. The Count de Tullenville was weeping openly, and the English couple staggered up the steep steps, clinging to each other desperately, at the end of their tether. Hamidou fought the crowd, pushing in on both sides, to make passage for the Christian girl. She was dressed in black, startling against the white and blue walls of the cobbled streets. The slave was also in black. Both wore black mantillas to cover their heads. They seemed instinctively to use the material to hide their faces from the curious, hostile crowd, the strange cadences of Arabic striking the vibrant air like the shrieks of the high-flying vultures above the city. Suddenly the girl stumbled and Hamidou shot out his arm to steady her. She leaned heavily on him; her face, despite the tears streaming down, was of an admirable hauteur. Her maid's face showed absolutely no trace of emotion whatsoever, just a certain resigned curiosity. After all, Angélique was thinking, one couldn't be a slave twice, could one?

They were taking the captives directly to the Mechouar, the administrative palace, where the Reis's take would be registered, evaluated, weighed, counted, processed and distributed by lots. Forty portions for the Dey, thirty for the Reis and twenty-five for the crew. It was only then that the captives would be taken to the slave quarters for the night, in the old Christian catacombs that had been the ancient Roman baths.

The cortege passed the black slaves' corrals, the end of the line for the caravans of the Sahara which brought Nubians and Sudanese and Guineans for sale in Algiers and Cairo. The slave trade in Cairo was the largest in the world.

The slaves had been herded pell-mell into the caravan's seraglio. Men, women, young children, infants at their mothers' breasts, and

young boys still suffering the terrible effects of the castrations they had
suffered farther up the Nile at Abutige were covered with dirt and flies.
The hum of a hundred different dialects filled the air, unperturbed by
even a hint of a sea breeze. And there were hundreds upon hundreds of
slaves corraled there.

Angélique, her eyes wide with horror, began to shake uncontrollably,
all her bravado dissipated by the scene before her. She began to vomit,
her body convulsed with dry heaves, her stomach so emptied that only a
thin line of bile emerged. She thought of only one thing: a Negro sold in
Algiers was as much a slave as one sold in America.

Angélique began to imagine ways of killing herself.

Her mistress had seen the slave market in Port Royale with her
father. Angélique, as a house servant, had never seen such horrors. The
newly arrived Africans were no better or worse off than the ones before
her eyes except that this time *she* was a part of their condition. She, like
the blackest of them, could have her life snatched from her now, or any
day, by the whim of any master. And she wanted to live.

All the slaves, except for the very young, had arrived on foot; the
camels of the caravans were used only for the transport of water, vict-
uals and other merchandise such as gum arabic, elephant teeth, tama-
rinds and ivory. Slaves had the advantage of being the only merchandise
that could carry itself. The cortege, guided by Ghellabis, slave drivers,
was hurried along by means of whips.

Water, the most precious commodity of all, was rationed to the limit
of human endurance. Caravans of five hundred to one thousand slaves
of all ages and sexes arrived three or four times a year. For a boy of ten
to fourteen years of age, the price was 50 to 70 Spanish piastres; for one
of fifteen to eighteen, 70 to 100 piastres. For a girl of eight to twelve
years old, the price was 35 to 50 piastres; for a woman of fourteen to
twenty years, 70 to 90 piastres; for a eunuch of ten to twelve years, 160
to 200 piastres or more.

The Reis and their prisoners had arrived at the courtyard of the
administrative palace and stood milling around the vast esplanade of
white sand enclosed on three sides by white arched colonnades. Crowds
had gathered, and the Turkish of the official administration mingled
with the Arabic of Islam, to which was added the confusion of the
Berber dialect of the desert. At the far end of the esplanade sat the
Keznapar, the Minister of Finance to the Dey of Algiers. He was surrounded by his officials, his scribes and his notaries, ready to register
the captures of Memmou and the other Reis. Reis Memmou joined the

Keznapar on the platform, taking Hamidou with him. To one side he recognized the English Consul. The French Consul had already been notified and stood ready to negotiate for his nationals.

"The French Consul is here. The girl is safe," the Reis whispered to Hamidou. Hamidou heaved a sigh of relief. God had answered his prayers. . . .

After a long conversation with the British Consul, the English couple were taken out of Memmou's line and placed to one side in the shade of the arches. As was expected, the sailors of the *Argus* were regrouped and sent to the galleys as slaves. The French Consul came forward and, after a long and agitated conversation, negotiated the ransom of the Count de Tullenville and the young girls. Hamidou could have cried with joy. He tried to signal with gestures and smiles to the uncomprehending girls that they were safe! The registering continued, with each person stepping out of line at the sound of his name while a secretary inscribed the information necessary and the laconic notations: slave market, ransomed, appreciated by the Dey of Algiers, apportioned to the Reis Memmou.

All of a sudden, Hamidou saw a tall, imposing figure step out of the shadows of the colonnade behind the Keznapar. He was dressed in a white caftan trimmed in silver cord and wore a huge white muslin turban attached with a large expensive stone and an ostrich feather. The Ottoman held a quick and quiet conversation with the secretary who, after nodding in comprehension, turned in surprise and began to protest in Turkish. The French Consul, who had also heard and understood what had been said, began to protest vigorously as well, gesticulating impatiently as the imperturbable Turk refused all conversation.

In the name of the Ottoman Sultan, the Christian girl, the red-blond one, was being appropriated as the levy imposed on every tenth slave sold. She belonged now to the Sultan Abdulhamid, not the Dey Baba Mohammed. Hamidou, who was beginning to understand, went pale. The Reis began to curse under his breath. Moreover, the Turkish official himself was personally appropriating the *other* American, the black one, for his own harem. One had to be blind not to see a jewel of a woman under that ridiculous tent she was wearing from the waist down. The amber skin, the long black hair, the yellow eyes . . . he intended to take this slave as a wife! The other would be sent with the tribute Baba Mohammed had owed the Sultan for the past six years. The ship was already in port and in the process of being loaded.

The young Hamidou thought he was going to faint. Reis Memmou

chuckled under his breath. There was going to be a hell of an administrative row over this between the Sultan's representative and the very
independent Dey. True, the Ottomans had a perfect right to levy every
tenth slave. But the little Christian girl had been marked for the Dey
himself. Baba Mohammed was not going to stand for it. Making an
obscene gesture, the Keznapar banged his registers closed. The Sultan's
official had darkened with bureaucratic righteousness. Was he or was he
not the representative of the Padishah of the Ottoman Empire? Was or
was *not* Algiers a vassal state of said Empire? Did he or did he not have
the right to every tenth slave? Was he or was he not exercising this right
in the name of the glorious Padishah of Turkey? The girl was the most
expensive of the lot, and it was normal she be appropriated for the
Sultan. As for the other American, she was his! He had always wanted
an American wife. . . .

"We'll see about that," replied the Keznapar. "I'll bring this up with
the Dey himself."

"You do that," said the Turkish controller.

"I intend . . ." began the French Consul.

"You shut up," snapped the irritated minister.

As for the two girls who were the subjects of the hot dispute, they
stood side by side forlornly, in the empty bleached courtyard under the
hot sun, their lips moving silently in prayer, their rosary beads clicking
against their skirts.

Reis Memmou shook his head warily. This dispute could go on for
years. It was as fundamental as the relations between the Empire and
Algiers. The poor girl was being haggled over like . . . well, like what
she was, a piece of meat, a candied orange, a rich loukoum, the
"throat's rest." At any rate, no Ottoman was going to dictate to the
Dey. It would be just like him to keep the Creole just for spite and just
like the Sultan to start a war over her. Everything was a matter of
saving face, as it always was in the Orient.

The boy, Hamidou, stood by helplessly, his eyes filling with tears. He
had taught her her first words of Arabic. Each day had drawn him
further and further into his adoration. They had tried to speak, one to
the other, realizing that they were both but children. He had learned
her name and she his. He had tried to quiet her fears as best he could
and to withstand the rowdy humor of the crew, who teased him mercilessly. . . . And then he had finally hit upon a plan to rescue his Christian from what they called *a fate worse than death,* as the pilot, Lyon,
had so vehemently insisted.

"You want to do WHAT?"

"Marry her."

"What?"

"Mar . . ." Before he had managed to get the word out, the hippo-potamus-hide whip of Reis Memmou had come down on his left shoulder, almost breaking his neck.

"You dog-fucking idiot. Do you know what you are saying?"

Hamidou was kowtowing with pain.

"You still have seven years before MY mast and after that you will be one of the richest, most feared, most hunted Reis on the Barbary Coast and you want to throw it all away on a vixen-eyed CHRISTIAN. An infidel! A Giaour. A Giaour! Allah help me in my sorrow! You, a good Moslem boy, son of your mother . . . not in a thousand years . . . not even if you could afford the gold chain with the heathen cross she wears around her neck! How do you intend to pay for her on what I pay you, may I ask? Lock her in a miserable room in the Kasbah while you go back to sea perhaps? Or perhaps you have decided to retire to your estates in Tripoli, you are such a rich man???" Hamidou still could not speak from the pain, which seemed to melt into the burning, indignant ache in his heart.

"A harem he wants."

He heard the others laughing behind him, but he could neither get up off his knees nor turn his torn neck around to scream at them. "A Giaour who would just as soon poison you in your sleep!"

Reis Memmou had laid down his whip and was tearing his hair. "I forbid you to set eyes upon her again. And if you as much as touch the hem of her skirt you will be off to the eunuch market before you can jerk off, you hear me? Aie, aie, aie, you are like my own son! You have the courage, the ardor, the balls to become a great Reis, with your own ship, your own fleet of ships, the greatest pirate on the Barbary Coast, and you have to fall in love with an infidel, the most expensive one I've ever seen to boot! She is destined for the Dey of Algiers himself! Do you like your head? Or would you LIKE to see it roll around Execution Square in Algiers? Allah! What have I done to deserve this!"

All this had taken place before the eyes of the Christian captives; his only solace was that they had had no idea what they were witnessing. Hamidou had failed in his first attempt to deal with the world as it was, but that day he vowed never again to allow anything to come between him and what he desired. And what he desired most besides his green-eyed Christian was the fame and fortune of a great Reis.

It was a question of face, thought Baba Mohammed as he smiled into his long hennaed beard. He scratched his nose, then his balls, and squinted nearsightedly at his agitated minister of finance, then at the two Giaours on their knees before him, their strange skirts billowing around them, their heads bent, their rosary beads clicking.

"You know I'm too old for this sort of thing, Suleiman Pasha."

"But Your Highness, it's . . ."

"A matter of face," finished the Dey. "And Abdulhamid after forty-four years in the 'Cage' and a harem of two hundred is too old for this sort of thing also. Although I hear his harem is quite active. More than I can say for mine. . . ."

"Sire . . ."

"Yes, yes, *yes*. I will not let the Ottoman minister dictate what I can or cannot do. But I really don't want a row about this, Suleiman. . . . I'm too old. I've got more important things on my mind. . . . How many Christian slaves did I promise the Sultan for his coronation?"

"Fifty, Your Grace."

"And how many have we sent?"

"None, Your Grace, we never got around to sending him anything for the coronation. Our tribute is six years late."

"Perfect then. I promised him fifty Christians—and I'll send him fifty-one as a *personal* gesture of friendship. One that I'd choose for myself, an 'extraordinary.' She will go with the tribute."

"And the other American?"

"The Ottoman minister can *have* her. I hope they'll be very happy together. He will find to his surprise that Americans in the dark are the same."

The minister looked up at his master, Baba Mohammed.

"Phew," sighed the Dey. "Get those two women to my harem and *bathed*. Verify the virginity of both, although there can be little doubt. Have them depilated and get them some clothes. But the blonde is to be presented to the Kizlar Aga in Istanbul in what she is now wearing. The Sultan will find it extraordinary. Get all her European frocks cleaned and in order, as well as a more conventional wardrobe. . . . This is my personal gift to Sultan Abdulhamid."

The Dey of Algiers rose and approached the two girls. He raised the chin of the first, the white one, and looked into her face, bringing his own close to see if her breath was sweet. He was surprised at what he read there. Of course, there were terror and disgust, but there was also something else: intelligence, willfulness, courage, insolence and fierce pride . . . most of all, pride. If she knew the real meaning of pride, he thought, that is, in the masculine sense of the word, something Orientals didn't teach their women, she would make an interesting gift to the Sultan. She might even, thought Baba Mohammed, manage to poison him if she got the chance—or turn traitor, or double agent. With eyes like hers, one never knew if one would survive the night . . . and she was only fourteen. . . . What would she be at twenty-two? he wondered. He felt himself stir. Perhaps he should keep her for himself. . . .

He turned to the second, the brown one. A rare beauty despite her darkness, he thought. And here too he read fierce pride, but of a different nature, and also pure hatred, deep, profound and abiding hatred. He would not trust *her* with a dagger either. Did she understand that she had been saved from the slave market and was destined for great luxury and the sacred doors of the harem of the third most powerful man (at least on paper) in Algiers? That she now ranked above her ex-mistress? Baba Mohammed motioned to his interpreter.

"Tell the black one that she is to be one of the wives of Keznapar Pasha, with the rank of Sultane. She is ordered to serve him faithfully and that he will be honor-bound, as Ambassador Plenipotentiary of the Ottoman Empire, to provide her with his protection, food, shelter, clothing, jewels, slaves and a private revenue. My condition is the following—that as a personal gesture of thankfulness, she should renounce her false prophet and embrace the true Faith of Allah who in his wisdom has given her such a fine husband. It is indecent for an African to be a Christian once the light of Islam has shone upon her."

Angélique and her mistress listened with disbelief to Baba Mohammed's words, as interpreted by a dragoman. The white slave in horrified stupor and the black one in alert resentment. When the interpreter had given the conditions of Angélique's marriage, her mistress's hand had flown to her mouth and she had cried out. But Angélique had made no gesture. She had not in effect moved a muscle from the beginning of the interpreter's speech to the end. Her eyes, which had stared straight ahead, had not blinked nor had her body flinched at the words "false prophet." There played about her fine lips a small smile.

"You are willing to renounce your Christian God for the God of the Prophet Mohammed, Allah the Powerful?"

"Oui, Sire." Angélique nodded.

"No, Angélique, you will burn in hell," her mistress cried out.

"Where do you think I've been living all my life?" replied Angélique. "And my mother, my father and my brother . . ."

The surprised interpreter didn't translate Angélique's words to her mistress for the Dey. It was, after all, only a conversation between women.

"What, Monsieur, is a harem?" Angélique asked the interpreter boldly.

"The word harem," he said, "comes from the Arabic *haram,* which means sacred, forbidden, unlawful. The holy cities of Mecca and Medina are considered *haram.* Women's quarters are *haram.* The harem is women's sanctuary, their holy place, the most respected place in a Moslem's house," replied Sid Huseyin, the Greek dragoman. "The place a Moslem is willing to die for."

The Dey Baba Mohammed fingered the large sapphire ring on his left hand and turned to the other girl. By the look on his amused face, she knew there was no appeal.

"You will be sent to Istanbul as part of my much belated tribute to the Sultan, Allah's Shadow on Earth. I urge you to renounce your false God and embrace Islam, for Allah, Lord of the Creation, is the only God and Mohammed is His Prophet."

"Jamais! Jamais! Never will I renounce God the Creator, the Lord Almighty, whose only son, Jesus Christ, died to save us!"

"It is just as well," said Baba Mohammed. "If you had embraced Islam, I would not have been able to send you. These women are dismissed. Inform the French Consul of my irrevocable decision. Strike her name from the registers."

His world, thought Baba Mohammed, was full of such moments and he cherished them.

The two girls were raised to their feet by female slaves to be taken to the baths. For one moment they faced each other over the schism that now separated them. Angélique was not pretending. She had renounced God. Despite herself, Angélique's ex-mistress shivered with fear and indignation. Angélique's godmother was her aunt! Angélique had renounced the only thing in the entire world that mattered: salvation. Her mother's African soul had been saved by her family and now Angélique had thrown it all away in the name of . . . of what? Not freedom! But survival, the harem, another prison! It was as if Angélique's whole life had been wiped from her soul. Not one word of comfort, of tenderness, of love escaped from Angélique's lips—and she *knew* she loved her!

"Angélique," whispered her ex-mistress.

But Angélique did not answer. Two negatives make a positive, she thought. And two Gods canceled each other out in her eyes. She no longer believed in anything or anyone. Her Pasha would come to fetch her and she would not have a backward glance.

The drama being played out in pantomime amused the Dey, for even if he was illiterate, Baba Mohammed could read human faces. He saw the hurt, the desolation and the fear on the face of one girl and the vengeance, the hatred and the sorrow on the face of the other.

Never, vowed Angélique's ex-mistress, would she renounce the Faith of her fathers, her race, her color. Never. Never. Never. There was only one God and Jesus Christ was His only Son. It was from that moment that she took to praying without cease, her lips constantly moving, her hands incessantly counting her rosary. In hysterical exorcism, she prayed out of fear. Repeating the same formula thousands and thousands of times in hope of keeping her terror away. She would never renounce her Faith. She would die first.

Sid Huseyin Oukil-Hardy, the Greek dragoman, checked the inventory of the gifts as they were loaded onto the Dey's personal sloop:

15 lions, 52 silk belts, 60 coral rosaries, 1 ivory rosary, 2 amber rosaries, 22 woolen blankets, 10 gladiators, 10 pistols decorated in coral, 10 muskets, 10 powder-horns, 10 cartridge pouches with gold ornaments, 10 gold watches (without music), a diamond ring for the Sultan, 60 shawls of fringed silk, 30 red haiks from Biskra, 10 lightweight haiks for women made in Morocco, 50 red haiks, 80 Tlemcen haiks, 80 Beni-Abbés haiks, 60 Saharan rugs, 35 svelte Negresses, 16 Negroes, 51 Christian slaves, a pair of gold pistols for the Sultan, encrusted with pearls, 150 tobacco pouches, 2 black eunuchs, 2 flags embroidered in gold; Mohammed Pasha remits to the Sultan's private treasury: 16,000 gold mahbouts, 2,000 gold dinars and 10,800 French francs.

—Chouel 1189 (Friday, September 10, 1781).

The sloop skirted the last of Africa. The little white huddle of Sidi Bou Said was visible in a distant line of red earth. Far away inland rose the lonely blue silhouette of the Bou Kosein and behind it, as faint as a ghost, the peak of Djebel Ressas. . . . Africa faded. There were only the vast and endless sea, the interminable flat horizon, the monotonous blue that touched it.

For weeks they sailed within the confines of the Ottoman Empire.

Tripoli and Alexandria slid by. The Syrian coast seemed a mirage, and for several weeks they put in at Smyrna. Then one day, several weeks later, the forlorn waters of the Dardanelles widened into the milky blue of the Marmara. The ship drew nearer and there, standing on its seven hills, wrapped in the Bosphorus and the Golden Horn, rose imperial Istanbul.

The Greek and the captive stood looking out upon the thousands of domes and minarets lit by the westerly sun reflected in the waters of the Archipelago, immobile as a lake, tinted in rose.

"This city is Istanbul," said Sid Huseyin. "And verily, it is the jewel of the world. . . . How many times have I arrived in this port and how many times has Istanbul disillusioned me? Never. She is universal and sovereign before the poet, or the Prince, the ambassador, or the sailor. The son of the north or the son of the south, all judge this city as the most beautiful place on earth."

The boat dropped anchor just beyond the entrance to the port of Istanbul in order to arrive later in the morning. The ship's cannons boomed in salute.

The Golden Horn was overcast by a light haze behind which the young Creole saw the city rise confusedly out of the mist, as if the same gauze that veiled Ottoman women veiled the city. In the distance, the quay and docks seemed deserted. But it was by order of the Kizlar Aga himself. Slowly, one by one, black and precise, the cypresses of Istanbul began to outline themselves against a dazzling ribbon of light like an army of slim giants. Behind the cypresses, suddenly the four minarets of Santa Sophia became visible. Then, from hill to hill, mosque to mosque, into the infinite distance, all the minarets, one after the other, turned amber; all the cupolas, one after the other, turned silver. Terrace by terrace, mezzotint by mezzotint, the dawn descended to reveal Istanbul in its totality; magenta on its heights, bluish and lilac along its banks, it rose from its own waters and its own reflection, as if freshly bathed. The entire, stupendous profile of the imperial city delineated itself against the horizon with such flair and finesse of color that the young girl could count at every rise each cypress, each minaret, each pyramid that crowned her strange destination: Seraglio Point and the Palace of Topkapi. The resplendence before her was like the blast of trumpets. The white slave thought of the first day of creation . . . and for her it *was* the first day of creation. . . . She knew only that she wanted to live. For if, as she gazed for the first time at Istanbul, she had had to describe her adventures up until that moment, she would have had to have more recourse to imagination than to memory, for her other life suddenly and irrevocably faded into fiction. . . .

Overhead, flocks of wild white birds circled and circled. Sid Huseyin looked up and said: "No motive can be assigned for their appearance. They do not seem in pursuit of any prey. They are never seen feeding or alighting, either on land or water, and take no notice of the shoals of fish and flocks that follow in their wake, but are impelled by a restless instinct to keep perpetually in motion. . . . It is for this reason that they are called the 'damned souls.' No one I have ever spoken to has ever heard the sound of their wings."

Sid Huseyin escorted her toward the tumult of the harbor below. Above the ships, the great mass of the Seraglio sat on its promontory between Asia and Europe, its great seawalls clasping it like a giant aquamarine. The cypresses and umbrella pines rose black and chill beside the battlement walls that stretched almost beyond view. And guarding it all was the Sublime Porte, the Bab-i-Humayun, the only way in and the only way out of the fabulous world of Topkapi. Sid Huseyin had said even the horses trod softly there.

Before the white slave realized it, she was being handed over by the Captain to the Kizlar Aga himself, the redoubtable Chief Black Eunuch, the Third Officer of the Empire, who had come personally from the palace to fetch the "extraordinary." Her rosary in hand, her lips moving in prayer, her black skirts billowing in the wind, she looked up to find a man as black as any she had ever seen dressed like a King. She thought he was the Sultan. She cried out suddenly and threw herself into the arms of the startled Kizlar Aga, to his great surprise and to the terror of Sid Huseyin, who saw his head separated from his body as the palace Halberdiers and the Kizlar Aga's personal bodyguards started toward them, sabers drawn. But the Chief Black Eunuch recovered his dignity, rearranged his robes and smiled speculatively to himself as he eyed the new captive. Why had she done such a thing? he wondered. He had learned that so much power over life and death made gratuitous actions almost a necessity to sanity. He could choose to take this child and throw her into the sea and no one would dare raise his eyes, let alone his voice. Or he could fling her before the startled gaze of the Sultan and ensure her fortune forever. Such was his power. Such was his choice. He flinched at the roaring of the fifteen caged lions, part of the Dey's tribute, now deposited on the dock. But the Kizlar Aga had suddenly decided how to present to the Sultan this green-eyed creature with the stubborn jaw who had embraced him, and so paid no attention to the lions. The prize stood staring at the Kizlar Aga's ruby buttons, her lips constantly moving in prayer, her Christian worry beads dropping one by one from her steady hand, her transparent gaze blazing like gems set in alabaster, her red-yellow waist-length hair billowing three feet above her head in the wind.

The Black Eunuch had an idea, but it was so audacious that he would have to consult with the Kiaya, the Lady Controller of the harem. There was no Valide, as the Sultan's mother was long dead. Yes, he would consult with Kiaya Kurrum. And it would be a hilarious parody of Hasan Gazi Pasha . . . the insufferable Grand Admiral and the inseparable Agony. . . .

The next day, the Black Eunuch mounted his coup. It delighted and amazed the jaded Sultan Abdulhamid. The Creole was presented to him in a cage placed among the fifteen cages of live lions that had been sent in tribute in the gardens of the Fourth Court, near the kiosk of Baghdad. The captive was dressed in black, European style, wearing the most voluminous of her crinolines. She was jewel-less and wore a mantilla of black lace thrown over, but not covering, the immensity of her wild waist-length hair. She stood, slim waist emerging from the huge circle of the black silk skirt that completely hid the bottom half of her body, presenting the most bizarre form the Sultan had ever seen. As the Kizlar Aga had hoped, she held the rosary in her hands in front of her and her lips moved constantly in silent prayer, the beads falling continuously one by one from her clasped hands.

The Sultan was so delighted, he unclasped a sapphire brooch and pressed it into the flattered Kizlar Aga's hand. He clapped his hands like an astonished child.

"Who is she?"

"An American, Sire."

"Why are her lips continually moving? And why does she finger tespi which is not the correct number?"

"It is a Christian rosary. She is praying to her God, which she has never ceased to do since she set foot in Istanbul. Her beads are used much as we use ours to mark off the ninety-nine names of Allah."

"How extraordinarily beautiful to me that her lips move like that so silently amidst all this clamor. . . . If only our women were to make so little noise with their lips. They have only to move their upper lip and the sound is like the roaring of these lions. . . . A quiet tongue . . . she pleases me."

"She is not yet prepared to serve you, Sire."

"Yes, I know, but soon. Soonest. Put her in the care of Kiaya Kurrum."

On a whim, the Kizlar Aga had achieved a sensational entrance for his prize, but at what price? he wondered. He had put the newly arrived slave in mortal danger. She had become in one day Gozde, "in the eye," noticed by the Sultan. This was already the third rank in the harem, the desire of hundreds of women. The jealousy of the other harem inmates, their natural propensity for intrigue and even murder, would be put to use. To be noticed by the Sultan sometimes took years, in most cases it never happened at all.

"I shall call her *Naksh* for 'tongue,' " said Abdulhamid, "which also means 'heart,' and *dil* for 'broidery,' *embroidered tongue,* for she has a golden yet silent tongue which has touched me. Call her Naksh-i-dil."

"Naksh-i-dil," repeated the Black Eunuch like a judgment.

CHAPTER THREE

THE BLACK EUNUCH
1781

For there are eunuchs which were born from their mother's womb;
and there are eunuchs which were made eunuchs by men; and there
are eunuchs which made themselves eunuchs for the Kingdom of
Heaven's sake. That those who can, accept.

—MATTHEW, XIX: 12

Edris Kizlar Aga, the Chief Black Eunuch, unlocked his private
rooms, choosing carefully his own key among the hundreds on the great
ring stuffed in his sash. He entered the narrow doorway of his cell. His
high white turban towered twenty-five inches above his head like a huge
sugarloaf. Diamonds and rubies sparkled on his temples and down his
chest. The rich brocade of his gown of flowered silk and his sable-lined
pelisse brushed against the young eunuch standing guard, saber in
hand, and the even younger one sprawled on the floor in front of the
door. The arrival of Naksh-i-dil and her successful presentation had left
a bitter taste in his mouth rather than exultation. The pleasure of the
Sultan was his aim in life, but there had been something about the
young girl that had touched him.

The history of the Ottoman Empire, he knew, was a long testament
to the enormous power wielded by women. And this cowering yet defi-
ant child, with her hypnotic gaze and, he decided, the most beautiful
green eyes in the Archipelago, could with luck become one of them.
There were more than three hundred women in Abdulhamid I's harem,
some of whom had lived through years of treachery and danger, bicker-

ing and intrigue. The harem was a hermitage, thought the Black Eunuch, not of sexuality, but of power. Ambition ruled the harem: women locked in internal politics, natural acquisitions, the advancement of protégés, and above all . . . the accession of their sons. . . . This was the foreign and domestic policy of his domain, he thought.

When the Black Eunuch had decided to separate himself from himself and with one blow deprived himself of the function of father, and the name of husband, he had been seventeen years old and in love. His adored wife, Tityi, had died in her fifteenth year giving birth to his child, who had also died. He had known then, as sure as God had forsaken him, that he would never love again. And so he condemned himself by his own hand to the dreadful prison of the castrato. He lamented neither his fate nor his pain. Not that he could say that he had had one day of calm or serenity since.

He had wanted to be free of the onset of love by his powerlessness to satisfy it, and he had finished by loving total strangers. Those who were in the best position to keep him rich, safe and unwronged. Eunuchs were objects of contempt to the rest of the world and to the rest of mankind, thought the Black Eunuch. Thus he had need of the Sultan. For there was no man who would not think he had the right to take advantage of a eunuch. But there was a reason a eunuch was superior to all others in fidelity. Eunuchs were not weaklings. He had drawn his conclusions from other species; vicious horses and bulls when castrated lose some of their spirits, but they are not deprived of their strength or capacity for work. In the same way, dogs when castrated stop running away from their masters, but are no less useful for hunting or guarding. One could say that men, after all, were not animals. Yet men, he had found, became gentler when deprived of desire, but no less careful of that which was entrusted to them. They were no less efficient horsemen, no less skillful lancers, no less ambitious men. His misfortune, thought the Kizlar Aga, was what the world thought him to be, depriving him of his pride.

The suite of the Kizlar Aga was small and compact. It included several rooms, and his favorite was the delightful coffee room he was sitting in. It was an octagonal, domed space, covered from ceiling to floor with fiery red tiles. Only one Armenian in all of Constantinople had known how to make them, and he had taken the secret of their color to his grave. The dome was gilded in white and silver, and flower motifs adorned the outer rim. From a small opening in the center of the dome, light filtered into the somber interior, entirely bare except for the

Kizlar Aga's silver coffeepot on a low table whose form repeated that of
the room. A glass lamp and a brazier were placed near a low divan
resting upon a pile of carpets. Surrounding this most private chamber
were a bedroom, a smoking room, his baths, a lavatory and a writing
room.

I am a rich man, mused the Kizlar Aga. His personal fortune
amounted to some twenty million piastres. The list of his personal
slaves outside of the harem read like a census of the Empire: 52 Bosni-
ans, 24 Circassians, 22 Hungarians, 16 Albanians, 7 Croats, 7 Franks, 4
Abazinians, 3 Germans, 3 Greeks, 2 Georgians, 2 Mingrelians, 1 Russian, 1 Walachian.

He sank onto the divan in his coffee room and adjusted the silver-
embroidered cushions behind him. A slave came forward to light his
water pipe, and his eyes slowly adjusted to the darkness of the room,
which overlooked the myriad galleries, alleys, gates and subterranean
passages leading to the treasury or to prisons, courtyards, dormitories
and cells of the black eunuchs.

The room overlooked as well the door to the harem and the Golden
Road, which led from the harem to the Sultan's chambers. It was the
only route from the harem to the Sultan.

The Chief Black Eunuch was not only chief of the women, but Nazir,
inspector of the Vakfs, the religious endowments of the imperial mosque
as well as those of the holy cities of Mecca and Medina. He was commander of the Baltaji, or Halberdiers, held the rank of Pasha with three
horses' tails. At the same time he was the messenger between the Sultan
and the Grand Vizier, and confidant to the Valide. He alone could
approach the Sultan at any time, day or night. And he alone could
touch him.

Every Wednesday, the Kizlar Aga participated in the Divan, the
privy council of the Empire, and was consulted on all nominations to
the palace and government. His salary was the highest of all the officers
of the palace and his fortune augmented by unending presents from
men and women wishing to gain favor. During the coronation of a new
Sultan, the imperial sword was given to the Sultan by the Kizlar Aga.
The Grand Vizier took the right arm of the Sultan, and the Chief Black
Eunuch his left arm. At the death of a sovereign, it was the Chief Black
Eunuch who announced the news to the Grand Vizier and then to the
hereditary Prince. It was he who was charged with rendering the accounts of the personal fortune and jewels accumulated by the defunct
monarch during his lifetime to a council of ministers. At funerals, he

alone represented the eunuch class. When the Sultan took his boat out to sea, he was immediately followed by the Silahdar, his bodyguard, in his boat and then by the Chief Black Eunuch. During the ceremonial periods, like all the courtiers of the palace, he offered the sovereign expensive gifts, along with a scribe who neatly wrote down in a ledger their name and nature and price. A law made the presence of the Kizlar Aga compulsory at a Prince's wedding. At the time of an imperial birth the Queen Mother would send to her Chief Eunuch a bedspread and a puside, a small blanket for the feet, decorated with golden thread. It was the Black Eunuch who took possession of all gifts that arrived at the harem.

The Imperial Sultanas received their living allowances from the Black Eunuch according to a memorandum established by him. He was Third Officer in the Empire. First, the sovereign, then the Grand Vizier, and third, the Chief Black Eunuch.

Anyone wishing to gain favor with the Sultan through the Valide would only be able to do so through him. And he was Kizlar Aga for life. If he retired, he received a handsome pension. He had no fear of being killed for his wealth, since everything returned to the Sultan; but for his powers, he could die a violent death.

Ever since the struggle of power between the white eunuchs and the black eunuchs for ascendancy in the harem, the post of Kizlar Aga, the Dar-u-Caaden, Keeper of the Door of Felicity, had been a position fraught with danger, power and money. Eunuchs of both colors had existed in the palace under the reign of Bayazid I, and all the eunuchs had been under the direction of the Chief White Eunuch, the Kapi Aga. Under the reign of Sultan Murat III, two hundred years before, the Black Eunuch Mehmet Aga had succeeded in seizing control of the palace eunuchs by eliminating the Chief White Eunuch.

This was the first time in the history of the Ottoman Empire that a black became the Supreme Chief of the eunuchs. His successor, the Black Eunuch Server Aga, had caused such misunderstanding between the occupants of the palace and those of the provinces that he was evicted from his post. The direction of all eunuchs returned to the hands of a white eunuch, a Bosnian. Finally in 1595 a black eunuch retook control of his peers, and this control had remained ever since in the possession of the blacks.

The Kizlar Aga sighed. For him, life would finish either tragically or in a manner quite picturesque. If by order of the sovereign his execution was not to be carried out by the Dar, he would finish his days in Egypt.

There was also disposition, thought the Kizlar Aga, in general the day on which the procession transported the imperial gifts to Mecca. That day the Emir-i-Abur of the palace was placed in the hands of the Chief Black Eunuch, the reins of the camel burdened with rich presents. The Chief Black Eunuch guided the camel three times past the Sultan and the dignitaries of the palace. If the Grand Horse Master did not take the reins from the Chief Black Eunuch's hands, it was the sign of his dismissal. He would leave by the middle door, the Orta Kapi, in the care of a commander, who would exile him somewhere in Hedjaz. If the Grand Horse Master *took* the bridle, it meant that he had retained his post and he would appear before his sovereign and receive his due, the gift of an ermine coat. But even a disgraced and exiled eunuch was not always safe. Death could pursue him even to his place of exile.

Still, despite all his sinister burdens, he felt from time to time a lifting of the heart, a kind of tremor mixed with melancholy and tenderness. He felt the weight of all these women. The footpaths that he crushed under his horse's hooves heard the swish of their silks. The arches of the small colonnades surrounding him resounded with the childish laughter of Princes and Princesses. He alone gazed upon these women, cried innumerable names, called them once, a hundred times, and heard some voice reply somewhere far away. Slave flesh.

The Hazinedar Aga, the Palace Treasurer, had been standing before the Kizlar Aga for several minutes before he realized his presence. The Treasurer, being a slave, would never have dared by a movement or a word to make his presence known. He knew what the Kizlar Aga wanted and he proceeded with his accounting. The dazed Black Eunuch, brought back abruptly from his reverie, listened. The Hazinedar Aga proceeded to read out his inventory.

"Gifts sent by Baba Mohammed Pasha to the Sultan Abdulhamid I, the tenth of September, 1781, from the vassal state of Algiers."

The Kizlar Aga said nothing. The gifts were satisfactory. Naksh-i-dil was spectacular. The arrogant Algerians always managed to send their gifts so late, and on foreign boats, so that their Reis had no chance of being held ransom for more tribute, thought the Black Eunuch.

The Hazinedar Aga took leave of his master, bringing his left hand to his forehead and down again, saying:

"We pray to God that sweet sleep closes your eyelids and gives rest to your body, and that your guardian angel watches over you this night and that the sun, every day more beautiful, rises tomorrow to shine upon you. . . ."

The irony of his treasurer's leave-taking was not lost on the worried Kizlar Aga.

This fictional world in which he lived that was the Great Harem of Topkapi was like no other. And everything changed with the changing of the despot: the Sultan. His will passed through this small world like a current of tenderness and melancholy. . . .

The Black Eunuch pulled his sable-lined caftan across his chest as if he were cold. His eyes closed. The young eunuch standing in the opposite doorway lurched forward as if summoned.

The Black Eunuch sighed.

"Tulip."

The adolescent boy, who had been waiting and watching, dashed across the polished teak floor of the Black Eunuch's coffee room and prostrated himself at the feet of his master.

"Master."

"I want coffee, and I want my writing materials."

Both were brought by the bright, devoted eleven-year-old. An Asagi, a debutant eunuch charged with keeping constant guard before the multitude of doors and passageways in the harem. The Kizlar Aga paused, then lifted the strong, steaming, aromatic liquid to his lips, relishing the stolen hour of his precious time. Then he laid out his writing materials. Tulip stood immobile by the coffee tray at his side, for he knew this was the way he liked to work. The Black Eunuch fingered his pen, the papyrus parchment and the rich black Egyptian ink now arranged on the low table before him. With infinite joy and clarity, he began a new poem for Tityi:

Pul	*Derdime derman bul*
Jonquil	Have pity on my sufferings.
Kihat	*Biilerum sahat sahat*
Paper	Each moment I burn.
Ermut	*Ver bize bir umut*
Pear	Allow me some hope.
Sabun	*Derdinden oldum sabun*
Soap	I am sick with love.

Chemur	*Ben aglarum sen gul*
Coal	That I could die so that my years would join yours!
Gul	*Ben aglarum sen gul*
Rose	I would shoulder all your hurts in exchange for your happiness.
Hazir	*Oliim sana yazir*
Straw	Vouchsafe to make of me your slave!
Jo ha	*Ustune bulunmaz paha*
Cloth	Priceless one.
Tartsin	*Sen ghel ben chekeim senim harqin*
Cinnamon	All my worldly goods are yours.
Gira	*Esking-ilen oldum ghira*
Match	I burn, I burn, my flame consumes me.

In the name of Allah, the Clement, the Master of Mercy, that the Greetings of God and His unshakable Blessing fall upon our Prophet Mohammed, on his family and his friends. Amen.

Change. It was the one thing not required in love. Just as perfection required no change. Change and perfection were as contradictory in government as in love. He had achieved the perfect love at seventeen. And he had dedicated his manhood to it with one unchangeable act. That act had been the perfect response to his ethical situation. With it he had defined himself forever. Castration was prohibited by the Koran. His act therefore was one of sin that required a lifetime of penitence. What better penitence for a castrato than to live one's life in a world of women. . . .

The dazzling calligraphy slid over the page embellished with the flourishes and inventions required. The Black Eunuch shut his mind to everything else.

His destiny was to be in this place, as if his hand had been guided by forces as supernatural as those that had brought Naksh-i-dil's ship to grief, and her to Topkapi.

• CHAPTER FOUR •

THE LAZARIST 1781

Eunuchs were made to be the custodians of women and girls, to observe their conduct and to prevent them from doing anything against their chastity or their conjugal duties. And apparently to that usage the Eunuch has correctly been defined; for the word signifies bed guard or bedroom guardian. It is still for that use that they are made in the Orient.

—COMTE D'OLLINCAN, *Traité des Eunuques*, 1707

Constantinople, April 4, 1781

Superior General Father Brzozowski
The Company of Jesus
St. Petersburg

My Reverend Father,
The Peace of our Savior be with you.
You commanded me to give you an exact account concerning the practice of eunuchism in the Empire of the Ottomans and especially in its court, where they number more than a thousand. I hope that this information written to honor my engagement will contribute to the conversion and health of the souls of the persons that I have the honor to speak to you of.
In the case of eunuchs everybody knows that the condition is not natural, but is a terrible mutilation imposed by one male upon another. The effect is seen—and heard—the reason generally appreciated; but the methods by which the mutilation is carried out

and the different degrees to which this can be done appear to be hardly known at all. The general ignorance is certainly not due to lack of interest in the subject, but to several distinct factors—the scarcity of information, the secrecy which has always surrounded the infamous trade of making eunuchs, and the consequential disinclination of those connected in any way with it to discuss the subject at all.

It is more than four thousand years that one speaks of eunuchs in this world: Sacred History and profane history mention to infinity persons of this nature that range neither in the ranks of men, neither in the ranks of women, so that they are called a *third kind of man.* We have seen such a great number of them throughout all the centuries and in all the countries, and one sees so many still that one cannot permit oneself to doubt that there have been, there are today, and there will be forever, eunuchs.

I shall trace as briefly as possible the origin of the use of eunuchs, the route by which the custom came to Europe, how the Turkish supply is obtained. This information is little known in the West, and merits more than ignorance.

The original home of the eunuch appears to have been Mesopotamia, the cradle of so many institutions to be transplanted westward. The contention of Ammianus Marcellinus is that the first person to castrate men was the Semiramis Queen Sammuramat, widow of Ninus, mother of Nynias, and who ruled Assyria as Queen Mother from 811 to 808 B.C. According to tradition, she dressed like a man, raised her son like a daughter and was murdered by one of her own eunuchs.

It is proved from extant texts that eunuchs were employed in Assyria, and their constant mention in the Old Testament tends to support this assertion. With the eunuch priest of Ephesian Artemis, Atargatis, and the Cybele-Attis cult, we are not concerned, nor does our brief inquiry touch religious sodomy, wide-spread not only in Africa but also among the ancient Semites.

Eunuchs were employed in Persia, in the kingdoms of the Egyptians, by the Phoenicians, the Carthaginians, the Greeks and the Romans. There existed on the islands of Chios and Delos and in the city of Ephesus veritable entrepôts of eunuchs, famous throughout the Oriental Mediterranean.

As you well know, there is the question of the two eunuch officers of the Pharaoh that Joseph meets in prison. Putiphar who bought Jacob's son was himself a eunuch and chief of the guards of the Pharaoh. The Prophet Samuel announced to his people that the future King of Israel would have eunuchs in his court and, in effect, eunuchs made their first appearance under King David and others such as Achab and Joram up until the capture of Jerusalem by Nabuchodonosor.

It would seem that there are several kinds of eunuchs, quite apart from those born entirely impotent. The early Christians naturally followed Matthew:

> For there are eunuchs which were so born from their mother's womb; and there are eunuchs which were made eunuchs by men; and there are eunuchs which made themselves eunuchs for the Kingdom of Heaven's sake. That those who can, accept.

Critics of this passage tell us that the word "eunuch" is used symbolically, and the meaning is that those who have entirely devoted themselves to the interests of the Kingdom of Heaven cannot satisfy the claims to married life. However, Origen lived to repent his too literal rendering of this passage. It is interesting to note that Mohammed also uses the word in a symbolic sense when he condemns the making of eunuchs, and adds "Castration in Islam may consist only in fasting."

In classical times the varieties of eunuchs were as follows:

1) Castrati, clean-cut—both penis and testicles
2) Spadones, whose testicles only are removed by a process of dragging
3) Thlibioe, whose testicles are bruised and crushed, the seminal glands being thus permanently injured—chiefly applied in the case of the very young

The *thlasioe* were almost identical with number three above. In the East, there are three kinds:

1) Sandali, or clean-shaved. The parts are swept off by a single cut of a razor, a tube (tin or wooden) is set in the urethra, the wound is cauterized with boiling oil, and the patient is planted in a fresh dunghill. His diet is milk, and if under puberty he often survives.

2) The eunuch whose penis is removed. He retains all the power of copulation and procreation without the wherewithal; and this is sometimes supplied.

3) The eunuch, or classical thlibias and semivir, who has been rendered sexless by the removal of the testicles (as the priests of Cybele were castrated with a stone knife), or by their being bruised, twisted, seared, or bandaged.

The operation is performed in this manner: white ligatures or bandages are bound tightly round the lower part of the belly and the upper parts of the thighs, to prevent too much hemorrhage. The parts about to be operated on are then bathed three times with hot pepper-water, the intended eunuch being in a reclining position. When the parts have been sufficiently bathed, the whole —both testicles and penis—are cut off as closely as possible with a small curved knife, something in the shape of a sickle. The emasculation being effected, a pewter needle or spigot is carefully thrust into the main orifice at the root of the penis; the wound is then covered with paper saturated in cold water and is carefully bound up. After the wound is dressed the patient is made to walk about the room, supported by two "knifers," for two or three hours, then he is allowed to lie down. The patient is not allowed to drink anything for three days, during which time he often suffers great agony, not only from thirst, but from intense pain, and from the impossibility of relieving nature during that period. At the end of three days the bandage is taken off, the spigot is pulled out, and the sufferer obtains relief in the copious flow of urine, which spurts out like a fountain. If this takes place satisfactorily, the patient is considered out of danger, but if the unfortunate wretch cannot make water he is doomed to a death of agony for the passages have become swollen and nothing can save him.

Eunuchs who often nurse their grievances for years take their revenge if opportunity offers, as is well known from the history of Hermotimus the Pedasian, the most favored of all the eunuchs of Xerxes. According to Herodotus, Hermotimus was taken by an enemy and sold to one Panionius, a Chian, who gained his livelihood by purchasing boys of remarkable beauty, castrating them, and selling them at Sardis and Ephesus for large sums. Chance brought Hermotimus in touch with Panionius later in life, and he persuaded Panionius to move to Sardis with his wife and children.

Having thus got his old enemy into his power, Hermotimus forced him to castrate his own four sons. Not being yet satisfied, he then made the sons castrate their father. "Thus the vengeance of Hermotimus overtook Panionius."

There is, however, considerable difference of opinion among scholars about the derivation and meaning of the best-known word of all—"eunuch." Several German philologists suggest that the Greek εὐνοῦχος is a loan word from the Semitic. I can, however, find no proof of this whatever, and inquiries from Assyrian and Hebrew scholars have yielded nothing in support of such a theory. It would seem, then, that the old derivation, from εὐνή, "bed," and οχ, the ablaut stem of 'ἔχειν, "to keep"—the word thus meaning "he who has charge of the bed"—should still be adhered to.

The only Assyrian connection appears to be through the Hebrew sārīs, "eunuch," which is a loan word from the Assyrian ša rêši, meaning, as a passage in a medical text explains, la alidi, "he who does not beget." Thus these words are self-explanatory, whereas "eunuch" tells us nothing of the physical condition. It should be noted, however, that the Hebrew sārīs has two distinct meanings—in fact, there were really two separate words—one being "eunuch" and the other "captain," "high official," or "chamberlain." The latter occurs chiefly in the Old Testament (Deuteronomy, 2 Kings, Isaiah, Jeremiah, etc.), while in Matthews, Acts and Romans, the former is the meaning intended. There are several other words connected with castration that are informative, as they show us that the condition was brought about by crushing, striking, cutting and pulling.

The method of striking or crushing is apparent in such words as the Latin capo, "capon," from the Greek κόπτω, "to strike," the Greek θλᾰδίας, "eunuch" from θλάω, "crush." Cutting connotes the Latin word castro, "to castrate," or the word "eunuch," from the Greek τομίας, from τέμνω, "to cut." In Sanskrit nirasṭa means "castrated," from aśri, "edge" or "knife." Finally, the operation of pulling or dragging appears to be implied in such words as the Greek noun σπάδων, "eunuch," from σπάω, "to drag."

It is above all in the Roman Empire of the East that the use of eunuchs was brought to its fullest realization. In Byzantium eunuchs were personages of great importance and the most influential after the Emperor and the Empress. It was Constantine VII who complained that the imperial palace was crawling with as many eunuchs as a horse stable with flies in the summer. In Byzantium it was usually the Armenians who were in charge of the office of castration. The Latin poet Claudian in his *Invective Against Europe* spoke in these terms:

> Up hastens the Armenian whose sure steel always knows how to change the sex of man . . . draining from his double reservoir the source of fecundity, ravishing with one blow at the same time, the victim of a father's function and a husband's name.

In Russia eunuchs existed in the harems of the Russian Princes, and in the eleventh century it seems that there are voluntary Russian eunuchs who made of their castration a profession of Christian Faith and asceticism. This sect is called Skoptsy and numbers over 100,000.

During the Middle Ages, it was mostly the Jews and the Abyssinians who practiced the eunuch trade. The first furnished *white eunuchs* and the second *black eunuchs.* Amongst the goods transported between Europe and Asia, the eunuch figured along with silk, furs, swords, musk and other merchandise.

The custom lingers in the Levant, and when the Turks first began to seclude their women, the Byzantines were able to supply the necessary eunuchs for a time. White eunuchs were obtainable from many of the conquered areas, but they often proved delicate, and the mortality was great. The Negro was tried, and proved both cheap and successful. The slave traders soon taught the African chiefs that a living prisoner was much more valuable than a dead one.

Here I must digress a moment, Reverend Father. The Ottomans borrowed from the Byzantines, of course, the custom of using eunuchs to guard their harems. But the use of black eunuchs exclusively has a twofold reason. First, their greater resistance to the mutilation itself and its aftermaths and secondly, the fact that a black man leaves traces of his race on his progeny that are a double insurance against a badly done or incomplete castration. A white eunuch could generate an infant that would be hard to prove was not that of the Sultan, but there could be no doubt that an infant engendered by a Negro was not the child of the Sultan;

the evidence would be beyond doubt: a black or, if you wish, mulatto infant. Indelible proof of transgression. . . .

According to Mohammedan law, slaves captured in war become the absolute property of the victor and, as any title to property, can be transferred. The slave dealer, having procured his slaves from an African chief or Arab kidnapper, can legally commit his right to any Mohammedan customer who cares to pay the price. Consequently, there is a lucrative trade. The chief locality from which the Negroes are obtained is in the upper reaches of the White Nile, chiefly Kordofan, Darfur and Dongola, as well as the Bagirmi district to the southeast of Lake Chad. Others come from Abyssinia, whence they proceed to the Red Sea ports of Massawa and Suakin to begin the journey to the chief emporiums, such as Smyrna, Beirut, Jedda, Mecca, Medina and Constantinople. For the most part of the White Nile Negroes are taken up the river to Alexandria in tiny boats, or else they are made to cross the Sahara partly on foot and partly on camel, finally reaching the coast.

It will thus be realized, My General, that eunuchs are not an invention of Moslem people, but that the Ottomans have adopted the Byzantine custom of employing eunuchs to guard their harems.

The secrets of the harem are also sacred in Islam, the harem being the sanctuary of sanctuaries, the word itself coming from the Arabic haram, meaning unlawful, as opposed to halah, that which is lawful; thus the whole region for a certain distance around Mecca and Medina was haram owing to the sacredness of these holy places. The Ottomans softened the word into harem and they apply it to that portion of the Moslem house occupied by women. The Turks are very careful to use only those eunuchs who are fully emasculated. White eunuchs—Georgians and Circassians—are given jobs that will never bring them into close touch with the women, as in most cases their castration is incomplete. But as regards the Negroes, the highest prices are paid for those who, besides being entirely rasé, possess the ugliest and most revolting faces, it being imagined (correctly or not) that this is a further guard against any profligacy on the part of the women. The Seraglio doctors not only inspect the eunuchs on admission, but examine them every few years just to see that everything is in order and that nothing has grown again!

Indeed, the fact that the eunuch who has lost only his testicles can have erections for a considerable time and enjoy sexual intercourse is fully recognized whenever such people are employed. This motif (if so it can be called) forms the main theme of the "Tale of the First Eunuch, Bukhayt," in the *Thousand and One Nights.* A Negro youth seduces a young girl and suffers castration as a punishment. He is then made her Aga but continues to have connection with her until she dies. It was said that his erectio et distentio penis would last as long as his heart and circulation kept sound. Hence the eunuch who preserves his penis is much prized in the zenana, where some women prefer him to the entire man, on account of his long performance of the deed of kind; but chiefly, I may add, because abortio non est opus.

Every form of sexual indulgence in the Seraglio and a eunuch in touch with the outside world can easily smuggle artificial phalli and similar erotic succedania into the harem and to a certain extent play the part of Lesbian, which by its very novelty and perversion might help satisfy the cravings of bored and neglected women. A eunuch, then, may marry. It has been said by one eunuch's wife that her husband practiced the manifold plaisirs de la petite oie (masturbation, tribadism, irrumation, tête-bêche, feuille-de-rose, etc.) until they induced the venereal paroxysm. At the critical moment she would hold a little pillow for her husband to bite, who otherwise would have torn her cheeks or breasts. There is ample evidence to show that eunuchs often have a deep and genuine affection for some of their charges, entirely free from any question of subsequent gain. It is more difficult to appreciate the technique employed by the woman to induce culumonus in the eunuchs, and no satisfactory accounts appear to exist. The procedure probably centers about the region immediately surrounding the opening of the urethra, as eunuchs sometimes report erotic sensations in that area. Anal massage would also play its part, while the knowledge and use of aphrodisiacs would assist.

Thus into the harem, so strongly and strangely eroticized, in which each sex defines itself in opposition with the other, a third sex is introduced, the eunuch, a chimeric being that carries within himself the confusion of attributes that breach the frontier between men and women and dilute the darkness and the light of these irredeemable opposites. One of God's creatures is mutilated: a sacrilegious and *sacrificial* act that serves to foil the primordial significance between slavery and mastery by creating a composite human being, neither male nor female, that assumes certain characteristics of both. The eunuch is then a victim who seems to have inherited the worst of each sex. The eunuch reflects in his body and in his soul the inversed image of the hyper-virility of men and the nymphomaniac weakness of women. He is at the same time, slave of the master, master of slaves, and being black, slave of slaves. His disquieting power which is most ambiguous makes this theatrical and somber personage one of the most significant in Ottoman institutions.

It is to be remarked that whenever we speak of Oriental eunuchs, we always represent them as persons of obesity with a triple chin, breasts and stomach overflowing their silk sashes and bouffant pants. In the Ottoman palaces, one surely sees such phenomena. I must say, Most Reverend Father, that in all truth I have never seen such a personage, but having known only one black eunuch, I cannot vouch for the entire race. Leprosy, gout and baldness never attack the eunuch.

To conclude, there is very little literature devoted to the eunuch. I might say that I myself am at work on Eunuch nati, facti, mystici ex sacra et humana litteratura illustrati.

I can recommend the work of Hieronymus Delphinus, Eunuchi conjugium; hoc est, scripta varia de conjugio inter eunuchum et virginem juvenculam anno 1666 contracto.

I should add here, Your Excellence, that of all the virtues that should render perfect a missionary of our company, comprehension and erudition are my humble aspirations. . . .

I beg you, Most Reverend Father, to pray to Christ, who descended from heaven for the fanaticization of our souls and for whom I try to live a fervent and penitent life, to grant me an equally fervent death. By the Grace of our Lord, My General, I remain

> Your very humble and obedient servant,
> Father Visitor, Delleda,
> S.F. of the Company of Jesus

Father Delleda rested his pen beside the sheaf of finely written paper that was his letter. Instinctively his hand passed over his thigh and between his legs. He could still hear the confused voice of his only friend, the Black Eunuch Edris Aga:

"But I do not understand. We are both eunuchs. I by nature, you by vows. We both have the same function: the control of women. You Christian eunuchs called priests, with your confessionals, are no different from a Moslem eunuch who guards the secrets of the harem. I too am confidant and confessor. I administer punishments, albeit a bit stronger than your 'Hail Marys,' but nevertheless for the same reasons: to keep the women under my control in the strict ways of virtue, modesty, chastity, and the laws of Allah, better to serve their master and husband, Allah's Shadow on Earth, the Sultan. I do just as you profess to do in the service of *your* master the Pope who is *your* God's Shadow on Earth. On one hand the *opposite* of chastity, procreation is even more sacred. Yet for you chastity is virtue in its purest form. I cannot understand that, not knowing what sort of virtue it is that produces nothing."

"Virtue is its own reward," Father Delleda had answered.

Even here in the privacy of his rooms the reply sounded hypocritical, but face to face with the Black Eunuch, it had been totally ridiculous. Whatever else he was, the black man was a theologian.

The Black Eunuch's voice, with its intolerable lesson in suffering, came back to him with all the force of the first time he had ever heard his story.

"I was born in 1744 in the upper reaches of the White Nile and named Edris Usâma-Ibn-Munquidh. My father was not an inconsequential man and I was his eldest son. After my act, he was so horrified he disowned me and I sold myself to a slave trader for a very high price which I gave to the bereaved father of my dead wife, Tityi, as my father refused to return her dowry. I was taken by boat down the Nile to Cairo. The transportation of human merchandise being a naturally tedious and risky affair, certain stopovers had been established along the way. On the Nile route, castration of the young boys took place at such places as Khartoum and Aswan. I was not insensitive to the sufferings of the other boys at the mercy of unskillful knifers, boys sold by their families or stolen or captured in war. The violence done to them I had done to myself, but with an unregretful comprehension and a passionate deliberation none of them possessed. My own heart and body were hardened by my immense suffering, but I did what I could to alleviate their misery and terror. The operation was so dangerous, with only the warm sand to use as a styptic, that mortality was very high. I would have gladly died in the place of any of those poor boys, but it had been the will of Allah that I had survived my own hand, and I determined to rise to great power and wealth in the greatest of all seraglios, that of the Ottoman Sultan Mustafa II. I had no doubt that I would succeed. My ambitions, my desperation and my courage were unlimited. By luck, I was sold directly to the Seraglio in Constantinople as I had vowed, for an extremely high price, being a very beautiful boy indeed. It was there, under the Kizlar Aga Abou Bakr, that I achieved my apprenticeship and formulated my sole goal in life: to one day take his place.

"We boys were watched and disciplined by the other youths of the Seraglio, till at a certain age we were ready for service. We were removed thence and sent to the women and placed under others in the service of the Valide, being under the command of their chief, the Kizlar Aga, Head of Virgins. We had a considerable allowance, of sixty to a hundred aspre a day, two robes of finest silk, and other things for our needs throughout the year, besides what was plentifully bestowed on us from other quarters. We bore names of flowers, such as Hyacinth, Narcissus, Rose and Carnation. As we were in the service of women, we were required to have names suitable to virginity, whiteness and fragrance. My harem name was Orchid." His friend had smiled.

"As soon as the Chief Black Eunuch knew my character, I was made Yayia Bashi, or Harem Lieutenant. He mentioned me more and more to the Sultan, saying I would be capable of carrying out his ideas and of taking over the post that he held. He was not put off by my extreme youth, believing that my assiduity would compensate for lack of experience.

"It was under this great master that I learned the difficult art of commanding women and trained myself in the principles of inflexible government. Under him I studied women's hearts. He taught me how to take advantage of their weaknesses and not be imposed upon by their imperiousness. He would often enjoy driving them to the furthest pitch of obedience, then he would gradually let them come back and, for a time, seemed to give way himself. But he had been at his best at moments when he found them on the brink of despair, full of entreaties and reproaches. He endured their tears without emotion, and would take pride in this kind of triumph. He personally conducted the chosen Kadine to his Sultan's bed every night.

"I am in the prime of life, yet I can look at a woman without emotion, like you. A greater connoisseur of women does not exist, the more so because they cannot catch me off guard. With me, the impulses of the emotions do not distract the eye. I never forget that I was born to command them, and it is as if I become a man again on the occasions when I give them orders. I hate them for being alive when Tityi is dead. So I face them with indifference and my reason allows me to see all their weaknesses. Although I keep them for another man, the pleasure of making myself obeyed gives me the secret joy you must be familiar with. When I deny them everything, it is as if I was doing it for myself. . . .

"Blind obedience and unlimited indulgence are essential. That," he had said with satisfaction, "is how to control women. It does not alarm me that there are a lot of them: better many who obey than one who does not. If the women whom I watch over should want to depart from their duty, I make them give up such hope. I am the scourge of vice and the bastion of fidelity. I have never been beyond the walls of Istanbul. Like the Grand Doges of Venice, I have not the right to sleep one night outside the walls of the palace," he had said proudly. "Thus I rule without malice or envy in that state of perfect virtue the Christian priest and dervishes of both sexes call chastity and for which they take a vow in perpetuity.

"Between the two sexes disorder and confusion arise because their rights are reciprocal. But I form part of a new and harmonious scheme: Between women and myself I create hatred, and between women and men, love. Thus I rule in that state of perfect virtue you Christian priests call chastity. . . ."

Geronimo Delleda's appearance was almost a caricature of the Oriental. The languid, half-closed eyes, fringed in long heavy lashes, were large and light brown, flecked with yellow. The black brows met across a perfect aquiline nose. His complexion, which had always been that of a beautiful woman, contrasted with his tonsured graying hair worn long, curling over the white of his cassock. In one ear glistened a small diamond, an Oriental conceit which he steadfastly refused to explain to his superiors and which badly contradicted his vow of poverty. Moreover, his refusal to remove it contaminated his vow of obedience, and compounded his coquetry, making it at least sacrilegious, if not insidious. Nevertheless, he thought, it was his own business. His predilection for wearing white caftans instead of black fitted cassocks when wandering the streets of Constantinople or visiting Turks was his own business as well. He had, after all, served his General well.

There was one other thing he refused to compromise on—the baths. The Turkish custom of daily or twice daily bathing had appealed to his sense of fastidiousness as soon as he arrived in Constantinople, and he had enthusiastically embraced the custom, which was seldom practiced among the Occidental aristocracy and practically unknown among his brethren. The Turkish bath was a hygienic form of spiritual purification, a delight to a man whose first impression of the Hall of Mirrors at Versailles had been its indescribable odor.

Father Delleda sighed. He had an appointment at six this evening at the public baths at Galata, and he flexed his long legs in anticipation. Upright, he was over six feet tall, a false slenderness concealing what was really a heavily muscled torso offset by narrow shoulders and exceptionally long, strong and well-made legs hidden under his skirts. His hands were surprisingly small for his build, and his long Turkish-style nails were immaculately cared for. Delleda fingered the diamond in the lobe of his ear. He loved Turkey. He had been stationed in Pera for sixteen years before the papal decree had come from Rome lifting the excommunication of the Jesuits. He had witnessed the most amazing feat of Abdulhamid rising Lazarist-like from the tomb of the Topkapi Kafes after forty-three years to become Padishah of one eighth of the world. *That,* he thought was a resurrection. He shook his handsome head in wonder and horror. Yes. He loved Turkey.

The bath was part of every Moslem's life, both male and female, both rich and poor. His was at Galata, one of three hundred public baths in Constantinople and of great beauty.

The complex of rooms of the baths was Byzantine, reduced from the ones of the ancient Romans. At the entrance of the bath was a room shaped like a church, round and domed with lead and with marble arches, one surpassing the other in beauty, all in black and white. The floors were also of black and white marble and the walls were occasionally encrusted with multicolored mosaics. In the dome was a series of round holes about a half foot in diameter over which was concave glass made in the shape of bells as Venetian mirrors.

A small amount of light filtered through the round glazed holes in the dome, which gave the effect of a crisscross of shimmering columns. In the middle of this hall was a beautiful basin of fine marble with a fountain of four jets around which were long brick seats so high from the ground that a man sitting could not touch the floor with his feet. Censers were kept burning at all times and the walls were dry and the air temperate. As Father Delleda entered this vast empty space, he would meet the silence he adored and perhaps sought more than anything else. The array of towel-clad figures, looking like so many mummies waiting to be buried, only added to this strange attraction. The only sound that broke the silence would be the splash of water in the marble fountain in the center and the occasional shuffling of some bather on his wooden pattens as he made his way to a warmer room. The hall was surrounded by low couches and cubicles, and to the far end were huge wooden towel-drying racks. Father Delleda would speak softly to the custodians stationed around the walls of the room and then to the cashier, and when this was done, he would undress in one of the cubicles, rolling his cassock into a bundle and wrapping a red towel around his body. Then he would glide into the second room. Here the rise in temperature would be quite noticeable and steam visible in the atmosphere. In the middle were a fountain and a pool of hot water with large copper bowls for pouring the water over one's head. To the left and right, there were small rooms, some for massage, some for depilatory operations and barbers, while others were lavatories. The removal of all body hair, including pubic hair and any superfluous hair in the nose, ears or anus, was indispensable to Moslem men and women for both religious and sanitary purposes. This hair was shaved, plucked or removed with a dangerous paste called rusma. The massage consisted of two distinct parts: massage with glove and massage with bare hands. Rolls of dried skin and dirt would be triumphantly shown to him by the masseur. Then, the glove having been discarded, the manual massage would begin with a severity that made the feeble collapse, the priest thought. Powerful fingers would work between his shoulder blades until they cracked. His backbone would be pressed so hard that he could only just endure it without crying out. His arms and legs would be pulled to their furthest extent. Then his entire body would be lathered from head to foot and he would be left to recover.

In the third room, the Yeni Kaplija, the temperature was really excessive with no outlet for the steam. The priest remembered his first reaction: a strange mixture of shyness and actual fear. Everything had seemed transformed. The atmosphere heavy. Figures lay around or moved slowly like shadows in the underworld. The priest had had the feeling he was in purgatory and the feeling had stayed with him until now; it had become literally an obsession. He knew it was this feeling that nourished his increasing dependence on the baths, and the strange silent specters appearing and disappearing in the steam-laden gloom. Suddenly the clank of a copper bowl, the noise of shuffling pattens, or the splash of a swimmer would bring him back to his senses and the enveloping fog. Yet the illusion that he was in some unworldly place never left him, even as hollow vaporous laughter at some joke rang out from a living, breathing man. All was so pure, so cleansing, so soft, warm, embracing as death itself. He would pass the naked bodies lying prone on the floor, or crouching in odd corners, or seated, or standing, or bending over a wall fountain, looking for all the world like life-sized figures descended from a Greek vase. Time stood still, and, as with the lotus eaters of old, no thought for tomorrow ever entered his head as he surrendered to the warm contentment and safety only the baths gave him. Slowly he would swim in the almost boiling water as if crossing the river Styx. Slowly he would return to the second room to cool off with bowls of tepid water. Slowly he would walk in his simple pattens made of boxwood with a leather strap nailed to the hollow of each side, floating six or seven inches off the wet floor. He would discard the red towel he had worn up until now over his muscular, hairy body, which the custodians had finally gotten used to seeing, but which always provoked stares and nervous laughter from a newcomer who didn't know him. But the regulars were used to his appearance now. He would receive fresh towels and wrap a fourth around his head like a turban. And always at this point, the feeling of bodily satisfaction, cleanliness and freshness transcended the ken of the mortal man he was and elevated him to . . . to . . . what he could only describe as ethereal heights. He knew it to be a sin. Every time he went to the baths, he went to confession.

Finally, he would lie on his marble couch and clap his hands, Oriental style, for coffee. The priest hoped only that his burnt offering reached the throne of Olympian Zeus, if not that of Jesus Christ, or at least to the Prophet Mohammed in the palms of whose hands he lay. . . .

It was wise to discover what happiness was made of, thought Geronimo. The baths, the presence of goodness, the affection of a few people, and sunshine. After these came a sort of daily beauty, like this spacious view before him, and after that perhaps expressions of the same desire, an atmosphere of continuity like the different rooms of the baths, a regular processional sequence and not a disorderly scramble toward eternity.

As he turned, the sweet, sharp, mounting tones of the Muezzin calling the faithful to evening prayer broke loose from the towers of a thousand mosques; sounds neither male nor female, neither human nor divine, most approaching the haunting tonality of the Italian castrati, gathered over the waters and echoed like the cries of wild birds mating over Europe and Asia. The hairs rose on the back of the Lazarist's neck.

Nowhere in heaven was there a more haunting sound. Nowhere on earth was there a more beautiful or more complex city; set on its promontory between East and West, between the Bosphorus and the Golden Horn, between God Almighty and Allah, Constantinople/Istanbul was as multilayered and theologically impregnable as the Islam that he, a secret Jesuit, was determined to penetrate, even to the peril of his soul.

BOOK II

ST. PETERSBURG
·1781·

• CHAPTER ONE •

ISHAK BEY 1781

"But this is what my uncle Count Ivan Ilyitch told me, assuring me
on his honor that it was true. Tchaplitsky, you know, the one who
died a beggar after squandering millions as a young man, once lost
three hundred thousand, to Zorich, if I remember rightly."

—ALEXANDER PUSHKIN,
The Queen of Spades, 1834

The courtesans surrounded Abraham. They found themselves each in
his own way, to treat with deference the new favorite.

—ALEXANDER PUSHKIN,
The Negro of Peter the Great,
1827–32

A card game had been going on for some seven hours in the white
night of late summer two thousand miles from Istanbul, in St. Petersburg, capital of the Russian Empire. St. Petersburg, which sat at the
mouth of the Neva River in the Finnish Gulf, was greater in surface
than Paris because of the obsessive building of its Czarina Catherine II.
The city was yellow, rose and pastel blue touched with white and gold.
In the peculiar light, one distinguished these colors very distinctly, as if
they had been invented for a metropolis that was light half the year and
dark the other half. The city spread in baroque palaces, multidomed
and gilded cathedrals, and vast squares along the two shores of the
river, wide and deep but subject to terrible flooding. The palaces hid a
city of wood and peat, prone, as was Istanbul, to terrible fires. A part of

the city had several islands connected by canals, which had given it its name: the Venice of the North. In the center, between the left bank of the Neva and the Moika Canal, were the luxurious mansions of the very rich, culminating with the Admiralty and the Winter Palace. It was here that the brothers Zanovich had established their gaming house.

The curtains were drawn against the light. Amongst the carved gilt tables, scattered throughout several salons illuminated by rows of forty-branched candelabra, was a table which seemed a miniature Istanbul. Watching the slap of macao cards with the same religiousness were a Turk, a Serb, a Greek, a Negro, a Russian Countess, and the hosts, the mysterious and ambiguous Zanovich brothers. Everyone was seated on French armchairs covered in the same brocaded silk that covered the walls, symbolizing the victory of the Russians over the Ottomans at the Battle of Chesme. The silk had been especially manufactured in Lyon for the Czarina.

"The only thing missing," muttered Ishak Bey, "is Hasan Gazi and his castrated lion. . . ." The Grand Admiral Gazi would have been the fourth hero of Chesme whose posterior would be interlaced between branches of laurel (the victory), ermine tails (the Russians), and a sinking frigate on which a green flag (the Ottomans) flew on a pale blue silken sea. . . .

Ishak shook his superb turban of silver lamé although he was dressed as an officer in the Ottoman navy. He had no more than a hundred rubles in his pocket. He was two thousand miles from Istanbul and home, in an enemy country, without any means of livelihood except handouts from his friend Zorich or, if he was lucky, a possible pension from the Empress Catherine II herself. He was without hope and without plans. . . .

Who would have thought, mused the exiled Turk, that a prank would have gotten him into so much trouble? It had brought the wrath of the Grand Admiral of the Ottoman navy down upon him, resulting in his flight from Istanbul, his death warrant in absentia. Russia, he thought suddenly, the hereditary enemy of the Ottomans for six centuries! Had he really weighed the consequences of the crime he had committed against Islam by his stupid prank?

Ishak Bey was a subject of Sultan Abdulhamid. Born the son of a Capidji-Bachi, and the great-grandson of a famous Grand Vizier, Deli Pasha, who had married Sultana Safiye, he bore with perhaps an excess of pride the family name. His grandfather had given Ishak and his brother Ismail an entrance into the imperial school for pages in

Topkapi. Ishak had become part of the clan of imperial pages who spent their boyhoods with Abdulhamid's eventual successor, Prince Selim. Because of their exceptional beauty and their inseparability, Ishak and Selim had become known by the clan as the archangels Michael and Gabriel. Ishak Bey smiled. Selim, who was blond with dark eyes, had been Michael; and Ishak, who was dark with light eyes, had been Gabriel. It had been a long time, he thought, since anyone had addressed him as Gabriel.

Ishak was most out of place with his turban. But Ishak was very fond of dressing as an Ottoman ever since he had achieved notoriety in Paris as the "Beau Turque."

The Beau Turque, Ishak, had been an officer of the palace by the age of twenty, his function being to present each day to Abdulhamid his towel after the Sultan's official ablutions. It had not been an occupation for a young man with a thirst for life and adventure, and Ishak had gotten permission to join the navy. He had survived the disaster of Chesme, where the Russians had completely destroyed the Ottoman fleet, and had attached himself to the Grand Admiral Hasan Gazi, the only military man to have escaped with his reputation intact. The Grand Admiral or, as he was called in Istanbul, the Kapudan or Captain Pasha, "Last of the Romans," was one of those energetic but isolated men whose talent and character disguised his real nature from a nation whose decadence he had arrested if only temporarily, thought Ishak Bey. A ferocious and intransigent enemy of Russia, Hasan Pasha lived in a state of barbarity as natural to him as the lion that accompanied him everywhere.

Ishak Bey looked across the table at someone Hasan Pasha himself would certainly bite on sight: the mulatto Admiral General Ivan Abramovitch Hannibal. Ishak studied Ivan Hannibal as he plopped down heavily in one of the gold and white armchairs, his legs sprawled before him. Ivan Hannibal was small with a tiny head, yellow hands and prominent forehead. He had bright golden eyes and curly gray hair, generous purple lips and a rich, wide sculptured nose. He was wearing the uniform of a Russian Admiral, a bottle-green military tunic that was tight at the waist in an old-fashioned cut, and wore his powdered hair in a pigtail.

Ivan Hannibal's exotic origins as well as his distinguished career had always been a source of bemused admiration for Ishak. Who could have invented such a bizarre and marvelously unbelievable story? Ivan's father, Ibrihaman or Abraham Hannibal, had been kidnapped from Abyssinia as a child and sold to Selim's grandfather Sultan Ahmed II's Seraglio in Istanbul. The Russian Ambassador, Count Raguzinski, had smuggled the adorable slave out of the Seraglio and had given him as an exceptional gift to Peter the Great. Peter had loved the boy from the start and had had the child baptized in 1707, giving him the name of Abraham Pyotr Hannibal. His godmother was the Princess Christiana of Poland. It was then that he had become known as the "Negro of Peter the Great." Abraham Pyotr Hannibal had remained with the Czar until 1716, when he had been sent to Paris to be educated. As a Generalissimo, Hannibal had witnessed and served the reigns of four Czars. His abduction from the Seraglio of Istanbul was not the most exceptional thing in his life. After Peter's death, he had been sent to measure the Great Wall of China by a jealous Czarina Elizabeth, only to return alive and with the correct dimensions. His first marriage had ended in a monumental twenty-seven-year-long divorce trial, the most sensational Russia had ever seen. The judge and jury had been faced with deciding whether or not a pure-white child could be born to a black man and a white woman. Hannibal's first wife had claimed yes. The judge and jury had not had the inkling of an idea. But Hannibal, with no scientific knowledge except his years in Istanbul and his bar- rack-style common sense, decided NO. He had sued for divorce after obtaining a confession of adultery from his wife by locking her in her own castle and starving her into submission. Meanwhile, he had mar- ried Ivan's mother (making himself a bigamist) and had proved his theory by fathering eleven children by her, not one of them white. His son, the Admiral General Ivan Abramovitch Hannibal, seated before Ishak Bey, was a rich brown.

"Nine," announced Ivan Hannibal. The white-gloved lackey standing behind his chair swept up the thousand-ruble notes on the table. Ishak Bey sat back and glared at the black man facing him. Ivan Hannibal had begun his career by conquering Navarino and had been named commander of this former Turkish fortress. In June '70 he had been part of the Russian division that destroyed the entire Turkish fleet un- der the command of his former patron, the Lord Admiral Hasan Gazi, in a spectacular battle in the Bay of Chesme. Admiral Hasan Gazi had not lost his head but had never recovered from the blow of Chesme, nor had he, who had been there, thought Ishak Bey. The Ottoman navy had been smashed into oblivion for a decade. For this exploit, Catherine had made Hannibal a Major General and a member of the College of the Admiralty. Hannibal had gone on to found the city of Kherson before retiring as a Lieutenant General to his great estates west of St. Petersburg. He had never married (probably the experiences of his bigamist father were too much for him), and he lived with his adored aunt, Countess Capitolina Pushkin, in a palace on the south bank of the Neva River. Ishak Bey eyed the once superb Countess speculatively. The dead brother of this arrogant card-playing Countess, Sergey Lvovitch Pushkin, had been violent and cruel.

"I raise three thousand rubles," the aristocratic voice of the Countess rang out.

Both the General and the Countess were heavily built. The Countess was enormous, her ramrod-straight spine held away from the support of the chair, her huge gray head with its large regular features and oversized teeth held erect as if in a vase. The General's halo of mixed-gray curls matched exactly those of his aunt and, strangely enough, resembled Ishak Bey's extravagant turban.

A lackey set another glass of water at the Countess's elbow. She had just raised another 5,000 rubles. She had an ace of hearts, an eight of diamonds, a red nine.

The Zanovitch brothers, who made their fortunes by winning promissory notes from the Russian nobility and paying their losses in cash, were crooked, skillful, cold-blooded gamblers. At this point, they held the bank.

Macao was the game in vogue. The beau monde of St. Petersburg was still talking about the sumptuous reception given by the Empress during carnival. Catherine had made sure its magnificence surpassed anything conceivable in any other European court. The dessert at supper had been set out with jewels to the amount of two million rubles. Huge stakes had been wagered that night, and at the macao tables, the Czarina Catherine had given a diamond worth 50 rubles as a bonus to anyone who drew a nine. In this manner she had distributed 150 diamonds.

One of the recipients of the Czarina's beneficence and one of her most hated rivals, the sumptuous "Greek" Madame de Witte, this night sat next to the ancient Countess Pushkin as if in sheer malice. Madame de Witte was also from Istanbul, and also via the slave market. . . . Abandoned in Jassy by her master, a Frenchman who had bought her on the block when she was fifteen, she had married an English Colonel who had taken her to Poland. At twenty, she had left the Colonel for a Polish Prince who had taken her back with him to Paris, where she had won the title "La Belle Phanariote" (Phanar being the name of the turbulent Greek Quarter of Istanbul), and where she had turned every head in Versailles. Potemkin had lost his head over her when she had been presented at court. She was the only woman, it was said, ever to invoke the jealousy of Catherine II.

"Eight," said La Belle Phanariote as she laid out her cards and glanced up at the Beau Turque. Ishak Bey was apprehensive as well as bored. In fact, he hated cards. He believed good luck was a matter of intelligence, not chance.

"Nine," announced the Countess with a grin.

The unmarried, retired General stared at the man facing him. Although nothing in his well-bred manner revealed it, he didn't approve of the Serbian General, Count Simon Gavrilovitch Zorich. Nor of his Turk, Ishak Bey. Count Zorich was not even supposed to be in the capital. Two years had passed since his hour of glory as Catherine's favorite. Zorich was such a beauty that the Empress had the habit of calling him the despair of sculptors and the shipwreck of painters. He was still an extraordinarily handsome specimen of the human race, mused Hannibal.

Zorich's neck stretched as if Hannibal's stare were a blade of cold steel against it. His perpetually bronzed complexion had gone pale and although his hands didn't tremble, his soul did. He wondered why. He had eight, the best score being nine. But his stake was uncomfortably high. It was all the cash he had. Next he would be wagering serfs and land. Small beads of perspiration appeared on his high forehead and under the mesh of hair that had fallen over one eye. He knew this sensation that had suddenly overwhelmed him. Many officers had experienced it on the field of battle just before sudden death. It was a common phenomenon, as if the soldier had been given one more chance at life but only at the price of living the rest of it in fear. And Simon Zorich knew that living with fear was the shortest and surest route to certain death when your profession was war or cards. Simon Gavrilovitch Zorich was a Serb whose real name was Nerantchitch. He had been adopted by an uncle, Major Zorich, inscribed in the Hussars and was already a Corporal by twelve. At sixteen he had been a Lieutenant. And in 1770 during the Russo-Turkish war, he had been wounded and held prisoner for five years in Istanbul. It was there that he had met Ishak Bey. Once liberated, waiting to be exchanged, Zorich had made his living playing chess in the cafés of Pera. Ishak Bey had beaten him roundly one night, but had also fallen under the spell of Zorich's spirit and beauty.

They had loved each other at first sight, the dark beauty and the fair Adonis: The happy-go-lucky, exuberant Zorich and the measured, cautious Ishak became inseparable. Until one day Zorich had decided he wanted to see the inside of a mosque, and Ishak in a lighthearted mood had obliged him, disguising his Giaour-Russian friend as a Moslem and sneaking him into the mosque of Aya Sofya, a profanation that now made Ishak shiver. They had been caught. His behavior with an infidel had been reported to his superior, the Captain Pasha, Lord Admiral Hasan Gazi. They had had to flee for their lives, for Hasan Gazi had put out a death warrant on both their heads. Zorich had returned to Russia with 5,000 piastres borrowed from Ishak. And Ishak had been smuggled out of the country by the French Ambassador bearing a secret letter from the hereditary Prince Selim to Louis XVI, and had taken refuge in France under the tutelage of an Orientalist called Louis Ruffin. In other words, treason against the reigning Sultan Abdulhamid. Neither of their lives had ever been the same. Hasan Gazi had never forgiven his favorite Lieutenant and surrogate son, Ishak, and had never lifted the price upon his head. And Zorich had never forgotten that magical night when he had gazed up into the infinite blue depths of the dome of Aya Sofya, the Byzantine cathedral of Santa Sophia that had exchanged cross for crescent when Constantinople had been conquered by the Turks. Zorich, a fervent Orthodox Christian, had fallen to his knees, tears streaming down his face.

Zorich took a deep breath and his chest expanded under his relucent white and gold uniform. It was bandied about St. Petersburg that Zorich was dashing only in two costumes: his Hussars uniform or nothing at all. . . . For eleven months he had remained the Russian Empress Catherine's favorite, receiving 1,800 serfs for his "debut" performance. In less than a year he had spent three million rubles. The envious said this dethronement was due to the fact that he couldn't walk across the waxed parquet floors of the palace in his boots without slipping. But the fact was he had bored Catherine to tears. Zorich had been ousted with the help of Potemkin by the twenty-four-year-old Ivan Nicolaievitch Rimsky-Korsakov, who had already been replaced by the twenty-three-year-old Alexander Dimitriyev Lanskoy.

Zorich had been sent packing with one million rubles, seven thousand serfs and estates at Shklov. But his greatest claim to fame was not his eleven-month reign as favorite but the five years he had spent as a prisoner of war in the dungeon of the Castle of Seven Towers in Constantinople. There had even been a popular ballad written about him. He began to hum the tune under his breath:

> *Zorich for his motherland, for five years*
> *remained in chains . . .*

And *his* motherland . . . thought Ishak. He looked with tender exasperation at the source of his exile and the cause of all his troubles. When Zorich had become favorite to Catherine, he had begged Ishak to come share in his good fortune. Ishak, who had learned from his brother Ismail on a short secret trip back to Istanbul from Paris that he was still persona non grata in the capital, had leaped at the chance. But his trip had been so long—Naples, Leghorn, Florence, Vienna, (always avoiding Ottoman territory, where he risked being arrested)—that by the time he had arrived, Zorich had already been ousted by Potemkin and replaced as favorite. He had never even recovered the 5,000 piastres he had loaned him to get back to Russia. His friend's hour of glory had been sweet, but short.

Ishak Bey was appalled at the excesses his friend was capable of. He had wept upon seeing him arrive in St. Petersburg, but he was capable of killing a man in cold blood. He, Ishak, was a chessplayer, not a cardplayer. The passion of a Slav he realized could never be reconciled with the detachment of an Oriental. The scene Zorich had made when he had been replaced by Rimsky-Korsakov had been of terrible violence.

It had taken place in Catherine's new theater, the Hermitage. Prince Potemkin had presented Zorich's successor to the Empress: a tall Russian officer with large white teeth, green eyes and curly hair, one of Potemkin's adjutants. Catherine had paid the officer a great deal of attention, and Zorich had completely lost control of himself. Once again he was about to discard the only good card life had ever dealt him. As Catherine was about to leave the room, he had turned on Potemkin violently, cursing him, then finally challenging him to a duel.

"I know well I'm going to get kicked out but, by God, I'll cut the ears off all the Hussars in Russia!"

"I don't like fusspots," the Empress had said.

But in the end, thought Zorich, Potemkin had gotten the better of him, being a much more artful and clever man. He had bowed finally to what his old friend Ishak Bey called kismet. With a doubled pension, an immense sum of ready money, a sumptuous diamond parure consisting of matching diamond cuff links, three diamond-encrusted buckles (two for his shoes, one for his waist), a diamond clip for his uniform, a diamond brooch for his fur toque, twelve diamond vest buttons, twelve diamond redingote buttons, a diamond-encrusted sword, a walking stick and snuff box, and an additional seven thousand serfs attached to his estates, he had been sent packing. But he had left without the title he had so craved. He had wanted the title of Prince, but despite tears and tantrums Catherine had made him a mere Count. He had had only the stupid satisfaction of knowing that his successor had not been proclaimed favorite until everyone, including Catherine, was sure he, Zorich, was safely out of town.

When Zorich had arrived back at his estates in Shklov, he had found Ishak Bey sitting on his doorstep demanding the 5,000 piastres he had lent to him in Istanbul. Zorich had never been so glad to see anyone in his entire life. Crying like a baby, he had kissed him a hundred times, deciding then and there never to allow Ishak to leave Russia. The two of them decided to open a military school for young nobles, an efficient training ground for officers, which existed in Europe, but not in Russia. The two young men's lives had been filled with balls, masquerades, supper, parties, banquets, military maneuvers, and gambling and luxury! Ishak and Zorich had even formed a corps de ballet. The Beau Turque had formed the first ballet school in Russia, imitating the other great courts of Europe, importing French and Italian artists to develop the already spectacular acrobatic folk dancing.

Zorich looked up at his friend. Their mutual beauty had almost a hypnotic effect on people. Even in the still-crowded gambling rooms, at three in the morning, people would pass, stare, then, shocked, turn again before they passed. Ishak Bey, in his gorgeous ermine-trimmed naval uniform and silver turban, was a young man whose appearance had always been more mature than his age. His build was tall, elegant and slim. He carried his turban-draped head with the graciousness of the well born. His regular features, blue eyes and straight nose gave a classic startling beauty to his dark skin. His chin, that part of a man's face which gives it its basic character, was firm and well molded. The sum total was attractive rather than imposing. One had the impression of a man who preferred to be loved rather than feared. He had less of the adventurer about him than anyone seated at the "Istanbul" table. It was as if his thoughts carried a certain weight like that of a nation or a people and that he was conscious of that weight like a stone. There was timid modesty in his glance. Ishak Bey was too apprehensive and too homesick to play the role of adventurer.

Zorich, known as "The Adonis," was thirty-six with the halo of a military hero. He was a tall golden blonde with steel-gray eyes, perfect teeth, and, like Ishak, a ravishing smile. His sculpted nose and high cheekbones gave him the appearance of an eagle, while his beauty eclipsed the entire Russian officer corps. On becoming the favorite, he had been made a Lieutenant General and in his white and gold General's uniform trimmed in Persian lamb, he was astounding. He wore neither powder nor wigs, but affected one diamond earring as a souvenir of his imprisonment in Constantinople. Zorich was famous. People spoke of him with awe. Foreigners wrote about him abroad. Now his golden hair shone in the candlelight, its bleached waves falling on his high-braided collar like flax.

Zorich had won upward of 400,000 rubles, which lay before him in heaps of gold and bank notes. Footmen bustled around him in expectation of rich tips. Ishak Bey fingered the borrowed diamond buttons on his vest nervously. He was wearing the entire collection of diamonds given to Zorich by Catherine.

"Simon," he whispered. "Let's go."

Something had begun to happen that was fairly frequent in macao. Luck clung for example to a red number and remained there ten or fifteen times in a row. This had been Zorich's winning streak. He now put 200,000 rubles on red and lost. In anger, he pushed toward Zanovitch another 200,000 rubles and won on a red seven. He now had his original winnings back. He felt like a conqueror. He no longer feared anything. He would show Catherine a thing or two! He flung the entire pile on red and won. The bank was broken. Ishak saw the two brothers exchange glances. People had begun to gather around them, talking, then silently waiting.

Zorich turned up a nine again on the first try, and then, all at once, he recalled neither the amount nor the order of his stakes. As in a dream, he won again and again. The house was silent as he suddenly dropped 100,000 rubles in three unlucky hands.

Ishak Bey's hands hovered over the diamond buttons on his vest, to ward off the evil eye.

"Simon . . ." he began.

But Zorich pushed his last stakes on the table, including an IOU on his estates at Shklov. He waited almost mechanically and won again, and again, then four more times in succession, always turning up a seven, eight or nine. They had recouped almost all their winnings. Nine had come up for Zorich six times in a row. Now, experienced players know the meaning of such freakish chances, but with a strange perversity Zorich deliberately went on staking the bank. Zorich was on top . . . Zorich had a hard-on . . . Zorich was *in* Catherine . . . Zorich was again *favorite*. He would be talked about again. He would astonish the brothers and the spectators. Zorich was overcome by a terrible craving for risk, like sex or alcohol or death, thought Ishak later. Perhaps Zorich's soul, passing through such a wide range of sensations, was not saturated but exacerbated by them, their demands on his spirit becoming more and more powerful until, like copulation, it reached its final exhaustion.

Zorich staked the bank and nine came up for him for the fourteenth time.

Suddenly the Countess Pushkin rose and passed close to Ishak Bey. "Tell him," she said, nudging him in excitement. "Tell him to stop, tell him to take his money as quickly as possible and leave. He'll lose. He'll lose everything he has in the world, the whole lot!" Ishak turned, stunned by the outburst in French of the Countess, but before he could reply, she had disappeared.

The brothers Zanovitch put 40,000 rubles on the table. Zorich rose to the occasion.

"Nine," he announced. Then in two more hands, Zorich doubled, then tripled his stake. He had won 576,000 rubles from the brothers. It was Marc now who held the bank. Zorich staked the entire 576,000 rubles. The brothers would have to pay him 2,880,000 rubles.

Zurich turned up a nine. A deep sigh went around the table.

"That's almost three million rubles, Simon. Let's go home," whispered Ishak to Zorich, the chill of the Countess Pushkin's words still with him. "Let's go!"

"Are you crazy?" muttered Zorich between clenched teeth. "This is the day I've been waiting for!"

He gazed at the "Istanbul" table scattered with louis d'or, Talers, rubles, little piles of gold and ten-centimeter rolls of silver. . . . Zorich as a soldier had risked his future innumerable times, but gambling was more than that. He craved the card that would *change* his past. It was Zorich getting it up once more! Zorich who renounced life, sex, art, society and duty. He renounced friendship as well. Ishak was like a ghost in his life at this moment. At this moment, he was totally alone in the world. His desires went no further now than eight, seven, nine. . . .

"Simon!"

"I raise one hundred thousand rubles."

It was seven o'clock in the morning. The gaming room was almost deserted. Only the professionals, fools and the genuinely desperate remained. The Zanovitches, who again held the bank, had been observing Zorich all evening.

Ishak Bey was never quite sure afterward how it happened. Everyone had dropped out. Zorich now played the bank alone. A new pack of cards was unsealed.

Zorich attacked at once, staking 100,000 gold talers at a time.

"Stake, stake," Zorich nudged Ishak Bey. Ishak obeyed.

"How many times have we lost our stake?" the ex-favorite asked at last, grinding his teeth with impatience.

"Simon, we've staked twelve times already. We've lost one million two hundred thousand rubles! I tell you, Simon, we've got to stop! The brothers Zanovitch already hold over a million rubles in promissory notes!"

Zorich won.

"You see! You see!" he whispered. "We've got back almost all we lost. We'll stake it all once more and I swear to you, Ishak, I'll never play again!"

The gaming room was almost deserted. Those who remained gathered around the table. A hush fell over the company as the rumor spread that the game of the century was about to be consummated.

Zorich turned up an eight.

Ishak sighed in relief. They had won! But Zorich turned on Ishak, glaring at the diamond studs he had forgotten to wager.

"We should have staked more! *You* talked me out of it!"

"I talked some sense to you, Simon, and now let's get out of here. . . ." He turned to La Belle Phanariote, who looked around nervously.

Then one Zanovitch brother turned over his card. It was a seven. Then the other Zanovitch turned over his two. They made a nine.

Zorich had lost his entire fortune in a single night: 14,000 serfs; 3 million rubles; 300,450 hectares of land; and 5 villages. Ishak Bey's features screwed up in horror and compassion, but even this grimace did nothing to mar the beauty of a face touched from boyhood with the vacuity that came from pleasing too many men and too many women too often and too soon in life. Zorich slumped down in his chair, his golden head drenched in perspiration. His magnificent white uniform

was dark along the shoulder blades and armpits. The brothers Zanovitch stared impassively at the duo. They had just annihilated the ex-
favorite of the Czarina. They now owned Zorich and everything he had
possessed.

Ishak Bey thought he was going to die. Tomorrow, the card game
would be famous in Russia. Tomorrow, he thought, as he looked out of
the window at the bright northern light. It *was* tomorrow. He continued
to look out of the window in order to avoid looking at Zorich. Suddenly
Ishak Bey was two thousand miles away in Istanbul, thinking of the
undisciplined dawn rising over the Bosphorus, as the immobile sun
brightened over the multicolored, onion-shaped domes of Catherine's
Venice of the North. He had been in exile for seven long years. Thirty-
one years old and he was no closer to returning to Istanbul . . . home.
Home. Zorich's ruin was his. Not because of the money but because the
incident of the mosque had bound them together in some supernatural
way.

Zorich rose, or rather stumbled to his feet. The table was deathly
silent. Furtively Ivan Hannibal crossed himself in the shadows and the
silence. But Simon Gavrilovitch had never felt more alive than at this
moment. Blood pounded in his temples and he listened attentively to his
own steady heartbeat. His beautiful mouth turned up under his sumptuous moustache. In Russia as in all despotisms, fortune and favor were
won and lost at the blink of an eye. Without rhyme, reason or compassion. He looked at Ishak Bey. What, after all, was beggary? What was
beggary in comparison to mediocrity? The only real point was that one
turn of the cards, like one nod of a despot, could change life itself . . .
in a second, everything could be different. And he and Ishak were
bound to the caprices of despotism forever. The two young men's eyes
met as they had that first time in Istanbul, Ishak's full of compassion
and Zorich's of defiance. They still had their youth. And they had
nowhere to go but up.

Impassively the brothers Zanovitch left their lawyer's card with
Ishak Bey.

The next day, nothing was spoken of in St. Petersburg except that the
Czarina's Zorich was a pauper.

At ten o'clock the news reached the imperial palace.

At ten past ten the screams of the Czarina would be heard all the way
to the Admiralty.

"Verily, it isn't sufficient enough to have a son like Paul! I have to choose a favorite like Zorich." Catherine stopped screaming long enough to regard her present favorite, the twenty-two-year-old Lanskoy, who was openly satisfied with the news.

"And you, Misha, *you* think you're better than Zorich? General Zorich?"

"He'll be here by five o'clock to ask you for money," Lanskoy said complacently.

"In that case, I suggest you leave before. The General will chew you up and spit you out like an enraged lion!"

"You intend to receive him?"

"Of course."

"Over my dead body."

"As you prefer."

Catherine turned on her heel and headed toward the Hermitage, her steps lighter and more agile than the speechless Lanskoy had ever seen. He trotted alongside as she stormed through the palace filled with her exquisite collection of paintings, sculpture, porcelain; her thirty thousand books, her ten thousand engraved precious stones, her cabinet de curiosités with its hundred thousand specimens of natural history, and her new theater installed in two immense halls. All the while she calculated how many paintings, drawings, precious stones, sculpture and books Zorich had lost in one card's throw. She looked around, suddenly surprised at where she found herself, her rage dissipated.

She had been reduced by age, she thought ironically, to traveling the three thousand paces from her apartments to this haven of beauty.

Catherine smiled dreamily. What a pleasure, she thought. Her mouth went dry, her eyes brimmed with tears as she contemplated the beauty of the objects she had paid for with mere money. Every object—the paintings, the sculptures, the engravings—brought her closer to Europe, to power, to God, to creation. Every work of genius she possessed made her wiser, richer, younger and more beautiful. Every beauty she bought changed, diluted and revoked her own ugliness to which she was bound like a serf to the land. And beauty was greatness.

The Empress was not a beauty. Yet her figure was tall and imposing, while lacking suppleness. She had a noble carriage, although affected by a somewhat ungraceful walk and increasing weight. She had a long face, especially about the chin, and an eternal smile on her lips that was quite irritating. Her smile fascinated in the beginning, but then it seemed painted on—like a china doll's—for her eyes never smiled. It was as if there were always a portraitist at her side insisting that she smile for eternity. . . . She had a slightly aquiline nose, small bright blue eyes, a deep-set mouth and a complexion marked by chickenpox. Yet Catherine's face inspired violent feelings.

Catherine was in a state of extreme agitation—thus the swift walk through the oppressively opulent halls of her Hermitage. In the throes of war with Sweden, she had thrown herself into a veritable whirlwind of literary and historical activity. She said it was to dull the anxiety of war. But she knew it was also because Potemkin was lingering in his luxurious court at Jassy, organizing the redeployment of the Russian army in view of the Prussian threat; and he was also conducting a passionate love affair with his cousin, Praskovia Potemkin.

And now Zorich! It was really too much! The Empress stormed.

Lanskoy, seeing Catherine in an alarming and rare moment of weakness, burst forth with a jealous tirade that he would never have dared utter otherwise. It was not jealousy of Zorich. As in all servile situations, his jealousy was not of her but of the others.

"You love me?"

"Yes," Catherine said tiredly. "I do love you, Misha."

"But you are always pointing to Potemkin as an example for me to follow . . ."

"A better example of intelligence, courage, humor and singularity I cannot think of," replied Catherine.

"You've never done for me what you did for him. You've not made me Prince!"

"Oh, for God's sake, you sound like Zorich."

"It is Potemkin's fault that I am not twice as rich as I could be."

"It is my fault, darling, because it is *my* money. . . . Zorich too wanted to be Prince. He couldn't be satisfied with the title of Count— oh no! Do you know how much Simon Zorich cost me in one year? Three million rubles!"

"It's true, Madame, the intensity of the love of a despot is measured in titles."

"Lanskoy!"

He had hardly gotten the words out of his mouth when a priceless fifth-century Chinese porcelain vase came crashing down on his head.

"It was easy and I shall do it again." Catherine chuckled, her deep gray eyes gleaming with good humor. What was she doing with this idiot boy? she wondered for one fleeting moment. Lanskoy had been declared favorite on St. Catherine's Day, November 24, 1779, as a surprise from Potemkin.

She smiled sweetly at Lanskoy. But the twenty-three-year-old wasn't finished. His jealous tirade continued as Catherine waited patiently for him to run down. She would never make another favorite a Prince, not as long as Potemkin lived. Potemkin was the only one of her favorites who had understood that power, real power, never came from sexual favors. A lover never possessed the *power* of a loved one as he possessed the body . . . he only *reflected* it like a mirror. Potemkin had achieved real power only after they had ceased to be lovers. . . . An empire and an erection, thought the Empress, were very different things. She was doing her best to train and guide her young lover in statecraft and government. She used him as a channel for requests and petitions, but almost at once in his blind jealousy of Potemkin, he had begun to intrigue against the Prince. She knew that her secretary, Khrapovitsky, famous for his laconic descriptions, called Misha duraleyushka, "Little Fool," behind her back, but she was determined to make a silk purse out of a sow's ear. She had failed with Zorich, had ruined his simple, passionate nature; but in alliance with her advisors, maybe Misha would learn something. She knew Lanskoy's rise meant her own decline. Zorich had been her last real man.

Now, in her old age, weighed down by pounds of tormented flesh, she could still hear, if she listened carefully, the svelte little German Princess wailing to be let out. Her bulk equaled the weight of her power, she thought. She glanced sideways at Lanskoy's immaculately chiseled profile.

Then Catherine looked around her. The furor to build, she mused, was diabolical. It literally devoured money, and the more one built, the more one wanted to build. It was a sickness not unlike the addiction to opium. Almost from her accession, she had reacted against the lush baroque which Bartolomeo Rastrelli had so amply provided for the Czarina. The architect Quarenghi had introduced the new classical style she loved. She personally favored the Scot Charles Cameron, who had remodeled her private apartments in Tsarskoye Selo, and she admired the English Adams brothers. But it was here, where Giacomo Quarenghi had built her Hermitage theater in the Palladian manner like the theater of Vicenza, that she was most happy.

But she was proudest of all of Falconet's statue of Peter the Great in which she had insisted on her claim to equality with Peter I: *Petro Primo, Caterina Secunda.* The hell with Catherine the First! She, Catherine II, was heir to Peter's greatness, not any other. She liked to be portrayed as Minerva, both warrior and law giver, standing with her

Nakaz, "Great Instructions," in her hand. Potemkin had even tried to persuade the young Mozart to enter into Russian service. She and Potemkin had decided more than four years ago to go their separate ways. The great romance of her life was over.

She was old enough to be his mother (his grandmother) and she was sick and tired of his whining. The men with whom she had shared love, danger, treason, war, power and assassinations were all behind her. Including Potemkin. Zorich had been the last. What could her sweet Lanskoy do for her except bring her the joys of a mother? Finally, all her men represented a failure of her soul, her femininity or her career. She recalled her tearful answer to Potemkin's jealous recriminations.

"I took the first because I was compelled to and the fourth because I was in despair. . . . As for the other three, God knows it was not from debauchery for which I have never had any inclination. If in my youth I had had a husband whom I could have loved, I should have remained faithful to him all my life. It is my misfortune that my heart cannot rest content, even for an hour, without love."

And what had they represented? Peter, the husband: father of her dead daughter, Ann; Sergey Saltykov: perhaps Paul's real father; the brothers Orlov: treason, coup d'état, ascension to the throne and, finally, accessory to murder; Stanislas Poniatowski: compassionate, impossible love; Gregory Potemkin: fatal love, which had led to Pierre Zavadovsky, and, finally, to Simon Zorich. . . . Peter had been murdered, but she had had nothing to do with it. That Paul was not a bastard, she was much less certain . . . much, much less certain. Besides, Paul was so stupid he *couldn't* be her son. . . .

At five o'clock in the afternoon, Catherine received what she had been dreading all day: a request from Count Zorich for an audience. She made him wait until after dinner to underline the inconvenience of the visit.

The first thing she said was: "I'm surprised to see you in Moscow." She was determined not to help him explain his situation. Zorich, understanding that she knew already and was pretending not to in order to humiliate him, plunged ahead.

"I've lost everything. The details you already know."

"I don't see why you have come all the way from your *estates* to tell me this." Catherine wanted a confession. Zorich understood this too. But he wanted two things: not to be humiliated and money. He decided to play on Catherine's masculine vanity. Catherine, on the other hand, was thinking of her failures with men.

"It's your fault if you find me here."

"*My* fault! What am I to understand by that? That I've failed you . . . corrupted you . . . spoiled you? Simon, what are you talking about?"

"What I'm talking about is the only revenge an ex-favorite has when he is no longer in power and the courtesans no longer respect him; the only revenge is money or complete contempt for money. I choose the second argument."

"Simon, I've had a great many favorites. None of them has acted in your stupid, babyish way. The problem is that your vanity is too small for an Empress. Great vanity instead of stupid vanity would have shown you how to *profit* from your situation. *Our* situation. Other favorites have known how to participate in power, share it; you thought only of yourself. *You* believed yourself irreplaceable. It was that that undid you. You acted just like a woman."

"The others were rich or noble or both!"

"Not Potemkin. And he is the best and he's still here. Stronger than before . . . you are being ridiculous . . ."

Zorich passed to the offensive. "I was the only one of your Harem who loved you disinterestedly," he said.

"No love is disinterested. And every man and every woman would like to have a harem; the secret is to acquire the *power* to impose one's dreams and desires on others—if they like it or not."

"In Istanbul the love of a Sultan is measured in the number and length of pearl necklaces."

"And *your* pearl necklaces, Simon. You were my most expensive favorite. You went through three million rubles and you never gave me a present to match Orlov's."

"Orlov! It's not a ninety-nine-carat diamond, it's the thought behind it!"

At this Catherine burst into laughter. Zorich was close to tears.

"There are only two debts I ask you to pay, Madame."

"And what are they?"

"One is a moral debt: the cadet and ballet schools. The last things I have done for Russia that I can be proud of. I don't want them to die."

"Granted. The schools will be the charge of the State. Next?"

"A debt that stems from my imprisonment in Constantinople. . . . I owe Ishak Bey . . . ten thousand piastres."

"Granted. I will see to it personally. I will command those two crooks to rent you back your estates and I will pay the rent. But you are never to set foot in Saint Petersburg again. I never want to see you again. This was once *your* court. Now it is your exile."

General Zorich bowed, turned and started toward the door. At that moment the aged Empress called out:

"Simon." The tall, handsome Count turned. The Empress took off the huge blue sapphire brooch surrounded by a river of diamonds that failed to dwarf its size, scintillating on her bosom, and placed it in his hand.

"And Simon, don't try to understand."

It was neither pity nor love. Merely the tribute of a Czar.

• CHAPTER TWO •

CATHERINE 1781

In Russia, the government is despotism
mitigated by strangulation.
—MADAME DE STAËL, 1822

Catherine placed her short, plump finger on Ishak Bey's lips. "Don't speak," she said. "The first one who speaks after making love always says something stupid."

Ishak Bey had no difficulty making love to Catherine, neither aesthetically nor morally. He had made love to men and women, to angels and whores, to English, French, Armenian, Hungarian, Rumanian, Italian, Ottoman, Egyptian, Tunisian, Tripolitan, Algerian, German, Russian, Austrian . . . he wondered if there was anyone to whom he hadn't yet made love in his life . . . dwarfs, lilliputians, eunuchs, monsters of face, figure and, moreover, soul . . . he placed Catherine in that category: a sacred monster, a goddess, a monument, and most of all a ticket out of St. Petersburg. He couldn't really ask Zorich for anything after his grand disaster. He wondered if this came under the heading of consorting with the enemy. He supposed so, but if Catherine thought she could get him to spy for her, she was dead wrong. Not that he had led her to believe she could. That was the weakness of despots, to be unable to conceptualize another human being's thoughts.

Physically Catherine even pleased him, since his Ottoman taste for small breasts, tiny waists and enormous haunches was fulfilled by Her Imperial Majesty's physique . . . and, besides, Catherine, whatever she was outside of bed, in bed was all Oriental woman: passionate, attentive, expert, lavish and grateful.

He thought suddenly of his grandfather crawling on his hands and knees to the bed of his Sultane wife and being either admitted or dismissed to the harem. Perhaps it was this childish fantasy that played such a great part in his affection for the Czarina.

He was exhausted. The Empress had prodigious reserves of energy at the advanced age of fifty-two. She was in fact insatiable. For not only did her official favorites service her, but uncountable "occasionals." Butlers, valets, merchants, Hussars, sergeants, secretaries. Yet there was no more decorous court in all Christendom. Transgressions were punished promptly and severely. This too was very Oriental, he decided. Scratch a Russian and you find a Turkoman. In bed she was a classicist. The woman on her back, knees upon her breasts, and the man on top. He had attempted a little fantasy and had been promptly discouraged if not outright repulsed. How boring it must have been for Zorich, he thought suddenly. But then Zorich had never had much imagination. . . .

Catherine gazed at Ishak tenderly. She might have named him favorite if he hadn't been a Turk. . . . He had passed with flying colors.

"Were you happy at the court of Versailles?" she asked, breaking the silence. "Happier than at the court of St. Petersburg?" she said coquettishly.

But Ishak ignored her heavy-handed plea for flattery and gallantry and instead launched into a recital of his adventures in France that made the Empress laugh until she cried.

"Try," laughed Ishak Bey, "to find a latrine in a cathedral or in all of Versailles . . .

"I was the bane of Comte Vergennes, the foreign minister's existence, money flowed toward me like the tides, and I swept it back to sea like a gale wind . . .

"I took up with Suleiman Aga, the Tunisian envoy to the court. Despite a fondness for terrifying bullfights at Pantin and boring horse-races at Sablon and a disgusting interest in animals, Suleiman Aga was a wonderful friend. He stayed for five months in Paris. He had been chosen as envoy to the Barbary States: first for his business sense, second for his good health and third to accomplish the *suppression* of the presents the Deys of the Barbary Coast had been sending each year to the King of France. In return the African ministers would diminish the incredible number of embassy people who ordinarily accompanied them. . . .

"Anyway, my old French professor, Louis Ruffin, was in charge of Suleiman's arrival in Toulon with his baggage, his horses, his presents, his retinue of thousands. . . . We had a wonderful time once he got settled at court—theater, salons, shopping. . . . The presents he bought to take back with him took up literally all of his and my time . . .

"Ruffin, having already lived in Istanbul . . . Constantinople, and knowing from experience the impossibility of ever satisfying all alone the multiple, imperious demands of fifteen to twenty barbarians (in the geographical sense)—and knowing the meticulous, troublesome, obtrusive and fastidious character of Orientals in general—asked me to help him. Suleiman Aga and I hit it off immediately. . . . He had arrived with his aides, his cook, his barber, his coffee maker, his soldiers, and all who had charge of the lions. He was charmed by Paris, but disconcerted by the quality of the guests at dinner and the hubbub they made, the sight of the women, the length of the dinners saying that even a lion would have been disconcerted in such an assembly. We went to the Jardin du Roi to see the animals, and he insisted on handling the snakes! Ugh . . . I have never found animals worthy of observation except the human animal. . . . He is facinating because he is so unpredictable, since he is the only animal who lies. . . .

"The Ambassador installed himself in the Hôtel Sartine, and he presented his credentials dressed in a sensational ermine pelisse that was soon the talk of Paris. We saw a lot of the Comedie Française at the Tuileries, which he loved, that and the Comedie Italienne. In March we had an audience with the King. We were magnificently dressed. I had a two-feet-high turban of white gauze trimmed in gold and a white fox pelisse over a red robe and the uniform of an Admiral in the Ottoman navy. . . . Versailles opened its arms. . . . The present from the King of France to the Bey of Tunis was fixed at fifty thousand pounds. On our way back outside of Paris we stopped at a rich Armenian who had the only Turkish bath in France."

"And the King," said Catherine. "How did you find him?"

"Very well. Like our Sultan, he doesn't say much. The ministers do most of the talking. The Queen was magnificent. . . . She was very impressed with our turbans. . . . Did you know they had bullfights in Paris? . . . They make cocks, dogs, tigers and lions fight too—I was quite offended at the dogfight, dogs are sacred to Moslems—they go to heaven. As for the bullfight, it was disgusting. . . . But you would have loved the King's garde-meuble, tapestries, objets in precious materials, vases, cups, the diamonds of the Crown with the Regent and Sancy diamonds, the stunning presents brought by the Ottoman Ambassadors. . . . One day in May I left Suleiman for Tunis. I took leave of Vergennes and Ruffin, my tutor. I rendered my farewells to Versailles, we went for the last time to a concert where the King and the Emperor of Austria, Joseph II, traveling incognito, were. . . . Suleiman embarked from Marseilles on *L'Alamène.*"

"And you?" asked Catherine.

"Hardly what I expected, Madame. Suleiman Aga almost didn't leave, for the day before an Armenian sailor, newly arrived from Constantinople, told him that my Lord Admiral, the Captain Pasha Hasan Gazi, had vowed to kill me. . . . But old Ruffin had received the same information from Istanbul. The Armenian told us in no uncertain terms that I was not to show myself in Istanbul until the Captain Pasha had fallen into disgrace or had forgotten your favorite Zorich and the mosque! I took the long way home via Algiers where I sailed with the fleet."

"But why were you safe in Algiers or Egypt when they are part of the Ottoman Empire?"

"The men of the sea have more solidarity than our Empire, Your Majesty. The Ottoman fleet is autofinanced. Thus each navy depends upon itself and its prizes to pay its expenses. This way the Ottomans have the greatest fleet in the world, but its sailors do mostly what they like. The Algerians certainly weren't going to hand me over to Hasan Gazi."

"Yes, but your Lord Admiral's hatred is all out of proportion to the crime! . . . His reaction so . . . oversized . . . it is almost Russian!"

Ishak Bey said nothing, but he thought: scratch a Turkoman and you find a Russian.

"Well," said Ishak, "it is a bit fanatic . . ."

"Je suis Allemande" said the Czarina. "I have never really understood the Russians. Everything in this Empire is . . . is oversized"— she looked down at herself—"even me. . . . I have to strain my imagination to keep up with myself. Here, one cannot just have a lover, one must create a *favorite.* That costs a fortune. A diamond can't just be a diamond, it has to be the size of a fist like Orlov's. One cannot simply gamble in Russia, one must absolutely ruin oneself like Zorich. One can't attend a play, one has to build the damned theater! And to have a place for my collection I had to build the Hermitage! To make love one has to fight a duel. And to cuckold a husband, my God, one has to kill him! . . . I may be a despot," sighed Catherine, "but with a country like this, one has to be!"

"I see that all Russians are fanatics." Ishak Bey smiled. "Like all pagans who have been converted to Christianity. . . ."

"The Catholic religion is less tolerant than the Moslem. But we too have our gaga over holy wars against the infidel. But the Russians are capable of *real* passion, whereas we Orientals are not. You *think* you are because you are violent. But you, my Beau Turque, are not passionate. You will never be. The Oriental is too fatalistic. Too measured. The harem proves it!"

"How so?" asked Ishak.

"One simply *can't* have more than one wife—one can't love more than one person at any given moment. I have never loved two men at the same time. . . ."

Ishak Bey said nothing. Catherine was so used to gallantry, adulation and flattery, to contradict her would simply put his future plans in jeopardy. But his pride got the better of him.

"To make love to someone you don't love is a sin, at least in your religion," he sulked.

"My Beau Turque, ordinary women use sex to obtain power. I use power to obtain sex."

Ishak was sorry he had spoken so lightly. His Oriental pride was hurt to the quick.

Catherine looked down at her bosom. If only he wasn't a Turk, she thought. But at least he speaks French. . . . Ishak Bey was also examining her bosom. Catherine wanted something from him . . . and it wasn't what she had already had.

"When do you return to your own country?" she asked innocently.

Ishak Bey knew what Catherine wanted from him. Treason. She wanted him to spy for Russia. It was time, he decided, for him to exit. Before things got out of hand in their usual way and he had to exit against his will. If there was any spying to be done, he would do it for the Osmans, thank you.

"I cannot return home. I have not a ruble to my name, Empress. Zorich owed me five thousand piastres but, as you know, your 'Sima' finds it impossible to pay."

"But he came to see me, Sima. And I promised him to personally settle with you the sum of ten thousand rubles."

"What?" asked Ishak Bey as if he hadn't understood.

"How much more do you need?" asked Catherine.

"But, Majesty, I had no intention of implying . . ."

"I'm the one who promised. And I add to the sum my own contribution: twenty-five thousand rubles."

"But," gulped Ishak. Then he was silent. Catherine's attentions, not his, had a high price. Too high. But he was going to take the money anyway, and run.

"With it, you can go home . . ."

"I can't go home, Matushka Gosudarynya. . . ."

"You would render your country the greatest service," said Catherine. "You are brilliant, traveled, cosmopolitan. . . . You know the world and the differences between races. You are not weighted down with superstition, dogma and religion as are most of your countrymen and mine. Teach them and your homeland will perhaps owe you its resurrection," said Catherine, as though the thing she wanted most was the resurrection of the Turks.

"As God is my witness, I have no other desire beyond the good of my country. How can your Sultan resist the unlimited power of an absolute Prince governing a warlike people?" she asked. "He rules the largest empire in the world," she said, grinding her teeth. "He has the largest fleet in the world, he rules one eighth of the world and still some of its richest parts!" (Ishak Bey appreciated the "still" but said nothing.)

"Why are you so backward in the arts, science and music? What do you do with your vast revenues? Your treasure? Where are your monuments?" she asked. "It is against justice and the Christian religion to make men slaves. . . . I want all people to obey the laws, but not be slaves. . . . Servitude is damaging to the State, it kills emulation, industry, the arts, sciences, honor and prosperity. . . . Nineteen out of twenty of our serfs die—what a loss to the State! We need populating. We must make our huge deserts swarm like an ant heap and I see no point in forcing those of our people who are not Christians to adopt our religion; far from it: I am in agreement that a plurality of wives increases the population. . . . Opulence must reign. Progress and modernity are the most important things in the world. I have built a hundred forty-four new cities, created twenty-nine new governments, concluded thirty treaties, won seventy-eight victories. I work twelve to fifteen hours a day. In this world it is not enough just to manage. One must move with the times, change, build. I am an aristocrat. That is my job."

Catherine paused for breath. She was flushed and excited. . . .
"Where are your monuments?" she repeated.

Our monument is the Istanbul you so covet, thought Ishak Bey to himself. But out loud he said: "We don't build monuments to Allah's Shadow on Earth. That is idolatry. We build fountains, public gardens, baths, mosques, hospitals and libraries. Everything that is made for the pleasure of life."

"But an empire like the Ottomans', *Alexander the Great's Empire,* can't be ruled by fountains, mosques and a Sultan who is kept locked up in a cage! What about legislation? I have issued 123 edicts to improve the lot of the people!"

"We have the law of the Koran. And we have a dynasty which is one thousand years old [by fear and courtesy Ishak made no reference to the brevity of the little German Princess's pedigree], that is and always will be Osman. It is for my own private satisfaction that I travel, read and study. When I return to Istanbul—"

"Constantinople," Catherine interrupted.

"—I will be very careful to hide all that I know, to despise, in appearance at least, all the arts and knowledge of Christians who according to us are born of demons. I will take care to follow all our absurd customs. . . . I will be as stupid and as ignorant as my compatriots, for otherwise I will not keep my head on my shoulders a week."

A man could go crazy, thought Ishak turning on his side, just simply thinking too profoundly about opening or closing a door. . . .

BOOK III

TOPKAPI
·1781–1787·

• CHAPTER ONE •

GEDICLI 1781

Political genius develops fully at times in the favorite Sultanes, admitted as they are to all the confidential secrets of governments and the intrigues of the court. Long and great reigns have been founded and governed by some of these beautiful slaves. . . . They are often the hidden mechanisms behind the greatest of events. Favorites, they serve, wives, they inspire, mothers, they covet and prepare the reigns of their sons.

—LAMARTINE, *Voyage en Orient,* 1835

It was not the august Kizlar Aga who led Naksh-i-dil through the Bab-i-Sa'adet, the Door of Felicity, but the Kiaya Kadine, the Lady Controller of the harem. She was a tall, red-headed Russian named Kurrum. Immense, wrinkled, rouged and animal-eyed, she wore the most enormous and precariously placed turban on her head that Naksh-i-dil had ever seen; it was at least two feet across and the same in height. The whole white mass was festooned with strings of pearls, ostrich feathers, diamond stickpins, ribbons, real flowers, silk flowers and sashes of gold gauze. It bobbed up and down independently of the corpulent body beneath, as if it had a mind of its own, threatening at any moment to topple over and send the woman crashing with it. But all Naksh-i-dil heard was the groan and then the deep boom of the harem doors, eighteen feet high and a foot thick, slamming behind her. Her heart sinking, she heard the swish of steel on steel as the eunuchs drew their swords, and the hollow echo of the door reverberated like a bell tolling. From now on, each door would be unlocked and then

locked again as she and the Kiaya traveled deeper into the harem. The
Kiaya fumbled with the ring of keys at her waist and the sound brought
back memories of the plantation and the sounds of keys being turned in
the padlocks of the slave quarters. She and the Kiaya were standing in a
spacious courtyard, shadowed by trees and cooled by a marble fountain
in the center. There was a colonnade that circled the courtyard, which
was empty.

Holy Mary, Mother of God! whispered Naksh-i-dil, still clutching her
rosary beads. *Pray for this sinner.* She was being buried alive. She
lurched forward, following the Kiaya.

Naksh-i-dil presented a serious problem of protocol. There was a
rigid and absolute hierarchy among the women in the harem, decreed
by law and centuries of usage. It took years to advance from one caste
to another. Sometimes it never happened. The first and lowliest degree
was Gedicli, or slave girl, attached to the personal service of the Sultan
and who aspired to his bed. They were sometimes referred to as Odalisques. The second caste was Gozde, or "in the eye," a woman in the
harem who had managed to gain the attention of the Sultan. Third,
there were the Ikbals, women who had become favorites of the Sultan
and slept with him occasionally. The fourth and supreme caste was
Kadine, "official" wife of the Sultan, who had been allowed the maternity of a royal Prince or Princess. This little green-eyed vixen was not
really Gedicli, because she was already Gozde, "in the eye of the Sultan." But she was not really Gozde because she totally lacked the training, comportment and manners of a Gozde and an aspirant to the Sultan's bed. . . . She had everything to learn about Topkapi, the
Seraglio, the harem, and . . . staying alive. Why, she didn't even know
where the toilets were, thought the Kiaya. At a first lesson, the Kiaya
decided to show her what she had escaped as a Gedicli. She led the
terrified girl down into the depths of one of the ten harem kitchens,
where hundreds of black and white slaves toiled. Here the female slaves,
destined for the personal service of the Sultan, the Valide and the
Sultanes, lived and worked. Naksh-i-dil was struck by the lack of light,
and the lack of sound. With all these women, she thought, there should
be a racket of chatter, conversation, gossip. Yet there was a strange
hush. The high vaulted wooden ceilings were blackened with smoke
which rose to an opening where she could see the sky. Bursts of startled
laughter and snickering followed the new inmate as she and the Kiaya
crossed the dark heated space, darting amongst the white-clad slaves.
There was a low drumlike moan rising from the clatter of cooking pots

and hushed conversation. Many of the slaves bowed to the Kiaya as she passed, her imperial staff of silver in hand.

Naksh-i-dil was cold with terror. She pulled the hand of the Kiaya, who held her firmly and easily while she clutched her silver staff, the symbol of her authority, with the other hand.

"Gozde," the Kiaya said sternly, "you should have pity on the Queens, Princesses and courtesans who do not stand in your place! I would give my whole fortune to stand where you stand, and I would not sell it for a province! You are in the 'eye of the Sultan.' Many have been here for years without ever achieving that goal! The world, this world, can be yours at the drop of the Sultan's handkerchief."

"I don't want . . . this world," Naksh-i-dil whispered in horror.

The Kiaya Kadine slapped Naksh-i-dil full in the face. "Idiot! You will learn, and you will learn to submit! To me, to the Sultan, to Allah."

She shook the trembling girl, judging her firm, full flesh under the disgusting black costume, which to her nostrils smelled of pig. "You filthy little girl. I showed you this to frighten you, to warn you of what can happen to you and your beauty if you do not obey me and the rules of the harem. Now, you are going to be clean—cleaner than you've ever been in your life, and you will leave that filthy rag behind you!"

The new slave and the Kiaya Kadine left the teeming kitchen courtyard, and followed a long arcade of arches supported by nine pillars elaborately decorated at the top. The Kiaya kept up a stream of information, admonishments, regulations, historic recollections, vindictive recriminations as she escorted the new inmate through a labyrinth of corridors, alleyways, courtyards, hallways, arcades and gardens, each time locking each door. There were small pavilions called kiosks with strange shapes and silver-plated domes, grilled windows and heavily bolted doors, decorated in arabesques and flower motifs in blue and white. A narrow stairway would suddenly descend into a secret court. They passed abandoned buildings, deserted apartments, a small village of wood, marble, stone, greenery, lead, bronze, porcelain and water. Women crossed their paths, one hundred, two hundred. Some of them were beautiful, some ugly, others like ghosts not made of flesh and blood in their white shirts and pleated drawers, gauze turbans and embroidered tunics, their open vests fitted with multicolored scarves and necklaces. All the women stared at Naksh-i-dil's strange bell-shaped black dress. There was no black among the galaxy of colored materials and textures, although Naksh-i-dil was to learn that the Sultan favored black and wore it excessively. Several of the women nudged each other, and bursts of malicious laughter followed her.

They arrived at a large open courtyard, around which ran still another colonnaded gallery and two stories of balconies. Naksh-i-dil thought of the houses of her island and their gingerbread decorations. A series of doors gave onto the balconies one after the other. The windows were Venetian glass. There must have been, thought Naksh-i-dil, fifty of these small cubicles. The gallery below was supported by slender fluted columns that seemed to stretch on into infinity. The courtyard was paved in white marble, the walls tiled in blue and white and yellow. Behind a window on the ground floor, Naksh-i-dil saw a shadow. On the second balcony, a woman stood.

"This is the Courtyard of the Favorites, the Gozdes and the Ikbals," said the Kiaya. "From here, we enter the baths. . . ." The Kiaya pushed open the only unlocked door at the far end of the courtyard. They entered the hammam, the baths. In the vestibule Naksh-i-dil was divested of all her clothes and led into the first chamber. She caught her breath at the high vaulted cupola from which light descended from hundreds of rounded openings no larger than the size of a melon. The illusion was that of a cathedral; the rays of light converged halfway down into an amber mist of diffused sunlight and vapor and the breaths of hundreds of women.

The Kiaya inspected the nude girl, shaking her head at the profusion of down and sinful pubic hair that was beginning to reappear on the new slave's body. The Kiaya handed her over to three slaves, who began by washing her; then after depilating her completely, carefully inspecting nostrils, ears and anus, they draped her in a muslin shirt, which did nothing to hide the outlines of her body, and led her to the first hot chamber. Naksh-i-dil tried, unsuccessfully, to cover herself from the nonchalant gazes of the fifty or so women in the first chamber, some of whom were draped, some not. Her eyes wandered over figures as beautiful and as varied as she imagined was possible in the world. There were matrons with opulent forms that their ferigees outlined; tall, with dark eyes, humid lips, dilated nostrils, aristocrats who could make a hundred slaves tremble with one glance. There were young girls her own age, completely naked, with high, hard breasts and long narrow torsos and legs that seemed like those of boys. There were others, small and plump, on whom everything was round: the figure, the eyes, the nose and mouth, and who had such quiet demeanors, who were so childish and young, even in Naksh-i-dil's eyes, with such resigned and docile appearance that they seemed born to be playthings and to have their mouths perpetually stuffed with sweets. In passing by them, Naksh-i-dil had the impulse to fill their half-open mouths with sugarcane bark as mothers did in Martinique. There were others too. Young wives rose, vivacious and healthy, cheerfully gossiping or drinking lemonade, their eyes full of astuteness and caprice. One thing surprised Naksh-i-dil: their manner of looking and laughing, without exception, was so ingenuous that it excused the most reckless and curious behavior.

The Kiaya Kadine followed, rattling on in her Russian-accented French as she unwound her turban. "If the Sultan wants a favorite for her sensuality, he chooses a Berber, if he wants handsome and numerous children, he chooses a Persian, if he wants servility, he takes a Greek. You, Naksh-i-dil, will live to be an Ikbal or my name isn't Kurrum . . . perhaps"—she paused—"even a Kadine. . . . After all, Sineprever Kadine started without great beauty. Yet she achieved perfection. She unites the willingness of a Greek with the virtuous adoration of an Egyptian, the lascivious movements of an Algerian with the hot-bloodedness of an Ethiopian. She combines the shamelessness of a Frank"—she eyed Naksh-i-dil with amusement—"with the consummate science of a Hindu, the experience of a Circassian with the passion of a Nubian, the narrowness of a Chinese with the muscular violence of a Sudanese, the vigor of an Iraqi with the delicacy of a Persian . . ."

Naksh-i-dil's head began to turn with the rush of words, the running water and vapor. Slaves passed to and fro with pipes, water, dinners. The scene was so strange, so new, Naksh-i-dil thought she had passed to another universe.

"The Iraqi women are more exciting," continued the Kiaya, "the Syrians more affectionate, but the most desirable of all women are the women from Hedjaz. . . . Turkish women," she added, "have cold cunts, get pregnant the first time and have nasty characters. But they are intelligent. So intelligent," chuckled the Kiaya, "they never marry a Sultan . . ."

"What?" asked Naksh-i-dil.

"No, free Turkish noblewomen are not allowed to marry the Sultan, for it would be blasphemy for the Sultan to raise another Ottoman to his level."

Naksh-i-dil was silent for a long moment. She remembered her humiliating presentation to Abdulhamid.

"Here the Circassians, the Georgians and the Caucasians are

adored," the Kiaya rattled on. "Over there is Kontayaki, and there is Shah Sultane; back there, I see Ayşe . . ."

"Is not the Sultan a man?" asked Naksh-i-dil.

"What?"

"A man," repeated Naksh-i-dil angrily. "A man who thinks and feels and talks and dreams, like *I* think and feel and talk and dream?"

"The Sultan is Allah's Shadow on Earth! How should I know if he talks or feels as we do, impertinent child!"

"Well, I know," said Naksh-i-dil. "I know."

"You know nothing," said the Kiaya. "But you will by the time I finish with you." She squinted. "You could be Caucasian, you know, with your red-gold hair and your slanted eyes. . . ."

The slaves had led Naksh-i-dil from one chamber to the next, from unbearable heat to cooling pools, to tepid showers, to breath-snatching steam. Now they had laid her down on one of the marble couches in the last chamber and had begun to massage her, bring the blood to the surface of her pale skin. Despite herself, Naksh-i-dil groaned with pleasure under the expert hands, her skin flushing rose. She squeezed her eyes shut and tried to pray, but nothing came. It was as if the baths had washed her brain as clean as her glistening, polished body, leaving no trace of thought or ambition or regret. She fell asleep. The Kiaya stared down at the sleeping girl. She couldn't in all justice put her with the Gedicli. . . . The Kiaya raised her hands in supplication. What was she to do with such raw material? How was she to please a Sultan of such jaded and exhausted tastes as Abdulhamid with the likes of an . . . American?

Kiaya Kurrum sat down, her head resting on her fists, her elbows upon her knees. Without her turban, her red hair was peppered with the gray that henna could not keep at bay.

There were 383 women in Abdulhamid's harem, and no Valide (may she walk in heaven) since Abdulhamid's mother, Rebia, was long dead. Abdulhamid's first Kadine, Rushah, on whom he had spent his passion and his pen, had obtained his permission to make the pilgrimage to Mecca and had never returned. That had left her, the Kiaya, with a great responsibility. Two days ago, there had been 384 women in the harem, but last night the Ikbal Lelia had died mysteriously. She had already left the harem by the Door of Death breached in the ramparts of the harem at the end of the gardens. It was the only possible way to exit from Topkapi—feet first. And now this little thing had arrived to take her place, so to speak, so that if for a day there had been 383, today there were again 384. Inshallah, thought the Kiaya.

When the Kurrum had entered Topkapi, Mustafa III was reigning and there were 480 women and that had been thirty-five years ago. She shook her head sadly. She had been a magnificent creature then, almost six feet tall, svelte, with blazing red hair to her waist. The years had passed, and so had the Sultan's handkerchief. She had been passed by. And it was during those years of waiting that she had found her vocation. She had observed the jealousies and intrigues of hundreds of women, she had seen their plans go astray, their abortions, their strangulations; infanticide, poisoning, repudiation, suicide, murder. Slowly she had resigned herself to another kind of life, another goal. If she couldn't be favorite, she would be guardian, ruler and maker of favorites. She had learned every language spoken in the harem, every art of medicine, every aphrodisiac, every possible feminine coquetry, studied every technique and manual of love, and she had arrived at her position of power by gradual advancement in all aspects of harem training, except, she thought ironically, the only one that counted: the chance to become Kadine. Passed over by love, at any rate male love, maternity had been denied her, and now all she could hope for was the maintenance of her high position and to die a nonviolent death. Kurrum Kadine was without real bitterness toward the life Allah in his mercy had dealt out to her. The harem of Topkapi was the largest and most flourishing in the world. It projected its shadow across the whole Empire. Women from every corner of the realm lived and died here. The lucky ones copulated, gave birth and triumphed here. But, mused Kiaya, they *still* died here, no matter what their triumphs. As she would. So be it.

She looked around at the reclining, chattering, sleeping, eating and dreaming women, the odor of female flesh making her nostrils dilate. She was responsible for this mass of imbecility, desperation and cunning. She had under her orders the Lady Treasurer, the Hazinedar Usta, who ran the highly complicated accounts of the harem, including the payments of pashmaklik, "slipper money," and the pensions for those who were exiled for whatever reason to the Eski Serai, the "Palace of Tears."

After Mohammed II had taken Constantinople, he had built a palace on its third hill in 1454. When ten years later a larger palace on the first hill replaced it, the former became known as the Eski Serai, or Old Palace . . . the Palace of Tears. It was a six-feet-thick, walled-in

square of one mile and a half. The widows of dead Sultans, their sisters
—if they were not married—the nurses of their children who couldn't
or didn't marry, all found their lodgings there. The lady who by age and
prudence had acquired merit had the care and conduct of the others as
Mother Superior. She was called the Kiaya Kadine, the Great Lady.
The Great Lady presided over the wren's nest of courts, gardens, kiosks, villas, pavilions, mosques, and cells much like those of nuns which
made up the buildings enclosed behind the high seven-gated walls.

It was a palace, a fortress, a sanctuary, a harem without a Sultan, a
city within a city, a citadel of women, august and magnificent, guarded
by an army of black men. There was one way in and only one way out:
power or death. And death came so much more often than power,
thought the Kiaya. The other members of her cabinet were the Wardrobe Mistress, the Bath Mistress, the Keeper of the Harem Jewels, the
Reader of the Koran, the Quartermaster. . . . Upon her ample shoulders rested the destiny of the harem, and every woman in it. The Kiaya
gazed at the sleeping girl, her own aging flesh aglow from the vapor and
perspiration. How many of the young and fair had she seen come and
go? One needed more than youth, beauty, French arrogance and American ignorance to survive here, mused Kurrum Kadine . . . one drop
of arsenic, one flacon of acid. . . . She shuddered.

Naksh-i-dil woke to the sound of running water and women's voices.
In terror she looked around her, trying to hide her nakedness, understanding nothing. A woman came toward her and started to speak.
Naksh-i-dil stared up at her in incomprehension. The woman insisted
for a while, then shrugged and turned her naked back to Naksh-i-dil.
Naksh-i-dil started to cry. "Don't worry," said the Kiaya. "No one here
speaks the same language . . . we are used to speaking to one another
and not being understood and not understanding. Mostly we talk to
ourselves. There are no nationalities here, yet there are all nationalities . . ."

Suddenly, from the direction of what the Kiaya knew to be the hospital, a long, wailing scream was heard.

"Come," said the Kiaya Kadine nervously. "It is dinnertime, Naksh-
i-dil, and you have not yet seen your room. . . ." The Kiaya had decided she couldn't put Naksh-i-dil in the Odalisques' dormitory. She
might not last out the night.

The scream echoed and reechoed through the colonnaded gardens,
perfumed with jasmine and pine, following them as the harem bell
sounded the hour. The scream followed them all the way to the courts

housing the Gozdes. It was the Sultan's fourth wife, Humashah Kadine, whose five-year-old, Prince Mahmud, had just died.

Naksh-i-dil followed the Kiaya out of the baths. She was dressed in a gomlek and a pair of linen drawers, her European clothes a bundle in her arms. The Kiaya led her into the Odalisques' dormitory. It was a long, wide hall with windows on both sides and down the middle rows of painted chests. The walls were whitewashed and decorated with floral patterns and bouquets. The deepening light slanted in columns from the narrow windows. The room was empty, the floor bare. Here too was the same babble of voices and languages. . . . The Kiaya beckoned to the girl nearest her, who bowed. She said something to her in a strange language, and with gestures the girl went to one of the chests and pulled out a neatly rolled mattress and undid it. Then she rerolled it expertly. Here slept the Odalisques, under the strict supervision of the Harem Mistress. At night the mattresses, which were now hidden in cupboards, would be laid out side by side in rows twelve inches apart on the two levels, accessible to the keen eyes of the Kiaya Kadine.

"There," said the Kiaya, "this is how you make your bed and how you undo it. Try it."

Naksh-i-dil knelt and with trembling hands attempted to roll and unroll the mattress.

"No! Not like that! Let her show you again. . . . No. No. No. Again, again, until you get it right!" The Kiaya gave her a violent shove. Naksh-i-dil swallowed and began again. When the Kiaya was satisfied, she pulled Naksh-i-dil to her feet and led her through the length of the dormitory, down a stairway, through a grille to still another courtyard. It looked deserted. The Kiaya unlocked one of the cubicles on the ground floor, and led Naksh-i-dil inside. The room was about the size of a slave cabin and had a high barred window. There was a tray of food on a low table and a chest like those she had seen.

"You rise at five. The harem bell rings."

The Kiaya put down the new Gozde's bedding and, executing a temennah, her right hand lowered, then lifted to her lips and then her forehead, left her without another word.

A full moon frosted the lead domes of the Seraglio and whitened the contours of the cypress and plane trees which spread their great shadows over the vast courts where the lights of innumerable tiny windows were extinguished one after the other. The spires, the white mosques, the minaret points, the suspended crescents spiking the sky, shone between the dark green forests of gardens.

The three great harem doors had just been shut, their iron keys still vibrating in the hand of the black eunuch. The thirty men who guarded the Door of Felicity stood erect against the walls with their sabers drawn, as immobile as bas-reliefs, their dark faces navy in the even darker shadows. Hundreds of invisible sentinels stood watch from the heights of the walls and the towers looking out toward the sea, the port and the gloomy narrow streets of Istanbul. In the kitchens of the First Court, the comings and goings of lanterns lighted the last of the day's work; then suddenly all became darkness.

Something or someone stirred in the Second Court, just beyond the Kizlar Aga's apartments. In the labyrinth of the harem, black eunuchs passed through the deserted alleyways, circling the darkened kiosks and closing the last shutters to the sounds of rustling trees agitated by the sea and seconded by the wind and the monotonous effusion of silver-white fountains. The imperial city slept in a state of suspended animation, interspersed with sudden spasms of defiance and fear.

Nocturnal thoughts rose from slaves, soldiers, prisoners, servants and Sultanas. They broke through the walls of the Seraglio and drifted off to the farthest niches of the earth, searching for loved ones, wild spaces, abandoned lovers and mothers, for the strange and terrible events of the past, as denuded of meaning as the deaf-mutes were of speech. The murmurs of a hundred different languages combined with sighs as the most disinherited lay beside the most fabulous riches, separated only by a thin wall. Great physical beauty lay beside deformity, vice, unhappiness and all the possible adulterations of the spirit and the body. The black eunuchs sat under the courtyard trees, their eyes fixed on the feeble gleams filtering through the kiosks' grilles, their souls corroded by bitterness and bewilderment, their fingers on the handles of their daggers.

Naksh-i-dil looked out of her tiny window toward the serene horizons of Asia. The graceful shadows of fountains and archways made patterns on the walls. The perfumes of the gardens filled the air which penetrated her whole body, as only the perfume of an Antilles night had been capable of doing. It penetrated the foot-thick steel-nailed doors, the chained and bolted locks, the iron-grilled windows, awakening all the voluptuous grief of her capture. For the first time, the Creole, who would never again be called anything except Naksh-i-dil, wept. For even in her ignorance, she knew this was the hour to measure, in shock and desperation, the infinite distance that separated her from the power that ruled her. That mysterious force that deprived this one of his liberty, that one of his power of speech, another of his human form, a fourth of his virility, and gave everything to a single man: the Sultan.

The wake-up bell tolled, as Kurrum had promised, at five in the morning. The Kiaya did not leave her Gozde's side the first days. Naksh-i-dil learned that the harem was a kingdom of its own: with a ruler, the Valide; a prime minister, the Black Eunuch; and a cabinet, the Kiaya and the treasurer. It was a true community of women, completely autonomous, with its own administrative discipline and responsibilities. Three hundred women had to be housed, clothed, fed, serviced. This peculiar institution was an integral part of the Ottoman Empire, its administrations, politics, religion. Total power were conferred on the woman who had borne the Sultan, the Valide. Kiaya Kurrum dreamed of the possibility of the Sultan honoring her with the title of Valide, for his mother was long dead and there was no reigning Valide. This joy had not yet arrived, but it could. . . . She was convinced it would. How many times had it been predicted by the astrologers? she told Naksh-i-dil. How many prayers had she addressed to Allah?

The routine of the harem was as strict as a convent.

"Kiaya Kadine! Where is the American lioness?" The high-pitched voice rang out like a clarion in the high-vaulted marble-lined torpor of the hammam. The sixteen-year-old Hadidge Sultane, eldest daughter of Mustafa III, Abdulhamid's predecessor, and sister of the hereditary Prince Selim, had tiptoed into the baths accompanied by her Lala and the infant Sultana, the Princess Esma, daughter of Abdulhamid and his Third Kadine, Sineprever. The four-year-old Esma clung to her aunt's hand and gazed silently and pensively at the strange new Gedicli. Esma was dressed as a miniature adult, her tiny hands and feet hennaed, her lips painted, her cheeks rouged. The already married Sultana Hadidge had spent all her life in the harem. She was like a daughter to the Kiaya. The Lady Controller turned and embraced the beautiful, willful and spoiled young girl.

"Where is the American lioness?" little Esma repeated.

"There, in front of you," replied the Kiaya Kadine.

"No! *That* creature?"

"What did you expect, a *real* lioness?"

"Well, from the gossip circulating, I didn't know *what* to expect!

She's beautiful," said Hadidge in French, eyeing Naksh-i-dil speculatively.

The two girls gazed into each other's eyes, those of Naksh-i-dil, pools of incredibly wide emerald, the other's, of the palest yellow jade. Hadidge had touched Naksh-i-dil's left breast and her hand remained there, nonchalantly, with a certain proprietariness. Naksh-i-dil blushed, but the female body held no mysteries for Princess Hadidge. She was married to a powerful and distant Pasha, although she remained in the harem. Hadidge Sultane continued to caress Naksh-i-dil's left breast, then pinched her nipple.

The Kiaya Kadine laughed.

"Little minx," whispered Kiaya Kadine to Hadidge. "She is not a plaything you know, or a doll . . ." But Esma, her huge liquid eyes filled with adoration, seemed to think otherwise.

"Nor is she a lion," said Hadidge imperiously in Osmanli.

They left the baths to inspect the opposite side of the court occupied by the Head Nurse. They passed the laundry where the Chief Laundress, an enormous Sudanese, bowed to Hadidge Sultane. In a procession of four, headed by the Kiaya, followed by Naksh-i-dil, Hadidge and the baby Sultana, Esma, they filed across a sunlit courtyard.

Naksh-i-dil's black dress was gone. She was now dressed in rose-colored trousers, white kid slippers and a gold-embroidered tunic worn over a chemise of fine linen. Her hair hung loose to her knees, and perched on her head at an angle was a small, round, pillbox-shaped hat, neat and close-fitting and embroidered with seed pearls.

The Head Nurse's finely tiled apartments led onto a balcony where the cradles of the Sultan's children were put out for airing. The balcony looked out into splendid gardens and the Bosphorus ahead, and the Marmara Sea to the right. Naksh-i-dil marveled at a beautiful golden cradle encrusted with precious stones and draped in white satin. The Kadine Benigar had just given birth to a Prince who would not survive his third birthday.

"And the story of America?" asked Hadidge Sultane in her broken Frank dialect.

"What story of America?" Naksh-i-dil asked.

"Why, the story of the Vac Vac tree! Is it true?" Hadidge asked.

"The what?"

"The Vac Vac tree!" repeated Hadidge.

"Vac Vac," repeated Esma Sultane and clapped her hands.

Naksh-i-dil looked at the miniature Princess with the imperious ways in total incomprehension. The Kiaya Kadine was staring at Naksh-i-dil with renewed interest. What luck! She had completely forgotten about the American Vac Vac tree. . . .

"In the islands of America," continued the Princess Hadidge, "where *you* come from, slave, there exists a tree called . . . the Vac Vac tree. I have seen *pictures* of it. The fruit that hangs from its branches is in the form of a lady . . . a woman, and when the fruit is ripe, it falls to the ground, opens its mouth and cries 'Vac vac.' The people of the islands of America love to gather this woman-fruit, but after only two days it turns to dust. During the festival of Douolma, we in Turkey plant a full-sized tree and hang painted ladies, cut out of cardboard, on it and inside each is a little machine that makes them fall off the tree and go 'Vac vac.' "

"It is the harem's favorite tree," inserted the Kiaya excitedly.

"Is it true that you have actually seen a Vac Vac tree and its 'women-fruit'?" asked the Princess. "Will you help us make a *true* one in the gardens at the next festival? We have never known an American who has actually seen one . . . who comes from the country of the Vac Vac tree!"

Esma clapped her hands together and put her arms about Naksh-i-dil's hips. The Kiaya smiled. What a story this was going to make . . .

Of the whole conversation, Naksh-i-dil had understood nothing. She had no idea what a Vac Vac tree was.

Together they returned to the courtyard and, crossing over to the other side, came to large double doors that opened onto a long flight of stone steps, broken at intervals by small landings that gave access to small rooms. This was the harem hospital. Neat white rows of canopied mattresses lay in a row on the floor. At the bottom of the stairs, Naksh-i-dil found herself in a charming courtyard full of trees surrounded by an arched colonnade supported on eight square columns each side. Naksh-i-dil had never seen a more peaceful, sequestered or romantic spot.

At this moment, a woman of medium height wearing a large turban came out of the baths. She smiled, showing perfect white teeth, when she saw Hadidge, but when she noticed Naksh-i-dil in her new clothes and her hair a mass of gold in the sunlight, her smile faded.

Suddenly the courtyard was invaded with women as a bell sounded the hour. Slaves, Odalisques, Ikbals all hurried to and fro in a confusion of scents, silks, laughter and languages. The new Gozde, Naksh-i-dil, tightened her grip on Hadidge's hand, and Hadidge squeezed back.

Hadidge led the Gozde through a warren of cells, tiny rooms, coffee rooms, bedrooms, kiosks, galleries, colonnades and staircases that finally led to the Valide Sultane's apartments, silent and majestic. They had been empty for fifteen years. Naksh-i-dil's eyes took in the beauty of the dark abandoned rooms, beautifully tiled with large floral designs, painted and gilded ceilings, hung with luxurious wall hangings and on whose floors five layers of silk carpets shimmered. In the corner lit by a window was a prayer rug, and upon a pearl-encrusted stand, an open copy of the Koran.

"From here, the harem, the Seraglio, and sometimes the whole Empire have been ruled by strong women," Hadidge said proudly. "Would you like to know what we eat here?" she asked.

Naksh-i-dil realized that the harem, let alone the palace itself, held thousands of people who had to be fed each day. She looked up curiously at Hadidge.

"Well," began Hadidge, "the Ashji-Bashi, or Chief Cook, has fifty cooks under him. There are ten kitchens . . . one of them only for the Valide, one only for the Sultan, one for the Kadines, one for the rest of the harem. The Chief Black Eunuch has his own kitchen, and there are five others, one for the Divan, one for the Sultan's pages, one for the other women, one for the slaves and one for the Sultanas. The Chasni Jir-Bashi, the Chief Taster and Chief of the Cupboards, brings the Sultan's dishes with his own hands, and he has at his command a hundred valets. The Mutbakh-Emini, the Steward of the Kitchen, has a secretary and earns twenty piastres a day. There are a hundred Ajem-Oghlans who transport the wood for the palace, and ten Sikkas who bring the water on horseback in leather sacks. There are twenty thousand people to feed on the days of the Divan, but on other days there are five thousand. From Egypt come dates, plums and prunes, honey comes from Walachia, Transylvania and Moldavia. Oil comes from Messenia. The salted butter, which we eat a lot of, comes from Moldavia, like the honey, and from Tana and Caffa by the Black Sea route. It comes in enormous—" Hadidge waved her hands in the air—"oxhides. It is stored in warehouses and when there is too much, it is sold in the city. We do not care for fresh butter, but prefer yogurt."

"Yogurt?"

"Yogurt is what an angel taught Abraham to make. Hagar and Ishmael would have perished in the wilderness but for a pot of it she took with her. It is made of boiled milk, soured over the barm of beer and allowed to ferment. Of this fermentation, two spoonfuls are poured into another quart of milk. This is repeated until the taste of the barm is lost and only the sour milk remains. . . ."

"Abraham?"

"Why our ancestor!"

"But Abraham is *our* ancestor."

The Kiaya Kadine, who had followed behind with Esma, held up her forefingers behind Naksh-i-dil's head and then crossed them vertically, making the sign of the cross, meaning "Christian."

Hadidge nodded before continuing. "Well, each year in the autumn, the Sultan orders pastromani for the royal kitchens and it must be from cows in calf because their flesh is more savory and salted. It is dried or made into sausages or hash, then preserved in barrels for the whole year. For the year we use 400 cows, 200 sheep, 100 lambs, 400 calves for the eunuchs, 30 pairs of geese, 100 pairs of guinea fowl, 600 pairs of chickens, 100 pairs of pigeons. . . . We use from seven to eight thousand kilos of bread (the flour comes from Bursa), thirty-six to forty thousand kilos of corn from Greece.

"You shouldn't be surprised at the large quantity. Apart from the ordinary service, all the married Sultanas, all the Pashas, all the grandees, and many more have their daily allowance of bread from the chilier, which is the store, or else from the Sultan's supply. The Sultanas receive twenty, the Pashas ten, the Mufti eight, or as determined by the will of the Grand Vizier . . ."

"Hadidge, that's enough for today," said the Kiaya.

"Oh, do let me tell her about the ice! The palace is supplied with ice from great ice pits where snow is stored. On procession days the 'snowmen' wear turbans made entirely of frozen snow, they come with wagonloads of snow the size of a cupola. This is for the sherbet for the harem . . ."

Hadidge Sultane rambled on in Arabic while Naksh-i-dil understood nothing.

The women she saw were richly dressed in silken cloaks down to the ground. They wore babucress, or closed-up boots, right to the ankle. In the baths they wore eight-inch-high wooden pattens like those worn in Venice. Everyone wore trousers and chemises, either of very fine linen or of muslin dyed red, yellow or blue. Unlike Hadidge, who was blond like her brother Selim, most of the women had black hair, or if it was fair, the hair was dyed red like the color used to dye the tails of the horses. The dye, she had learned, was called henna, and the women used it on their nails, sometimes their whole hands, and their feet. Some dyed the pubic region and four fingers' length above it. They removed all the hairs on their private parts, the Kiaya had said, because it was a sin. Their hair was decorated with ribbons and left loose to spread out over their shoulders. Covering the hair was a thin silk veil, like a priest's stole, with long fringes at the end. The veil was attached to a cape. The women wore small round caps, neat and close-fitting on their heads, which were embroidered with satin damask or silk. Only the Kiaya wore a huge turban. And, thought Naksh-i-dil, they wore more cosmetics than any French actress. Their eyebrows were painted with very thick black stuff, and she had noticed that some of them made their two brows look like one by painting the space between, which she found very unsightly. They painted their lips red. Many had big breasts and crooked feet, which, she would learn, came from sitting cross-legged. They wore a kusak over their shirts which was used to carry money and handkerchiefs, and draped knotted flowered sashes, as wide as towels, around their hips.

Hadidge Sultane, reverting to French, took Naksh-i-dil's hand. "This is the Golden Road that leads from the Valide's apartments to the men's part of the palace. It is called the Golden Road because it is where the Kadines go when they sleep with my uncle . . ."

The Golden Road was a long narrow corridor, tiled in yellow and blue of flawless glaze, which ran along the side of the Valide's courtyard between the apartments of the Kadines and Ikbals, past the harem mosque and up to the courtyard of the Kafes, or Cage.

"It leads to the Kafes," murmured Hadidge.

Naksh-i-dil looked in the direction Hadidge was pointing.

"That's where my brother Selim lives," Hadidge said. "He is the hereditary Prince, and so has to stay there until my uncle dies, and he becomes Sultan. Otherwise, he would be killed."

Naksh-i-dil gazed uncomprehendingly into the candid, golden eyes of the Sultana Hadidge. But the Princess contemplated the death of her brother with complete serenity.

• CHAPTER TWO •

GOZDE 1783

Palmire: How can I be yours? I am not even mine!
—VOLTAIRE, *Mahomet*, 1714

Naksh-i-dil opened her eyes one moment before the harem bell, a wooden machine fixed with iron hammers, rang the hour. It was five ante meridiem. The wooden bell announced sunrise and sunset, mealtime and prayertime, reverie and curfew, each day at the same hours. Topkapi was regulated with a precision that only the Black Eunuch, who held supreme but invisible power, could modify. It was now more than eighteen months since she had stood before Sultan Abdulhamid in the harem gardens, and it had been the last time she had seen him or the Kizlar Aga. Had she been abandoned forever in this godforsaken cell to die of boredom, isolated and solitary for the rest of her life? Naksh-i-dil's green eyes moved like those of a small trapped animal. She was fifteen years three months old, and she wanted to live!

She had survived her smallpox vaccination, which had left no trace on her skin, only terror in her heart at what the harem doctor had done to her. He had deliberately contaminated her with the pox! Only slaves, the lower classes and their families had themselves inoculated. The clergy and the nobles staunchly refused. Abdulhamid had refused to have any Prince or Princess submit to the process and thus, according to the Kiaya, had lost three of his children. Abdulhamid's nephew and heir to the throne, Prince Selim, bore the traces of the pox on his face and body. Naksh-i-dil was forever free of the dreaded disease that periodically ravaged Istanbul and the Empire. The process had been painless. She had been placed in the harem hospital and an incision made on her underarm. A specimen of pox had been applied to the open wound, and her arm bound tightly. In three days she had felt the first fever, which had raged for a week. The blisters had appeared. She had stayed in the hospital for three weeks attended by the Venetian doctor of Abdulhamid, Tabib Gobis, and a strange Florentine doctor, Lorenzo Noccioli, who was Prince Selim's physician.

In the months that passed, she had learned the language of the Bazam-dil-siz, the most important lesson of the harem. The language of the forty Bazam-dil-siz had become part of her life. It was the unofficial language of the court, for there was no one who could not and did not make use of it on occasion for the sake of secrecy and silence. The Bazam-dil-siz had invented a marvelously efficient sequence of hands and lips signs of pantomime hieroglyphics, often naturalistic, which sometimes rendered it obscene and because of its great velocity was always aggressive in aspect. For the Bazam-dil-siz were the killers of Topkapi; deaf-mute eunuchs who officially had the titles of Bostanji, palace gardeners, but who, upon orders of the Sultan, strangled with the strings of their bows.

The deaf-mutes announced themselves with a kind of monotonous hollow panting that resembled the sound of the sea breaking. They advanced toward their victim, holding before them their silk cords; the mark of prompt and infallible death, for there was no trial, no jury and no grace. Privileged executors of the Sultan's politics, vengeance or anger, they were the true aristocrats of the Seraglio.

Its simplicity made it even more sinister, thought Naksh-i-dil. Nightfall was the hour prescribed for execution, the silence of the demi-men who had no voices other than this distinct and deadly sound issuing from their windpipes as they seized their victim. Yet, with hand signs, body positions, yelping, barking noises, lip movements, gestures or a combination of any or all of these, they did, to her amazement, readily and easily understand the intentions and sentiments of each other. They even expressed abstract concepts, marveled Naksh-i-dil, as in a mutual dialogue. . . . This communication dated from beyond written history. Inherited from the Byzantines, who were the first to use deaf-mutes in the court, it had been, Hadidge had told her, transmitted from Oriental antiquity. Naksh-i-dil wondered if some worthier cause than murder could be had for such a language. . . .

The first sign she had learned was the one for "Christian": laying the forefinger of one hand upon the other. The second was that for "Moslem": a crescent formed with the thumb and forefinger of one hand. The first sentence she made signified that she was a Christian, not a Moslem. Ironically the answer she received was an open palm in a horizontal position turned upward in front of the body, signifying: "It is a matter of indifference to me whether you are Moslem or Christian."

Naksh-i-dil learned the court language easily, which was a strange and beautiful mixture of Turkish, Arabic and Persian. She learned some words of Greek and Armenian, a rudimentary Russian and a respectable Arabic. She discovered she had a special gift for languages. She even managed to recognize a few lines of the Koran, the only book allowed in the harem. She had improved her embroidery, and had learned to play the tchegour. She now hennaed her hands and feet, kohled her eyes, rouged her lips and plucked every trace of down from her body. She had been put on a diet and was slick and smooth with extra fat. She spent every day in the steam baths, and her skin was ravishingly beautiful from the constant steaming. She had become conscious of her body and her capabilities of voluptuosity. She had learned to whiten her skin with almond and jasmine paste, elongate her eyelashes with Chinese ink, tint her eyelids, powder her neck, circle her eyes, paint her mouth, and accent her dimples with rouge. She alternated the scents ordered from the imperial apothecary, and would perfume herself every day with musk, or rose, or sandalwood, or orange, or geranium. She had analyzed the beauty of the harem women: the whitest of faces, two black eyes, a tiny mouth and an expression of sweetness. It was necessary to have a pure-oval face; a small nose slightly arched; a round chin, preferably dimpled; a beautiful, strong, opulent and flexible neck; small hands; minuscule feet; a round, full-bodied figure that flirted with actual fatness; large breasts; a high waist; heavy hips, thighs and buttocks; and a seductive, undulating walk.

The Gozde learned the second most important lesson of the harem, bakshish, "the obligatory gift." The law of bribery was the law of the harem, of the Seraglio, of the Empire. Everything and everyone had a price in gold or silver or flesh. Anything and anyone could be bought . . . or sold. And was. The Empire was a society built upon that principle. Each act, every favor, every social or commercial exchange was accompanied by it. It was as much a part of life as breathing, eating, sleeping. . . . And everything emanated from the Sultan in what was called the "Circle of Equity." There can be no royal authority without the military, called Askeri. There can be no military without wealth.

Wealth is produced by the Re'aya, or subjects. The Sultan keeps the Re'aya through his justice. Justice requires harmony. The world is a garden, the walls are the State. The State's foundation is the shari'a, the holy law of Islam. There is no shari'a without royal authority: the Sultan, Allah's Shadow on Earth . . . and at the center of it all was the slave, for within the category of Askeri were the Ghulams: slaves and slavery.

The harem routine held no secrets for her now, only a chilling finality. The harem bathed itself in falsehood, and a dream of happiness. The harem never ceased to have recourse to the law, to order, to cleanliness, to questions of legitimacy. The women never ceased to use all sorts of amazing tactics against its power by applying reason, intuition, imagination. All this produced a most astonishing paradox: a life together, yet alone.

Naksh-i-dil murmured and turned on her narrow cot. For weeks she had been having the same dream, and night after night she would awaken to echoes of the screams of dying horses in her father's burning barn, set on fire by the same rampaging slaves who had killed him less than two years ago. The ringleader had been a man named Abraham, and she had stood on the veranda of their stone house surrounded by thirty thousand hectares of sugarcane and forest, while her father had fought to free himself and his frightened horse from Abraham's grip. He had seized the reins of her father's speckled bay, Plato, and struggled to unhorse her father and prevent him from warning the other planters. The marooners, fugitive slaves, had organized a raid on several plantations that night, and the struggle between the black man on foot and the white man astride had continued, it seemed to Naksh-i-dil, for hours, etched against the conflagration of the flaming outbuildings. The white man who was her father and the black man who was her slave, and the gray horse had become one writhing beast, turning upon itself to the music of the cries of the uncontrolled horse, the curses of her father and the maledictions of the slave.

"Abraham! Abraham!" her father had shouted, and his voice seemed to lift the red cinders spraying from falling timbers into the air. Her father had finally killed the renegade slave, crushing him under Plato's hooves. He had then ridden off into the night to warn the other planters and to form a vigilante party to track the runaways back to their camp. He had left her and her slave Angélique clinging to the oak post of the veranda, the smell of burning wood and horseflesh to become forever impregnated in their white cotton nightgowns. "Papa, Papa," she had shouted.

"The attic. The attic," he had shouted back. "Lock yourselves in and don't move until I come back for you."

But he had not come back for her. The next time she had seen him, he had been carried down a mountain in a litter, his left leg amputated and his life hemorrhaging away. The other planters had laid him in the plantation courtyard under an avocado tree. It had taken her father two weeks of agony to die, but the slave revolt had been put down, the ringleaders caught. From Three Islands to Salty River black bodies had hung from every tree. Her father had lived long enough to receive from the Governor himself the Cross of Merit of King Louis. That decoration hung on her rosary, the only possession left to her. It had been decided to place her in a convent, for she was an orphan; her birth in the wild, doctorless tropics of Antilles had caused her mother's death.

Naksh-i-dil sat up and lit a cigarette. She then called for her little servant, Issit, who would bring her first meal of the day. Issit, with her intense, delicate black face, and who never left her side from morning to night, was an echo of home.

It was Hadidge who was her lifeline to the real world outside the harem. It was Hadidge, more than the Kiaya, who had instructed her in the mores of the harem, for as Sultana, an Imperial Princess, she could go anywhere, see everything. Naksh-i-dil understood that this Princess with the mentality of a six-year-old, the experience of a forty-year-old, and the morality of a barrack guard was her key to survival in the harem. Hadidge had introduced her to another Sultana, Fatima Sultane, daughter of the Grand Vizier Halil Hamid Pasha. Fatima's father had already served as Grand Vizier under Mustafa III, Sultan Abdulha-mid's brother, and he shared Sultan Mustafa's desire to open to the West and reform the Empire from within. It was Hasan Gazi who opposed him. Fatima had been taught French and Latin. She had draw-ing lessons with foreign artists in the Danish Embassy, and lived as a Western young girl would live. Fatima was timid and gentle, singularly sensible and intelligent. The Sultanas, Hadidge and the little painted Esma, indulged by a fond Kiaya and all the harem women, on the other hand, submitted to no discipline whatsoever and ran wild in a world of women, dwarfs, slaves, eunuchs, guards and the Bazam-dil-siz. Hadidge was even allowed to visit her brother Selim in the Prince's Cage where he lived with his pages, his Kadines, his doctors.

"You mean he can never leave his apartments?" Naksh-i-dil asked her again.

"What for?" replied Hadidge. "He has his mignons, Kuchuk Huseyin, Ebubekir Ratib, Shakir. He has his wives . . ."

"His wives?"

"His Kadines, you know . . . the slaves he sleeps with. Except he isn't really very interested in sleeping with women . . . he prefers men."

"Hadidge!"

"His favorite page, Ishak, left the Seraglio and joined the navy and then had to leave Istanbul forever. . . . It is all very complicated. He even ignores the no-bet-geçesi—the night of love due to each of his Kadines!

"I visit Selim every day. We play gammon. He reads me the Koran . . . I tell him court gossip and stories. . . . Sometimes we play chess. I love him very much."

Hadidge Sultane had stood with her head cocked to one side looking at Naksh-i-dil with disdain: This Giaour understood nothing, but she liked her anyway. Perhaps Fatima could make her understand. . . . Hadidge had been dressed sumptuously in yellow silk trousers and a blue shirt tied at the waist with a black and gold brocaded sash. Perched at an angle on her head had been a yellow velvet toque encrusted with pearls and rubies with garlands of pearls descending in loops on one side to her shoulders. Her long hair had been coiffed in hundreds of tiny plaits that fell to her waist. Naksh-i-dil was smiling at the memory when Issit entered the room with her meal.

Naksh-i-dil leaned back on her pillows and sipped the coffee Issit had brought.

Naksh-i-dil learned that Sultan Abdulhamid had also been confined to the Kafes—for the duration of his brother Sultan Mustafa's reign . . . forty-four years. He had spent forty-four years in the Prince's prison only to emerge seven years ago, at the age of forty-nine, to rule. If, as was said, he acted like a blind man who has suddenly gained sight, so rejuvenated that he had produced up until now nineteen children, most of whom had died, who could blame him?

Naksh-i-dil had learned that from the spacious Gate of Bab-i-Humayun, the imperial city was divided and subdivided into smaller and smaller spaces until it reached the ultimate space—the door of the harem, the cell of a Kadine, the room of a Gozde like herself. And over

the Door of Felicity were inscribed the words in stone: LÂ ILÂHA ILLA
LLÂH, MUHAMMAD RASUL ALLAHI.

No one had ever breached the sacredness of the harem door in the
hundreds of years of its existence. Rebellious Janissaries still stopped
short of crossing the threshold. Servants who had spent fifty years in the
harem still lost their way. But inside, thought Naksh-i-dil, the place was
neither imposing, commodious, nor magnificent. All the pavilions were
wooden, painted with gold leaf and open to the sky, their windows
giving onto beautiful sites, brilliant seas. The inner courts were formed
by light and shadow, fountains, wells, springs, horizons framed in the
delicate filigree of grilled windows and arched doorways. Hundred-
year-old trees, dark cypresses and paler plane trees, gave an illusion of
space; terraces were planted with gardens; and surrounding all, the sea,
infinite, variable at every moment of the day and night, changing with
the tide, with the hour, with the light—the only element truly free.

"There is no God but God, and Mohammed is the Apostle of God."

At the Gate of Bab-i-Humayun, the outside world, the citizens of
Istanbul gathered every morning to see if a head of one of the notables
had fallen during the night and was nailed to either side of the door in a
niche specially made for that purpose. Then they rushed to see if there
was some other notable's head, and the accusations against him, in the
silver basin of the First Court. Piled pell-mell at the gate's entrance
would be the bodies of those condemned to the bowstring (not having
had the honor of beheading and exposure), the flesh trampled underfoot
by horses and pedestrians. From this gate, one passed the First and
Second courts, from which the silence of the palace deepened until it
reached the tomblike silence of the harem . . . the heart of the Sultan,
the place through which the arteries of the Empire passed. Through the
silly hearts, thought Naksh-i-dil, of a thousand women—for there were
a thousand women in this place. And of these, only a handful escaped
real slavery; and of that handful, only seven became Kadines; and of
those seven, only one became Valide. Sixteen courts, two hundred Odalisques, Ikbals, Gozdes, Kadines and their courts; six hundred black
eunuchs to guard them, eight hundred guards, forty deaf-mutes, dwarfs,
musicians, the blind, the dumb, the female masters of music, painting,
embroidery—all terrified of poison, sickness, disfavor, boredom, madness, the terrible breath of the Sultan. And even more, the terrible
futility of every gesture, every function, every thought—for nothing
counted here except the master . . . except the dreaded and hoped-for
sign from HIM.

"Mistress is ready for her bath?" asked Issit.

"Your Mistress is going to the baths with me," came a lovely voice from the doorway.

Naksh-i-dil looked up in surprise and real pleasure. It was not Hadidge, but her beloved Fatima.

The baths were the harem's theater. Kadines, Ikbals, Odalisques and Gedicli went, as did Fatima and Naksh-i-dil, in groups of two or three or in veritable troops of ten or fifteen, carrying cushions, rugs, toilet articles, sweets and sometimes their dinners. There in the innumerable cells and dimly lit great hall, long bars of light fell on a hundred women and their slaves, nude, or wearing silken gauze shirts. They carried perfumed towels, lotions and henna as if to a sacred place. "The most sacred element, according to our Prophet Mohammed, is water," Fatima said.

There were Odalisques as white as snow side by side with Gedicli as black as ebony; the Sultan's powerful Kadines and Ikbals who represented the panorama of ideal Turkish beauty. They had heavy hips and thighs, small waists and torsos, high bosoms, minuscule feet and hands, endless black silken hair in thousands of tiny plaits, invisible mouths and overwhelming black eyes. Others, younger, were more lithe, long, and with hair so short they resembled young boys. There were Circassians with hair of gold falling to their knees; Armenians with a hundred black tresses spread out over breast and shoulders; Greeks with hair divided into a thousand separate, disordered coils that gave the effect of enormous wigs. One had an amulet around her neck, another a string of garlic around her head to combat an eye infection. Some had tattoos on the palms of their hands, their arms, their backs and buttocks. Naksh-i-dil and Fatima took in the gracious and bizarre groups without joining any. There were women smoking stretched out on Oriental carpets, others having their hair brushed by slaves. There were women embroidering, women singing, laughing, rinsing their bodies with enormous sponges. Some moaned under the hands of massaging slaves, others screamed under the cold showers, or perspired beneath woolen towels. Arranged in circles or grouped in corners, they gossiped about their neighbors. And in unveiling their bodies, they unveiled their souls. Scattered phrases reached Naksh-i-dil's ears: "I am so beautiful," or "Do you realize you are more beautiful than I?" Another said, "I'm passable," or "I cannot deny that I am upset about this blemish." Someone would reproach a friend or another Gozde with "But look at Farahshah, how fat she's gotten eating all those dolmas . . ." "Rice balls are better," another would reply complacently. And when there was a Kadine or an Ikbal present, she would be surrounded and asked a thousand questions or offered courtesies, for she represented power.

Souls shriveled in the endless steam and running fountains without any of the restraints that education could give. They dissolved into excessive and brutal passion and never evolved into anything but an instinctive desire for youth and beauty. All these provocative curves hid the infantile characters, the most shameless caprices, pursued with fury which had to be satisfied at any price.

She had noticed, especially in the baths, that here the women, inferior by birth and education and far from men who would by nature restrain them, fell into the habit of using the most crude and incredible language. They knew no nuance of expression. They spoke in a language as nude as their bodies. They loved obscenity, dirty words, filthy jokes, which now made her blush in comprehension. From those lovely, languorous and perfectly formed mouths came the most obscene, impertinent and gross language imaginable, mordant and insolent. All the frustrations and helplessness found expression in the language of the gutter; curses, insults, inexpressible lewdness were propounded in Greek, Russian, Persian, Arabic, Turkish, Polish, Lithuanian, Bosnian, Rumanian, Albanian, Egyptian and Hebrew. The walls of the harem were covered with crude graffiti.

And the tyranny the inmates had endured was transferred to their peers or their inferiors. It was a tyranny more capricious than that of the most ruthless despot since it was administered by the powerless. Fatima had seen riots break out in the baths, mêlées of incredible violence and beauty, as raw and nude flesh massed into one sensuous animal of twenty arms, legs, breasts, heads, shoulders, hips, knees. She watched now the curve of an arm draped almost in an attitude of flight; a flexed knee, open thighs, bent backs, heads thrown back in attitudes that could be ecstasy or the last throes of death; hands pressed on every part of the body absently. As if in desire to touch oneself or stem an open wound. The heavy mist and the slow movements seemed more a vision than reality. Heads, arms, shoulders appeared and disappeared in waves of steam that supplemented one another. Barely discernible features would suddenly become as sharp as a painted porcelain tile, a disembodied hand would reach out, a voice from nowhere would suddenly ring out in laughter, the heavy swish of water on tile and marble, the tap of wooden pattens, sighs and whispers unneedful of a national language to be understood rose on the hot air. Long tresses of wet hair gleamed on white shoulders. Rosy nipples and white turbans shot with gold thread, the splash of cold water on warm skin, dark hands handling the heavy hair of an Odalisque, raised arms arranging a chignon of red-blond tresses, the flash of a ruby earring in a pierced ear, the slap of flesh against flesh . . . all this was the baths where Fatima and Naksh-i-dil were washed, shaved, steamed, perfumed and purified every single afternoon. Fatima and Naksh-i-dil sat side by side in silence. Fatima glanced at the Gozde, but she seemed lost in thoughts of her own. The baths were not only a stretching out of endless time, Fatima knew, but a savoring of forgetfulness, a detachment comparable to that of a narcotic. Naksh-i-dil's eyes had glazed over, but she was not, as Fatima imagined, in a state of detachment or forgetfulness. Naksh-i-dil was remembering her first true lesson of slavery. . . .

The Kiaya had led her into a small cabinet in the baths, and Naksh-i-dil had trembled instinctively, as if she realized some ritual was about to take place. She had made no protest as her transparent shirt was lifted by the Kiaya and pulled over her head, leaving her totally nude. The Kiaya had then sat down heavily on the stone bench lining the tiny cubicle.

Wordlessly the Kiaya had reached over and pulled her over her knees so that her torso rested on the Kiaya's outspread thighs. Naksh-i-dil's head was thrown back, her neck arched and exposed, her legs stretched open and bent with the heels flat on the warm tiled floor. She had cried out, but was too afraid to move. She had never felt so open, so exposed, so vulnerable. With all the expertise and tenderness at her disposal, the Kiaya began to explore her body with her hands, testing her reactions. She had realized that the Kiaya was required to gauge to the narrowest guess the erotic and sensual possibilities of her new charge. She had gone about her job coldly but not sadistically. It was part of her responsibilities. Her huge hands had caressed her innocent flesh, pressing and pulling the nipples which had become erect at the first touch of the Kiaya's hands, testing for firmness, texture, the rising of the blood to the surface skin, the odor, the beauty and color of its complexion, its softness. The Gozde's navel was perfectly placed, said the Kiaya, her neck was an opulent, round column with the required three rings of beauty.

Suddenly Naksh-i-dil had begun involuntary movements in response to the insistent hands of the Kiaya. A moan had escaped her lips. The Kiaya's hand had ridden down the lifted rib cage, waist and flanks of the childish body laid across her knees. Naksh-i-dil had opened her legs wider, and the Kiaya's fingers had entered the soft tiny slit between her legs; she had opened the lips and inspected her *kouss*. "It is royal," the Kiaya had said, "a fit throne for a Sultan." The Kiaya's hand softly caressed the wide-spaced, hard, round breasts of her prisoner. With a soft downward thrust of her fingers, the Kiaya had moved her hand on her, careful not to bring about a full climax, until the Gozde had been bathed in perspiration and writhing with unknown and unrealized pleasure. Her back had arched as tightly as a bow. The Kiaya had bent over her flexed body and kissed her on the mouth. She had opened her lips and allowed the Kiaya's tongue to enter and explore at will. Violently she had clung to the Kiaya's mouth; her arms, which had been dangling, had come up around the Kiaya's neck. But Kurrum Kadine had pushed them back brusquely.

"You are to make no move, Naksh-i-dil. You are only to submit. You have no right to take the liberty to return my kisses . . ."

As if to underscore the breach in decorum, the Kiaya had lifted Naksh-i-dil's legs onto her own stomach with the crook of her arm and had thrust the fingers of her left hand rhythmically into her widened kouss, careful not to harm the precious hymen. Methodically the Kiaya had continued until Naksh-i-dil had swooned with pleasure, crying out as the other woman brought her to her first climax. The Kiaya had watched her open-eyed reaction coldly. Naksh-i-dil found herself in the throes of a muscular spasm which she had prolonged with sharp breaths and motions and cries she hadn't known she possessed, but which had pleased the Kiaya. In the months that followed, she had learned all the techniques of lovemaking in the Kiaya's repertoire, but her own sensuality frightened her. For it was not artifice or acting. The Kiaya had been satisfied. Naksh-i-dil had wept from the prolonged pleasure the Kiaya had given her, which had also pleased the other woman.

Kurrum Kadine had allowed her to touch with her small hands the pendulous amplitude of her breasts and place her hands between her thighs. Next time, she would show her how to bring pleasure to another woman, she had said. For the moment, the Kiaya had taught her to bring pleasure to herself. She was to try it alone in her rooms . . . every night.

"You are to allow no one to touch you as I have, Naksh-i-dil. Do you understand? If you do, *everyone* will know it. *I* will know it and you will be spoiled forever for the Sultan. He will never touch you. . . . You believe me?"

"Yes," she had whispered, still lying supine on the outstretched knees of her mentor.

The Kiaya had slipped her hands under Naksh-i-dil's hips and cupped her buttocks, opening and closing them in rhythm to Naksh-i-dil's moans. The Kiaya had continued to do so, faster and faster until, without touching her, she forced Naksh-i-dil to experience those strange spasms again and again as the Kiaya bore down on a new place. "A good sign . . . perfect for the two doors of love," the Kadine had said.

"Now, Naksh-i-dil, touch yourself like this. Yes. Now. See if you can make your own pleasure, but think of the Sultan . . . think only of him . . . not so fast . . . No. Harder . . . now softer . . . now downward . . ." The Kiaya had watched, noting how she did so, and what movements brought her pleasure. There were women who could satisfy themselves without touching themselves at all, Kurrum had told her, by merely closing their thighs. The Kiaya had said that the next time she would paint the nipples and the nether lips of Naksh-i-dil with hashish . . . it evoked a most enduring effect. Kurrum Kadine had then bent down toward Naksh-i-dil and with surprising strength had picked her up in her arms and laid her face up on the marble slab, her legs apart hanging over the edge, not touching the floor. Then she had taken Naksh-i-dil's small narrow foot in her hands and covered it with kisses. The Kiaya had moved upon the tiny inert foot with more and more pressure and force until the narrowest part was inside her. Then she had flung herself upon the outstretched Gozde, clasping the edge of the marble couch, forcing more and more of the flesh inside her with violent movements, her turbaned head flung back, her eyes closed. Finally she had shrieked with pleasure. It had been a strange animal sound, half bird, half beast. A sound that Naksh-i-dil had never heard before . . . it revolted her as nothing ever had . . .

Naksh-i-dil told Fatima of her humiliation at the hands of the Kiaya. "It is nothing," sighed Fatima, and she put her arms around Naksh-i-dil's neck and held her while her friend sobbed with shame and incomprehension.

"Desire," explained Fatima, "should not lead only to procreation. It is a reality of life. . . . The pleasure that accompanies its satisfaction is comparable to none other. It should make us dream of the sumptuousness promised us in paradise . . ." Fatima looked away. The Kiaya had only been doing her duty . . . testing Naksh-i-dil's reaction to a real phallus—that of the Sultan.

Naksh-i-dil and Fatima left the baths. They returned through the odors of perfumes, the murmur of water, the shadow of slaves; and the mountains of Asia, remote, cold, silent, pierced through the black steel of the grilled windows with a rustling branch of honeysuckle, evoking an inexpressible melancholy: fragile impressions that expressed themselves in time, trailing, inconclusive gestures, unfinished sentences, unstructured thoughts, and a kind of blindness of the mind.

Tears were not tolerated in the harem.

"And you are never afraid for your father?" Naksh-i-dil asked Fatima one day.

"My father?" Fatima smiled. "Why? He is respected and respectful and has greatly aided his Empire and his government. He knows we *must* face the West. We cannot hide forever in Asia. We *must* modernize the army, rebuild the navy, which under Barbarossa was the greatest in the world. We need military advisers from the West, a new way of fighting war. . . ."

The sharp-eyed Fatima noticed the wistfulness in Naksh-i-dil's voice. She said: "From this place, you can know nothing of the weakness of this enormous Empire ruled by a Sultan who is a prisoner of his own desires and his own ignorance." Fatima stopped short. This was not the kind of thing to discuss with a Gozde, even an intelligent Western Gozde who would one day, Fatima thought shrewdly, be Kadine. It was almost as if it were written. There were hundreds of women in the Sultan's convent, but only a few were chosen. Chosen by chance, circumstance and history out of the thousands of women who passed, like an army of phantoms, unknown and anonymously, through the harem. But, thought Fatima, this one was different. She didn't know why.

Naksh-i-dil turned as if someone were following her. She had had a strange dream this night and now she must have it interpreted. She had a premonition that the long, uneventful hours were inexorably coming to an end. When she and Fatima entered her rooms, the Kiaya Kadine was waiting for her.

"The Sultan has sent me for you," said Kiaya Kadine triumphantly.

"He has sent the handkerchief with a message inside: 'Where is my tamed lioness?' "

Kurrum Kadine was beside herself. Fatima Sultane looked away.

"Fatima! Don't leave me!" cried Naksh-i-dil. But Fatima was more horrified than Naksh-i-dil . . .

The Kizlar Aga, whom she hadn't seen for a year, burst into the room without knocking and started pacing up and down. One by one the heads of the different departments entered Naksh-i-dil's small cell. The Keeper of the Baths took her off to supervise her toilette, despite her protestations that she was quite capable now of doing it herself. When she had finished being bathed, massaged, shampooed, perfumed, having her hair dressed, her body shaved, her nails dyed, her teeth polished, her gums rouged, her breath sweetened, her eyes darkened, and her eyelashes elongated, she proceeded to the Keeper of the Lingerie. In a swirl of silk and gauze, exquisite lace and embroidery, she was literally taken over by the Wardrobe Mistress who had already decided on her costume: azure green for the color of her eyes, gold silk for the color of her hair and camellia rose for the color of her skin. Costumes were draped and tied and untied, adjusted then discarded; dark blue velvet vests brocaded in silver, silver slippers, an azure turban draped in emerald chains. Now the Keeper of the Jewels began to drape her from head to toe with the most gorgeous of the harem jewels. She devised a way to attach tiny diamonds to Naksh-i-dil's tresses. She placed a diamond necklace in such a way that it covered her shoulders and reached down below her bustline. At last, everyone was in agreement. She was ready for her royal lover.

Her chance had come. To do what? wondered Naksh-i-dil. Avenge her father was the only thing she really wanted to do in life: to kill the man who had killed him. To kill the man who had enslaved her.

It seemed incredible to Naksh-i-dil, surveying the frantic agitation surrounding her. She had always dreamed that her visit to Abdulhamid's apartments would be private and secret.

It was time to go. Two silent black eunuchs came to fetch her. Accompanied by the Kizlar Aga himself, Naksh-i-dil was escorted along the Golden Road leading from the harem to the Sultan's apartments. Complete silence had fallen outside her cell, as if what was to follow were as unreal as a birdless sky.

Mary, Mother of God, pray for this sinner, murmured Naksh-i-dil. Her footsteps and those of the young eunuchs fell noiselessly as they moved along the silent corridor. At the door of the Sultan's apartments, the Kizlar Aga inspected her for the last time. With a nod of approval, he bowed low before her, kissed the sleeve of her gown and executed a temennah, lowering his right hand toward the ground, then raising it to his lips, then to his forehead. He opened the huge heavy oak doors with an enormous key taken from the ring at his waist. Once the doors were opened, he left her without another word.

The door opened into a huge penumbral chamber where two ten-feet-high torches burned, one at the door and the other at the foot of a dais. Two ancient black slave women sat in one corner. On the dais, raised a foot above the marble floor, sat Sultan Abdulhamid, the "Lord of the Two Seas and Two Continents." He wore a simple white robe edged in ermine. The dagger at his waist was studded with opals, and the plume of a white egret in his turban was held in place by a cluster of diamonds and rubies. The room was heavy with perfume, incense and amber-scented coffee. The Sultan was much taller and much more robust than she had imagined him. His eyes and beard glistened in the torchlight. The black slave women did not move, for they were meant to stay. From the corner of the room, she imagined that one of them, crouched there, spoke to her with a long-ago voice.

You will reign as a veiled queen . . . where slaves without number, thousands, will serve you.

Abdulhamid gazed at the Gozde. Her red hair reached to her knees. Her darkened eyebrows arched over the limpid green of her eyes like the cloudy line of an approaching storm. Her cheeks were perfect ovals. She had an elegant nose, a graceful mouth, a long throat and a strong neck. Yes, thought the Sultan, the Kizlar Aga had chosen well . . . His eyes traveled further. Her waist was perfect, her bosom and belly were well shaped and marked. She had small hands and minuscule feet of surpassing elegance, plump arms and lovely . . . lovely shoulders. The old man cleared his tightened throat.

Naksh-i-dil dropped to her knees, bowing her head so that her entire body was covered by her red-bronze hair that fell in wavelets, spreading out upon the floor. She began to make little moaning sounds, and real tears started in her eyes as she began, under the tent of her hair, to caress herself as she had been instructed by the Kiaya. She moved slowly, toward the couch and Abdulhamid, placing one thigh before the other, her knees scraping the cold pavement. The White Slave didn't know whether the pain was the result of the tremors of excitement that shook her or the tremors of excitement were the result of her pain.

⋅ CHAPTER THREE ⋅

IKBAL 1784

Decrepit husband, despotic husband,
Slit my throat, burn my flesh
I have the heart of a lion and I
fear neither dagger nor fire.
—ALEXANDER PUSHKIN, Zem
Fira in *The Bohemians,* 1827

The first thing Naksh-i-dil saw was a pale-blue pelisse lying on the floor by the bed. In a heap next to it were the Sultan's clothes of the night before. The Gozde knew she had a right to all the money to be found in the pockets. On her pillow lay a knotted handkerchief. With trembling hands she opened it. Inside was a sapphire as large as a hen's egg, a deeper blue than the pelisse, and a handful of piastres. She looked around dazedly. The eternal black witches were still there. The torches still burned in the dawning light. The Kizlar Aga entered beaming, still without announcing himself, forcing the Gozde to scramble for the pelisse. His grin turned into a triumphant parade of white teeth when he saw the pelisse draped over the naked girl's shoulders. Naksh-i-dil was Ikbal!

Now, thought the Chief Black Eunuch, the real struggle for power begins: maternity. He eyed Naksh-i-dil curiously. If only last night . . . his thoughts began but then stopped. Naksh-i-dil's first night with Abdulhamid and each succeeding one would be fixed by his own hand with the date, the time, the duration and the position of the stars in the book he kept for that purpose. He gathered this information in the event the Sultan had procreated, and in the event the Sultan dispensed one of his rare prerogatives: to allow his slave her maternity.

Naksh-i-dil looked boldly into the face of the pleased Kizlar Aga. A small smile played around her mouth. But the Black Eunuch, knowing women too well, detected disgust mingled with pride and already a terrible loneliness.

Naksh-i-dil, like so many before her, could be forgotten in a night, he thought, two nights . . . The Kizlar Aga looked on as Naksh-i-dil picked up the Sultan's outer coat and put her hand into the slit under the arm. There was a purse heavy with piastres. In the other pocket she found an opal necklace. Her eyes sparkling like a greedy child's, Naksh-i-dil went through the trouser pockets of Allah's Shadow on Earth, making little exclamations of surprise and joy after each discovery.

The Kizlar Aga had only one thing on his mind: finding Mihrishah Sultane, the mother of Prince Selim and Hadidge Sultane. She had been the Kadine of Abdulhamid's brother Mustafa III and had given birth to the hereditary Prince in 1761 and Hadidge Sultane in 1763. She had been sent by Abdulhamid to the Eski Serai until her son succeeded him to the throne. At the Eski Serai the Kizlar Aga recounted the triumph of the little American Gozde, who could be useful to her.

"Did it hurt?"

"No."

"Did you crawl to the bed on your hands and knees as you were supposed to?"

Naksh-i-dil burst into laughter and put her arms around Hadidge Sultane. "Well," she began, "I started . . ." She choked on her own giggle. "I started to do what the Kiaya told me . . . I started crawling toward the divan . . . making sounds like a lioness, actually I sounded more like a cat than a lion . . ."

"And then?"

"And then—but don't tell a soul, Hadidge—the Sultan practically fell off his couch laughing . . ."

"What!"

" 'Well,' your uncle said, 'this is certainly a stupid and charming idea of my Kiaya's. Will you stop making those terrifying noises, child? This is a bedchamber. You are not a lioness, you are a slave about to be deflowered. Stop meowing, for heaven's sake. I am not so old that I need pantomime. I have deflowered more than a thousand women!

Comport yourself well, and I will make you an Ikbal . . .' He couldn't stop laughing, I tell you."

"And then he took you in his arms . . ." Hadidge added excitedly.

"No. He got up off his couch and picked me up with both hands, like a doll, and I kissed him right on the mouth without even asking, and he began to laugh again."

"And then?"

"And then," said Naksh-i-dil matter-of-factly, "he got on with it. I did everything Kiaya Kurrum told me to do. We giggled a lot and he kissed my feet."

Naksh-i-dil didn't tell Hadidge everything she had found out about Abdulhamid that night or the nights that followed in quick succession. She had found a lonely man, hungry for the illusion of the life that had passed him by. He had spent more than three quarters of his life in the Cage, surrounded only by eunuchs, Odalisques, slaves, astrologers and doctors. He was afraid of the Divan, afraid of dying, afraid to lead his armies into war with Russia, afraid of the Ulemas, afraid of the Janissaries, afraid as the lowest slave was afraid. Thus he had the mentality of a slave, and she had ruled slaves since she had been born, and she would rule this slave. He was, as much as she, a prisoner in his own palace; as much as she, a slave in his own Empire. She neither hated nor feared him.

When Abdulhamid had ascended the throne in 1774, the doctors of the Seraglio had composed for him a manuscript, *From Age to Youth.* The first part consisted of an ancient pornographic calendar composed of 8,760 dictates on how to benefit from life's pleasures each hour of the day and night. The second part was made up of precautions to take to preserve one's virility. The third part consisted of recipes for aphrodisiacs. In other words, three volumes to convince her Sultan that life flowed backward instead of forward. Three volumes he believed in more than he believed the Koran. For Abdulhamid, *Allah's Shadow on Earth,* was a desperate man . . .

"I will be Kadine," she whispered to Hadidge Sultane. Hadidge said nothing. The problem of her uncle was not to have Princes but to keep them alive.

The Kizlar Aga and Kiaya Kurrum led the Ikbal Naksh-i-dil to her apartments, which had been readied in twelve hours. In each room there was a low couch, which also served as a bed, against which were placed cushions. At one end of the divan extended a table in the form of a chest, which reached to shoulder height of a seated person. The divan had a soft down mattress covered with silk on which one sat, Ottoman style, legs cross-folded and tucked up under oneself in a lotus position. The mattress and the linen would be removed every morning and stored in the huge chest carved of black wood and ivory, more voluminous than the divan and waist-high, where the Ikbal could begin to accumulate the private property that would become her dowry. To Naksh-i-dil the chest seemed as large as a cathedral. She had her first key. . . . In winter, woolen shawls or fur blankets would be added. Naksh-i-dil possessed a large Venetian mirror on columns and a kavouklouk on which her hats were placed; these were scattered around the room, as were small tables made of mother-of-pearl holding candelabra, or precious boxes, or a water pipe, or small silver trays filled with sweets.

Naksh-i-dil stopped short, then took a step backward. At the end of the second room, on the floor, there was an embroidered silk prayer rug with one corner folded over. She lifted the cover. Under it were a Moslem rosary and the small veil that women used to cover their heads when praying. Facing the rug and in the same embroidery was a small thin cushion. The Kiaya and the Black Eunuch said nothing. Naksh-i-dil turned questioningly, her face burning with outrage. She was a Christian! There was nothing in life that would change that. Not all the verses in the Koran, not all the veils in Bursa, not all the prayer rugs in Kharpont, not all the gold in Tripoli.

"In winter, a copper brazier is added to heat your apartments," said the Kiaya absently. "The walls will be covered with tapestries or velvet hangings to guard against the humidity. If you like, you may choose the colors and design. . . . even the material. . . ."

Naksh-i-dil said nothing. The force of the prayer rug held her captive.

Mary, Mother of God, pray for this sinner. . . .

The sweet voices of the Muezzins of the palace broke the silence with the call to evening prayer like the voices of a dozen sirens.

"Mary, Mother of God . . ." she repeated even louder to drown out the sound.

The Captain Pasha, Grand Admiral Hasan Gazi, sat in the shadows of his salon at the Arsenal. His half-tamed lion, which went by the name of Agony, was curled up at his feet in a stupor of overeating. The heavy black head and the high yellow turban of his rank as Captain Pasha mingled with the shadows, making it impossible to see Hasan Gazi's features distinctly. But his features were strong, regular and crosshatched with scars. His piercing black eyes were direct, open and honest. He was a man with one wife and one master. The soft and surprisingly small hand of the Captain Pasha reached down and stroked the lion. He smiled. Only his valet and a few dozen of his servants knew that he, Gazi the Victorious, walked around with a lion that was in a constant stupor from overeating. Gazi doubted if the lion would have been able to digest a man even if he had caught one. But he bore the marks of two attempts by Agony to kill him. The lion had terrified every foreign Ambassador at the Porte, several miladies, a butcher; had killed or mutilated several of his slaves. Agony was like Catherine of Russia, thought Gazi, curled up in quietude, digesting the latest chunks she had bitten off the Ottoman Empire.

Hasan Gazi, the "Crocodile of the Sea of Battles," originally Persian, had been the most famous pirate of the Algerian fleet. Chosen by the Divan as Grand Admiral in hopes that he could terrify the diverse Regencies of the Ottoman fleet by the sheer power of his authority as the most ferocious and courageous Reis in the Mediterranean. The Ottoman fleet was the largest in the world. The problem was that it didn't exist. The Empire found it very convenient to command a fleet without spending a piastre, thanks to its piratical activity. But the result was anarchy, autonomy and indiscipline. Terror of the Mediterranean, disaster in great sea battles with another maritime power. That was the fleet. Chesme. Chesme haunted Hasan Gazi.

Gazi had defended the Empire as best he could for ten years. He had modernized the navy after the disaster at Chesme. He had built new shipyards on the Golden Horn, the Black Sea and the Aegean. He had established, once and for all, a career navy with barracks at the Arsenal itself, and he had turned Baron de Tott's mathematical school into a full-fledged naval school. The fleet had, at this moment, twenty-two new ships and fifteen new smaller frigates. But his men lacked quality, that he knew; conditions aboard the ships remained as archaic as ever. But it was not his navy which preoccupied him at the moment, it was Abdulhamid's loss of provincial authority to the notables. During the last war, they had used the government's revenues to build their own treasury, armies, administrations, making them virtually independent. Abdulhamid's sovereignty was a myth: in Anatolia, in Egypt, in Syria, in Arabia and in the Balkans. Crimeans were beginning to emigrate to Anatolia, a refugee movement from lost provinces which, if not stemmed, would mount into millions, creating major problems that the

Empire was ill equipped to handle. Iran was supplying arms to Iraq and supporting raids into the province of Anatolia.

But the hardest blow of all had been the Sultan's acceding to the annexation of the Crimea by Catherine at Ainali Kavak. Abdulhamid had given in to the Russian demands. Potemkin had advanced into the peninsula. The Sultan had been forced to accept the Russian annexation *in so many words.*

The Lord Admiral's visceral hatred of all infidels, but especially the Russians, made him gnash his teeth. Hadn't he exiled his own adored Ishak because of his philandering with a Russian? He knew that another war with Russia was inevitable. Catherine's greed for Ottoman territory was insatiable and the annexation of the Crimea had only whetted her appetite. And he was tired—so tired. He now had proof that Halil Hamid, the Grand Vizier, was involved in a plot to depose Abdulhamid and place his nephew, Prince Selim, on the throne. If only he could convince the Sultan to get rid of the Grand Vizier before it was too late. The warmongers, determined to regain the Crimea by force, were gaining in the Councils of the Divan. He sweated revenge with every pore in his body, and he had vowed on the head of his mother to regain the Crimea, but he also knew he was weak, that the British and the Austrians had offered only empty words, not concrete military aid.

Hasan Gazi put his yellow-turbaned head in his hands. He resembled Agony, who was fast asleep. He would have to put down the revolt in Egypt himself, but he feared leaving Istanbul to the weakness of the Sultan.

The harem reception room for the Sultan, the Hunkar Sofasi, was the highest, widest and most richly decorated in the harem. The canopied ceiling of silk covering the cedar-laminated cupola, the blue-, white- and red-tiled walls, each tile embellished with a bouquet of flowers, dazzled the eye of the new Ikbal, Naksh-i-dil, who was allowed into the vast hall for the first time. The gifts from foreign diplomats clashed with the rich brocades and satins of endless sofas, oceans of Persian, Caucasian, Syrian and Mameluk silk rugs slid underfoot while English clocks, French-lacquered Chinese chests of drawers, Venetian mirrors and Chinese vases mingled with the hundreds of Kadines, Odalisques, Ikbals, Gozdes and slaves. The beauty of Lyonnaise silk was undermined by the richness of Venetian brocade, which paled beside the gossamer Chinese silk muslin and the heavy Russian velvet. Bouquets of flowers were everywhere, as were flowering trees. Precious jewels, priceless pearls, ivory fans, ribbons, scarves and veils were lit by beautiful candelabra of immense size and were reflected a thousand times in the gilded mirrors and glazed tiles. A movement from the salon doors signaled everyone present to rise. The Sultan entered and took his place on the raised three-tiered platformed divan. From this elevated position, he surveyed his garden of delights, from his latest acquisition—a pale-eyed, dark-skinned Abyssinian—to his black, deaf-mute, hump-backed, castrated dwarf, the rarest of his collection. To his right, on a lower platform, sat Ayşe Sineprever, mother of his Prince Mustafa. Then, descending like steps, came the Kadines, Benigar, Neveser, Fatma Shebsefa and the Ikbals Hatice, Binnaz and Nusrefsun. Scattered about on cushions lounged the Gozdes. The Odalisques who served the harem population hurried to and fro. With the various courts, slaves, eunuchs and dwarfs, the total was over 1,500 persons. The massed beauty of silk and satin costumes enhanced with every imaginable jewel; the richness of the rugs, tapestries, cushions, the brilliance of the illuminations, the silent lines of black eunuchs seemed to hang like a stage drop framing the Padishah, the Sultan himself. Abdulhamid sat on the throne in black robes edged with sable, a dagger studded with diamonds at his waist, a white egret plume in his turban and his bejeweled water pipe at his side. The room was heavy with the mingled perfumes of the women, the incense of the braziers and the amber-scented coffee.

Nothing was more ambiguous than a visit from the Sultan, which brought to a head the eternal jealousies and never-ending bickering in the harem. There occurred a familiarity, an event, that weakened the strict hierarchy of the harem and posed opportunities for victories as well as defeats. This was the Seker Bayram, the Sugar Festival. During three days, visits were rendered, presents given, the rich dressed the poor, and parents dressed their children. Forty days hence would come the celebration of Abraham's sacrifice; but between the two holidays, the most glorious of all the harem entertainments would occur: the Tulip Festival.

The Coffee Mistress placed the Sultan's zarf to his right, and the Kalfas, charged with his tobacco, lit his pipe of amber and gold. The Chief Black Eunuch brought the box of the gilded opium pills. The Sultan began to distribute them among his favorites. The fumes from the incense and perfume and coffee seemed to Naksh-i-dil the smell of lavishness, ambition and success. The boredom of the harem, the fear, the lassitude and the desperation seemed to fall away from all the women. The rising heat of three hundred female bodies was palatable, like mouthfuls of loukoums. Even the narrow, thin mouth of the Sultan moved as if he were chewing, savoring and swallowing the vapors exuded by his women. He supped off the faces, bodies, objects, voices, music and laughter that broke the sternness and silence of the Seraglio for a night.

The spectacle was about to begin.

The orchestra was made up exclusively of the most talented female musicians of the harem. They took their places on the podium behind the Sultan and began their concert. Following this came an obscene shadow play, which was met with childish enthusiasm. For the occasion five white eunuch boys slid with naked feet into the rich multicolored marbled hall, followed by an orchestra of blind musicians—for no man who had eyes was ever allowed into the harem. Guitars, zithers and violins began to produce a music that was acidulous, promiscuous and nostalgic all at the same time. The dancers began to move slowly, almost imperceptibly, swaying rather than moving to the dense captivating music as weighted as the perfumes and incense that filled the hall. With the opium, the company began to see what did not exist: the most beautiful images in the world. The Sultan had found the only arm against the jealousy of the harem. Slowly the rhythm increased and with it larger gestures were added to the soft undulating belly movements that imposed themselves like a heartbeat upon the music. The thin muslin veils that covered the dancers outlined every gesture like a sharp stiletto, no matter how minute; each ripple of muscle was more seductive, tantalizing, stimulating and obscene than the last. The muslin lay upon leg, thigh, armpit like liquid light marrying itself to waist and chest as honey to bread. Naksh-i-dil felt her head as a wave of heat engulfed her. Unknowingly she was swaying with the music, as was the entire silent company. There was hardly a breath of life while contortion after contortion climaxed in a debauch of sinuous pelvic movements as if, out of nowhere, a new rare animal had been roused and had begun to speak.

Sugar.

Everything became tactile, even anger, jealousy. Enemy touched enemy. Sugar, in every conceivable shape and form, circulated: marmalade, syrups, sherbets, pastry, honeycomb, loukoums, baclavas. Suddenly the harem was Sugar. The red and white drugs, opium and sugar, melted into wheels within wheels. The music became more languid, plaintive and tormented. It spoke loudest to the Kizlar Aga who knew it was the only way to control the uncontrollable: three hundred females whose beauty had been eroticized and then locked behind doors for life. He ordered more. Sugar and opium floated from one island of females to another. The sweets produced an unbearable thirst that could be quenched only with chilled water, which circulated incessantly.

Sugar.

The taste in Naksh-i-dil's mouth was the familiar one of childhood, dense, heavy, full-mouthed sugarcane molasses, churning in a galaxy of degrees of dulcification and stickiness, dribbling from the corners of mouths, swept up furtively by pink tongues. Manners became the dulcet, gentle, the gestures of love. Sugar. Sugar. Sugar. The whole hall was drunk with sweetness. The very scent was sweetness. Sweetness seeped into skin and soul. It was usually at this point, having done his duty, that the Black Eunuch left what he could not judge. . . .

Naksh-i-dil glanced furtively at the Sultan. His face, half hidden by the black beard, was impassive, his eyes emblazoned and blind, like the gaze of the eunuchs. Like the gaze of the women. Naksh-i-dil pressed herself back into the cushions, only to find other hands and bodies pressing in upon her. The whole harem seemed to be pressing in upon her thighs, breasts, shoulders. . . . She dared not close her eyes and succumb to the delicious sensations the bodies were creating. Instead, she stared blindly ahead. Then she reached out, to intolerable, promiscuous sensations. The Sultan slept. The reception was over. The Ikbals and Kadines little by little came to themselves. The sun rose. Naksh-i-dil would never know who in that tumult of faces, scents and perfumed bodies had given her such illicit and dangerous pleasure the night of the Seker Bayram.

Now that Naksh-i-dil was Ikbal, she had her own retinue and was responsible for her own court. The Kizlar Aga, as one of his functions, had found her a cambist who invested her money, made loans, bought land, haggled over the price of perfumes she bought or the jewels she sold. Naksh-i-dil communicated with him through the Black Eunuch. The Kizlar Aga was an expert, his personal fortune was guarantee of his good advice. Moreover, he was paid a commission. It was in the interest of the Sultan. The richer the Sultan's women were, the less they cost him and the State.

Naksh-i-dil received a monthly pension from the treasury of the harem plus rations of coffee, sugar, eggs, fruit, jams, honey, wool wax, wood and coal. Her daily rations were two pounds of meat; three chickens; two pounds of butter; ten ice blocks in summer; a bowl each of curds, of cream, of yogurt; a pound each of honey, of fresh fruit; twenty eggs; four cocks; five pounds of vegetables and ten of rice. The food was much too much. It was redistributed from caste to caste. Her servants and slaves ate the leftovers from her meals. Everything, from the last morsel of bread to the lowliest of slaves, was administrated and redistributed. What was not eaten personally represented barter, friendship, loyalty, delicacy, sympathy and service, or silence. For food in the harem was power. And when the rhythm of this chain of power was broken, it was broken by the opposite of food: poison. Everyone in the harem, including the Sultan, ate alone, except slaves. Food was prepared in the harem kitchens, and the Ikbals, Kadines and Gozdes were served in their rooms by their personal servants. The Odalisques ate in the corner, the slaves ate on the floor, and everyone feared poison.

Naksh-i-dil's servant Nittia supervised the food and tasted everything she ate. Nittia also controlled incense and perfume as it was a favorite way to poison. White arsenic, the most reputed poison, was also the easiest to procure. It was Fatima who had warned her of the danger. The smell of garlic was characteristic of arsenic. Myriad systems were invented to smuggle arsenic into the harem, despite the vigilance of the Kizlar Aga. One's life could end in the Eski Serai if caught with white arsenic, henbane or nightshade. Arsenic joined the two other powers of the harem, and if sugar was Prince and opium King, arsenic was Emperor.

Arsenic could be introduced in incense, fruit and perfume. Fabrics could be dipped in arsenic which, when inhaled, would cause depression, lethargy, weakness, fever, loss of hair and, finally, death. Or it could be given in large doses, causing vomiting, paralysis and death. Ground glass in coffee was another popular means of dispatching a rival. It was the one method for which there was no antidote, and it was the most difficult to detect. It produced excruciating pain, internal bleeding and a long, agonizing death. As with the bowstring and the dagger, death by poison was as much a part of the harem as were silence, boredom and loneliness.

Vengeance, elimination, mutilation or punishment—all were good enough reasons to use poison—for the sane as well as the insane, since many of the women, Naksh-i-dil was convinced, had gone out of their minds. There were many accidents because there was a thin line between drugs, aphrodisiacs and poisons, and many potions used in the harem contained arsenic, belladonna and opium. The poisons were usually those that suffocated rather than paralyzed. They generally came from Africa: iron of calabar from Niger, the bark of the tali tree, the terrible arrow poison from Guinea.

Death had a hundred faces. A bewitching gold rattle could be impregnated with hemlock; a deadly spider or a hibernating wasp could, by secret mechanisms, be released into the mouth of an infant Prince or a new favorite. Rings, gloves, boxes, flowers, scarves, even jewels could contain or disseminate venom. Poison, the weapon of the weak, could change in a few moments the physiognomy of the palace and the politics of the Ottoman Empire.

The more Naksh-i-dil had come to know the inmates of the harem, the more they had come to resemble young girls of good families raised in the country. Like her, they were no longer children but not yet adults, and they committed the thousands of blunders and stupidities that a mother would frown on in exasperation. Yes, thought Naksh-i-dil, exasperation was exactly the word she wanted. It was comical to see a stunningly beautiful Odalisque, lounging serenely on a divan and goddesslike in the most sublime and seductive position, suddenly cross her hands behind her head, or pull her knees up to her chin, or absently scratch her crotch, itching in protest from countless depilations. The liberty of the harem gave a woman the license to do anything she wished with her body, commit any kind of outrage to decorum, because in the harem there was no decorum. Decorum suggested "society," a society of real relationships between men and women, and this did not exist, thought the Kadine. Only the ever-present enemy, boredom, existed. Everything was tried to relieve it. Each day was a continuous fight against that obstinate monster; waiting, waiting, waiting. Seated on cushions or rugs and surrounded by slaves, the inmates ornamented innumerable handkerchiefs, played various instruments endlessly, fingered their tespis, or Oriental rosaries, a thousand times, counted to the highest number possible, or recited the ninety-nine names of Allah. They gazed for hours out of grilled windows, cried, smoked opium pipes, ate pounds of sweets, chain-smoked the blond cigarettes made especially for the harem. When they tired of smoking, they ordered Syrian coffee or Egyptian oranges, made a sherbet last for a half hour, brushed their teeth and polished them with pumice, chewed a bit of mastic to take away the taste of smoke, tried a new hairstyle, counted their jewels, picked their noses, plucked hairs from their bodies, drank lemonade to take away the taste of the mastic they had just chewed to take away the taste of the cigarette they had just smoked to take away the aroma of the coffee they had just drunk.

Naksh-i-dil closed her eyes, listening in her head to the shrill nervous laughter that was everywhere. Women dressed and undressed and then dressed themselves again, sometimes in every stitch of clothing in their clothing chest. They stuck French mouches in the forms of stars or crescents in the middle of their foreheads, to the left of an elongated eye, at the corner of the mouth or high on the cheek. They combined dozens of mirrors and hand mirrors in every manner possible in order to get a better view of themselves. They inspected their underarms for telltale hairs, their vulvas for the same reason, their ears and their nostrils. They painted their nails, applied henna to their palms against perspiration; but the fiend boredom always caught up with them, and every day they lost the race against time. They ordered fifteen-year-old slaves to dance until they dropped, ordered another to repeat a fable for the fiftieth time or demanded a blind musician to play a song until his fingers ached. But boredom was ever present. They went down into the gardens, played on the swings, climbed the trees, returned to say their evening prayers, reclined on divans to play cards awaiting dinner; and then the infernal cycle of cigarettes, coffee, lemonades, sherbets and opium would begin again. Two female wrestlers would put on an exhibition which would finish with a kick and a humorless cascade of laughter, yet the monster boredom sat hunched in the corner, reflected in every mirror, every path, every face, every window. . . .

The women of the harem tired easily of any prolonged attitude. They lay down on their sofas, they turned continually, twisting and arranging the long trains of their gowns into a thousand draped effects. Naksh-i-dil watched Benigar, the Third Kadine, sit down, then take her feet in her hands, then put a cushion under her knees, then stretch out, then pull up her knees, then twist herself into the position of an enormous cat, then roll off the divan onto the stacked rugs beneath her feet, then from the rugs to the marble pavement, and finally fall asleep where she lay like a child. The women were all in the habit of assuming positions in which they could always take each other into their arms, like round things, soft and yielding. The most severe position was sitting up straight and cross-legged, a position acquired in childhood, and it left almost all of them slightly bow-legged. They smoked thus, they played cards or gammon, they conversed, they played their instruments and sang thus. There was a black Odalisque named Zeineb who had the most beautiful voice in the harem. It was said that another Odalisque had fallen in love with her voice without ever having laid eyes upon her, and would listen in a trance to her singing for hours. But, thought Naksh-i-dil, with what grace they were able to seat themselves. It took years to be able to let oneself fall to the ground in one gesture and remain seated without the aid of one's hands, to be immobile like statues for hours, and then rise again all in one motion and one gesture, suddenly, like a spring bow. She loved the grace of Turkish women, the art of putting in evidence their beautiful curves, languid gestures of sleeping beauties, their heads thrown back, their hair undone, arms hanging, the art that extorted gold and jewels from any man and deranged the blood and reason even of women. . . .

Sometimes, thought Naksh-i-dil, a real event would take place; an outing to the sweet waters of Asia, moving to the summer harem in spring, a troupe of French acrobats, a theater of Egyptian dancers. A jewel merchant would come with diamonds from Golconda, Ormuz sapphires, Tibetan rubies, necklaces of opal, emeralds in the shape of flowers and starfish, Ophir pearls, agates, garnets and lapis lazulis. A Bohemian from Serbia would stay for weeks telling everyone's fortune by the lines in the hand. Dr. Lorenzo, Selim's doctor, would come to predict if an Ikbal was to give birth to a son or daughter by taking her pulse. . . .

The Tulip Festival took place in April. Wooden frames with shelving on both sides to hold vases filled with tulips were erected in the main courtyards of the Selamlik, the men's section of the Seraglio, and the harem in the form of amphitheaters. Vase-shaped lanterns decorated in gold letters alternated with flower-filled chalices of the same shape. Hanging from the topmost shelves were water-filled glass balls of various colors, and canary cages. The reverberation of light from the colored water fascinated Nittia, Naksh-i-dil's nine-year-old slave, who couldn't keep her eyes off it.

The Sultan's kiosks displayed the lavish gifts sent by the Pashas, Sultanas, Governors and grandees of the court. The Chief Black Eunuch pointed out each gift and its origin to Abdulhamid. With such an opportunity to please, ambition and rivalry strove to create anything new to catch the attention of the Padishah. And whatever was lacking in originality and rarity was made up for by its richness and magnificence.

When all was ready, Halvette, total privacy, was proclaimed by Abdulhamid. All gates leading to the gardens were closed. Palace sentinels stood guard on the outside of the gates, while black eunuchs took their places on the inside. The entire harem population and those Sultanas living outside the palace had been invited, and the Kizlar Aga presided. First the grilled protected bridge doors were opened, then those of the corridor leading from the Seraglio to the harem, and finally those of the harem itself. The infant Princes and Princesses, followed by the Kadines and Ikbals and their courts, swarmed along the narrow street. Behind them came the Chief Kalfas and the Odalisques, and then all the rest flowed out in a cascade, spreading out over the walkways and arcades, climbing the trees, running, jumping, whooping and screaming like children. It was the first outing the Kizlar Aga had permitted since autumn, and with all the disturbed desperation of imprisoned bodies and spirits, the women filled the gardens with squeals of laughter, clouds of muslin, almost one thousand strong. Tables were set under the plane trees, and the Black Eunuch, as always, was amazed at the gaiety and the skill and art the occasions brought about: the little games invented, the graceful dances, the melodic voices, the elegant dresses, the coquetry, the ecstasies, and, he realized suddenly, what could even be called expressions of love. The Kiaya Kadine rushed back and forth, brandishing her silver baton to hurry or to slow down the slaves. The women were here and there: dancing, singing, playing instruments, eating sherbets or sweetmeats. All came to the Sultan's kiosk to pay their respects, each heart beating in fear or anticipation of a sign, a nod or a gesture from Abdulhamid himself. Many congratulated Naksh-i-dil, for the rumor was that after so many years the Sultan anxiously awaited a child by the new Ikbal. The Black Eunuch began the distribution of presents. Abdulhamid had given Naksh-i-dil a perfume bottle carved out of a single two-inch-high emerald. After the long winter enclosed within the harem, Naksh-i-dil wanted only solitude: to be away from the crowd of females. Not today. Not this chattering, stupid and hysterical mob. Not with the happiness she carried within her own body. She did not even crave the attention of the Sultan.

Suddenly she almost collided with the First Ikbal, the Armenian Nusrefsun. "Naksh-i-dil, come share my sherbet with me."

Naksh-i-dil smiled, and took the ice held out to her in a gilded cup. She sipped it politely, the delicious cold lemon sherbet sliding down her throat as easily as the hot sun embraced her face and loosened her hair. Naksh-i-dil looked curiously at Nusrefsun whose eyes never left hers. She wondered who had ordered Nusrefsun to make peace with her—the Kiaya, the Black Eunuch, the Sultan? Naksh-i-dil looked down at her own expanding contours. She was more than five months pregnant, and expected to give birth before Ramadan. A wave of fear assaulted her, but was resolutely put aside. She had nothing to fear. She had the love of Abdulhamid, and she had proof of that love. A Prince! She was barely eighteen. Nusrefsun was twenty-four.

Naksh-i-dil looked around. In a few hours, all would be silent again, as silent and as deserted as though some great catastrophe had wiped them all off the face of the earth. Each face so clear now in her mind, each body seen daily at the baths, each strand of hair, each eye, each living soul would suddenly disappear behind grilled windows as if the women had never laughed, or run down a rose-lined pathway, or caught a butterfly, or felt the breeze of the Marmara Sea across their faces. . . . The black eunuchs would make their last turn at sunset, sweeping the deserted gardens to see if by chance a girl had fallen asleep in a corner. And when they were satisfied that all the women were enclosed, they would shut the Door of Felicity, the huge iron keys grinding in the metal locks.

Naksh-i-dil turned almost at once from Nusrefsun and, leaving Nittia to enjoy the decorations, walked slowly toward the farthestmost reaches of the gardens. When she reached the thicket, her head felt heavy and she touched her temples tentatively, then her throat, before her hand dropped as if she could no longer control the muscles of her body. She pulled at the scarf around her neck and let it fall to the ground. Naksh-i-dil looked down, and the ground seemed to swell and rise like the sea before engulfing her. She found herself face up on the soft moss growing under a plane tree. She gave in to the seductive temptation to rest for a moment. Vaguely she heard the calls of "Halvette," "Halvette," but they seemed as far away as Martinique and had nothing to do with her. She lay with her arms and legs outstretched as though nailed to the soft cushion of moss, the fullness of her kusak encircling her while above her the swirling green leaves unfurled like the Sacred Standard of the Prophet. . . .

At the last cry of "Halvette," the gardeners and sentinels of the palace gardens retired. The black eunuchs took their places, spacing themselves at intervals along the walls and archways, shouting in their strange sexless voices the last warning of "Retreat." But Naksh-i-dil couldn't move. The tulip amphitheater, the colored waters, the chirp of the canaries evaporated into nothingness.

Naksh-i-dil woke with a start. The gardens were dark and the half-moon shone silver-gray in the horizonless darkness. Naksh-i-dil stumbled to her feet and began running toward the harem doors. She had missed the curfew! The punishment for such a breach of discipline was seclusion for months, privation, the displeasure of the Sultan, even disgrace! And where was Nittia? Why hadn't she awakened her? Had the black eunuchs searched for her, or had they completely forgotten her in the overcrowding of the festival? She was heavy and awkward, and her breath came in gasps; her trousers and shirt were damp with perspiration as her slippered feet flew over the pavement. She tripped on the heel of her pantouffles and fell. Now she was really frightened, and she discarded the backless slippers that prevented her from gaining speed. Her veil caught on a branch. The harem gardens which seemed so safe and serene in the daylight had taken on a sinister aspect. She saw no one; yet she knew that the gardens swarmed with guards, dwarfs and deaf-mutes at night. She looked up. The slim cypresses leaned over her like sentinels. She passed the abandoned well of Isma the Concubine. Then she heard it. The sound of the sea breaking. There was a movement, then steel hands grasped her from behind and began to drag her toward the abandoned well. The Bazam-dil-siz struggled with the terrified girl, using one hand to stifle her screams. Naksh-i-dil found herself being pushed backward over the edge of the bottomless dry well. With fiendish strength she struggled against the rancid, malevolent weight, a trickle of vomit escaping her compressed lips as she bent back against the well edge. Then, just as she felt the release of the man's body against hers, she gasped. A fine length of bowstring had tightened and sliced into her neck. She clawed at the invisible hands holding it, trying to insert her own hand between her slashed throat and the deadly wire. She slumped to her knees, her head crashing against the stone well. She was losing consciousness as with bleeding fingers she pulled at the bowstring. This time an unknown force slammed her head and body against the rim of the well. The man against her jerked silently and slid across her as if in an embrace, and fell soundlessly to the ground. Unable to scream, making the same hollow sound in her slashed windpipe as the Bazam-dil-siz, Naksh-i-dil raised her head.

A black man stood outlined in the moonlight. He was holding the dagger that had dispatched her assailant. He was one of Hadidge's eunuchs. He smiled at her in reassurance, his white teeth flashing in the darkness until they suddenly clamped shut in a death grimace, the dagger remaining in his hand, as he turned and slumped over the man he had just killed. Where he had stood was the Obadachi Fatima, Prince Selim's old nurse, one of the Kiayas who reigned in terror over the harem. In her hand glistened the poisoned stiletto that had dispatched the eunuch with one thrust in the back of the neck. Naksh-i-dil saw still another body place itself behind the grotesque form of Obadachi Fatima. It was the Kizlar Aga. A pain ripped through Naksh-i-dil's body.

When she awoke, she was in Hadidge Sultane's apartments and the Black Eunuch was leaning over her solicitously. She had lost her voice. "She is mute, but it will pass," said Dr. Lorenzo. "It is only fear. A few days of rest and she will recover the powers of speech."

But not her Prince, thought Naksh-i-dil, as the doctor avoided her pleading eyes. Her hand went to her womb, then to her neck, where an almost invisible red line crossed her white throat from ear to ear.

Naksh-i-dil's beloved Nittia was found in a niche of the gardens, strangled. The five deaths Naksh-i-dil's ascendancy had engendered would be only the beginning. Naksh-i-dil's unborn child was wrapped in linen, anointed and burned. The ashes were put in a silver box, placed on a silver tray and presented to Abdulhamid by the Kizlar Aga who announced the death to the Sultan. Of Abdulhamid's now eighteen children, only five remained alive and only one, Mustafa, was male. The Sultan wept for the death of his unborn son. Ikbal Nusrefsun's punishment was quick and pitiless. She was sewn alive into a linen sack and thrown into the abandoned well to which she had condemned Naksh-i-dil.

Naksh-i-dil decided on a course that was as familiar to her as her name.

"What you call Obeahs, Naksh-i-dil, we call Golias, and of course you can have one to protect you, if that will make you feel safer. . . . But I don't have to go all the way to Algiers to find one. Istanbul is full of Golias! The first of May is their feast day, you can have the best Golia money can buy. The best in the Empire." The Black Eunuch looked down at the prostrate, quivering Ikbal. Normally he never interfered with the affairs of the harem unless it was absolutely necessary. But murder in the harem, blatant triple murder in the harem, was an affair of State. He and he alone, thought the Kizlar Aga, was responsible for the Sultan's most prized possessions, the shawl of Fatima, the keys to Mecca, the harem. The attempted assassination of a pregnant Ikbal was the crime of lèse majesté. He should, mused Edris Aga, have Kiaya Kurrum tortured in public. This was the prescribed punishment which would also serve as a warning to the whole harem. Now he must wait for another pregnancy. Not so easy, thought the Kizlar Aga. But this insistence on a Golia astounded him. Where had she learned about the powers of the Golia? What did she know about their magic and how much did she believe? wondered the Black Eunuch. And as if she had heard his questions, Abdulhamid's Ikbal began to speak.

"Euphemia David was her name. She was the most famous Obeah on the island of Martinique. She was the one who predicted my destiny, my kismet." Naksh-i-dil looked up at the Black Eunuch and the worried Kiaya. "She held the secret of life, of medicine, of poisons, of remedies against the evil eye. She could read the future, the past and the present. She was feared by all, black and white. She could kill a grown white man as easily as if she were breaking a straw . . . with black magic. . . ."

The Black Eunuch looked surprised. "You are a Christian . . . you believe in magic?"

"I am not *that* Christian," replied Naksh-i-dil. "I grew up with the slaves I owned. I believe, just as every white person in the islands of America believes."

"Then, let it be so."

The Black Eunuch gazed at the Kiaya, who avoided his eyes. He too had avoided the question of how to deal with Kurrum Kadine. She was governess of the harem. If Naksh-i-dil had died, she would have been held responsible. Even now, the Kizlar Aga knew he should have her executed in the mortuary field or dragged to the Eski Serai. As a Kiaya, she could have the honor of being decapitated, but never had a female head been displayed on the doors of the palace. . . . The Black Eunuch guessed what was going on in Kurrum's head. Personally it made no sense to take out his frustration on the Kiaya, but protocol and discipline demanded it. What should he do? Send her to the Eski Serai or merely remove her as Kiaya? Have her executed or merely banished from Istanbul?

For Ikbal Nusrefsun's transgression, the Kiaya Kurrum had her left foot chopped off in public and was retired to the Eski Serai. Six months later, thanks to her fortune, she was married to an Aga from Persia who took her back with him to his province. The still-grieving Naksh-i-dil never saw her again.

The Festival of the Negress took place in Istanbul on the first of May. On that day almost every black woman in Istanbul would join her comrades and crowd into oxen-pulled, flower-draped carts which would take them to a field near the cemetery. The festival would provide the Golia the Black Eunuch needed for Naksh-i-dil without his going to the slave markets of Egypt or Algiers. Those women, who were believed to have communion with the spirits and the occult, were easily recogniz-able, for they enjoyed an immense prestige amongst Moslem and non-Moslem. The Kizlar Aga looked around nervously. He had bowed to the favorite Ikbal's wishes, but he wanted no part of Istanbul. Plague had broken out in the city and had spread as far as the Crimea. He wanted to get himself and his ward safely back to the Seraglio and the summer harem as quickly as possible. Even being here, thought the Black Eunuch, was playing with death. Who knew where the plague would strike next or which of these women were already contaminated?

A crowd had gathered around the field to watch the ceremonies. In the center of the prairie were great boiling pots of food. The day would pass in singing, eating, playing the tambourine, dancing, nervous cries and fits of possession.

Naksh-i-dil peeped out of the grilled slot of her ox-drawn closed carriage, which was placed slightly on a rise just beyond the area and offered the spectacle of the black women in red ferigees and white yachmachs that transformed the prairie into a field of wild color, black faces and white teeth. The cost of the festival was borne by all the slave women except the Golias—for it was really their celebration. Undulat-ing waves of songs, screams and laughter swept up to the very wheels of Naksh-i-dil's carriage.

"If it so pleases you, Naksh-i-dil, this is a Golia. I have found her free and willing to enter into your service."

The woman standing before the carriage was as tall as the Kizlar Aga, and as black. She was veiled, her head and hair covered by an enormous red turban, and only her extraordinary eyes were visible. They took in the equally veiled Ikbal, who held her gaze. The two veiled women's kohled, unblinking eyes engaged as the Kizlar Aga looked on. Neither Naksh-i-dil nor the Golia flinched while the long survey contin-ued. Between the two women passed a kind of idiom. The Kizlar Aga had not failed her: This was a real Golia. She would never bend to Naksh-i-dil's will, but she would defend her with her life if she so chose.

The Golia suddenly bowed her head and backed away, executing a temennah expertly. She then turned her back and started walking away from the carriage. The Black Eunuch turned to follow, but Naksh-i-dil stopped him. "She will return. She has decided to serve me." As Naksh-i-dil spoke, the Golia returned to the carriage carrying a sack slung over her shoulders and leading a goat and an ox—all she owned in the world. Without another word the woman attached the goat and the ox to the carriage, opened the door and got inside.

The Ikbal leaned out of the tiny opening of the carriage, her hands working expertly in the sign language of the palace deaf-mutes.

"No one is to know there is a Golia in the harem."

The Black Eunuch laughed inwardly. In three hours everyone in the harem would know there was a Golia who served Naksh-i-dil.

"Yes, Mistress," he answered by placing his left hand palm up and crossing it with his forefinger from top to bottom.

Naksh-i-dil dropped her pearl necklace into the Kizlar Aga's wide sash.

"You will be called Angélique," began Naksh-i-dil.

"My name is Hitabetullah," said the woman, "and upon my life, in one year, you will give birth to a Prince."

Naksh-i-dil told Hitabetullah about the prophecy.

· CHAPTER FOUR ·

THE PROPHECY 1784

The entire middle class of 18th century shipping
is more or less slave dealers.
—PROFESSOR GASTON-MARTIN, *Histoire de
l'Esclavage dans les Colonies Françaises*

It was midday on December 19, 1776. The stone fortress sat on a promontory looking out toward the sea; its steep seawalls enclosed on two sides gave it more the air of a pirate's nest than a nobleman's mansion. Luxury on the island of Martinique was rude, scarce and imported. The most imposing houses had foundations of stone to withstand hurricanes and the rest in local wood, with huge columned verandas surrounding them on all four sides. Through the open windows women in white could be glimpsed, seated in the drawing rooms, darkened against the heat and the light. They were discussing three-month-old gossip from Paris and six-month-old fashion. There was a haughty provincialism about them and most of them had received their letters of nobility less than fifty years before. The island belonged to these Grandes Blanches, who were for the most part the descendants of adventurers, penniless younger sons or men with something to hide. The plantation lay under a haze of smoke coming from the barbecues of fresh kid and pig that had been set up by the kitchen slaves for dinner. The smoke hung lazily over the tops of the palm and banana trees surrounding the villa and the savory odors of burning hickory and roasted meat mingled with the ever-present stench of the sugar factory, five hundred yards behind the big house. The barbecue pits, which had been dug during the night, were now troughs of rose-red embers, the meats turning slowly on spits above them, the juices trickling down and hissing onto the coals, each spit tended by two or three slaves who seemed more fascinated with the fiery embers than with watching and basting the meats. The long trestle picnic tables, which had been covered with the finest of the plantation's linen and decked with huge bouquets of wild flowers, stood in the shade, with armchairs from the salon, benches, hassocks and cane furniture scattered around them. Bouillabaisse had simmered in huge iron caldrons. A dozen slaves rushed back and forth from the kitchens. Behind the kitchens, another picnic was set up for the servants, valets and coachmen of the visiting families.

The men were involved in a long debate over whether it was more economical to work one's slaves to death in seven or eight years and buy fresh ones from the traders, or whether it was more prudent to work them less hard so that they survived longer. Negroes stood in each corner of the salons slowly waving huge fans of ostrich feathers on long bamboo sticks. Smaller fans of every description fluttered in the darkness: palmettes and ivory, mother of pearl, silk, peacock and ostrich, ebony and sandalwood. Stony-faced Packeys in livery passed sherbets and iced coffee on trays and the air was full of Creole laughter and excited talk. The ball would start at six and people started to wander toward the laden picnic tables.

The meal ended, lazy somnolence set in and people began to drift off to their méridional, the traditional island siesta. The men assembled in the billiard rooms. In the bedrooms on the floor above, the children, in an unending hum of high voices punctuated with squeals of laughter, assembled along with the young women of the ruling families of Martinique. On the beds, couches and hassocks, the girls were resting, their stays loosened, crinolines upturned.

Little by little the voices calmed. The slaves had pulled the shutters closed and except for the stirring of the hot air of the ostrich fans, this time held by young female slaves, the only sound was the regular breathing of the Grandes Blanches. Downstairs the men talked: "On this island there's an age when you get no value at all. . . . My Theodore, who's seventy-eight now . . . however, a nurse is worth one hundred pounds, a child from two on, two hundred to four hundred pounds. A ten-year-old, twelve hundred to fifteen hundred pounds and an African, three thousand pounds, a sugar refiner, a carpenter, a mason, four thousand pounds. . . ."

The excuse for the gathering was the christening of a newborn Grande Blanche. Everyone had gathered around the French slaver, Captain Marcel Dumas, who had just arrived from Nantes with 730 prime Negroes.

"Any Atlantic port from Dunkirk to Bayonne may rightly be called un port négrier," he explained. "But to Nantes and Nantes alone is reserved the title La Ville des Négriers, the City of Slavers. There has grown up in Nantes great commercial dynasties rooted in the 'institution' and bound together, in the French bourgeois fashion," he added, by arranged family marriages: the Montaudoins, the O'Schiells, the Wailshes, the Bouteilliers, the Grous, the de Geurs. The greatest slavers in Nantes are an Irishman and a Swiss! These Nantian merchant princes pool their resources to fit out slaving expeditions," explained the Captain, "whose ambition was to marry into one of these slaver families before it was too late.

"Such family patterns," the Captain continued, "exist in every French port to a more or lesser degree, and they exchange merchandise of scarlet cloth, mirrors and glass objects, copper and brass pots: Those objects which were formed by the love of that which glittered or made noise stimulate French home production. But though the Saintonge, the Nantes country, and the Basse-Normandie can supply the brandies, Berry can supply serge and druggets, Choletais canvas, Mazamet bolts of linen, and Rouen the fake Indian and Guinea cotton, dyed with indigo from the French Antilles, we French slavers still have to import mirrors, knives, arms and clay pipes from Flanders, Holland and Germany." (Captain Dumas had arrived with French silks, fine glassware and Sèvres porcelain for the Martinique planters.) "However rich you French merchants investing in the slave trade may become," the Captain continued, "you are still way behind the English."

The planters had listened attentively. Prosperity was ever at the mercy of poor crops, hurricanes, slave epidemics and revolts, and of enemy raids, invasions, malaria, typhus and cholera. Many planters went bankrupt, their health ruined by the climate or their own debauchery, and the cultivation of sugarcane, the sweet source of such riches, became as precarious as it was tough.

"The English city of Liverpool is in ascendancy at the moment, with five eighths of the English trade in slaves and three sevenths of the whole slave trade of all the European nations combined," said Captain Dumas.

"Liverpool, it is said, is cemented with Negroes' blood," a voice commented.

"But what an ugly city they have made with such a mixture," said another.

"On the contrary, Nantes is one of the most beautiful cities in the world."

The ball, like all things Creole, was extravagant to the extreme, as if the French fashions had been filtered and heated through the tropical sun, delicately changing what had been born under the white and gray of Paris into the lush colors of the Antilles. The sherbets were a bit sweeter, the gowns a fraction wider, the décolleté slightly higher, the materials of the costumes more vivid. There was less white and pale green and more rose red and yellow; less striped and solid color and more embroidered florals, gold and silver. There were more old-fashioned crinolines, more ribbons, more bows, more encrusted pearls, shot silver and gold, more organdy. It was not very often that the ladies got the chance to exhibit their imported finery, and even though it was months behind the latest Paris dictates, all was new to the isolated Creoles. The men still wore the old-fashioned wigs and wide-cut jodhpurs instead of the new skin-tight breeches. They had, of course, done away with powder and rouge in the tropics, since after ten minutes, they would have been running down their cheeks in tricolor rivers. The ladies protected themselves from the savage Martinique sun with mittens, bonnets, parasols and veils. The men wore wide Panama hats.

The ball started outdoors to the music of the slave orchestra, and with the coolness of nightfall, it moved indoors to burning torches and hundreds of candles, while outside the cedar torches burned on the lawn, giving off light like the breaking of day, and the servants, who waited and watched their masters and mistresses, threw long shadows across the illuminated lawn. Later, there would be fireworks over the lawn and a shadow play by a roving theatrical group of the island. Handkerchiefs fluttered and floated between the perspiring dancers, and the perfumes of Paris were overwhelmed by the heavier and stronger perfumes of millions of tropical blossoms. Barely cleared vegetation menaced over the edges of the well-kept lawn as if to break in upon the dancers at any moment with all the outraged fury of savage beasts held at bay. Once loose it would sweep across the whirling figures in an avalanche of twisting vines, ferns, equatorial orchids and liana. The brittle rustic music also had an undercurrent of something more robust, sensuous, than the music heard in the ballrooms of Paris. Wild tropical birds swooped over the miniature figures below, their cries mingling with the mandolin guitars and flutes held by the work-scarred hands of the slave musicians.

The Grandes Blanches of the colony were out in force. The men as usual outnumbered the women by more than three to one, just as the slaves on Martinique outnumbered the whites six to one, and a new class of bastards, the free mulattoes, sons and daughters of the whites of the colonies, were day by day becoming a greater and greater part of the population. They now equaled the white population and would soon surpass them. New arrivals, gossip and the latest fashions from the court made news, as did commissions, fiefs, commercial treaties, the slave trade and business transactions in Nantes. The old-fashioned brocades and watered silks swept and floated past the newer muslins and velvet chenilles. There were also more exotic fabrics from the Empires of China, Ceylon and Turkey, such as fringed shawls of cashmere and silk, gold-stamped taffeta, transparent gauze overlying deep, rich indigos and sulfur reds.

Once the large and noisy ball was under way after the siestas, in the late afternoon, the Ikbal told Hitabetullah, she and two other Grandes Blanches had slipped away, followed only by her slave Angélique, and had made their way along the beach to the hut of a famous Obeah, Euphemia David. Of the three of them, only one truly believed in black magic. The young girls had held with one hand their wide-brimmed straw hats, and with the other, the white crinoline skirt of the friend preceding her. The Ikbal smiled. Together they had made a six-legged prancing animal . . . one at the head holding in both hands a bouquet of favorite flowers, lilies, as if they had been the plumed headdress of a trotting pony. This was to be their offering to the witch.

Euphemia David, a mulatto daughter of an Irish adventurer called John David, was the property of the High and Mighty Madame Marie-Euphemia Désirée Tascher de la Pagerie Renaudin, the Ikbal recalled, and she lived on the Le Robert Plantation. There was no plantation in Martinique worth the name who didn't have an Obeah. And Euphemia David had been the Obeah at Le Robert for years. Africans, Creoles, mulattoes revered, consulted and feared her. Because of this, every precaution was taken to conceal her from discovery by white people. But the three Grandes Blanches had arrived when Euphemia David least expected it. It had been a holiday for the plantation and so there had been a meeting of slaves. The lookout had spied the girls coming up the hill on foot holding on to each other's ball dresses. They had been frightened, coming to see the Quimboiseur, the Magician, the Obeah, so feared in the colony that when a young slave merited a few lashes, he was threatened instead with Euphemia David. The three Grandes Blanches had found her in her hut surrounded by dark and silent people who murmured surprise when they had pulled back the woven palm curtain covering the entrance. There had been total silence. They had stared at the circle of black faces. They imagined a tempest rising out of the witch's head, or the hissing of a hundred serpents around her body, but prosaically she had said:

"Well, children, you won't see me exhaling strange vapors, or smoke and flames, or whirlpools of sulfur. No, beautiful Creoles, don't regret to have honored me with your presence."

The Obeah had faced east and made the sign of the cross. This was not the Christian cross, but the equal armed cross that stood for the four cardinal points. She had said, "Protect me from all evil approaching from the east," and she had raised her hands over her head. Then she had faced north, south and west, repeating the same, "Protect me from all evil coming from the north. Protect me from all evil coming from the west. Protect me from all evil coming from the south." Then she had drawn a circle clockwise from east to south to west to north following the direction of the sun. The circle was not only to keep at bay evil forces outside it, but to concentrate the forces of nature inside it. She had placed a small brazier inside the circle and lighted it. She began to burn her herbs. The fumes attracted the spirits and the spirits could make visible forms out of themselves in the smoke. She threw herbs onto the fire: coriander, hemlock, parsley, liquor of black poppy, fennel, sandalwood and henbane. She had thrown on the fire asafetida, civet, henbane, galbanum, musk, myrrh, mandrake, opium, scammony, sulfur, and the powdered brains of a black cat. She had peered through the fumes at the three white, white children before her and had begun to speak to the eldest girl who was twenty-one, Mademoiselle Du B**.

"You are blessed with a certain maturity and the talent for administration that your mother has, so necessary to the government of many houses. You will marry your cousin, a Grand Blanc from Guadeloupe, and give birth to only one child, a daughter. You will pass most of your life far across the ocean. Your role on this planet will be transient, but material fortune will always be yours."

Then, Euphemia's eyes had rolled back in her head. Her voice had been like Mont-Pelé thunder. She had begun to speak to another

Grande Blanche, the thirteen-year-old Joséphine Tascher de la Pagerie. The Ikbal recounted:

"You will be married to a fair man promised to another in your family. This young person will not live much longer. A Creole that you love you will never marry and one day you will even be called upon to save his life. Your stars promise you two marriages. The first of your husbands was born in Martinique, a noble, but lives in France. He is a military man. You will have some moments of happiness with him but infidelity on both sides will disunite you after which the Kingdom of France will know revolution and great troubles, and he will perish tragically, leaving you with two small children. Your second husband will be very dark, of European origin and without fortune or name. Nevertheless, he will become famous and will fill the world with his glory and conquer all the nations. You shall be famous and celebrated, more than a Queen, but one day, most of the ungrateful world will forget your good deeds and remember only your bad. You will regret the sweet and easy life you lead in our colony." She paused for a moment. *"You will return to this island, but you will leave it for France and when you do, a great comet will light up the sky, a sign of your stupendous destiny."*

Then the voice of Naksh-i-dil lowered as in a confessional. And Euphemia . . . began to speak to the third girl, Mademoiselle de S***, a ten-year-old orphan with red-gold hair and green eyes. Suddenly the Ikbal's voice became the remembered, frightening hoarse voice of the Martinique Obeah.

"Your new guardian will soon send you to Europe to complete your education. Your ship will be taken by Algerian pirates. You will be taken captive, and not long afterward you will be imprisoned in a convent for women not of your nation, or a prison. . . . There you will have a son. This son will reign with glory over an empire, but the steps of his throne will be bloody with regicide. As for you, you will never enjoy public honor or glory but will reign as a veiled Queen, unseen, occupying a vast palace where your every wish will be a command and where slaves without number, thousands, will serve you. At the very moment when you feel yourself the happiest of women, your happiness will vanish like a dream and a lingering illness will lead you to your tomb."

The three girls had recoiled. They hadn't known what to expect on this fine dry December day, but it had not been this. They had taken lightly the power of Obeah. Angélique had known better, thought Naksh-i-dil.

Euphemia David had risen to her full height, rising and rising until she seemed to be levitating and the people in the room had begun to move restlessly and groan so that all had known that the spirits were still there. Then, they, the Grandes Blanches, had fled, the day of the ball indelible forever in their minds.

They had left the Obeah in the darkness of her hut, with her spirits. Euphemia David had been unable to shake them off, unable to come to terms with them, so she had put on a seamless dress of black and gone to her chicken shed. She had taken a black hen that had never been crossed by a cock, and, seizing it by the throat, so that it made no noise and thus dissipate the energy now sealed within, she had taken it to the crossroads and waited until midnight. On the stroke, she had drawn a circle on the ground with the rod of a cypress and, concentrating all her magical powers, had torn the live bird in two with her bare hands.

Then she had turned to the east and commanded the devil to leave her. He left.

She lay on the ground as if dead, feeling the damp seep into her bones. The day's summer heat had still been enough to warm a tired body. This island was hers, she thought, as much as any Grand Blanc. It had belonged to the Carib Indians long before they had come with their sugar, long before Christopher Columbus set his foot on its soil. Her only desire was to drive the Grands Blancs from her land, from all the islands of America, from all the sugar they so craved, and the black flesh that made it all possible. What evil had brought sugarcane into the Antilles, sweeping masters and slaves into the same common grave, oppressor and oppressed into one bottomless pit?

Naksh-i-dil closed her eyes, remembering the Sugar Festival.

Sugar, sugar, sugar, sugar, sugar, sugar . . . Martinique was Sugar Island.

Sugar was overseers in nankeen trousers and cutaway jackets and huge cartwheel Panama hats, holding long snakeskin whips, driving lines of hoeing slaves. *Sugar* was cane shoots planted in flatlands, harvested with evil-looking machetes. *Sugar* was copper caldrons that a man could fall into, in the infernal heat of the boiling house. *Sugar* was the fecal stench of raw cane which invaded skin and clothes, and hung like a nauseous gas over the plantation. *Sugar* had come in 1640. *Sugar* was not an easy crop to rear. It demanded precision, exactitude, implacability, low plains, rich soil, tropical heat, great humidity and violent sun.

The essence of the planting was synchronization achieved by the whip. The holes had to be dug in a straight line and when one line was completed, the slaves had to fall back in formation to begin the next. Woe to those worn out or weak who dared to break the line. Holes had to be made all at once, together. And the slaves had to work or stop, together. Then the cane shoot was dropped into place and the whole thing started again.

Sugar. When the sugar crop was being harvested, the crushing mills and the boiling houses worked twenty-four hours a day. The sugar mills crushed the bundles of canes twice with heavy rollers. The trash was used as fuel while the precious juice ran off in lead-lined gutters. It continued on its way along another leaden gutter into the boiling room. Here it mixed with white lime, cooled and passed to the curing house. Work in the boiling house during crop time was hell. . . . The heat induced dropsy, the swelling of the arms and legs and open running sores. Drowsiness from long night shifts led to loss of fingers in the crusher, or life itself in the boiler coppers.

Sugar. The working day began just before sunrise, when the slaves were awakened by a bell tolling or the blast of a conch shell. Sometimes the watchman would confuse the blue-white radiance of the tropical moon with the rising sun.

A cluster of mountains in the north and another in the south, and a line between them, formed a kind of backbone; deep ravines, escarpments which culminated in the north, were reduced to quiet undulations by the drapery of tropical forests that shrouded them. In the hamlet of Trois Ilots where the witch lay waiting for the dawn on the chilly ground, Mademoiselle de S***, Mademoiselle Du B**, and Mademoiselle Tascher de la Pagerie lay sleeping . . .

> *Thee I invoke, the Bornless one*
> *Thee that didst create the Earth and the Heavens*
> *Thee that didst create the Night and the Day*
> *Thee that didst create the Darkness and the Light*
> *Thou art IA BESZ*
> *Thou art IA APOPHRASZ, ELOY, ELOHIM, ELOHE,*
> *ZABAHAT, ELION, ESARCHIE, AHONAY, JAH . . .*

• CHAPTER FIVE •

ISHAK BEY 1784

The S.S. *Séduisant*, a seventy-four-cannon frigate commanded by the Marquis of Sainneville, and destined to conduct the Count de Choiseul-Gouffier to Constantinople as the new French Ambassador to the court of Abdulhamid, prepared to set sail from the port of Marseilles on the fourth of August, 1784, accompanied by the frigate *La Poulette*. Ishak Bey was aboard. He was returning once again to Istanbul.

The coach that Ishak Bey had taken to Marseilles had been followed by a wagon loaded with crates and trunks. He wondered when and if he would ever see France again, but with an infallible nose for trouble, he knew that France would soon be bloodied, and regicide, the unthinkable, was a distinct possibility. He stood on the wharf and inspected the multitude of frigates, schooners, sloops, destined for or coming from all parts of the world, their masts a forest against the bright sky. There were American and Dutch slavers, mercantile ships from England and Spain, and Portuguese warships, six-, nine-, thirty-six- and forty-nine-cannon frigates of surpassing beauty. Ishak bade his last adieu to Europe.

Ishak Bey had had his doubts about returning to Istanbul, and the superb, newly built *Séduisant* had served only to remind him of Hasan Gazi. After St. Petersburg, he had returned incognito to Istanbul and carried back to Versailles secret letters from Selim to Louis XVI. His departure from France despite his pardon from Hasan Gazi and his letters of recommendation from the Minister of Foreign Affairs to Abdulhamid for services rendered did little to calm his apprehensions. The passengers, Choiseul's wife, the Ambassador's secretary, his military aide, the Abbé Martin, the chaplain, a doctor, an astronomer, two young illustrators (for Choiseul-Gouffier had a penchant for commissioning drawings and signing them as his own) had all boarded. This fascinating boat, Ishak Bey thought, was taking him home.

The *Séduisant* had passed the island of Malta, the strongest citadel in the world, he thought, famous for having resisted Ottoman conquest. Ishak Bey began to feel better. All the fastidiousness of the court of Catherine and the court of Louis XVI slipped off him the way a smooth sable pelisse could slip off one's shoulders to the ground. He felt Osman again, after such a long time and such a long exile. Seven years. Seven years in which Abdulhamid had steered the Empire from one disaster to another.

The first sign came during the night of the nineteenth between eleven o'clock and midnight. A warship that puzzled Captain Sainneville, but which Ishak Bey judged to be a frigate of his old mentor, the Grand Admiral of the Ottoman navy Captain Pasha Hasan Gazi, signaled and blocked the vessel, demanding to know who they were, where they were going and where they had come from. The ship's megaphone spoke in Italian, French, Spanish and English without revealing the nationality or identifying the ship. A bad sign, Ishak thought. The Captain began to fear it was a pirate ship and, not wanting to satisfy the insolent questions hurled at him by God only knew who, took his megaphone in hand and requested a visit aboard. He then ordered a cannon fired but out of range of the taunting ship. Although it threatened to fire all its batteries, the mysterious ship allowed the *Séduisant* to outdistance it, the megaphone hurling a thousand insults at the Captain and his crew. The Captain, still in the dark about what nation the lone ship could belong to, prudently held his fire. But a cold sweat crept down Ishak Bey's spine and with good reason. At the break of dawn, the crew and passengers of the *Séduisant* discovered themselves facing the Ottoman fleet, composed of fifteen or so sails following the same course as the *Séduisant*.

"Oh, my God," thought Ishak. "It can't be true!"

Hasan Gazi ordered the *Selimie* to pull alongside of the *Séduisant*. Then, with his megaphone in hand, the Captain Pasha demanded to speak with Ishak Bey. Hasan Gazi already knew who was on board the *Séduisant*, and why they were there, except for Ishak Bey. What, mused the Grand Admiral, was his prodigal son up to?

"Oh, my God," repeated Ishak out loud, and the disordered, vaga-

bond travels of the past years swam before his eyes like the jeweled fish
that followed the caïques de luxe that sailed the Bosphorus. Slowly he
changed into his Ottoman naval uniform, leaving his elegant French
clothes in a heap on his cabin floor. His knees were shaking as he
climbed the hemp rope ladder down to the small boat launched by the
Captain Pasha's ship. Ishak remembered the time Hasan Gazi had
shown up at the Divan with his damned beast, and the whole council of
ministers, terrified, had jumped out of the windows or had almost broken their necks scrambling down the stairs, leaving the Grand Admiral
and his semidomesticated lion tête-à-tête. . . . And now, he had to
face his own tête-à-tête with his former master. . . .

"Where the fuck have you been for seven years?" shouted Hasan
Gazi, drawing up to his not considerable height of five feet seven and a
half inches, his feet apart, one hand on his cutting sword, as Ishak Bey
approached him.

"Fishing," answered Ishak Bey. There was a moment of silence. And
then Hasan Gazi threw back his head and roared with laughter. Agony
yawned.

"You son of a bitch!"

"*You* son of a bitch. I still love you."

"Welcome home."

"Is that true?"

"You are pardoned by me, by the Grand Vizier Halil Hamid, by
Abdulhamid. You are, of course, free to set foot in Istanbul . . ."

Ishak Bey scrutinized the Captain Pasha. He was in good form,
dresses as always in an old-fashioned caftan. He was still the same
courageous, brave, natural sailor he had served, but Ishak Bey knew
also he was still the same cruel, bloody and unmerciful beheader he had
fled.

"Assure your ship and the Ambassador that there is no plague in
Istanbul nor on our ships."

Ishak Bey had seen Hasan Pasha cut off the hands of a fugitive slave.
He had seen him throw a Janissary live into flames because he had been
slow in putting out the fire. He had seen him gather and smash to pieces
the most beautiful Greek sculptures in the Dardanelles, had seen him
pile severed heads in pyramids in front of the gates of recaptured cities. . . .

"What happened last night? Who tried to hold us up and insulted us
in such a bad-mannered way?" asked Ishak Bey.

"The Venetians," lied Hasan Gazi.

"There haven't been any Venetian ships in these waters since they lost Crete."

"It must have been a *lost* Venetian ship," repeated the Grand Admiral. "Come Ishak. Let's play some chess. But before we start, let me make something quite clear." Hasan Gazi sat down, then looked up at Ishak Bey, the white of his eyes luminous in the penumbra of the ship's cabin.

"You work for me from now on. Is that clear?"

Ishak Bey's heart slammed against his chest.

"Is that clear, Ishak?" the Grand Admiral repeated, evenly and coolly.

"Quite . . . quite clear . . ." said the young man.

"And one more thing. Despite rumors to the contrary, especially"— he paused—"in the Western kingdoms, Abdulhamid is still absolute master of our Empire. He and he alone contracts your destiny and mine despite his weakness for the harem. . . . England, France, Austria still dream of carving up the Ottoman Empire. But it will be over my dead body . . . And Russia still wants her window to the south at the expense of the Ottomans. . . . And *that* will be over my dead body."

"Czarina Catherine has only one ambition," Ishak said to his Admiral. "To pursue the dream of Peter the Great, and extend her frontiers north to the Vistula River and south to the Mediterranean. This we both know. Her aggressions and annexations will always be used as her official motives in the name of humanity." Ishak continued. "Her excuse is always the defense of the oppressed and the Russian Orthodox Church. If this means holy war against Islam, so much the better. . . ."

"Either Islam or Orthodoxy will rule this part of the world," said Hasan Gazi. "Czarina Catherine with her half-yellow Empire has turned her back on the Orient . . . forgotten that Russia is *Oriental.*"

"The Czarina," said Ishak Bey, "intends to pull Russia by its coattails or its balls into white Christian Europe . . . out of the shadow of Islam and into first eminence in the world . . . world power."

"By the way, how is she in bed?" asked Hasan Gazi curiously. And Ishak Bey, surprised that Hasan Gazi was so well informed, answered him frankly.

"She is sensual," replied Ishak, "and avid, nay, *starved* for love. Her position as Empress prohibits such a love; the love of a man, a normal love in equality, just as it is refused Abdulhamid. Thus she attaches herself to younger and younger favorites"—he paused—"Zorich, *you* remember him . . . was the last *man* favorite—now they are boys. . . . She attaches herself to these . . . boys like a female child attaches herself to her dolls. The Czarina is like our Sultanas who have been placed by law outside the *laws* of their sex. *Whore,* for those elected, is a title of glory. . . . The reigns of four Czarinas of dubious virtue have accustomed the court at St. Petersburg to the caprices of favorites, just as our Empire endures the caprices of our Sultanas. The Czarina is ugly," he continued. "It is said that in her youth she had what is called the devil's beauty: lively, fresh, alert, excellent horsewoman, unique, charming, in fact, highly capable of pleasing. For even Zorich, she was first of all an Empress."

"And this Potemkin?" asked Hasan Gazi, fascinated with this gossip about his formidable and bitter enemy. *"That's* a favorite. The Czarina did well to have married him."

"The Empress *obeys* him like a wife. They have mutually given proofs of innumerable reciprocal infidelities. . . . Yet I am sure these two people love each other," said Ishak Bey. The Czarina's submission to Potemkin, his total devotion to her, his jealousies, her humors, his desire to arrange Catherine's private life . . . all point to marriage," he said. "All her favorites have been handpicked by Potemkin without exception and Potemkin is, without a doubt, superior to Catherine as a human being." Ishak Bey chose his words carefully. "More energetic, more passionate, a much vaster intelligence, a more developed sensibility. . . ."

"The spectacle of an old woman changing lovers every year for their youth and beauty is disgusting . . . laughable," said Hasan Gazi.

"The Sultan does the same, Sire. . . ."

"He's a male!" exclaimed the Grand Admiral.

Ishak Bey kept silent for a moment. He felt a great tenderness for the painted, rouged, ravaged monster he had made love to.

"The function creates the weapon," said Ishak. "Catherine *is* male, as any *woman* of character would have to be in a similar situation. Catherine's femininity only furnishes her enemies with one more arm against her. She herself must be tough, ruthless, narcissistic but generous. The Empress has the irresistible necessity to cover her lovers with gifts [He did not mention his own rewards from Catherine to the puritanical Captain Pasha]. It suffices to have satisfied a woman who has never, never lost her lucidity, even in love. . . ."

"A formidable enemy."

"A courageous, dangerous and, I repeat, determined enemy," said Ishak Bey. "It is her or us."

Hasan Gazi fell silent. He took his mother-of-pearl chessboard out of its rosewood chest tenderly, sat it on the low table and placed the jeweled chessmen in position. Coffee was brought and the two men began their first game carefully, as if seven years had been but an interrupted afternoon.

"The Shah is dead," said Ishak Bey finally as he checkmated Hasan Gazi for the last time that night. "Long live Sultan Abdulhamid," said Gazi belligerently. It was four o'clock in the morning when Ishak Bey returned to the *Séduisant.*

"We thought you might have returned headless," joked Choiseul-Gouffier, "when we saw the Grand Admiral's colors. Wasn't he the one who craved your handsome head not too long ago?"

Ishak Bey merely smiled. Any confirmation Choiseul-Gouffier would get out of him would come straight from Hasan Gazi's own mouth.

Then he heard the twenty-one-gun salute Hasan Gazi was rendering the new French Ambassador. That old hypocrite, thought Ishak Bey. Sainneville returned the homage with the same number of cannons, and the whole morning was taken up with cannon salutes, first one ship and then the other. Ishak Bey found this both laughable and sinister. How close they all had been to being annihilated last night, he thought. And on top of that a dreadful accident subdued the whole party. They had lost a man in the cannonade. He had probably been on a cannon or just beside one when they had begun to fire their salute. The man had been blown overboard by the recoil, and, by one of those strange, incomprehensible events, one of his legs had been thrown back onboard. That night Choiseul-Gouffier sent marmalades, syrups, liqueurs and Turkish slaves he had ransomed in Malta as gifts to the Grand Admiral. The Grand Admiral's squadron continued on its course and the French frigate approached the Dardanelles. By the next day they were vis-à-vis the island of Chios.

"Vinum novum fundam calathis Arvisia Nestor," murmured Choiseul-Gouffier.

"Virgil, eclogue number five," replied Ishak Bey to the astonished Ambassador. The island was now one of the richest and most agreeable in the Archipelago, thought Ishak Bey. But he had other long-ago memories of Chios. For him the island of Chios was the Battle of Chesme. Chesme would remain with him to his grave, he thought. The screaming men, the burning ships, the gaming table in St. Petersburg

and Hannibal rose like specters before his eyes. Eleven thousand men
had burned in total rout. Tears rolled down Ishak Bey's face.

In June 1770, the Russian fleet under Admiral Orlov had chased
Hasan Gazi's Aegean fleet in and out of the Greek islands for a month,
Ishak remembered. Hasan Gazi had had no choice but to stand and
fight. He had chosen the channel between Chios and the Bay of
Chesme. He had had sixteen ships of the line, six frigates and some
smaller ships. The Russians had had nine ships of the line, three frigates
and some smaller ships.

The Ottoman fleet was anchored before the bay in the form of a
crescent, under the protection of the guns of Chesme. The Russians
attacked one of the horns of the crescent by firing a salvo and departing
leeway one after the other. But the Russian Admiral's ship lost its
rudder under the Ottoman cannon fire. Grand Admiral Hasan Gazi
boarded it. The two flagships lashed together immediately began to
burn as one, as the battle continued. Five hundred men in small boats
were sent by the Russians to help their Admiral, making the battle even
more bloody. The flames had become uncontrollable and the two flagships detached themselves. The first to explode was the Russian one,
with everyone leaping overboard. Hasan Gazi's burning boat drifted
like a mountain of fire on the sea into the center of his fleet, causing
such panic that all the ships fled into the cul-de-sac of the bay. The bay
was filled with sand banks and was too shallow and small for the entire
fleet, leaving it entirely immobilized. Immediately the Russians dropped
anchor at the entrance of the bay, blocking the exit and any possibility
of escape. Then they sent a squadron of fire boats, which set the entire
Ottoman fleet in flames. Each ship exploded and burned and in turn set
the next one on fire until the bay resembled the mouth of a volcano in
eruption. Men jumped or were blown overboard. Gazi and Ishak had
escaped by swimming ashore covered with wounds and gore. The battle
itself cost the Ottomans their entire fleet and eleven thousand men. It
had been a rout that had changed the course of history. That night had
marked the young boy Ishak's shame forever.

Ishak Bey thought of his old mentor. If his erudition had equaled his
nature, Hasan Gazi would have been a prodigious man. Hasan Gazi
was an escaped Persian slave. As an adolescent, he had escaped in a
rowboat from the Dardanelles to Smyrna, where he had joined the
Algerian pirates. He became famous as a result of several hand-to-hand
battles with lions in the desert, where he would go to hunt them with
such passion that he sometimes stole lion cubs and then had to fight off

the mothers. The hatred of a Dey resulted in a death sentence for Gazi. At this point, he again escaped, first to Morocco, then he hid in France, worked in Italy and fled to Istanbul from Naples. In Istanbul he joined the Ottoman navy. Working up through the ranks, he had become the Captain Pasha, the Lord Admiral of the fleet. The scars of a lioness still crosshatched his face, giving Gazi a terrifying aspect. And he still had, as a companion, one of the lion cubs he had stolen so many years ago.

Ishak Bey had not closed his eyes all night. He had undone his bed by his twisting and turning. To calm his nerves, he had tried counting up to one thousand, staring down at the white foam that formed about the prow of the ship, singing old nursery rhymes under his breath, even fingering his tespi. Nothing helped. He was feverish, his breath came too quickly. The lifting of the morning mist seemed to be interminable. Ishak made for the bridge, and suddenly there it was: the entrance to the Bosphorus, the arm of the sea that separated Asia from Europe and attached the Black Sea to the Sea of Marmara. To the right was Asia, ancient Anatolia, and to the left was Europe, ancient Thrace. The ship seemed to advance through the sheer will of Ishak Bey. He saw to the left the gulf, which formed a right angle with the Bosphorus and burrowed several miles into the profundity of Europe, infiltrating the sea's outstretched arm, making a curve that resembled the horn of a steer. This was the Golden Horn, the horn of plenty, where the riches of three continents converged upon the port of ancient Byzantium. And on that site, on that angle of European earth bathed by the Sea of Marmara and the Golden Horn, sat Istanbul . . . mother of the world, thought Ishak. On each of its seven hills rose a lead-domed mosque topped with its golden obelisk: Aya Sofya, all white and blue, the mosque of Ahmed II, flanked by its seven minarets, the mosque of Suleiman, crowned by its ten domes, the mosque of the Valide Sultane, which reflected in the black waters, the mosque of Mahmud, the mosque of Selim, the mosque of Murad, and on the last hill . . . the mosque of Bayazid.

Ishak Bey's face was ribboned with tears. The city rose before him and flaunted its immense contours, broken, capricious, white, green, rose, scintillating, golden, gracious, dressed in cypress, pine, turpentine trees, and gigantic plane trees, which spread their branches beyond the walls of Topkapi, making shade on the sea. The *Séduisant* and *La*

Poulette did not make their twenty-one-gun salute to the city as planned, for it seemed that one of the women of the Sultan was expecting a child and their homage would disturb the tranquility of Seraglio Point.

• CHAPTER SIX •

DR. LORENZO 1784

I sent some heads to Constantinople to amuse the Sultan and the
people, and some money to his Ministers, for water sleeps, but envy
never sleeps.

—ALI, Pasha of Janina, 1792

The little fourteen-gun frigate, *La Poulette*, sat bobbing quietly in the
calm waters of the Bosphorus, under the cypress and olive-dotted hills
of Pera. On board with the French Ambassador Choiseul-Gouffier, were
the Florentine doctor Lorenzo Noccioli, Ishak Bey and Father Delleda.
Choiseul-Gouffier scrutinized his guests. In a few days, he would be
officially received by the Padishah, Sultan Abdulhamid. To do this, he
needed information from each one of them. Father Delleda was in
charge of the hospital of St. Benoit for the French sailors in Constantinople. That had been the old Jesuit convent turned over to the Lazarist
community after the "suspension" of the Jesuit Order by the Pope.
Strangely enough, Ishak Bey had been witness in Paris to the arrange-
ment that had been made between Monsieur Ruffin and the Pope's
envoy, Monsignor Doria. Like the convent, Delleda had been turned
from Jesuit to Lazarist, and was thus under the authority of the King of
France. But secretly he was faithful only to his Father General, who
was now under the protection of the Czarina Catherine in St. Petersburg.

The dazzling, cobalt-eyed Ishak Bey, thought Choiseul-Gouffier, was
the most *modern* man he knew—no ties, no government, no nationality,
only constant motion, constant striving for what he considered the

world's "Horn of Plenty," as if all of life were a gambling table. As for the Florentine, Tabib Lorenzo, he was an adventurer and a paid informer for the French Embassy. He had arrived in Constantinople, like hundreds of others, to make his fortune by the practice of medicine. Probably, he was not a medical doctor but only a very clever man. Like Ishak, he had proceeded to make so many obliging friends, was the protégé of so many important people, that he earned his living serenely by treating his friends without killing them. By a stroke of luck, Selim, the nephew of Abdulhamid and the heir apparent to the throne, had fallen ill with smallpox, and Lorenzo had had the good luck to cure him. The father of Selim, the dead Sultan Mustafa III, not content to smother Lorenzo with gifts, had built the doctor a beautiful stone house in the middle of Pera. Being considered the savior of the heir to the throne, Lorenzo had been named personal doctor of Selim. The title had given him easy access to the harem, where his specialty was predicting male children for the Sultan's pregnant Kadines. But more important, he had also become the confidant and friend of Prince Selim. That was why he was on board, thought Choiseul-Gouffier, to use his influence on Prince Selim in favor of the French. Sought after by all foreign diplomats, Lorenzo, they said, was also on the payroll of the Austrians. Dr. Lorenzo had twice found himself involved in intrigues and affairs of State, and twice he had been warned and pardoned. The Ottomans were loyal to their protégés to the point of idiocy, mused the Ambassador. But he would not put his money on another chance for Lorenzo.

Choiseul-Gouffier eyed the long-legged, white-breeched Lorenzo, who affected Ottoman dress in the Seraglio but the latest and most becoming Occidental dress outside the gates of the Porte. His flashing white linen, his elegantly cut, silver-embroidered dark blue serge, cut wide at the waist and open on the chest, his impeccable yet discreet jewels, his long blond hair and thick grayish sideburns made him the image of Continental fashion, up to and including his mirror-image yellow-topped black boots. It was said that in Ottoman dress he was even more elegant. He was a fine specimen of mankind, thought the Ambassador. Even after the disappearance of Abdulhamid, Lorenzo's future (if he was careful) was assured. He had the affection and undying protection of the future Sultan, Selim III. Choiseul-Gouffier's job was to convince Lorenzo to use his influence on Prince Selim so that he would go along with Grand Vizier Halil Hamid's plans to dispose of Abdulhamid in favor of Selim as Sultan. As for Abdulhamid, Choiseul-

Gouffier had always considered him a "good" Sultan until he realized that he was merely a stupid one. He had already taken the measure of the Grand Vizier as well as the redoubtable Lord Admiral Hasan Gazi, in whose favor Ishak Bey was miraculously restored.

Choiseul-Gouffier had never been able to figure out Ishak Bey. Ishak expressed what he thought with great care, and he was even more expert in feigning contempt of Christian manners, customs and art. Yet he was in manners and temperament as European as any Westerner he knew. This double-faced Janus of East and West, still known in Constantinople as the archangel Gabriel, was speaking:

"I assure you, Hasan Gazi Pasha is very well disposed toward France. . . ."

"Perhaps," replied Choiseul-Gouffier, "but I would be more assured if he didn't go around with the bloody lion. . . ."

Ishak Bey laughed. "That lion is so overfed, he couldn't consume a mouse!"

"Perhaps," chuckled the Ambassador, "but I needed all my sangfroid in circumstances that were very far from my normal diplomatic duties, and far beyond, may I add, the call of duty, citizenship and downright common sense. There I was, having a normal conversation with Gazi, when at a moment of pleasurable animation, all of a sudden I felt something heavy and warm pressing against my knees. Squinting down, I perceived the enormous head of Gazi's bloody lion showing, believe me, more teeth than I have ever seen in my life. No one had warned me of this idiosyncrasy of Gazi's [Why hadn't Ishak told him?] and thinking that any brusque movement on my part would be, if not fatal, extremely disagreeable, I placed my hand casually on the animal's head and caressed it: 'Pretty pussy . . . pretty, pretty pussy,' I said. What else do you say to a lion?"

Ishak Bey burst into laughter.

"Mercy me," sighed Choiseul-Gouffier, "thank goodness Gazi lowered his voice, calmed down the interpreter and halfway between anger and panic called his servants and promised to kill the one who had allowed this third 'criterion' to enter. Once the lion was safely out of the way, I received Gazi's congratulations for my . . . intrepid presence of mind, and he told me that my personal boldness could procure even greater success for my country!"

"That lion, Mr. Ambassador," said Ishak Bey, "fascinated by your firm but vigorous gaze, yet still dangerous, is the exact image of Ottoman power; exasperated by the languor of the Seraglio but having lost none of its inherent ferocity, or its taste for blood, it quivers with impatience at the ties by which its European neighbors have enmeshed it, be they friends or enemies."

Lorenzo, not willing to commit himself, was silent. His situation required deference toward everything and consequently he was attentive but reserved even when he was in agreement. Ishak Bey was a fool, he thought, to speak out even in intimacy. He, Lorenzo, was constantly anxious never to compromise himself; and above all, to remain master of his secrets. And that secret was the eventual alliance between Austria and the Ottomans against France and Russia. Ishak Bey guarded, or thought he did, another secret, that of Selim's ambitions. Selim cherished only one thing, a kind of political testament of his father, Mustafa III, composed of abuses to be suppressed. Selim even dared speak of reestablishing, by war, the integrity of his Empire—an empire out of which every European nation in the world had taken a bite. It was he who had told Choiseul-Gouffier:

"I know what kind of consultation you want of me, and what has passed up to now between you and the Prince. My master doesn't confine himself exclusively to Ishak Bey's promises and he has ordered me to request of you, on your word of honor, if you think the King of France would welcome a token of his confidence and esteem in the person of a secret agent, accredited clandestinely, but received with honor and having at his disposal all the means necessary to his instruction. . . ." The secret messenger had been Ishak Bey, thought Lorenzo. This had at the time posed some problems for poor Ishak, especially in the way of image, up until this very moment. One could never really be sure which way he would jump. If he was really brilliant or merely lucky. . . . He, Choiseul, personally didn't trust handsome men. . . .

Ishak was ill at ease and anxious. In this little frigate, *La Poulette,* a so-called bastion of civilization, he suddenly felt superfluous, foreign, detached, parasitical and downright hostile. The arrogance, the superciliousness of these, these Giaours. Their ignorance, stupidity and puerility irritated him profoundly, although he had readily tolerated the same attitudes at Versailles, London and St. Petersburg. Contempt for the Ottomans he had encountered everywhere, even here on Choiseul-Gouffier's little frigate. The exaggerated pride of the Ottomans was their undoing, he knew. It so affected Westerners that they saw only the savage, the Oriental, the ignorant, the vulgar; a people incapable of "modern" civilization. . . . But he was after all indigenous to this most beautiful of all cities—so beautiful, it defied even conquest. And he was after all the stepson of a Sultane. . . . Moreover, his sense of danger had been honed to such perfection that he *knew* he was in danger. But from whom?

Choiseul-Gouffier thought he was working for Selim. Father Delleda thought he was working for the Russians. Lorenzo thought he was working for Halil Hamid. Halil Hamid, who had named him attaché to the Grand Vizierate, thought he was working for Choiseul-Gouffier—and Hasan Gazi thought he was working for *him*. Ishak Bey smiled. Only he and the Prophet knew who the hell he was working for, and sometimes he doubted if the Prophet really knew.

Tabib Lorenzo Noccioli was also impatient to be gone. Selim was waiting for him. But he knew that he was in for a long and tedious description of Choiseul-Gouffier's keen penetrations of the ways of the Orientals with all the finesse and intuition of an elephant. He settled back, his animosity toward Ishak Bey, his prey, expertly dissipated in one of the most charming and devastating smiles in all Constantinople. He looked around at the rich, smug, safe and handsome company in disgust. Abdulhamid was already a dead man, he thought, and nobody here knew it except him.

The Ambassador Choiseul-Gouffier and his cortege of about fifty persons had set out by moonlight for his audience with the Sultan. The streets were lined with Janissaries wearing their ceremonial caps made of thick white felt, having a scroll-like cylinder of brass, representing an upright spoon, in front and a long, broad flap hanging down to the small of the back behind, which represented the sleeve of Hadgee Bectash, the founder of the Janissary Corps. They had stumbled down the steep streets, their horses continually falling against each other and slipping, to a large mulberry tree where two paths branched off, one to the right, leading up to the Porte, and the other to the left, leading to the Seraglio. Here, along with Ishak Bey, they had waited for almost an hour for the Grand Vizier to descend from the Porte to lead the way. The French Ambassador was livid. He had been kept waiting under a tree, in a dirty street, for nearly an hour! They followed the Grand Vizier at a humble distance. At the top of the street was the Gate of Bab-i-Humayun. To each side were the usual piles of human heads. Most of them had been trampled into the ground. Some children had gotten hold of a half-dozen of these mutilated heads, which they were balancing on their toes and knocking one off with the other. Having entered the gate, the Ambassador's party found themselves in the First

Court, a large, oblong, irregularly shaped area with low barracks on each side.

The First Court was thronged with people. They passed into a chamber called the Kapi Arasi because it lay between two gates that formed the entrance to it from each court. Here were the torture chamber and the apartment of the Chief Executioner. Here pipes and coffee were offered and the Ambassador was kept waiting for another half hour. Then the party advanced into a second court, more silent and filled with full-grown trees. On one side of the courtyard were the kitchens, on the other, the Divan; and at the upper level was the entrance to the harem, the Door of Felicity, the Bab-i-Sa'adet.

Ishak Bey remembered it all so well: the mosque of the Sultan, the palace hospital, the treasury, the orangery, the Capidgi, the barrack kitchens, the mint, the famous plane tree of Ahmet II under which the condemned were decapitated.

The Court of the Divan was always filled with a multitude of people and, paradoxically, silence. From morning until nightfall, this court was a mass of humanity, out of which rose the hundred uniforms of the Empire, the turbans of the Janissaries, the helmets of the imperial guards, the bonnets of the eunuchs, the turbans of the Bostanji. The crowd of archers, lancers, guards, white eunuchs, black eunuchs, merchants, valets, officers with their woolen plaits hanging from their turbans, was so varied that one's head spun. Ishak explained that each costume was regulated by law. Choiseul was wide-eyed. Status and function in this apparent confusion were easily recognizable by the height of a turban, the cut of a sleeve, the quality and type of fur, the color of a lining, the ornament of a saddle. Even the shape of a beard or the length of a moustache. The Grand Vizier, for example, wore light green. The first six personages of the Empire—the Chief of the Emirs, the Judges of Mecca, Medina and Istanbul—all wore dark blue; the Grand Ulemas wore violet, the Sheykhs light blue; the Generals wore red boots, the officers of the Porte, yellow boots; and the executioners and torturers were recognizable by the dead silence that followed in their wake, and by the two rows of heads, touching the ground, between which they passed.

The Chief Black Eunuch passed through a forest of helmets and turbans lowered as if by an invisible hand. They found themselves before the Door of Bab-el-Selam, through which one could not enter without a firman, a command of the Sultan, upon pain of instant death. The executioners' cells were overhead, and a secret passage connected the courtyard to the Divan. A man could die between the closed doors of Bab-el-Selam and those of the Second Court, Ishak remembered. As one set of doors closed behind him and another set closed before him. . . . The Second Court was open to the sky, surrounded by gracious buildings with gold- and silver-plated domes. A long avenue of giant cypresses traversed the entire court. Everything was embossed, columns, bases, walls, roofs, doors, arcades. Everything was incised, painted gold leaf like a pavilion of lace embroidered with pearls. Ishak's heart stopped upon seeing this city of tents; one, two, or six hundred, he couldn't count, tents of every color, embroidered, hung with tapestries, festooned with flags and banners. Everything announced the presence of Allah's Shadow on Earth; the silence, the discreetness of movement— neither the prancing of horses nor the voice of workmen could be heard. In Topkapi, the closer one came to the Sultan—as our dear Ambassador has noticed, Ishak thought—the more charged and rarefied was the air, the more encompassing and imposing was the silence, troubled only by the occasional flight of a flock of skylarks, or the click of an iron key turning in a lock—for they were now standing before the Door of Felicity, the Bab-i-Sa'adet, sacred, closed to all except the Sultan, the door of the harem, forbidden territory for four centuries. . . .

The Sultans always fixed an audience on the day the Janissaries were paid, which was a ridiculous and ostentatious policy to display all the most imposing details of government to foreign ministers, thought Ishak.

The Janissaries, or New Troops, had been formed in the fourteenth century to replace the irregular and unreliable armies of the feudal Pashas, which had constituted the majority of the Ottoman army. They had once been the most brilliant invention of the Osmanlis: the first standing army in the world. Landowners and local despots could not be depended upon to be loyal to the Sultan. This militia, however, was a kind of proletarian household guard, loyal only to the Sultan, paid by him. Every time the Standard of the Prophet was unfurled and carried outside the walls of Istanbul, that was the cry of war. The Janissaries were apart from the civilian population, and were on occasion used against them. The Corps had originally been composed only of Christian children conscripted by force from their families, converted to Islam, and trained for war. They had been the most dependable soldiers in the world, without family ties either between themselves or with the Ottoman people and with marriage prohibited. In the seventeenth century, the Janissaries had been given a religious status by a famous and venerated dervish from Anatolia who had given them the name of Yéni-tchéri, which was not long in becoming famous in both the East and the West. A sacred character was attached to them because of the holy man's blessing, and their turbans represented the wide, flowing sleeves of the saint.

The Janissaries had numbered no more than 1,200 at their conception, but now, under Abdulhamid, they numbered more than 140,000 and were almost all in Istanbul. By now, however, the Corps had degenerated into intermarriage and life outside the barracks. Now, there were sons who automatically inherited a place in the Janissaries. They were of no military value except to terrorize the capital and overthrow Sultans. The Sultan was considered the paternal provider of the Janissaries and his mother, the Valide, was their maternal provider. Thus the ritual of feeding and paying them as well as their grades had been borrowed from the vocabulary of the kitchen. The Colonel was "the Master of the Great Soup Pot," the Captain, "the Master Cook," the Lieutenant, "the Water Carrier." The iron pot was the symbol of the regiment, the equivalent of a regimental flag, and to have it fall into enemy hands was the worst dishonor. To overturn the iron pot was for the Janissaries the symbol of revolt, the signal for insurrection. Insurrection was led by their Aga, one of the most important religious personages of the Empire. On the other hand, the apocalyptic spectacle of the Janissaries, on signal, throwing themselves on the rice offered by the Sultan, was the symbol of their submission to him. They were at once an aristocratic and religious army and an organized democracy, and each Sultan had to deal during his reign with this redoubtable Corps, which now imposed itself between him and his people.

The Janissaries were a motley group, and except for their hats, they were without any kind of uniform. They were, lined up on either side of the courtyard, waiting for the distribution of pilau, a kind of boiled rice with bits of lamb and vegetables. Porringers of rice and milk were set out in different parts of the courtyard, and at the signal, the Janissaries started for them. Whoever seized them first, kept them; so during the scrambling, they smeared and daubed each other with great gravity. In silence. For a Janissary not to take part in this humiliating ceremony was considered an act of revolt; the sentence was death. To refuse to eat was literally to lose one's appetite forever.

Ishak marshaled the French party through the confusion of this infantile yet frightening fiasco, into the Hall of the Divan. The hall where all the affairs of State were dealt with consisted of two apartments formed by domes and separated by a chest-high partition. In the middle and opposite the entrance sat the Grand Vizier, dressed in white satin robes and wearing a conical turban of snow-white muslin marked with a broad band of gold. Immediately above his head, projecting from the wall, was a little semicircular balcony about the size of half a hogshead. It was formed of very closely constructed gilded bars, through which a person sitting inside might hear and see but not himself be seen. Here, unknown to all except the Chief Black Eunuch and the Grand Vizier, sat Abdulhamid and the new favorite, Naksh-i-dil. Ishak Bey looked up more than once, furtively and at length, and caught the gleam of four eyes through the small aperture in the latticework. It was without a doubt Abdulhamid and one of his Kadines, he guessed. On the right of the Vizier sat the Captain Pasha in green satin robes; on the left sat the Black Eunuch wearing yellow satin. Behind the Vizier sat two Judges of the Empire, one for Roumelia, the European portion, and the other for Anatolia, the Asiatic portion. The French party were crammed into a recess at one side of the room and then completely ignored.

First came a lawsuit. This was followed by the payment of the troops with leather purses, piled into two heaps on the floor, four feet high and ten feet long. They looked the size and shape of potatoes about to be buried for the winter, thought the Ambassador. Each purse contained 460 piastres. Together the heaps amounted to 6½ million piastres in 30,000 purses, six months' pay for all the Janissaries in Istanbul. This took an hour. When all was done, the Vizier sent a sealed letter to the Sultan (who, Ishak could see, was still in the niche above the Vizier's head) saying the money was there. In about an hour, the "messenger" returned. The money was distributed as the pilau had been, and the purses were thrown into the air. The troops, like little boys playing ball, all rushed forward. This lasted more than three hours. Then they were fed, washed, clothed and made fit to be seen in the presence of His Sublimity, Allah's Shadow on Earth.

Naksh-i-dil looked down in horror at the Janissaries scrambling for food. She would never forget this squalid entertainment. Roast and boiled, sweet and sour, hard and soft were all clawed together by thousands of filthy hands, without knife, fork, cloth or napkin. She watched the Ambassador being washed and clothed in a ceremonial pelisse after this scramble, followed by the Vizier, the Captain Pasha and a lane of attendants, and she spied the advancing party of the Frenchmen all dressed in ceremonial pelisses. The Ikbal also looked down upon the famous Ishak Bey for the first time.

"I must now rush to greet my new French Ambassador, now that I have observed him."

Choiseul-Gouffier, the Grand Vizier Halil Hamid and Ishak Bey, accompanied by the Captain Pasha, the Black Eunuch and a delegation of eighteen advanced to the harem gate, which was decorated with the most beautiful display of Turkish sculpture and covered by a large semi-circular projecting canopy supported on richly carved gilt and embossed pillars. Around the entrance, with sabers drawn, were the black eunuchs in their richest dress, some in brocades shot with gold, which as they moved were quite dazzling against their dark skin. Some of them were boys of sixteen years, some were men of forty. While Choiseul-Gouffier stood gazing on the eunuchs in a kind of daydream, he was suddenly roused by being seized by the collar by two men, as were the others, and hurried, or rather dragged, down a broad, descending passage, between rows of guards, to the interior of the harem. Arriving at a gloomy courtyard, the delegation was led into a dark and dismal little chamber lighted only by one grated window. In the chamber there was a large throne, resembling in size and shape a four-poster bed without curtains. It was covered with an immense array of silks, satins and brocades in the form of cushions, embroidered with gold and pearls. On the side of this, with his feet hanging down like a man getting out of bed in the morning, sat the Sultan Abdulhamid. The Sultan appeared small, and older than his years. His beard was very full and as black and glossy as jet. Abdulhamid used artificial means to color it. The Sultan neither greeted the company nor made any gesture of recognition. At a signal the Chief Black Eunuch, the only person allowed to touch the Padishah, came forward and offered him a gilded opium pill. The Sultan never turned his head nor did he utter one word. Choiseul read his speech, translated by a trembling, terrified dragoman. The interpreter could barely see to read the paper he held, as it was blotted with large drops of perspiration dripping from his forehead. He had reason. His predecessor had just been executed. The interview did not take ten minutes, and as the last word dropped from the mouth of the dragoman, and without the slightest previous notice, the Ambassador was dragged back by his conductors, whose grips never left his neck for a moment. In stumbling backward, he trod on the tail of his gown, well-nigh prostrating himself without intending to. No one had the right to turn his back on the Sultan. The French delegation was twirled about and hurried along the passage, then flung off by their conductors as if they were things to be avoided, and whose touch could cause contamination.

It was, thought Choiseul-Gouffier, one of the many existing proofs of the stubborn immutability of a people who have been Europeans now for four centuries! And they have not adopted one European usage to ameliorate their own.

Naksh-i-dil listened, spying behind the iron grille of the blind (window) behind the throne, mesmerized by the sound of her own language . . . the elegant Parisian French of the new Ambassador washed over her like soft waves. Her whole body was seized by an uncontrollable tremor, part rage, part despair. She peeped through the light gauze curtains and glimpsed the ambassadorial party. Most were in shadow. Only an obvious Frenchman with powdered hair and rouged cheeks, in white smallclothes and a blue coat trimmed with silver over which was thrown a ceremonial pelisse of ermine, and Ishak Bey, the most handsome man she had ever seen, were visible to her. Abdulhamid had been completely silent as the presentation of the Frenchman went on and on, interminably.

Naksh-i-dil was trembling with emotion. She had only to step from behind the curtain that was hiding her and demand asylum of the French Ambassador as a citizen held in slavery for more than four years now, against her will. What could Abdulhamid do? Kill her there before the French Ambassador? Refuse his claim to her as a French citizen? Execute the representative of the powerful French nation? Naksh-i-dil thought of Abdulhamid: her master, her deflowerer. What could she expect in the outside world, a woman no longer a virgin, not yet a widow and never a wife? An ex-slave who was devalued forever in the eyes of white Christian society?

She didn't have the courage of an act that would surely cost her her life. Even her desperation was not profound enough to overcome her fear of death.

She watched the procession as it left. The proud Choiseul-Gouffier trod on the tail of his gown as he departed.

Ishak Bey was introduced into the Kafes by Dr. Lorenzo.

Selim received Ishak alone, in the Cage. Or at least apparently alone, as Ishak had become used to spies everywhere since he had returned. Shadows played on the Prince's handsome, pock-marked features. The dark eyes had filled with tears.

"Ishak," was all that Selim said. And the two friends embraced with emotion. Their rich robes mingled in a swirl of color and texture; Selim brought his hands up and held Ishak's face, searching it as if it contained the secret of his unhappiness.

Ishak had been prepared for changes in his friend, but not to the extent of having Selim transformed into a stranger. Yet he smiled bravely and embraced his Prince. Ishak's laughing beautiful eyes took in the ravages of the years spent in the Cage.

"Well, Michael," he blurted out.

"How you have changed, Gabriel!" said Selim.

Ishak smiled. "For better or for worse?" he asked.

"Oh, for the better, Ishak. You have seen the world. . . ."

The two friends stared silently at each other. A whole Empire stood between them, Ishak thought. Selim's dark eyes were clouded with mistrust and ignorance. Not only of the world outside, Ishak thought, or of him, but a totalitarian ignorance. . . .

Ishak Bey began to speak slowly about the outside world. Selim, who had never been outside the walls of Istanbul, listened to his messenger Gabriel ferociously, his eyes burning. Ishak described the court of Catherine, his sojourn in London, and finally, because it had amused the Czarina, he began to tell Selim about Paris, but in such a way as to incite him to revolt; revolt not only from his own position as Prince Hereditary, but from the Empire itself. He wanted to ignite in his Prince all the frustrations and longing for freedom that any slave would have.

"It is said in Europe," he began, "that you are the only hope for the Empire. That your uncle Abdulhamid, who was thought to be a good Sultan, is only a stupid one. . . . The attitude of the outside world to the Osmans is one of contempt and ridicule. We are considered barbarians (not to mention the worst, for it is blasphemy against Our Prophet), incapable of progress, of achievement, of modernism. Imagine that when the Bostanjis are enforcing the curfew with their sabers, the King of France is leaving for the theater and dinner. The streets are filled with people. No one has to carry a lantern for the streets are lit all night by torches posted certain distances apart. Arms are not allowed in Paris, nor are they sold in the bazaar! Think of our Janissaries with their sabers, the Yamaks, the Halberdiers. There is enough steel in Istanbul to cover the Black Sea. Women are safe to go out alone in this city of light. The court is the most brilliant in Christiandom. There are concerts, theaters, books, paintings, newspapers, gazettes. There is the Sorbonne, and such a concentration of thinking and invention that if we achieved even one tenth of its vigor, we would make the world sit up and take notice of the Ottomans. Medicine, mathematics, these were things the Orient discovered long before the Occident. But we have fallen behind. The hospitals and school of medicine in Paris are wonders.

"The Observatory is a place where one can go to look at the stars! The intensity of life and thought is so great that renowned inventors ask to enter a hospital, so exhausted are they with such intellectual activity. There are also business, trade, banking, delirious gambling. Imagine, men and women commit suicide over cards. Then in the winter, all of Paris gives itself over to the balls, which occur every night and go on all night. Carriages jam the streets, the salons are diamonds of light and color, men hold women in their arms, thus, and twirl around to music. Yet behind all this is a sense of security of the power of the State, or order, of serenity that liberates the spirit, and induces great thoughts. . . .

"By the will of God, you can take this kingdom out of the dark ages like Peter the Great did in Russia! *You* can be the Peter the Great of the Osmanlis. We have been a European Empire for four centuries, yet *foreigners* fight over us and divide our territory like a piece of meat! Your father knew the moment would come when destiny would make it imperative that you reach out to your natural allies in Europe—especially France. I would say that Louis XVI is only *waiting* for a word from you in order to express *his* friendship. By the will of God . . ."

Ishak had worked himself up to a lyrical pitch when he realized that Selim had sat down quietly at his writing table while he, Ishak, had been pacing back and forth, and was serenely composing a poem. His answer to everything. But when the Prince looked up, Ishak realized that his gesture was one of excitement, even anguish. The atmosphere was charged. Ishak walked over to him. It was as if Selim's pen had stopped his voice. Selim rose to meet Ishak's eyes level with his.

"Do you want to know what I've written?" he asked shyly. "A letter to King Louis . . ."

Selim's eyes burned with the excitement of Ishak's speech. The dreams of his life he now identified with Ishak. Ishak was a passage to the real world. From this lonely prison, only Ishak's touch could give him the illusion of freedom, of action, of life.

Ishak, looking into Selim's eyes, felt as if he were opening an unclosable door.

"I've missed you," said Selim. "How much I've thought of you these years. How much I've always loved you. How I wished you home. . . ."

"I'm here now."

"Splendid and faithful observer of the spectacles of the world, Ishak, Prince of men, I salute you."

• CHAPTER SEVEN •

FATIMA 1784

Fatima had made up her mind to convert Nakshi-i-dil to Islam. At first Naksh-i-dil had refused to listen, but Fatima was a true evangelist. She refused to give up. It was her duty to bring her friend to the light. A Giaour.

"Now," she continued her lesson, "I'll begin again. From the beginning. For once, Naksh-i-dil, *listen* to me! Your very soul is in danger! Jesus Christ is one of our prophets," said Fatima.

Fatima began to read from a text on the Koran. "We both believe in God and His angels, His scriptures, His prophets, the Resurrection and Last Judgment, in God's absolute decree, which is Prayer, Ablutions, Alms, Fasting, Pilgrimage to Mecca, Circumcision are prescriptions of the Koran. Both you and I worship the true God. . . . Both of us believe in the existence of angels. The two angels most eminently in God's favor are Michael, the friend and protector of the Jews, and Gabriel, who sounds the last trumpet at Resurrection. . . . We also believe that two guardian angels attend every man. They observe and write down our actions, and are called al moakkibur, or 'the angels who continually succeed one another.' The devil we call Eblis, who was God's favorite angel, Azzel, and who fell from divine grace for refusing to pay homage to Adam.

"As for the scriptures, the Mohammedans are taught by the Koran, as you are from the Bible. In the various ages of the world, God gave revelations of His Will in writing to many prophets. There are 104 sacred books. Ten were given to Adam; fifty to Seth; ten to Enoch; ten to Abraham; and the others, the Pentateuch, the Psalms, the Gospel and the Koran, were given successively to Moses, David, Jesus and Mohammed. Mohammed was the last of the prophets, and received the last revelations. No more are to be expected. All these divine books, except the last four, are irrecoverably lost, like the lost Ark. There is a gospel in Arabic attributed to Saint Barnabas, in which the biography of Jesus Christ is related in a manner very different from that which you Christians believe. Moreover, there is a passage in the Koran where Jesus Christ is formally asserted to have foretold Mohammed's coming under his other name of Ahmed, which is derived from the same root as Mohammed." Fatima paused. Her sweet voice had taken on a fervent tone and she continued to lecture to her friend.

"The number of prophets sent by God into the world throughout history is 224,000. There were 313 apostles sent with special commissions. Six of them brought laws. These were Adam, Noah, Abraham, Moses, Jesus and Mohammed. We believe *all* the prophets to be free from great sins and errors of consequence, notwithstanding the different laws and institutions which they observed. Thus, we include all thirty-three of the prophets, patriarchs and saints in the scriptures: Adam, Abraham, Job, Noah, Nehemiah, Ezra, Samuel, Joshua, Jacob, Esau, Levi, Zechariah, Zephaniah, Aaron, Malachi, Haggai, Habakkuk, Daniel, Ezekiel, Jeremiah, Isaiah, Obadiah, Amos, Hosea, Joel, Ishak, Jacob, Micah, Nahum, Suleiman, Jonas, Ismail. Jesus, Son of Mary . . . Like Christians, we believe in the Resurrection and a Last Judgment. When a corpse is laid in the grave, he is visited by an angel who whispers in his ear the answers to the two questions of two examiners. The two examiners are black angels called Monker and Nakir. They order the corpse to sit up, and they question him concerning his Faith, the unity of God and the mission of Mohammed. If the departed person was a believer, two angels meet him and convey him to heaven. We believe that a man's body is entirely consumed by the earth except for the bone called al ajb, which, being the first formed in the human body, will also remain the last, uncorrupted until Judgment Day. The Jews believe the same thing and call this bone Luz."

"What about the Resurrection?" whispered Naksh-i-dil.

"The date of the Resurrection is known only to God," said Fatima. "And even the angel Gabriel doesn't know it. But the end of the world is heralded by many signs: the decay of Faith among men; advancement of the most humble to eminence, the world much given to sensuality, Moslems holding hostages and inciting great disorder in the world. Iraq and Syria will refuse to pay their tribute. The city of Medina shall revert to King Ahab of Israel.

"Some of the greater signs are: The sun will rise in the west; and the anti-Christ, whom the Mohammedans call Mafid al Dajjal, that is, 'false or lying Christ,' will arrive. He will be one-eyed and his forehead will be marked with the letters C F R, signifying cafer, or infidel. The Jews give him the name Moshiah ben David and believe that he will restore the Kingdom of Israel to them. Finally, Moslems believe Jesus will descend on earth, and that He will embrace the Moslem religion, marry, have children, kill the anti-Christ and die after forty years. Under Jesus, there will be great security; plenty in the world; all hatred and malice put aside; lions, camels, bears and sheep will lie in peace together. There will also be war with the Jews at this time, in which the Moslems will slaughter a prodigious number.

"At the Resurrection Gabriel's blare of *consternation* will sound. The effects of this are very wonderful. The earth shall shake; mountains shall be leveled; heavens shall melt; the sun will darken; angels will die; the sea shall dry up or turn into flames, the sun, moon and stars will be thrown into it. Women who give suck shall abandon the care of their infants. Gabriel's second blare is that of *examination,* by which all creatures, both in heaven and on earth, shall die or be annihilated. The last to die will be the angel of death."

"And hell," said Naksh-i-dil. "What does·Mohammed say of hell?"

"Hell is divided into seven stories," Fatima continued, "one below the other, destined for the reception of as many distinct classes of the damned. The first is called jehennam, 'the receptacle for those who acknowledge one God,' that is, wicked Moslems who, after having been punished in that place according to their merit, will at length be released. The second, ladha, is assigned to the Jews. The third, al hotama, to the Christians. The fourth, al sair, to the Sabians. The fifth, al sakar, to the magicians. The sixth, al johim, to the idolaters; and the seventh, al hawyat, which is the lowest and the worst of all, to the hypocrites.

"But the most important practice," said Fatima, "is *prayer* combined with purification. Religion is founded on cleanliness, which is half of Faith and the key to prayer. . . . There are two purifications: ghost, bathing of the body in water, and woden, washing of hands and feet.

"*Fasting* is a duty of great importance. It is, according to Mohammed, the gate to religion: *'The odor of the mouth of him who fasteth is more grateful to God than that of musk.'*

"There are three degrees of fasting: restraining all parts of the body from lust; restraining ears, eyes, tongue, hands, feet and other members from sin; fasting of the heart from worldly cares and restraining the thoughts from everything besides God.

"We are obliged to fast the whole month of Ramadan, from new moon, to new moon, from daybreak to sunset, or to the hour 'when one can no longer discern the difference between a white thread and a black one. . . .' The month of Ramadan, the ninth month of the Moslem calendar, is the month that the Koran was sent down from heaven to Mohammed. Abraham, Moses and Jesus received *their* revelations in the same month. . . . A pilgrimage to Mecca at least once during one's life is commanded by the Koran," continued Fatima.

Naksh-i-dil was overcome by a strange weakness. "Enough for today." She signaled in the language of the deaf mutes. Her head was on fire. . . . It was the first of the spells that would come increasingly to her.

Neither Choiseul-Gouffier nor Dr. Lorenzo had counted on the assassination of Halil Hamid. His death destroyed the effects of the secret agreements France had contracted with the disgraced Vizier. Halil Hamid was sent to Tenedos, where he had been met by the bowstring.

On hearing that Halil Hamid's head had been nailed to the gates of the Porte, Ishak Bey had been filled with disgust. The suspicion of a Sultan could destroy the efforts of years of planning.

Halil Hamid had fallen victim to the intrigues of his political enemies, led by Hasan Gazi who had resented the prestige gained by the Grand Vizier. The story was spread that the Grand Vizier had been involved in a plot to overthrow Abdulhamid and put Selim in his place. Now he was dead.

On the twenty-first of July of the following year, a French warship slipped out of the harbor of Istanbul under cover of night. Aboard was Ishak Bey incognito. At the exit of the Archipelago, he changed to a French ship of the line headed for Marseilles. Ishak Bey was secretly on his way back to Versailles with what he sincerely believed was the Empire's last chance: a proposition that Selim ascend the throne occupied by Abdulhamid. The French foreign minister, the French Ambassador and Louis himself seconded this. Selim, thought Ishak Bey, *would* be to Turkey what Peter the Great had been to Russia . . . or so thought Prince Selim. It was in the secret letter Ishak carried to Louis XVI. The archangel Gabriel was still faithful to the archangel Michael . . . but if he didn't become Sultan soon, thought Ishak, he, Ishak, would never see Istanbul again. . . .

After Hamil Hamid had been deposed as Grand Vizier by Hasan Gazi and exiled, Fatima had been held hostage in the Eski Serai. When the news that her father was dead reached her, she escaped the eunuch guards and reached the ramparts giving onto the sea. There, according to those who saw her, she had hesitated for an instant, then, almost as if she could fly, her heel had lifted from the edge of the stone fortress, and she had hovered at least a foot above the broad heights before plunging to her death on the rocks below. There had been nothing left of her when the guards had finally arrived, for the birds had gotten there first.

CHAPTER EIGHT

KADINE 1785

When I rescued you from the hands of infidels and I bought you . . .
I thought to profit from Fate's decision over the destinies of men in
order to dispose of you as I pleased and to make of you one day either
my daughter or my mistress. The same fate has decreed that you be
both the one and the other, it being impossible for me to separate
friendship from Love . . . You might have ended the mistress of a
Turk who would have shared his tenderness amongst twenty others
. . .

—BARON FERRIOL to the ex-Circassian slave
Mademoiselle Aissé, bought in
Constantinople and taken to France in 1698

The crimson linen—the color of the Osmans—had been ready for
months, as had everything concerning the royal birth of Naksh-i-dil's
infant. The silver basin for the infant's baths had been readied, the
layette, extravagant pieces requisitioned from the imperial wardrobe,
had been woven and embroidered. Every major event—death, circumcision, marriage or birth—was a pretext to break the rigid monotonous
rhythm that ruled the harem. Winter had passed and the last snows had
melted from Aya Sofya's dome. Spring had brought the tulips in bloom,
and the triple vigilance of Hitabetullah. A birth in the harem constituted an event in which tragedy, superstition and plots all played a part.
Hitabetullah exercised all her powers of concentration to protect
Naksh-i-dil and the new life growing within her from everyone in the
harem. The collective exaltation that grew with the approach of Naksh-

i-dil's confinement focused on her as an excuse for the entire life of the harem. Now it was July, and her time had come. Naksh-i-dil found herself the center of attraction, for some three hundred women who would all vicariously live the end of her confinement.

"There is no way to escape it, Naksh-i-dil," said Hadidge as she moved the ostrich-feathered fan back and forth over Naksh-i-dil's bloated body. Hadidge regarded her with a mixture of tenderness and secret envy. As a Sultana, she would never have children. She was sterilized. But she was determined not to give in to despair.

"Hitabetullah swears it will be a male."

"Hitabetullah has never been wrong."

"And if it is a girl?"

"Well." Hadidge smiled. "She'll be like me . . ." She avoided Naksh-i-dil's eyes.

"And the news from the front?"

"All bad."

"Abdulhamid is taking it very badly. It is killing him."

"I know."

"What does the Czarina want?"

"She wants Istanbul. That's what she wants. She *has* everything else."

"What will happen?"

"No one will ever have Istanbul because all the world wants it for themselves—the Russians, the French, the English, the Austrians, the Greeks . . ."

"Not the French," protested Naksh-i-dil.

"Of course the French. Why not? Even the Chinese want Istanbul. . . ." Hadidge laughed. "But you know who will one day rule Istanbul?"

"Who?"

"You and your son. Hitabetullah told me."

"You imagine things, Hadidge. Selim, I am told, is young, vigorous and vengeful. Mustafa is almost six years old. . . . A son of mine will never rule Istanbul. . . ."

"Hitabetullah says yes, and I put more faith in her predictions than the Divan's. Besides, she is Moslem."

"What is Selim like?"

"My brother?" Hadidge paused at the question. "It is years since I last saw him. I loved him dearly as a child, and while he was more at liberty than he is now, we were great friends. But since the deposition of

Halil Hamid, the Sultan has kept him and his friends under strict surveillance. Only his doctor, Lorenzo, is allowed to see him," said
Hadidge innocently.

"It is such a strange law of succession."

"You mean because the eldest male member of the Osmans succeeds
rather than from father to eldest son?"

"I mean all the rest," whispered Naksh-i-dil. "That brother can kill
brother. That the heir to the throne must remain a prisoner for half his
life, or more . . ."

"You fear for your child?"

"Yes," Naksh-i-dil answered.

"It is true. . . . Someday, if he is a Prince, he will be taken from
you. Be resigned to that Naksh-i-dil. Don't fight it, or it will kill you."

At daybreak the floors of the harem and Naksh-i-dil's apartments
were washed. The Kiaya personally supervised their cleaning and pol-
ishing. She stood barefoot on a small square carpet armed with a silver
baton. Twenty or so slaves surrounded her, and at her command a
dozen of them threw pails of water on the floor, followed by another
dozen who sponged the marble dry and then polished it with pumice
stones. Rose petals were then strewn over the polished surface and the
incense stands lit. The harem deposited before Naksh-i-dil bouquets of
flowers, sweets and loukoums. The harem doors were closed to the
Sultan. Tea and coffee were served, gossip was exchanged along with
beauty recipes, jokes and riddles. In an eternal hunger to communicate,
the schoolgirl voices of a dozen women rose and fell in the deepening
day, while the Boulas, the midwives and the Kalfas, tespis in hand,
timed the labor pains. Fully dressed, Naksh-i-dil stood half crouching,
legs apart, and supported on either side by two midwives. To activate
labor, the Boulas had placed a wide leather belt across her stomach
which they pressed down progressively. Naksh-i-dil, biting a stick of
ivory to keep from screaming, clutched Hitabetullah's outstretched
hand. As the midwives held the crimson linen under her to receive the
child, Naksh-i-dil bore down a last time, surrounded by a horde of
Boulas, midwives, the Kiaya, the Kalfas, and the Black Eunuch, who
had been sent to ensure that there was no substitution for the child.
And in the midst of a terrible clamor, conversation, and to the strident
Zaraites expelled by the surrounding women, the infant glided between
the unwashed, wrinkled hands of the first Boula.

It was a male. The blood-curdling ululations of the women rose upward, vaulting against the arabesque-painted ceilings. Then began the rituals to ensure protection of the newborn and to ward off the evil eye. Lavender, sandalwood and boxwood were burned. Those wearing pearls removed them, for it was considered bad for the mother's milk and unfavorable for the birth of a second child. Boulas applied sugared oil to the infant's mouth, so "that he will have a sweet and amiable tongue." Then his eyes were painted with kohl so "that he may have beautiful lashes and a profound gaze." The child was held high in the air by the Chief Boula, who whispered a prayer that would place him under the protection of the archangels Gabriel and Michael. Naksh-i-dil's son was placed in a miniature quilted dressing gown, his limbs pulled straight down and tightly swathed. On his head was placed a cap of red silk with a tassel of seed pearls to which were attached a number of amulets against the fena guz, "the evil eye." He was placed in his silver cradle on a handsome red quilt, one corner of which was brought down over his head, and a veil of red gauze was thrown over all. Slowly each woman approached and laid a silver piastre on the silver cradle. A Koran, its cover encrusted with diamonds and pearls, was placed at his head. Naksh-i-dil was laid in the State bedstead used only on such occasions. It was spread with the richest quilts of the treasury, decorated with embroidery and sheets of fine red gauze with borders worked with red silk and gold thread. Half a dozen long red silk pillows covered with richly embroidered pillow cases were placed at the head of one side of the couch. A red kerchief was bound around Naksh-i-dil's head, and a veil of red gauze, to which were also attached amulets against the evil eye, was thrown over her temples. A head of garlic had been fastened to a stick propped up in a corner of the room.

The Kizlar Aga left to announce the birth, and shortly afterward, the cannon salute for a male child roared out. The celebrations of the birth of the still-unnamed Prince had begun. They would last for five days in a city illuminated day and night and festooned with garlands of flowers and sweetmeats. A miniature silver manger was placed at the palace door. A sherbet placed in crystal, held by a gold zarf, was sent to the new Grand Vizier. For three days and nights after the birth, no one was allowed to pass between the cradle and the braziers, lit by the midwives, which burned day and night. The child's name was not revealed so that a jealous woman could not place the evil eye on the newborn. After the third day, the infant's protection was assured by Allah. It was at this moment that Abdulhamid was allowed to see his son for the first time. In his immense joy, he had ordered illuminations and feasts unheard of before. Balls were held in the streets and loaves of bread and silver piastres were distributed to the population. Cannons roared day and night. One hundred white doves were released, and in the garden, an entire palace made of spun sugar and hung with colored lanterns was constructed. On the Bosphorus ships decked with flowers fired cannon salvos for five days. Flags and banners by the hundreds were flown while the crews of the entire fleet in port perched like flocks of birds on the mast. The Prince was named Mahmud.

"I never dreamed of such happiness so late," whispered Abdulhamid to his Seventh Kadine. "Allah be praised." He touched Naksh-i-dil's forehead and placed a kiss on her breast as he fondled his infant son. His tenderness touched Naksh-i-dil, although she knew that during her confinement he had taken a new Ikbal, Binnaz.

Naksh-i-dil was now almost twenty years old. She had survived an institution that had broken the spirit of all but the most resolute: Rushah, Sineprever, Hadidge. She had learned to pick her way through the minefield of physical dangers that was a court ruled by executioners and an arbitrary, suspicious and violent ruler, her husband. She had discovered the art of turning enemies into friends and spies into servants. She had never lost her heart to a man who had ceased to love her exclusively. But she had reached the position of supreme power and reverence in Islam—maternity.

Mahmud enchanted Abdulhamid, deprived as he had been of so many children. Hitabetullah had not only administered the medicines necessary and calculated the calendar that had resulted in the birth of Mahmud, but had protected her life from the first day. She had prevented deaths (or induced them) with her potions. How she kept her powerful hold over the population of the harem, neither Naksh-i-dil nor the Kiaya cared to know, any more than they cared to know about the fortune Hitabetullah was amassing.

Naksh-i-dil looked up into Hitabetullah's soft liquid brown eyes. Unfocused, and without a hint of rancor, they were the eyes of a dead woman. They had the same impermeability as granite, and were as unfathomable as a lagoon.

It had been one year ago. They had gone to the baths together. Hitabetullah had accidentally dropped the white cloth she always wore draped around her, and Naksh-i-dil had seen a long scar traced from the top of the V-shaped pubis to the opening underneath. For a moment, Naksh-i-dil had thought of the rigors of childbirth. . . .

"What did they do to you?" whispered Naksh-i-dil in horror.

"I am circumcised," she had replied. "From the beginning of time our women have been circumcised in the manner of the Phoenicians, the Hittites, the Ethiopians and the Egyptians. The Queen Nefertiti was thus circumcised."

"But," Naksh-i-dil had protested, "what does it mean? But what is this thing to which your race is submitted?"

"In my country," said Hitabetullah, "it is considered a mark of beauty . . . of property. . . . The heat, the perspiration, the continual brushing of clothes against the skin risk to excite . . . sexual desire —and so they remove our sex, close it. Otherwise, our mothers told us, we would have sicknesses, that this was the only way to preserve our health . . . besides, it was a sin to leave young girls to the temptations of Satan. . . ."

"But don't you realize that you are remaking the creation of God. It means that what God created is not *perfect.* It is as if you said, God, You have erred in Your creation of woman. You are wrong!"

Hitabetullah was very troubled by this. "But men are circumcised," she replied.

"But that is only a small piece of skin. They are not diminished or mutilated by it! Besides, the Koran commands neither one nor the other," said Naksh-i-dil with authority.

Hitabetullah was astonished at this. "I'm fifty-six-years old, excised in the Pharaonean manner . . . and my mother and her mother before her. Not to do so was to bring dishonor upon one's family."

"It is a sin against God," repeated Naksh-i-dil stubbornly. "It is even a kofr—an eternal blasphemy!"

"My mother said to leave her daughters in a state of nature would be to expose them to temptation . . . because it is a sensitive organ . . . the heat . . . the perspiration. Look at yourself in this mirror," Hitabetullah continued, holding a mirror between Naksh-i-dil's legs. "This is what a woman should look like." Then she had held the mirror to herself to show only a long scar and a tiny orifice the size of a matchstick. "The Pharaonean manner consists of the ablation of the clitoris, the small lips, the interior part of the large lips which are then sewn together." Naksh-i-dil tried to distinguish a feminine sex or something that resembled it but there was nothing that resembled anything she had seen in the baths, only a small closed plait.

"When I was seven years old, I was taken before the woman charged with its completion by my mother." Hitabetullah had taken a long breath as if she were about to plunge into an abyss from which she might never return. "When the sun began to set, the woman placed the leaves of a special kind of ortie [nettle] on each girl's kouss, which induced great swelling. My thighs were opened and held solidly by two matrons. The razor was cleaned in melted butter and my sex washed with butter and honey and then they proceeded. One may vow not to scream, but one always does. Once done, the pit of a date was placed in the opening to leave a place to urinate and to menstruate. The next day, the initiator seized and excised the swollen clitoris and all the flesh around it with a sharp knife. She then extracted from the flames a red-hot ember and applied it to cauterize the wound. At that moment precisely, great cries of joy arose from the women assisting, which also served to cover my screams. In this way there was no need to sew the wound together with acacia spikes and less chance of hemorrhaging.

"My legs were bound and tied from my waist to my knees. I was left several days stretched out on a mat, waiting for the scarring to take place. On the eighth day, I was allowed to join my friends during the season of excision and enjoy a big celebration. We took our first bath in the Nile while the drums played and songs filled the air and we were showered with gifts. The fortieth day, another ritual bath in the Nile was necessary. Five thousand years ago we sacrificed living virgins, now only virginal sexes. . . . Later we must be opened by our husbands by tearing. . . ."

Hitabetullah's voice had taken on a dreamlike quality. The sheen on her body from the steambaths had been augmented by the sweat that had popped out over her entire body, which was trembling violently. Tears flowed from her brown eyes. Naksh-i-dil could hardly see her servant through her own tears.

"But it is so unjust. . . ," Naksh-i-dil had begun.

"If by one chance in two, the urine passage had been blocked, the whole process had to be repeated. I was lucky. But my suffering was not over. On my wedding night my husband had to open me with the aid of a double-edged knife in order to possess me and impregnate me. He took me many times in order to open a way of access that would not reclose. Some husbands open and then sew their wives up again after every copulation. And when I finally gave birth, the same procedure had to be repeated to make enough space for the infant to pass. . . . But the thing I remember most was the old woman with a whip who stood beside me during the operation. When it was done, my mother cried out with joy, snapped the whip, and the others approached me, screaming and dancing, and forced me to dance."

Hitabetullah had stared at Naksh-i-dil through the haze of the baths and continued her narrative. "There is a circumcision which, if it is done with delicacy, does not affect the sexual pleasure of the woman. The second kind is excision, which eliminates all sensation. The clitoris is considered the organ of pleasure and therefore useless for reproduction. This is done to avoid all dissipation before and after marriage. And then there is what was done to me and practically all women of the Sudan and Egypt."

"You could have died . . ." cried Naksh-i-dil. Hitabetullah looked at her with something like contempt.

"A part of me did die that day forever. That part of me that lived as a female, full of hope and tenderness. My husband knew nothing of me, or even my children. Because in me, everything was dead . . . everything was empty. For I have never experienced pleasure or joy or comfort with a man. . . . It is God's will."

"No! *God* gave us ways to tell the difference beween salt and sour, bitter and sweet, hot and cold, the organs of men and the organs of women. If you destroy or mutilate this difference, kill its sensibility, you are taking away what God has given: pleasure. . . . You have made a woman inferior and less than 'a woman.' She is like a piece of wood," said Naksh-i-dil, remembering her conversations with Fatima.

"The men drug themselves to make the act last because their wives do not respond, and the women beautify their bodies with perfume and kofra, depilation . . . to keep their husbands happy, for he is the Sayed, the master," said Hitabetullah.

"But why? Why?"

"I don't know why. I don't know why."

Naksh-i-dil had reached over with trembling hands to bathe her face in cool water. What hatred and secret fear men had for women. . . . "How they must hate us all," she had whispered. She had known the violence of plantation life, the violence of harem life, but this violence perpetrated by women on women in the name of men seemed more than she could bear.

And as if in answer to Naksh-i-dil's unspoken question, Hitabetullah had added: "And what was I to do? Run away? Where? To become an outcast of my own tribe, my own village? An untouchable to my

mother, my sisters and all men? Not to have suffered this was to have
rejected the village, to have become a criminal in the eyes of my family,
future husband and for me, the world."

The Chief Black Eunuch paced up and down his apartments, his
yellow silk robes dragging on the blue-tiled floor after him like petals of
a daffodil. The death of Halil Hamid had been the sign he had been
waiting for. The Black Eunuch came to his decision. At the end of
Abdulhamid's reign, which, he read in the Sultan's face, would be soon,
he would tender his resignation, make his long-dreamed-of pilgrimage
to Mecca and retire to his estates in Egypt. His luck, his time, his very
heart had run out. His duty was to Allah now. And he was weary,
weary, weary of Topkapi's intrigues, the bloodletting. He was rich beyond measure, and he was alive, and he wanted to stay that way. In
anticipation of the harem bell that at any second would ring the hour of
prayer, he knelt on his prayer rug, turned the corner down and placed
his forehead to the ground, his arms outstretched. He would pray as he
always did, for Halil Hamid's soul and that of Fatima. Halil had been a
good man with a bad enemy, Hasan Gazi, and Hasan had won. . . .

His prayers over, the Black Eunuch returned to pacing up and down
ceaselessly, his thick fingers releasing pearl after pearl of his chaplet.
Beads of perspiration broke out on his forehead. The vision of his
paradisical retirement to Egypt, of his pilgrimage to Mecca, the enjoyment of his immense fortune and his well-furnished harem evaporated
like a mirage. The Black Eunuch bit his lip. And the little Naksh-i-dil
and her tiny Prince? What would become of them? And why, despite
himself, had he become so attached to them? Had it been Naksh-i-dil's
impulsive human gesture that first day? And if his *own* days were numbered, could he protect them? he wondered. Mahmud was a royal
Prince. His life and happiness were a matter of State. Naksh-i-dil was a
slave who counted for nothing in this world.

Edris Aga placed his writing table on his knees to calm himself. He
began to compose a poem. Now that his decision was made, a deep
serenity invaded him. He would be loyal to Abdulhamid for as long as
he survived. His brush flew over the whiteness of the page as his elegant
and perfect calligraphy sang across it. He envisioned the black-draped
square perfection of Mecca with milling hordes of white-gowned pil-
grims, the golden dome of the sanctuary which was haram, glistening in
the brilliant, sacred sunlight. He wrote:

La dina bi'l muruwali

There is no religion if not in virility . . .
I take my refuge in the Lord of David
Against the evil that He creates
Against the evil of a darkness when it
spreads itself
Against the evil of those who suffer on
burrs
And against the evil of the envious
who envy . . .

Why, mused the Kizlar Aga, was he so preoccupied with death? After all, Abdulhamid's reign had been less bloody than most.

Then he wrote:

Oh Lord, give me the daughters of Zanzibar
Who walk in ardent auras like those of the sun which burn
She disappears into her night and smiles into her dawn
I give her the power over my emptiness in search of flames
In search of Fire. . . .

Edris Aga put his head in his hands and wept.

The lonely young mother sat with her golden head, festooned with diamonds, bowed. Since her own world was lost to her forever, she would construct another for herself, here in Abdulhamid's library. It was the twenty-first of July, 1786, the day after Mahmud's first birthday.

She heard a harem gate close like the door of a convent. This place was now her convent, she decided. A place of worship and study, of devotion to Mahmud and prayer. The desires of the flesh would fall away as they did in true vocation, and eventually her body would no longer crave a man, a husband, a Sultan. One day she would no longer crave a caress, a tender touch, a rough possession.

Naksh-i-dil put down the Czarina Catherine II's Nakaz, the "Great Instructions." This French translation was in a way her inheritance from Fatima, for it was Fatima who believed in learning from one's enemies. . . . She had determined to read everything Catherine wrote and published, and to learn as much as she could about the powerful

Czarina. It was a kind of vengeance, stealing as it were the thoughts of her greatest adversary, whose armies threatened her husband's Empire. It was as if this rummaging for ideas, thoughts and weaknesses would give her clues to the Czarina's character: to her decisions of war and peace. She intended to know Catherine better than she knew herself.

Fatima's suicide had taught her how cheap life was in the Seraglio and how she must protect her precious new son. Hitabetullah was one guarantee. Knowledge of the outside world was another. The vow that one day she would be Valide would be her last. In order to teach Mahmud to rule, she must learn herself. And what better teacher than the greatest ruling despot of them all, Catherine II. Naksh-i-dil didn't think of the strongest and most potent of all her incentives to learn: fear.

What refuge did she have now except Topkapi? The pages of Catherine's Nakaz trembled between her clutched hands. The Nakaz was not a code of laws, but a compendium of the general principles of good government and an orderly society. Absolute power should be exercised within certain fixed and established limits. Fundamental laws, though few in number, are permanent and exist independently of the reigning sovereign. Power is limited. The arbitrary will of the ruler is limited by making the ruler and the State separate entities. In the chapters on crime and punishment, Naksh-i-dil read things that she had never heard of before—anywhere: No citizen should be punished until he had been proven guilty in a court of law; there was a difference between custody, investigations and imprisonment as punishment. Catherine condemned torture. Nobility was acquired and not innate; "the people should not be reduced to a state of slavery. . . ."

It was as if the Czarina were in the room with her; as if a predestined meeting had been arranged here in the twilight among the manuscripts of Abdulhamid. Naksh-i-dil knew she had to match the hatred and contempt the Empress felt for the Ottomans. With her own.

She would become more Turk than the Turks. She would have to forget where she came from in order to be what she vowed to be one day: ruler of all Moslem women. . . .

Mahmud must reform the Empire by snatching it from the state of slavery in which all its inhabitants were bound. One phrase of Catherine's rang in her ear like the harem bell and made her heart beat faster: "Russia will be a European state." This must be the cornerstone of Mahmud's life and rule. Turkey must one day be a European state, turned to the West rather than the East. How this was to be done and how long it would take, she had no idea. In a despotic society, time, just as life itself, had no measure.

Naksh-i-dil's trembling hands quieted. It was almost too much to bear—the hatred and the gratitude, the thirst for revenge and the recognition of true genius, the conviction of Catherine's evil and the longing for the power she held.

BOOK IV

CRIMEA
·1787·

• CHAPTER ONE •

KATHERINA KHAN 1784

In itself, all idea is neutral or should be; but man animates and projects his passion and his madness; impure, transformed in belief, it inserts itself in time, takes on the air of an event; the eclipse of logic is consummated. Thus is born ideology, doctrine and bloody farce.
—VOLTAIRE, *Essay on Tolerance*

The hardest blow to Abdulhamid had been the annexation of the Khanate of Crimea by Catherine in 1783. Russia had gained access to the Black Sea and the Khanate of Crimea had become a Russian protectorate. The Divan was no longer allowed to levy Christian slaves there.

The Crimea was almost an island, attached to the mainland by a narrow isthmus, the interior filled with the dead waters of lakes, mire and marshlands, and surrounded by the living waters of the Black Sea. Like nature, there were violent contrasts between the north and the south; to the north, vast plains frighteningly empty, steppes frozen by gale winds or burned by furnacelike heat; fields of grain, grasslands for sheep, cattle and camels. To the south facing the sea were miles of coast, beautiful low mountains with Tartar names, deep gorges, gracious bays and the lush sweetness of meridional Europe.

The Sultan had not been forced to accept the peace in so many words; he still held the Spiritual title of Khan. But Catherine had added eighteen thousand square miles to her Empire without firing a shot. The whole Khanate had been declared the new region of Tauris, the ancient Greek name for Crimea, and the Empress had given her favorite, Potemkin, the title of Prince of Tauris. Potemkin became the Viceroy of

South Russia and indisputable ruler from the Bug River to the Caspian Sea. Now, the Czarina set out to inspect her province.

At three o'clock on the afternoon of January 7, 1787, the white plains of snow in the winter sunset were crisscrossed by the fiery avenue along which the imperial cortege of Catherine, Empress of All the Russias, advanced. The Czarina had quit her northern capital, St. Petersburg, to journey to Sebastopol in the Crimea, the farthermost reaches of her domains and the frontier of the Ottoman Empire. The cortege had set out with 15 carriages, 124 sleighs and 42 other vehicles accompanied by 40,000 soldiers. The imperial sleigh was a veritable mansion on skates. Drawn by 30 horses, it contained a salon, library and office, walls all lined in furs. During the six days it would take to cover the two hundred miles, 560 fresh horses would be at each relay. And outside each city, townspeople would gather to greet the "Court on Wheels." The huge procession flew over the snow-packed roads, which were lit by immense birch torches by night. By day, there was only the broad expanse of dead white, broken solely by the grooved tracks of the innumerable sleighs.

Supposedly a festive tour, it was the political gauntlet thrown at the feet of Sultan Abdulhamid I by the new Prince of Tauris. Catherine had invited the whole of the diplomatic corps, Count Cobenzl, the Austrian Ambassador; the Austrian internuncio from Constantinople, Fritz von Herbert; the English Ambassador, Alleyne Fitzherbert; the French Ambassador, Count Ségur; the Prince de Ligne, Chamberlain of Austria; and Catherine's twelfth favorite, Alexander Mamonov. The travelers were bundled in sable, bearskins and beaver bonnets.

"Admit," said Prince Potemkin to the French Ambassador, who sat swathed in Persian lamb in his comfortable closed sleigh, "that the existence of Moslems is a virtual plague for humanity. If three or four great powers decided to ally themselves, nothing would be easier than to sweep the Turks back to Asia and thus deliver from that pestilence Egypt, the Archipelago, Greece and Eastern Europe. Would not such an enterprise be at once just, useful, religious, moral and heroic? Not to mention the fact that France would have . . . Egypt. . . ."

"My dear Potemkin," replied the urbane Count Ségur, staring at the one-eyed Prince, "life is more complicated than that."

"In fact, Count, I have never understood this strange and immoral political system that goes out of its way to support barbarians, brigands and fanatics who depopulate and devastate the vast territories they possess in Asia and Europe."

The Frenchman was silent and gazed pensively out of the glass window. He wondered if Potemkin really believed himself to be the opposite of a fanatic, a barbarian and a brigand.

"It is incredible," continued Potemkin, "that all the Christian Princes squander their help, prestige and reverence on a government that is barbarian, stupid, proud, and that despises us and our religion, our laws, customs and Kings to the point where daily we are called Christian dogs."

"Most honorable Potemkin," replied Ségur, not without a certain irony, "you are too wise and too enlightened not to sense that we cannot overthrow an Empire such as Abdulhamid's without dividing it, which would strain all our commercial interests, destroy the balance of power in Europe achieved after such long and cruel wars. . . ."

A political maneuver such as Catherine was undertaking was one thing, thought the Count, a religious war was another. "Besides," he continued, "it is as impossible to divide Constantinople as it is to find the philosophers' stone! Constantinople itself suffices to divide every single power you have to act together. Believe me, Prince, Emperor Joseph would never consent to see you master of European Turkey. He has never forgotten the turbans of Constantinople at the doors of Vienna, but he is even more afraid of Russian toques."

"We can always come to an agreement to destroy humanity, never to save it," said Potemkin, pouting.

On the ninth of February, the Empress arrived in Kiev, where she remained for nearly three months. Each foreign envoy had his separate palace, with its own furniture, porcelain and wine cellar. There was a succession of feasts and public welcomes from the wild Nogaus, Kalmuks and Kirghizes. Potemkin received Poles, Kurds, Georgians, Tartars and all the exotics of the Empire at his own court. Finally, on the third of May, the artillery cannons smashed the last ice sheets covering the Dnieper, and Catherine II embarked on seven specially prepared galleys, followed by eighty ships and three thousand troops, down the river. The galleys were wonders of comfort with sitting rooms, Oriental divans, silk hangings and orchestras for each ship. The Empress entertained on a second galley designed to seat up to sixty dinner guests. Small boats circulated continuously between the galleys, transporting fruit, wine, visitors and musicians. And all along the way, Potemkin had created illusions of a fertile land instead of desert, triumphal arches of flowers, serenades, military maneuvers and prosperous peasants instead of miserable slaves. Idyllic gardens and grottoes replaced desolate plains as if by magic. Young girls danced, the old and sick and the crippled were locked away; squadrons of Cossacks and Tartars emerged from the depths of Asia; enchanted palaces, temples of Diana, harems, nomadic tribes, all appeared from nowhere. Camels and dromedaries, towns, villages and country houses completely covered with flower wreaths sprang up from the desert. Huge herds of cattle dotted the grasslands.

Catherine was pleased beyond her wildest dreams. At every village she made a point of visiting the church, since she knew her peasants were so superstitious that they still set a place at their tables for Saint Nicholas. It was on Polish territory at Kaniev that Catherine had an unexpected meeting.

"Sima! My angel!"

The General Count Simon Zorich stood before her in all his splendor; his white and gold Hussar's uniform with the scarlet sash, his emerald-green-lined jacket fringed in ermine tails draped over one shoulder. His boots, burnished to a golden hue—the same color as his hair—glistened in the pale sunlight. Zorich's blue eyes mirrored an infatuation that denied the innumerable changes that had taken place in Catherine's appearance in eight years. Zorich saw her as he had always seen her, majestic, fascinating, intimidating and irresistible. Beside him stood his old comrade, Ishak Bey. When Zorich decided to join Catherine's cortege, he had begged Ishak, who was in Paris, to come give him moral support. This time Ishak had managed to arrive on time. The Empress smiled at the Beau Turque. Ishak bowed low and kissed her hand, but he wondered why the Czarina had chosen this moment to visit the Khanate of Crimea.

Catherine's weight strained the fastidious French robe she wore to disguise her heaviness. She looked at Zorich with pride. He had actually made a success of his military academy, and its renown had reached even St. Petersburg. He had been, she thought, the most beautiful, the most temperamental, and the dumbest of all her favorites. Ah, the lovely scenes he had made! Catherine lowered her eyes without rancor. He had no business here at all, but she did not have the heart to scold him . . . the absolute thunder of those eyes, that mass of wavy hair as thick as a lion's mane, *all* that Serbian beauty. It had all been hers, she thought. She had had his portrait painted a dozen times, but none had done him justice. Only this light, these steppes, this wildness matched his brilliance. If only he had been a *bit* more cultivated, she thought. She glanced at the sulking Mamonov.

"Little Mother," Zorich greeted her.

"Oh, how glad I am to see you . . . you look . . . you look wonderful."

"So do you."

"My dear."

"My dearest."

Count Simon Zorich did indeed look wonderful. Country life, far from the glittering balls and casinos of St. Petersburg, had done him good. Catherine gazed at him tenderly. Zorich took her hand, and she allowed him to kiss it.

She looked away from Zorich's eyes. She and he had become the center of attention. She was genuinely glad to see her beauteous General, for if she had ever not loved him, she had long forgotten why.

"Yes, yes, I know. You want to come back to Saint Petersburg. Well, yes. So be it. You may return. Your exile is commuted." She smiled her still lovely smile, and Zorich, moved beyond words, smiled back.

But it was Stanislaw Poniatowski, now King of Poland and former favorite, who was the most pathetic sight. "Stanislaw has spent three months and three million rubles to spend three hours with the Empress," snickered the Prince de Ligne.

It was true. The meeting between the two ex-lovers was the first since they had parted twenty-five years ago before the lynx eyes of a curious mob of malicious courtiers. But Catherine and Stanislaw seemed oblivious to everything but their sadness. The Empress and the King withdrew for a half hour. When they rejoined the entourage, they showed signs of embarrassment.

Thus Ishak and Zorich joined the army of survivors at Catherine's court. Ambassadors, ex-favorites, Kings, Generals and the new Prince Potemkin. If Zorich avoided Potemkin, Potemkin avoided King Stanislaw. Stanislaw avoided Mamonov and Mamonov avoided Zorich. Peace reigned.

Nine years after the founding of Kherson by General Ivan Hannibal, Catherine's cortege reached that city, rebaptized Ekaterinoslav, "The Glory of Catherine." A huge triumphal arch had been built with the inscription "The Road to Constantinople." Kherson was no longer the swampy wasteland Hannibal had found when he arrived to create a shipbuilding town in the middle of nowhere. The city now possessed 1,200 stone buildings and a population of 48,000, including 4,000 convicts. Catherine visited the dockyards Hannibal had built and inspected the warships she hoped would destroy Sultan Abdulhamid I.

The Czarina stood under the flower-decked double beams topped by an arrow, and stared out over the frighteningly empty steppes. Her heart was beating a bit faster after her meetings with Zorich and Poniatowski. She had long left them behind. Nine years. Twenty-five years. She was at the summit of her power. Nothing save death could stop her now. Old lovers like Stanislaw forgotten. Old favorites like Zorich forgiven. Old husbands like Potemkin producing miracles for her . . . Catherine's heavy body seemed to become lighter, straighter and narrower, as if by Potemkin's magic.

Her face, even when she was a young girl, had never been pretty, and now, with the weight of sixty years—twenty of those years as ruler of an empire of 11 million square miles and 111 million souls of which the most part were serfs—the mouth under the eternal smile was tight-lipped, hard and sensual. Catherine had abolished slavery in her Empire, but she had given away more than a million "State" serfs as presents. Her eyes, though sparkling with life and triumph, were cold. Her chin, decidedly too long, with age had become more prominent. While she had always prided herself on her femininity, she now nevertheless had a countenance of a male. But after being attractive to and attracted by so many men, of having lived so many passions, of inspiring such devotion which had withstood every test, she had no doubts of her charm, her power over men, her inquiring mind, her natural gaiety and her right to rule. . . .

She was Matushka Gosudarynya, "Little Mother" of her Empire, and she would be, she vowed, mistress of Byzantium. She turned toward the horde of courtiers approaching her, and she faced them; imposing, impenetrable, imperial, potentate. Absolute.

Her life was about to begin.

After each passage of the Czarina's big ships, the music faded, the "happy" peasants turned back into miserable serfs, the freshly painted "houses" remained false façades without roofs or walls, and Potemkin hastily dispatched the troops to serve in the next, upcoming decor. The new villages had been created along Catherine's route by the terror and ruin of several provinces. Money and lives had been squandered. Bands of serfs had labored and fifty thousand men had perished for an Empress's smile.

But just beyond the mouth of the river stood a squadron of Turkish warships under the command of Mahmud Pasha, and to his back loomed the imposing fort of Ochakov which blocked the Empress's route by sea. The magician Potemkin switched galleys for sleighs, turned the procession around and proceeded across the Crimea by land to Sebastopol and to the safety of the Russian fleet.

Overland the cortege advanced deeper into the Orient and the genius of the Prince became more extravagant than ever. Cities of multicolored tents covered the steppes of Nogali. Caravans of heavily laden camels made their way in endless file across the desert. In Bakhchisarai, the Mecca of the Crimea, Caucasian tribes played polo with a human skull on swift white ponies. And at last, Catherine sat upon the throne of the great Khans. But she and Potemkin had made a fatal error. They had misread their treaty with Abdulhamid.

The title of Khan, which they believed to be merely pontifical, was in fact, as far as Abdulhamid I was concerned, still his and he believed he still ruled.

The Empress reached the Crimea and Sebastopol in May. All along the route she and Potemkin had been greeted by cheering crowds, peasants and Cossacks. Catherine saw neither the unfinished houses, the starving peasants, the empty steppes, nor the cardboard ships and fake guns at Sebastopol, where fifteen warships and frigates lay anchored. As the procession approached, the sails were unfurled, guns fired and sailors cheered.

Abdulhamid drew his conclusions. In August, Humashah died. Thus, it was to the Kadine now elevated to her place of number four that Abdulhamid announced: "Naksh-i-dil, we have declared war on Catherine."

At the end of the winter of 1788, St. Petersburg scintillated in frozen opalescence. The city spread across nineteen islands, chained by arching bridges, laced by winding canals, garnished with unfinished stone palaces. To the northeast lay the dead white wild expanse of Lake Ladoga and to the west was the Gulf of Finland. Between them and frozen solid the broad shaft of the Neva River sliced the city down the center like an enormous ice scabbard. The northern shore was dominated by the red brick fortress of Peter the Great surmounted by a slim golden spire that soared like a note of music four hundred feet into the air above the fortress's cathedral. Stretching for three miles along the south shore was a solid red granite quay lined by the Winter Palace, the Admiralty, the embassies and the new Italian-style palaces of the nobility, including that of Ivan Abramovitch Hannibal.

The court ball had started at three, but it was already pitch-black. A polar wind that had traveled across the flat plains surrounding the city caught the uncovered leonine head of the Lieutenant General Ivan Hannibal as he stepped from the sleigh. The same wind lashed palaces, serfs and imperial platoons. The river Neva stood in ice nine feet deep, frozen as hard as tempered steel. Over the baroque golden spires of thousands of cathedrals, over the frozen canals, the strange aura of the northern lights mingled with the huge birchwood torches lighting the quay for one mile. The General's head bent against the almost physical wall of sub-Arctic temperature, the air full of invisible slivers of ice, battering into it as into a massed crowd, shoulder first, his dark skin ashen in the flickering torchlight. The southern colors stood out like painted gardens against the silver sky, the gray haze and the white Arctic latitudes which played tricks with light and time.

The General had arrived alone and now, cloakless, his tunic covered with decorations, his uniform jacket draped over one shoulder in the manner of the military and his Persian lamb toque under his arm, Hannibal pushed open the ballroom doors and waited until the tumult of the mazurka music subsided before being announced.

"His Excellency, Lieutenant General Ivan Abramovitch Hannibal, ex-commander of Kherson."

Catherine II had ordered a Te Deum and a court ball to celebrate the Russian fleet's victory over the Turks at Ochakov. The cries of "Peace" had greeted Lieutenant General Ivan Hannibal's sleigh as it drew up in front of the brilliantly lit palace.

The arrival of the handsome, black, immensely rich and unmarried son of Peter the Great's Negro always caused a stir. Hannibal's imposing figure, his mane of curly gray hair, his resplendent uniform, his letters of nobility and his incalculable fortune made more than one mother's heart leap with anticipation. At age fifty-one, and despite the efforts of the nation's matrons, widows and young eligible women, the retired Lieutenant General remained unmarried. It was one of the mysteries of the capital. He entered the ballroom surging with warmth from the huge porcelain stoves and the candles that topped the shimmering chandeliers. Officers in brilliant white and gold uniforms bristling with decorations and ladies in billowing white satin seemed to echo the whiteness of the northern lights outside. The mulatto General contemplated the bottles of champagne lined up before the lackeys, the buffets of cold sturgeon, creamed chicken, stuffed eggs and four kinds of caviar.

The General felt his blood tingling, despite his innate disdain for flesh, flash and anything French.

After paying respects to his hosts, Hannibal took a place near the banquet table and watched the milling crowd almost furtively under pensive heavy eyelids. He was an excellent dancer, and in a few moments he would throw himself methodically into the ball, but for the moment, his mind was melancholic. Russia was at war but nobody here, surrounded by laughter, perfume and human flesh, seemed to know it. One cannon shot would raze this ballroom, he thought, shatter bones and scatter blood and intestines all over these polished floors which gleamed like the white canals outside.

Hannibal flashed a white smile indiscriminately at a friend here, a Prince there; his heels clicked automatically in homage to a passing Princess or to a nodding Ambassador. Ivan Hannibal had a smile that was the mask of the Russian military—respectful but at the same time arrogant. He scrutinized the crowd with a mixture of wistfulness and condescending curiosity. What a sea of white shoulders and gold epaulets riding on the waves of white serge, red satin, black velvet, moiré silk and white mousseline. . . . He noticed the new cut of the ladies' gowns; the heavy capelike sleeves, the deep décolletés, the abundance of lace and pleats rather than ruffles, the enormous bell-like crinolines. Diamonds, emeralds and endless ropes of pearls scintillated in the steady glow of the chandeliers. The heavy scent of magnolias and gardenias from Georgia rose like a miasma around him, and he drew his breath inward as the scent filtered through the open ballroom windows, out over the snow-covered terraces, down into the endless gardens to the very river itself, frozen stiff and suspended in its flow toward the sea. His eyes stayed fixed on the hordes of chattering, laughing female guests making little turmoils of hot air with their ivory and lace fans. How they disordered everything, thought Hannibal, even the air around them. They had made bigamists out of his father, Abraham, and his two brothers, Pyotr and Osip. They had brought in their wake . . . dérangements, yes, complete madness and the opposite of all that he loved in life: order, honor, correctness, frugality, protocol, rank and war.

The warm ballroom, lit by ten thousand candles, was already deep in animation, awaiting the arrival of the Empress Catherine.

At the arrival of the Empress of All the Russias, Catherine, the aristocracy of St. Petersburg, festooned with gold, silver and multicolored silks, formed a double line and bowed as one. The exalting Empress, her triumph at Ochakov etched in a radiant smile, her voluminous body enveloped in silver cloth, glided between them. She was followed by General Potemkin and her new favorite, twenty-eight-year-old Alexander Mamonov. He was blond, virile, and his amused expression and generous mouth were as shrewed as his eyes, fringed in long black lashes, were astute. Hannibal liked him, that is, as much as one could like any of the Empress's creatures. He was, thought the General, the most cultured and intelligent of Catherine's young lovers; while hardly a Zorich, he was well educated, fluent in French, fond of music, witty, and passionate without ambition. It was rumored that poor Mamonov had fallen hopelessly in love with a young Princess and was finding his life with Catherine burdensome. The aging Empress propelled her heavy body forward through the crowd like an icebreaker plowing a frozen sea. Her spacious bosom was completely covered with a square meter of pearls, her head weighted down by a ruby tiara. No, everything was not as calm and triumphant as this ball. The Ottoman Empire was weak, but not prostrate.

Since Abdulhamid's declaration of war in '87, neither side had taken offensive action until the spring of the year the deadlock had been broken, when the imperial troops had occupied Bosnia and northern Moldavia. Then Ochakov had fallen. The Czarina had reason to celebrate. But Catherine's penchant for foreign Admirals had led to a colossal quarrel between the German Prince Admiral Nassau-Siegen and the American hero Captain John Paul Jones, whom he now spied across the room alone.

Hannibal considered Jones a corsair at best and a pirate at worst. He also had the reputation of a womanizer of very little couth. Most of the Russian and English officers had refused to serve under him. Hannibal ducked behind a gold and white column as he saw the Admiral making straight for him.

John Paul Jones ran his hands through his black, curly, unpowdered hair. Jones was a Scot, but a dark one with black curly hair and marine-blue eyes. His face was as ruthless as it was handsome, a combination that had cursed him with success and catastrophe with both women and men. The large, rather common face with its wide-spaced candid eyes, generous flared nose and high cheekbones belied the lower part of his face, which was virile and inflexible. Paul Jones flexed his body, which was of medium build and finely proportioned. His catlike walk was a remnant of spending almost all his forty-one years on moving vessels. So, he thought, Potemkin had won. . . . The Major General thought of the man he had come into so much conflict with, from their first meeting at St. Elizabeth to their last, just a few days ago. Potemkin was colossal, like Russia itself. Potemkin's mind, like his country, had cultivated districts and desert plains. In a word, he mused, even Potemkin's eyes, the one that saw and the one that was blind, knew it was he, John Paul Jones, who had defeated the Ottoman fleet, not Nassau, whose bravado was resounding throughout the courts of Europe. Nassau, who had been promoted two grades, had been given a valuable estate and several thousand serfs! All he had received, thought the distraught American, was the measly Order of St. Anna, which was not even a Russian decoration but German!

Order to our Admiralty College,
Having admitted Captain Commander Paul Jones to our service, we have graciously commissioned him as Captain of our navy with the rank of Major General and we have ordered him assigned to our Black Sea navy, and to that effect, we have issued an order to General Field-Marshal Prince Potemkin Tavrichesky.

E. Katerina, Czarina, 1788

This had been Catherine's answer to his pleas to prepare a brilliant campaign against the Turks: Major General!
"If Her Imperial Majesty entrusted to *me* the chief command of her fleet in the Black Sea, with a free hand . . . in less than a year, I should make Constantinople tremble," said John Paul Jones out loud to no one in particular, offended at Hannibal's deliberate rudeness.
John Paul Jones wandered off into the dazzling crowd, unaware that he had missed his last chance to greet the Empress and explain himself to her. For Catherine had in the sleeve of her ballgown a police report that effectively destroyed the career of the ambitious "Kontradmiral Pavel Ivanovich Jones":

I have seized four letters that will shatter two lives: I have seized four love letters of the Princess Anna Mikailovna Kourakina to the Admiral Jones and three letters of his to her, hereby enclosed: it is evident that they will not be able to communicate one with the other since the Princess has been sent to the Convent Novo-Devichy to await the birth of her child.

Count Beckendorf, Chief of the Secret Police

"You look worried, my General."

Ivan Hannibal looked up, surprised. The Empress and her entourage had stopped before him without his even knowing it. He bowed deeply and clicked his heels. "Only for your health and happiness, Majesty."

"You have been one of their most brilliant defenders, my Lord."

"I hope you remember me as one who did his duty. . . ."

"The hero of Chesme, the founder of the Kherson fortress. . . ?" The Empress laughed. "Where even now new ships are being put to sea? You mock me, my General."

The General bowed. The Empress moved on. The ball began.

Ivan Hannibal's eyes followed the solitary, rather pathetic figure of John Paul Jones. He was being unfair to the man, he thought. The Battle of Ochakov had proved him to be an admirable man. Why, then, could he not bring himself to admire him? "I wish to have no connection with any ship that does not sail fast: for I intend to go in harm's way," the Kontradmiral had said. And that is exactly what he had done. . . .

The Battle of Ochakov had inspired Hannibal's awe for the Kontradmiral Pavel Ivanovich Jones. At Ochakov, the Ottomans had outnumbered the Russians in ships and guns two to one. It had been in June a year ago, in the Liman estuary. The Russian fleet had drawn up in a line across the Liman about four miles east of Ochakov. The Lord Admiral, Pasha Hasan Gazi, had placed a detachment of his fleet inside the entrance. The first battle had begun on the sixth of June at two, mused Hannibal, with the German Prince Charles of Nassau-Siegen and John Paul Jones trying to cut off Gazi's retreat, but they had been chased back to their positions. The Lord Admiral had then committed almost his entire small-craft flotilla and part of his squadron, drawing them up during the night in two divisions close to the north shore. Favored by a northwesterly breeze, he had attacked Kontradmiral Jones's right flank. Pavel Jones himself had rowed along his front line, bellowing into his megaphone, trying to get the entire Russian fleet into action against strong headwinds. Hasan Gazi himself had arrived in a swift lateen-rigged galley. The *Kirlangitch* carried fourteen guns and began to punish the right side of the Russian line, but an unlucky change of wind easterly had enabled Pavel Jones to move five ships of his left wing into a right angle and bring the Lord Admiral Pasha under crossfire. Gazi had fallen into Jones's trap and lost two or three ships from firing licornes, charged with incendiary missiles.

Ten days later, on the sixteenth, the entire Ottoman fleet had gotten under weigh with a fair southwest wind and sailed into the estuary, determined to sink the Russian fleet and burn Kontradmiral Jones's squadron. And an impressive sight they were, thought General Hannibal, who was also an Admiral, under full sail with tall lateens spiraling among the square-riggers. They had come, before the wind, bearing down on the Russians with trumpets braying, cymbals clashing and loud cries to Allah for help in slaughtering the unbelievers, wine-drunken and pig-eaters. But, thought Hannibal, a naval battle was not a horde of Tartars sweeping down from the steppes of Asia Minor, yelling. . . . Because the situation suddenly changed. The Lord Admiral Pasha's sixty-four-gun flagship ran aground about a mile and a half from Kontradmiral Jones's flagship, the *Vladimir.* The rest of their fleet had then anchored in disorder. Prince Nassau hadn't detached at once, and the wind had veered to strong northwest, placing the Ottoman fleet directly windward so that neither the sailing nor the rowing vessels of Admiral Nassau's squadron could make headway.

It was only much later that the story of that night became legend, mused Hannibal. Rear Admiral Jones had made a personal reconnaissance of the Turkish fleet. In a small boat with a Russian sailor who spoke Turkish, he had rowed into the anchored squadrons! In due course, they had been challenged by two Ottoman frigates, but these had been manned by Crimean Cossacks with whom the Admiral's sailor could speak. The sailor had then gotten the countersign for the night by pretending he was bringing salt to Hasan Gazi's flagship and needed it to get by. When Jones had reached the ships, the password for the night had been given and he had answered. From there he had darted among the Ottoman and Algerian squadrons like a seagull. Some had threatened him, some let him through silently; here he crawled, there he swooped. Thus Pavel Ivanovich had approached Hasan Gazi's stern and held on to it. He had stood up in the boat while his sailor asked if the Ottomans' Lord Admiral Pasha didn't want some salt. "This is the one," Kontradmiral Jones is reported to have said. While the Cossack was haggling with the cook on board, Pavel Ivanovich Jones drew a large "X" with white chalk over the gilded insignia of the Lord Admiral, which seemed to say:

TO BE BURNED JOHN PAUL JONES WAS HERE

The next morning Jones positioned all the ships on the right flank of his line toward the center so that they made an angle with the left flank toward which Hasan Gazi was steering, hoping to squeeze the Russians in a vise as he had tried in the first battle. Hasan Gazi advanced to the attack. Meanwhile, the wind changed to northwest, affording the Russians a lucky break. A terrible mêlée followed without rhyme or reason. Hasan Gazi's fleet was undisciplined, his peasant sailors were impossible to control; only the Algerians fought systematically. First the Ottoman Vice Admiral's ship ran aground. Then, almost comically, Gazi's ship ran aground again, listing so that his guns couldn't fire. Their whole fleet had turned against the two stranded Turkish ships and completely destroyed them with licornes instead of boarding them. He guessed that it was Nassau, not Jones, who had been afraid of hand-to-hand battle.

Meanwhile, the Russians' main line had gone unprotected and the Algerians had sunk the *Aleksandr* with incendiary bombs. The Russians were losing. . . . But the chaloupe (longboat) of Jones arrived and managed to drive Gazi's fleet back into the mouth of the Liman, the estuary of the Black Sea formed by the Dnieper and Bug rivers, that night. And when on the night of the seventeenth, the Lord Admiral Pasha had tried to withdraw the rest of his ships from the mouth of the Liman estuary, the Russian batteries on Kinburn Point had opened up and so confused the Ottoman fleet that nine vessels were grounded. The Russians then burned seven of the Ottomans' grounded ships with licornes and captured two others. What an undisciplined massacre! thought Hannibal. In two days' fighting the Ottomans had lost 10 large and 5 small vessels, 1,673 prisoners and 3,000 men. The Russians had lost only one ship, the one the Algerians had sunk, and no men. Kontradmiral Pavel Ivanovich Jones had taken the day, thought Hannibal. Gazi had anchored under the ramparts of Ochakov. Potemkin had brought his army across the Bug River and attacked Ochakov by land and by sea. In the thick of the fight, Pavel Jones's chaloupe had directed the rescue of a Russian frigate carried outward by the current. Then Jones had taken the chaloupe out ahead of his fleet and seized five Algerian galleys. The American had then boarded the nearest galley himself and had it towed out of danger. Next he boarded the Lord Admiral Pasha's own galley, but again that stupid fool Nassau had bungled the towing and had instead set it on fire. . . . The galley had burned with all the wretched galley slaves still chained to the thwarts.

Potemkin's land army had by then begun the siege of Ochakov, while the Russian fleet had bombarded Ochakov. Gazi the Victorious had lost again, Hannibal chuckled. In October, Hasan Gazi broke through the

Russian blockade with a reinforced fleet, but it had been too little too late. Ochakov had fallen on the sixth of December.

The Admiral Lieutenant General Hannibal watched the whirling, swaying couples dancing the polonaise, the flickering amber lights of thousands of candles. He even saw the imperial orchestra playing, so he wondered why he heard no sound, like the silence after a great battle. Had he suddenly gone deaf?

Outside, surrounding the light, there was only pitch darkness. And in Ochakov 50,000 frozen corpses waited in bundles of 100 for burial when the thaw would make it possible to dig the mass grave in the spring.

• CHAPTER TWO •

THE SULTAN 1788

> The perfect condition of *slavery* is nothing else but the state of war
> continued between a lawful conqueror and a captive.
> —JOHN LOCKE, 1690

Snow covered the roofs of Topkapi. It hung crystalline on the branches of the plane and cypress trees, slid in avalanches off the roofs of the kiosks and the galleries, and whitened the dome of Aya Sofya. The winter silence deepened even more the silence of the harem. The blanket of white muted even the voices of the inmates as it softened frozen fountains in the gardens and courtyards. Her apartment was draped with furs and wall hangings. Excursions into the countryside were a memory until spring. The lack of proper clothing made it impossible for anyone to venture outside except the Kadines and Ikbals, who had the fur-lined caftans of their ranks. Slaves and servants froze on their journeys to and from the kitchens. The high grilled windows were not sufficient to ventilate the rooms and dormitories, and the air became close and fetid. The smells of perfume, incense, food, charcoal, tobacco and hashish all mingled together into one overwhelming scent. Naksh-i-dil's apartment was regularly sprinkled with orange blossom or rose water. It was dark outside, and Naksh-i-dil lay back on her cushions half asleep. Gradually she became conscious of a low, murmuring song, and opened her eyes to meet those of Hitabetullah.

"May the night be a happy one for you, Kadine Hanum," said Hitabetullah, her dark eyes meeting those of Naksh-i-dil.

"Is it late?"

"The Sultan, your master, awaits you," replied Hitabetullah. "I was coaxing your spirit back into your body with my song."

Abdulhamid sat cross-legged on the high dais, waiting for his Fourth Kadine. He was dressed in a simple white robe edged in ermine, a green turban perched on his head around which torsades of white gauze were wound and held in place by an aigrette in the form of a branch of leaves and flowers from which shot the stem of a heron feather. He watched her enter the room not without a tremor of excitement. Not since his first love, Rushah, had a woman remained so indelibly in his heart and mind. Naksh-i-dil was like Rushah Sultane in many ways, thought Abdulhamid, intelligent, proud, opulent in both flesh and feeling, astute, mercilessly hard, tough and courageous. Mahmud was now three years old; robust and healthy, Allah be praised. Mahmud was his reward, he thought, for he had been patient, generous and indulgent to the point of stupidity as far as Naksh-i-dil had been concerned.

Abdulhamid fingered the Persian dagger at his waist. He was small, well proportioned and prematurely aged with white skin. His large expressive black eyes were never still. A wide forehead and a narrow hooked nose gave his face a falconlike appearance. A brilliant, dyed-black beard hid a large, generous mouth, full of beautiful teeth. Abdulhamid's rare smile was melancholy. His movements were slow, proud and indolent. He spoke little and gesticulated not at all. His voice was deep and sweet. A simple man, intellectually impoverished, yet exact in his expressions. His character had been formed by the solitudes and ignorance of the world around him. Yet, lacking imagination, his judgment was sound. Lacking sophistication, he was rarely duped, for he could become wily and cunning if betrayed in his affections, which were loyal and passionate.

The Sultan regarded love as a sort of cruel sickness through which the elect were required to pass, and from which one emerged pale, wronged and defeated (through the weakness of love, he had allowed Rushah her pilgrimage to Mecca. He had lost her through error). There was—mercifully, he thought—a great repertory of errors impossible to those who recovered from the illness of love. Unfortunately, there remained also a host of failings as well, but at least he never again regarded any human being as a mechanical object, and he never again mistook servility for the whole conduct of life.

He was afraid of everything in a world in which he was the absolute despot. A world which seemed more hostile to him than to the lowliest slave. As Sultan, he spoke only in grave circumstances and only when he could make men tremble.

Sultan Abdulhamid was the last of the five sons of Ahmed III. He had survived his other four brothers. He had come to the throne in 1774 at the age of fifty-one to rule a degenerating empire. His nobles assumed that the supremacy of Ottoman ways would magically keep the Empire's enemies at bay, but he knew better; inflation, plague, food shortages, overcrowded cities, roving bandits, and insubordinate notables, Deys and provincial Governors prevailed throughout the Empire. In Egypt, Syria, Iraq and Algiers, the Beys had practically affirmed their independence. He held on to his power by the only means open to him: pitting one man against another, one political faction against another; changing ministers, using bribery, terror, execution or exile. Yet his Empire had known only humiliation. Against his better judgment, he had let himself be swept into a new war with Russia. Out of vanity and honor, his new Grand Vizier, Mussum-Oglou, had thrown an army of 400,000 men against Catherine. But the Russians had triumphed everywhere, led by formidable Generals whose very names were daggers in his heart, Solvokov, Kamensky, Rumyantsev.

Abdulhamid shifted his weight uncertainly. No more than four months after being crowned over fourteen years ago, he had been forced to treat with Catherine, open his seas, recognize the independence of the Tartars. But even this hadn't been enough for the greedy Catherine. . . . A state of war had existed between them for fourteen years now, which he suffered in silence, his government helpless, overwhelmed, not daring even to murmur against the Russian aggressiveness. And now, Ochakov. Russia defeated him. The European powers defeated him. Rushah had defeated him. Even nature had defeated him. Of all the royal births, thirteen in all, only two living sons remained, Mustafa, barely nine, and Mahmud, barely three. He had lost territory just as he had lost his own physical powers, as if one were metaphysically attached to the other. His doctors did everything to maintain his virility, but however avid he was for the joys of this life, they were escaping him. He reached out for Naksh-i-dil's hand.

He had possessed ten wives, seven Kadines and three Ikbals. Rushah, of course, Humashah, Ayşe Sineprever, Benigar, Mehtap, Hatice, Fekti-Seza, Fatma-Shebsefa, Naksh-i-dil and Binnaz. They had given him twenty-two children, ten sons and twelve daughters. His first son, born in 1776 by Humashah, had also been called Mahmud and had not survived his fifth year. A new Princess had been born only a few days ago, to Fekti-Seza. But daughters didn't count in this world. Seventeen of his children hadn't survived infancy. Only Mustafa and Mahmud, and, Allah willing, more sons to come, counted. Life flowed like a river and only in one direction, from cradle to grave, from its unknowing source into the boundless, eternal sea. No doctor, no Odalisque, no Kadine in the world could change that. Moreover, there was no end to it, mused the Sultan. How he regretted the death of Halil Hamid, Fatima's father. But he had had no choice. It had been a necessary death for reasons she could never know. Halil Hamid had been implicated in a foreign conspiracy against him. Abdulhamid fingered his tespi; the worry beads of gray amber fell in droplets.

"You are thinking about the Russians," said Naksh-i-dil.

"I am always thinking about the Russians," replied the Sultan.

Naksh-i-dil gazed at Abdulhamid. "Without speaking of love," Fatima had once said, "one could tell oneself a thousand things; one could reproach oneself, give oneself advice, warnings, news—this is the great occupation of the harem. Not to speak of love, but to learn its symbolic vocabulary and compose with it long, endless conversations." Naksh-i-dil had mastered the terms for sexual conjunctions, which numbered one hundred: mash, violent; za'ab, pouring forth to exhaustion; da's wa-'ard, piercing through and through mean, rough; hakk wa-hawn, pounding and grunting, denoting vigor; visa, resemblance to a small bird as it treads the female; fahz, the act with one girl in one room while another girl in another room listens to the sound; khawq, the act with a girl where one can hear the noise of going in and out; if hāk, lying down with one girl and finding felicity in another. She had learned that there was no concept of adultery in Islamic law, since a woman has no exclusive right to the person of her husband. "I commend to you fair treatment of your womenfolk for they are your prisoners . . ." said the Prophet. And never had she felt so much the captive. Never had she felt Abdulhamid's desperate clinging to his calendar of the impossible, his youth.

The Sultan sighed. He sensed Naksh-i-dil's hatred. There was nothing to be done, he thought. A man never entered his harem as a husband, that is, as a friend, a companion, a parent of his children; he entered only as a lover. He left at the threshold every thought that might trouble the pleasure he sought; every part of himself that had *nothing* to do with the desire. He entered his harem to forget his worries, his grief, and moreover, to anesthetize all sentiment; not to demand comfort from a serene spirit or consolation from a loving heart. Yet

Naksh-i-dil insisted upon this, much to his confusion. When he wanted consolation, he sought it from a man. Women were not made for that role. When would Naksh-i-dil understand this? If she ever would understand it. She always seemed to be . . . present, asking, willing, thinking. He had no need to think, surrounded as he was by a halo of glory, of brilliance, of science, of power. He was Allah's Shadow on Earth. Adoration was his due. Yet Naksh-i-dil seemed to expect *something* . . . to command it, wordlessly. His preference for her alone should be sufficient for her to accord him that sentiment of gratitude resembling love, or at least the kind of love he desired. However, she stubbornly did not accord it, holding on to her extravagant Western ideas. . . .

"What are you thinking?" asked Naksh-i-dil.

There, thought Abdulhamid, no other Kadine in his harem would dare pose such a question! And she *always* did it.

"Why," he asked, genuinely puzzled, "should you wish to know what I think? What need do you have of it? Why should I be thinking of anything at this moment?"

"Because men always think of *something,*" replied Naksh-i-dil, "even other women."

The Sultan rose on one elbow and surveyed his Fourth Kadine. "Do you know what we call women in our language?" he asked.

"Yes. 'The Veiled One.' 'The Hidden One.' 'The Foreigner.' "

"There can never be true thoughts between men and women because of this; because there is always a veil of senses that hides the infinite and abject difference of men and women. You understand this, Naksh-i-dil?"

"I don't believe that."

"Yet it is true. You belong to me. For you come from nowhere, like everyone in Topkapi, and you leave nothing behind you, for all returns to me, your Sultan and master to whom you owe love because only he can protect you."

Abdulhamid touched the nape of Naksh-i-dil's neck lightly. He had such power over this . . . this *foreigner.* He could if he wished crack her skull with his two hands, pierce her breast with the dagger at his side, close his strong hands around the white column of her neck. He could abandon her to the Eski Serai, have her burned at the stake, strangled by the Bostanji, slit with the saber of the Black Eunuch just outside the door, or poisoned by an Obadachi tonight, or tomorrow. Yet, he had engendered new life in this helpless body, his beloved Prince

Mahmud. His hand caressed Naksh-i-dil. Life. Life instead of death. This too was possible, he thought.

Lines of worry, fatigue and age were etched in his face, and the flickering light made deep shadows of his kohl-lined eyes and the gray pockets of flesh underneath them. The struggle was against the death of his own nature; his belief that his power lay only in his virility. His panic and fear resulted in his desperate search for still another aphrodisiac . . . still more pornography in order to prove that he still lived; that if he chose to speak, he could make men tremble. He confused the Empire with his own body. The trouble was he still needed an Empire of fresh slave flesh.

Could one not conclude that a man who had never been out of the Seraglio lacked the intuition of half the women in it? wondered Naksh-i-dil. She leaned over to serve the Sultan his coffee.

"Mahmud's hair will be cut soon and sent to Mecca. Soon he will be circumcised and put into the Prince's Cage," she said.

The coffee had already been brought in by a slave. The gold coffeepot was placed on hot cinders held in a small golden basin suspended by three chains attached at the top. The slave held the sitel by the extremities of the chains, being careful not to allow it to drag on or touch the floor. Two other slaves held a golden tray on which rested the delicate cups held in chalice-shaped goblets called zarfs. Naksh-i-dil always caught her breath at the sight of Abdulhamid's zarfs, engraved in gold and encrusted with diamonds, pearls, sapphires, coral and jade. On the tray was an embroidered silk rug. One corner of the rug was slightly folded inward, two others were held in the palms of the slave girls' hands, while the fourth fell triangularly toward the floor. Naksh-i-dil took the cup from the tray and placed it carefully upon the zarf. She then took the handle of the coffeepot with a small quilted napkin and poured the coffee. As delicately as possible, she took the stem of the zarf in her right hand and placed the base of it on the tip of the index finger of her left hand and held it steady with the pressure of her thumb. In a gesture of skill and grace, she handed it to Abdulhamid. The delicacy and the handling of each precious object during the slow ceremony pleased Naksh-i-dil. The automatic gestures of serving coffee soothed Naksh-i-dil's mind. She remembered with pleasure her apprenticeship with the Cahvedjiousta, the First Mistress of the Coffee. The coffee, as thick as chocolate and sweetened with honey, reminded her of home and the odor of boiling sugarcane. . . . With a flourish, she removed her thumb, and balanced the zarf on the tip of her index finger without a tremor. This was the prelude to their insatiable games of gammon, which led inevitably to Abdulhamid's insatiable taking of her body. They began to play.

Naksh-i-dil's game was swift and ruthless. Her long hands flowed over the open mother-of-pearl and ebony twelve tables board. Speed was everything. The dice had hardly touched the black-and-white saw-toothed surface, and her pieces were in place. Abdulhamid looked up in amazement at his Kadine. Her red-gold hair was held back in a net of cords and diamonds, giving her a severe, even masculine allure. Her azure-green eyes squinted unattractively in concentration. They had begun the thirty-second consecutive game of the night. Abdulhamid yawned. There were limits. He had initiated her into playing for money and he hated to think of the sums he had lost to her. Naksh-i-dil had earned a fortune by gambling with him. She was undoubtedly the best player in the harem. She even played with the Black Eunuch, who was the finest player in Istanbul. Naksh-i-dil smiled in satisfaction, her small white teeth glistening in the light of the oil lamps placed nearby. She loved to win.

A woman, thought the Sultan, who liked war games as a formidable opponent in or out of bed. She had gained ascendancy over Ayşe Sineprever. He loved her. And she was a courageous and astute gambler. Cold-bloodedness and piastres rarely went together and one could lose one's head more easily at gammon, a swifter game, than at cards. He had noticed that women, after tasting the joys of gambling, became more intoxicated and more passionate than even their most ardent male counterparts. He used their games as a prelude to lovemaking because they excited Naksh-i-dil even more than him. He watched Naksh-i-dil's eyes. He saw greed, an attribute he detested in a woman except for the greed of jewels. He clasped Naksh-i-dil's hand in his.

"It is time to stop, Naksh-i-dil, it is nine o'clock."

"Of course." She smiled. She had won over a hundred piastres.

Abdulhamid took out his pillbox and slipped a gold-coated opium pill into his mouth. He offered one to Naksh-i-dil, who shook her head silently.

Only on occasion would she condescend to accept opium. She was not as addicted to the drug as she was to winning his money. The Sultan smiled. Their games were the only thing that took his mind off the war he was losing. He was satiated with the flesh of hundreds of women, the blood of thousands of soldiers he had sent to die, the tribute of millions of souls for whom he was responsible and whom he had taxed to the utmost of their endurance, even their survival. Neither his power nor the Empire's wealth was infinite. He felt the walls of both closing in on him.

He reached out and took the edge of his wife's gomlek between his thumb and forefinger and opened it, revealing the snowy-white, blue-veined breast beneath the transparent gauze. He did not touch her. Her nipple rose immediately as if by magic. It was one of Naksh-i-dil's incredible feats, and the Sultan felt himself stir. Naksh-i-dil allowed the Sultan to unveil the other breast, still without touching any of the succulent whiteness before him. The Sultan remained motionless. The gauze of the gomlek opened like a theatrical curtain on her perfect bosom. Naksh-i-dil lifted her arms and placed her hands behind her head, lifting her chest. The Sultan blew gently upon the rouged nipples still without a touch. She sat cross-legged, contracting and pressing hard against the soft cushions beneath her. In a moment's concentration, she had drawn in the lips of her kouss in a climax, gasping and clutching her husband's shoulders. The blood rushed visibly to the exposed whiteness that arched toward the Sultan's hungry lips. With a low groan, he pressed his Kadine back upon the myriad of cushions and pillows, still without touching her now aching breasts. He opened her shalwar slit in the center, exposing the shaven white mound and the silky vermilion cleft now contracting a second time. He brushed them with his lips and eyelashes, bringing a groan of pleasure. He entered her and simultaneously brought his burning mouth to her breast.

He felt the interior dialogue of her kouss, which seized and released him, supporting his moments of weakness with their contractions, giving him the illusion of a vigorous power he no longer possessed. She was his favorite.

Naksh-i-dil released her hair with one hand, and thrust upward violently, triumphantly providing her Lord his pleasure in the slowly breaking morning. Abdulhamid cried out as he moved within her, reaching her center, her left and her right, his erection held by the opium and the unexpectedness of his desire for the sumptuous flesh beneath him. The two slaves watched silently in the corner, ready to spring forward with whatever service was necessary to the copulating Sultan and his Kadine. The games had so excited Naksh-i-dil that her reactions to her Lord's lovemaking were more than genuine; the familiar sensations that had been revealed to her so long ago by this same Lord and master. She brought to bear again and again until they were both exhausted. Abdulhamid lifted his weight from the full figure beneath him and turned her. One of the slaves washed him and applied an ointment. He entered his Kadine from the rear, pressing her sides with the open palms of his hands in rhythm with his own sharp movements. At a sign from Naksh-i-dil, her slave, Issit, pressed a gold-coated opium pill into her outstretched hand. Naksh-i-dil swallowed the opiate, allowing it to take possession of a body which did not belong to her, and a mind which did.

• CHAPTER THREE •

NAKSH-I-DIL, 1789

> Ramadan ends when one can no longer distinguish
> a white thread from a black one.
>
> —The Koran

When Abdulhamid died, the frozen bodies at the gates of Ochakov had not yet begun to thaw.

Naksh-i-dil knelt alone under the cupola of her husband's kiosk as Hitabetullah entered to warn her that the procession of mourners was on its way. The Kadine turned violently upon her.

"You promised," said Naksh-i-dil to Hitabetullah in a voice of steel. "You guaranteed the Sultan's safety and that of Mahmud! I *bought* you to keep them alive. Alive! They have killed the Sultan, poisoned him. . . ."

Hitabetullah turned on Naksh-i-dil coldly. "I say your Sultan died of heartbreak, my Lady, not poison. If anyone killed him, the Russians did."

Naksh-i-dil stared at her. Hitabetullah was holding Mahmud's hand. She looked down at her son for a moment and then asked her slave to take him from the room. She would never tell Mahmud what she suspected. She refused to see her son grow up like Catherine's Paul, in the belief that his father had been murdered. She looked down at the dissipated white face set in rigor mortis. In one hand she held a tespi and in the other, a rosary. The ninety-nine amber beads of the tespi weighed ten times heavier in her trembling hands. Naksh-i-dil looked from her husband to the beads. If the Oriental rosary represented safety, power and perhaps even divinity, the title of Valide, Diadem of the Veiled Heads, the other represented eternal damnation. And if the Occidental rosary represented the white race, salvation, civilization, all that she had believed in that now fictional Christian world, the other represented exile, slavery, martyrdom and eternal damnation. The Kadine brought her hands together in supplication, the two ropes of beads, one amber and the other ivory, colliding and intertwining one with the other like the worlds they symbolized. Naksh-i-dil made a sound much like that of a frightened, cornered small animal, a cheetah perhaps, or a desert fox.

On Tuesday, April seventh, 1789, Edris Aga had arrived at dawn, his face gray with fatigue and grief, his eyes red-rimmed, his huge bulk moving through the labyrinth of corridors of the harem like a wounded animal, swaying to and fro. He appeared to be roaming through the halls at random rather than making his way toward the Prince's Cage. He entered the Kafes and prostrated himself.

"Your Highness, Allah's Shadow on Earth. By the will of Almighty God, the throne of your ancestors awaits you. Come see the dead body of your uncle."

With these words Selim knew he was the new Sultan.

The twenty-eight-year-old Selim rose, his dark blond hair falling loosely around the angelic face that resembled his Circassian mother, Mihrishah. The dark green caftan he wore flew open with his movement, and he clutched it to him as if in protection as he followed Edris to the Sanctuary of the Hirka Serif. The Kizlar Aga opened the door of the Cage and proceeded toward the small kiosk where Abdulhamid's body lay. The room was not empty. Naksh-i-dil Kadine sat silently and motionlessly beside the shrouded body of her husband, her hand in his.

Edris started toward the weeping woman, but Selim stopped him and he obeyed. Selim was now the Sultan, the absolute ruler of forty million souls, and he, the Kizlar Aga, was his slave.

"Leave her," whispered Selim.

As he said this, Naksh-i-dil lifted her green eyes to Selim's dark ones. Naksh-i-dil's uncanny beauty unnerved Selim, not a lover of women, even more than the dead body beside which she was kneeling. The Kadine, who had never seen Selim, prostrated herself.

"My Lord . . ."

"No. Rise."

Naksh-i-dil rose and began to unbind the body of her husband.

"No, no. I don't want to see," said Selim. But as he turned to leave the kiosk, the booming voice of the Kizlar Aga stopped him.

"Lord, your dead uncle was a powerful and noble Sultan. Follow his example. The rulers of the world are not eternal. Eternity belongs only to God Almighty. Day and night, fear God, be merciful with your people so that in the shadow of your justice all may be happy. Ask God to aid you. Allah bless you."

Selim's elegant, narrow shoulders began to tremble, and he covered his head with his caftan.

The Black Eunuch left to announce the death of the Sultan to the Divan, his prerogative. He glanced back only once, and only once did he allow the fleeting thought of Selim's treason against Abdulhamid enter his mind. He had a new master. He would serve him as he had his predecessor.

When Selim arrived before the Door of Felicity dressed in pale yellow silk lined in ermine, with a silver-gauze turban on his head, he was more composed. The new Sultan raised his hand in salute to the 101-cannon salvo that greeted him. He would reign eighteen years, one month, twenty-two days, four hours and twenty-five minutes.

Naksh-i-dil waited in the shaded dark room. In seven days Mihri-shah, the mother of Selim, would enter the harem as the new Valide. It was she who would decide if Naksh-i-dil would be sent to the Eski Serai. There had been nothing in Selim's eyes or manner to suggest he had the least interest in her.

Her plans and dreams for her son were like ashes in her mouth. Selim would beget sons, and fratricide would eliminate Mahmud and his half-brother, Mustafa, as hereditary Princes. She was alone to fight against the overwhelming odds aligned against her and Mahmud. She was a Giaour, a Christian slave in a foreign land, separated forever from the world beyond the walls of Topkapi.

She lifted the winding sheet that covered the face of her dead husband. As the news of Abdulhamid's death spread through the harem, shrieks, cries and screams reverberated through the alleys and corridors, the dormitories and gardens of the palace. But the sound seemed far, very far from here. Abdulhamid had died in her arms this night to the crash of Ochakov. The victories of Catherine's army, the Russians' advance down the Danube had broken even this old cynic of a ruler, she thought. He had forgone his evening horseback ride, and had sent for their son.

"Mahmud, I leave you in the hands of God, and with His help may you never in this world or the next have to blacken your forehead in shame . . ." Amen, thought Naksh-i-dil.

Mahmud had gazed at his father uncomprehendingly. As one of his small hands clutched at hers, the other caressed the face of his agonized father.

"I swear on the head of my Prince, Abdulhamid, revenge against the Russians and against Catherine. In the name of the Father, the Son and the Holy Ghost . . . Mahmud swear," said the Kadine.

"Maman . . . Maman . . ." Mahmud had begun to cry and she held his trembling body steady before his father.

"Mahmud, repeat after Maman . . . I swear revenge . . ."

"I swear revenge . . ."

"On Catherine, Empress of All the Russias . . ."

"On Catherine, Empress of All the Russias . . ."

"And I vow to reclaim . . ."

"And I vow to reclaim . . ."

"The Crimea."

"The Crimea."

"So help me, God."

"So help me, God."

In the lightening dawn Abdulhamid had broken the silence of the room with the words "If Allah so wills." And Mahmud repeated the Moslem injunction. The doctors took the Sultan's pulse.

"Majesty, stay calm, but don't worry. Your pulse has simply accelerated a bit. Put yourself in the hands of Allah."

"Tabib Hasan Efendi, take it again. You are in the midst of losing your Lord and master," said the Italian doctor Gobis.

Hasan Efendi had begun to cry. Gobis began to murmur, "Poison . . . he is poisoned, Naksh-i-dil. He is poisoned."

Naksh-i-dil knelt, kneeling with self-absorbed grief, her head in her hands, her fingers interlaced in the now inseparable rosaries.

"Lâ ilâha illa-Llâh Muhammad Rasûl allahi."

Naksh-i-dil's green eyes had turned as amber as the tespi in the half-light. It was the only way to live in this jungle—the only way for her and her son to survive was to become like them. She had only to pronounce the sacred formula to find herself no longer in the land of strangers, but among co-believers. Naksh-i-dil knew the Koran by heart, and the New Testament had gradually faded into the Old. The prophets were the same and had become a confused and jumbled memory. For one moment, she held on desperately to the one thing she knew to be true, that Jesus was the Son of God. But in the small overheated space of the kiosk, she began to despair.

Oh Lord, she thought, keep me from sinking down, but what she said was, *"Lâ ilâha illa-Llâh Muhammad Rasûl allahi.* There is no other God but Allah and Mohammed is His Prophet. There is no other God but Allah and Mohammed is His Prophet." Her voice had risen now almost to a cry as she repeated, "There is no other God but Allah and Mohammed is His Prophet."

The Kizlar Aga stood staring at the Christian Kadine in astonishment.

"What did you say?" he asked.

Naksh-i-dil, her face contorted with the fear and horror of what she was doing, answered the Black Eunuch.

"I have just said three times that there is no other God than Allah and Mohammed is His Prophet."

Naksh-i-dil had just renounced the Faith of her fathers. She thought of her long-ago traveling companions, the lions. The lions and the Christian. She thought of how the flesh was weak. How unfathomable was her fear of hell . . . how much she wanted to live. . . . Survival, she knew from that other life, was *everything.*

Hitabetullah looked up into the shocked black face of Edris Aga as if his color was the key to her comprehension. This . . . this ferocious little Christian . . . this *fanatic* of the Prophet Jesus . . . this idolatress of the Virgin Mary . . . had become a renegade. The two black witnesses stood apart silently, each wrapped in his thoughts, watching the white Giaour wrestle with her conscience and her God before their very eyes. As if they didn't exist. As if this spectacle was not repugnant to them: a Moslem and an animist whose Gods preached prudishness, silence and the soft secret surface of one's prayer rug. The moans of Naksh-i-dil reached them, amplified by the tiny cupola. Edris and Hitabetullah approached the suffering Kadine at the same time, and at the same time, they wondered who she was mourning, her Sultan or herself? But Naksh-i-dil knew of no other way. She burned with a fervor that would serve her new God to the death and hate the God who had so long ago forsaken her.

BOOK V

RAMADAN
·1789·

The Moslem calendar is reckoned from the year 622 A.D.,
the year of the Hegira, based on lunar cycles of thirty years,
of which nineteen years contain 354 days and eleven years
contain 355 days. The ninth month of the Moslem calendar
is Ramadan, consecrated by fasting from sunup to sundown
after which every license is allowed.

• CHAPTER ONE •

MIHRISHAH VALIDE 1789

The harem did not attend the funeral of the Sultan.

The body of Sultan Abdulhamid, washed and dressed, was carried through the Door of Felicity by the black eunuchs. The Kizlar Aga handed the corpse over to the Grand Mufti, and as the funeral procession formed, the inmates of the harem watched through high windows the last of their master. If anyone mourned, it was for himself and the mortal danger any slave feels upon the loss of a master.

Preceded by the Mutafaraga, the Grand Mufti carried a turban of the defunct Sultan on the top of a lance to which was attached a horse's tail, symbol of temporal power. After him came the Janissaries, the Muallem Bostaniyan-i, the Svlachi Hassa, and the rest of the imperial guard. In the First Court the procession was joined by the officials and nobles under the direction of the Master of Ceremonies. The Halberdiers carried the weapons of the dead Sultan, and the last of them trailed the royal standard in the dust into which the Sultan would return.

The funeral cortege proceeded to the mausoleum of Abdulhamid. It was necessary for the Sultan to arrive in paradise as soon as possible and not linger on this earth. The sooner he arrived, the sooner he could answer the questions posed by the archangels Gabriel and Michael who, having received the correct answers, would open the gates of heaven. The two shores were lined with mourners, who tore their clothes and hair. The caravan serpentined the suburbs of Istanbul. The setting sun inflamed the horizon and threw back reflections of gold and purple.

At the gates came the Pashas and grand nobles of the Porte dressed in mourning, two panels of dark gray material falling before and behind like a monk's habit. Others wore small black turbans to which were attached long pieces of cloth that trailed to the ground. The standard bearers marched with the points of their flags turned downward. All the Sultan's stallions were draped in black velvet that trailed the ground. If men didn't weep for the Sultan, the beasts did. Pepper had been placed in their eyes and tobacco in their nostrils to make them whinny and weep. In the grand silence of the procession, this was the only sound, but it was a torrent of sound: the Sultan's only mourners.

In the harem all had settled down to await a new regime and a new Sultan. The women were subdued, the silence terrible.

Mihrishah, mother of Sultan Selim, was Valide now. She was Modest Lady, Diadem of Feminine Nobility, Queen of Queens, Empress of the Veiled Heads. And as Valide she had the power of life and death over the harem and everyone in it. After seventeen years in the Eski Serai, where she had pored over astrology charts and distributed forged horoscopes of her son's glorious destiny, she had emerged triumphant. The ceaseless warfare between the Sultan's Mother and his favorite Kadines was established by law. It would be Mihrishah who would arrange the marriages (if they had enough dowry) of the inmates of the harem—with a generous commission for herself and Yusuf Aga, her intendant and favorite. She would add to her already great fortune, mused Naksh-i-dil, by reselling part of the harem of Abdulhamid to the officers and Pashas of the realm, excluding of course the mothers of Princes, like herself. And one source of Edris Aga's fortune was to supply a description, profile of character and estimation of the fortune of each of the harem inmates to prospective husbands. The rise or the death of a Sultan made everyone richer, thought Naksh-i-dil bitterly. Indiscretions were in the hands of the Black Eunuch. Dowries in the hands of Mihrishah. Marriage contracts in the hands of Yusuf Aga. The rest of the harem would end up in the Eski Serai, the Palace of Tears, a charge upon the State until they died. The cries and wailings of the population drifted over the gold-flecked waters, and Naksh-i-dil imagined she heard murmurings from the deep as well, from the hundreds of corpses at the bottom of the Bosphorus welcoming still others to the unknown. Of Abdulhamid's eleven wives, who would remain in Mihrishah's court?

In the silent corridors, Sineprever's dark liquid eyes met those of Naksh-i-dil. They had never been friends. Sineprever's imposing beauty and haughty temperament had always held Naksh-i-dil at a distance, and she was not at all sure if Sineprever had plotted against Abdulhamid. At any rate, approaching Sineprever was no longer her problem. Protocol demanded that Sineprever approach her, as she took precedence over everyone except Mihrishah Valide. Sineprever also had a son to protect. Mustafa had been born in 1779, so there was six years' difference between the two boys. Mustafa would reign only if he survived Selim. The chances of Mahmud ever reaching the Ottoman throne were remote. Sineprever had nothing to fear from her—or did she? Could she imagine that she, Naksh-i-dil, would scheme against Selim or Mustafa in order to advance her own son? What, she wondered, did Sineprever believe her capable of? She tried to rid her own face of all expression as Sineprever scrutinized her without a shade of emotion ever passing her face. Sineprever's beauty resided in her darkness, her coal-black hair, dark straight eyebrows, fathomless and brilliant eyes, which were heavily lined with kohl and embellished with the longest eyelashes in the Empire. Her nose was long but aristocratic, her lips thin, her chin determined. Her high cheekbones gave a Slavic cast to her face, which could just as easily have been Greek or Italian or even English. Her body was generous and opulent. Yet, there was great feline grace in all her movements; the languor of the harem had seemingly been forgotten in her new role of mother to the hereditary Prince. Feminine rivalry had long been left behind by both of them. They were scarred and victorious survivors of the harem wars—their glances were those of artillery men at rest rather than of rival Kadines. Was Sineprever also wondering, as she was, thought Naksh-i-dil, if his wives had loved their Sultan? One thing they both knew: They loved their sons.

Mihrishah, like all Queen Mothers, had been and was a slave. She was a Circassian, the slave of the Grand Mufti Vely Efendi. Beautiful and talented, she had been given, at the age of nine, to Sultan Mustafa III. She had been noticed for her dancing and the extreme whiteness of her skin, the ocean blue of her eyes and the fairness of her fine and luxurious ash-blond hair, and she had received the honor of his favors. In 1761 Mihrishah had borne Selim. Selim adored his mother and it was evident, thought Naksh-i-dil, that Mihrishah would be a powerful Valide. And she was still Christian. She had already made known that her old master, who was still alive, Vely Efendi, doyen of the Ulemas, would enjoy her favor. The other man who would now have enormous power was also a former slave of Vely Efendi, Yusuf Aga, favorite of the new Queen Mother. Born in Crete, one of four sons of a poor cobbler, Yusuf Aga had been sold at the age of seven. He would be appointed Lieutenant of Mihrishah Valide as soon as Abdulhamid was in his grave. He was the perfect accomplice, intelligent and faithful.

Mihrishah Valide's genius, character and political astuteness had developed in the shadow of the Seraglio and the harem. Favorites and Sultanas were admitted to all the confidences of government and were involved in all the intrigues of the court. Long and great reigns had been founded and governed by some of these beautiful slaves, and Mihrishah Valide intended to be one of them. The law of the harem was clear: favorites served, wives inspired, mothers reigned.

Of all Abdulhamid's twenty-two children, thought Naksh-i-dil, as she sat in the dappled courtyard of her apartments, only five now survived: Prince Mustafa, Prince Mahmud, Esma Sultane, Hitabetullah and Durrushevar, his daughter born in the Cage. Of Abdulhamid's ten sons and twelve daughters, seventeen had died as infants, including those of the three Kadines who had followed Naksh-i-dil: Fekti-Seza, Hadidge and Binnaz. They would spend the rest of their lives in the Eski Serai, unless Mihrishah decided otherwise. Mehtap, Neveser and the First Ikbal, Fekti-Seza, would be allowed to marry officers of the State. Two of Abdulhamid's wives were dead, Fatma-Shebsefa and Humashah. Abdulhamid had erected on the European side of the Bosphorus, at Eyup, a bath and a mosque in memory of Humashah.

Twenty-four hours ago, thought Naksh-i-dil, she had been safe and loved, and Mahmud had had a father. Now the future was as uncertain and unknown as that of a newborn emerging from its mother's womb. And as fraught with danger. She bowed her head, the beautiful slender hands came up to cover her face.

"I am so afraid," she said out loud.

"I know. I have the power to protect you," said a voice above her.

"Why?" The word was out before Naksh-i-dil had time to raise her head.

"Because I want you. . . ."

Naksh-i-dil stared into Hadidge Sultane's pale eyes.

• CHAPTER TWO •

THE SULTAN 1789

The third day of Selim III's reign, April 10, 1789, was particularly clear. Overhead a single vulture circled, then swept down, shattering a peaceable formation of seagulls. Causing screams like maniac laughter.

The new twenty-eight-year-old Sultan had arrived at the Arsenal at noon, climbed the steep approach ramp to the palace garrison, followed by his suite. He ordered his Lieutenant General, Nasif Efendi, onto the treeless, sunbaked parade ground that flanked the blue and white buildings, and commanded that the Lieutenant General's head be severed from his body. The severed head rolled grotesquely toward its former master, dotting the curled and pointed toe of Selim's yellow boots like a question mark.

The population of the Arsenal who had been ordered to witness the execution was stupefied. Father Delleda, the new confessor of the Christian Valide and the only European among the Sultan's suite, fainted. The rest of the entourage stood in white-faced silence. It was the same fearful compliant silence that reigned within all three courts of Topkapi.

Selim had long suspected that the man he had just beheaded had rendered him sterile by the use of certain poisons. His first act of vengeance as Sultan was also a confession. Selim had been circumcised five months after Abdulhamid's accession when he was already in the Cage. This had given rise to all kinds of rumors of his unnatural inclinations.

The Kapi Aga, the White Eunuch who was standing in the Arsenal courtyard, broke into a cold sweat under his green and yellow ceremonial robes. And the Kapi Aga remembered that Abdulhamid too had begun his reign with a private act of vengeance, and his own life had ended in a violent death. For the White Eunuch was convinced Abdulhamid had been poisoned. The White Eunuch glanced toward the Black Eunuch and, as if at a signal, their eyes met. This singular act of cruelty would haunt Selim, both pairs of eyes seemed to say. The White Eunuch and the Black Eunuch knew there was no way to keep this execution secret. No way to keep the Janissaries from outrage and the astrologers from dire predictions.

The Kapi Aga watched as Selim turned on his heels and started down the steep incline, his dark eyes blazing. The Sultan was extraordinarily handsome, despite traces of childhood smallpox on his fair skin. He was dark blond, like his mother, under his elaborate white turban held by a diamond brooch and surmounted by an egret feather. Of medium height, he was slight but well built. His features were regular and his beard had been artificially darkened, almost black. His gaze was serene, even now, but at its center there was something ferocious. Like all imperial Osmans, he was short of leg and would always look better on horseback than on foot as he was now, his scarlet robes billowing in the sharp breeze coming off the sea, his turban feather quivering hysterically, his tunic parting to reveal the thousand-pleated silken pantaloons of rose silk that fell over his yellow-shod feet. Selim, like every Sultan, had been obliged by the laws of the Empire to choose an occupation. The Kapi Aga smiled. Selim had chosen lace-making.

But Selim, his body trembling with rage and emotion, glanced up at the hills of the Seraglio where he had been prisoner for so many years. He was a Mohammedan monarch and his palace was at the foot of Pera, a Christian city. He was the absolute despot of one eighth of the world and his metropolis, Istanbul, was filled with European powers who built their stone palaces, who dictated the policy of his nation, forced him to tolerate their intrigues and spying, believed themselves the masters of *his* destiny. Selim turned to look behind him at the troop of courtiers hurrying down the hill. He was surrounded by an army of parasites, sycophants and bodyguards who would kiss his footsteps if he so desired, yet he trembled continually for his life. He possessed a thousand women, chosen from the most beautiful on earth, yet he alone of all Moslems had no right to give any the name of Empress. It was not only because he loved men that he had refused the wives his uncle had offered him at age fourteen, but because he could have children only by slaves. He was called "son of a slave" by the same people who called him "Allah's Shadow on Earth." In the most miserable tribes of the most miserable provinces, in the mosques, the most solitary convents of the most savage lands, prayers were ardently offered for his life and his glory; yet he could not take one step in those same states without fear of assassination. For that part of the world which spread out before him, he was one of the most august and formidable monarchs of the universe, and for that part which spread out behind him, he was the weakest man who ever wore a crown. He was the Prince who, on entering the Cage at the death of his father, had vowed:

> If one day it is decreed that I mount the throne of the Empire, these shall be my colors: my head will roll like a cannonball on the battlefield rather than bow to a Russian sword or even less, to a woman, nor the devaluation of the religion of my fathers . . . my colors are vengeance. . . .

The scarlet-uniformed slave boy trembled visibly before him. Selim pushed him aside. Was he going mad? Was there no one he could trust? Ishak Bey was taking his own good time returning home. Except for his mother, Mihrishah, and his sister, Hadidge, Lorenzo was the only person he could trust. . . . It had been Lorenzo who had broken the solitude and ignorance of the Prince's Cage by smuggling books, money, information. But he commanded in himself a kind of defiance, a continual vigilance against even Tabib Lorenzo, even his mother. He would compromise himself with no one. No one. He would remain master of his secret. A secret that only Lorenzo and Ishak knew: conspiracy with France.

The treasonous letters he had written to Louis XVI while Abdulhamid still lived had been a youthful error, a stupid mistake. Fortunately, without dramatic consequences. To have dethroned Abdulhamid he would have done anything as Prince. But as *Sultan,* conspiracy was now *his* enemy. Agents, spies such as Ishak and Lorenzo, could no longer be trusted. They had had a taste of treason. And, moreover, they were witnesses to his own.

The White Eunuch, still on foot, looked up in horror at the contorted face of his master.

"Where is my Grand Vizier?"

His Grand Vizier, thought the Kapi Aga, was dead. His fleet had just been totally destroyed by the Russians. The Austrians were baying, like the Christian dogs they were, just on the other side of the Danube. And Selim himself had just decapitated the fleet's second-in-command—one of the best officers in the Ottoman Empire—a horrible . . . he searched for the word . . . lèse majesté. Everyone was wrong, mused the White Eunuch, to believe in a brilliant destiny for Selim; that Selim would avenge the honor of Moslem arms. Selim was deceitful, secretive, capricious, despotic. The White Eunuch stared upward at the screaming Selim. Selim was menaced by madness. . . .

The news from the Arsenal reached the harem in the midst of preparations for the procession of the Valide. In seven days, the Valide would make her public procession from the Eski Serai to Topkapi.

A new Sultan on the throne sweeps through the harem like an earthquake. Heads roll, destinies change, dreams shatter, alliances crumble and powers are granted or lost forever. In seven days, a very short time, all traces of the old harem had to disappear. In a kind of harem revolution, Abdulhamid's women were sold, married off or consigned to the Eski Serai. The richest were ransomed by their parents or by a pretender to their hand. The Ikbals and Kadines were especially sought after by ambitious second-class officers. For the mothers of Princes, the future was clear: Eski Serai. Their sons had become part of the Selamlik, the Men's Palace, to be locked away in the Prince's Cage for as long as Selim reigned.

In all the confusion of building new apartments for Selim's Kadines, the Kiaya managed to console the desperate Naksh-i-dil.

"Mahmud is only four. They won't take him yet, I'm sure. . . . They will wait another few years, especially if Hadidge asks Mihrishah."

"And Mustafa? Mustafa is ten!"

"Mustafa must go. He is next in line," the Kiaya replied.

Naksh-i-dil looked down at Mahmud, who was clinging to her trousers. He was dressed in ceremonial robes every day, for no one knew at which moment the Black Eunuch might appear to claim him, and he had to be ready. The eyes of the miniature Sultan at her side were bright with the excitement and confusion that reigned in the harem. Selim's useless Kadines, Husni-Mah, Afitab, Zibi-fer, Nefizar and Nourichemss, had already arrived with their slaves, their eunuchs, their jewel cases, cushions and furniture.

"I like that one," said Mahmud, pointing to Afitab.

Naksh-i-dil shook the small boy roughly, her terror communicating itself to Mahmud, who began to wail, his cries mingling with the screams, cries, orders and counterorders of the toiling slaves.

Oh, God, thought Naksh-i-dil. Don't let them take him. Not yet. Which God was she praying to, she thought suddenly, the One of the crescent or of the cross? Wordlessly Naksh-i-dil took the screaming child into her arms. What comfort could she give him? They would come, the men, as sure as death, and this small bundle of silk and brocade would be snatched from her.

"It is for the Valide to decide, Naksh-i-dil," whispered the Kiaya. "She may allow you to keep Mahmud for a while. After all, Mustafa is the eldest. Do not despair. Pity Sineprever, for Mustafa's fate is sealed. But at least she has Esma. . . . As for Mahmud, Mihrishah is known to be merciful, I hear." She crossed her fingers silently in the deaf-mute sign of the cross.

Naksh-i-dil's thoughts, however, were on Hadidge Sultane as she clasped Mahmud to her breast. Hadidge both repulsed and fascinated her. Hadidge was the only one who could convince her mother, Mihrishah Valide, not to exile her to the Eski Serai. She had received no word from Hadidge since her brother's coronation. Naksh-i-dil had spied her along with Selim's two other living sisters in the cortege of her dead husband. But not since. Hadidge had sent no message to her, nor had she appeared at the harem. Naksh-i-dil could only wait for Mihrishah Valide to appear. The new Valide's duty would be to control all passions and fears, to hold by sheer will, force and temperament all divergent elements of the harem. It would be the Valide, and the Valide alone, who could save her son, who would shape the comportment of the four hundred women under her command. She would choose the women for her son's bed. She would choose the slaves for the harem's kitchens. She could kill or banish. She would make and enforce the rules and regulations of the harem according to desire, tradition or caprice. It was she who would distribute power among her court, her favorite and the Sultanes. It was she who would decide Mahmud's fate and hers.

On the sixth day, the Black Eunuch came for Mustafa. Sineprever's screams and cries unnerved the harem until she too was taken away to the Eski Serai. Naksh-i-dil had once witnessed a slave mother being separated from her child. Little had she dreamed that such grief would come to her. She and Hitabetullah took Mahmud into the harem gardens, away from Sineprever's screams, away from the eyes of the Kizlar Aga. Perhaps he had forgotten about Mahmud after all. Naksh-i-dil squeezed her son's tiny hands in hers.

"Mahmud," she whispered, "I love you more than my life."

"Is Mustafa gone?"

"I will never leave you, Mahmud. No matter how many years we have left to live, I will always be at your side. I have renounced God for you. From this day, you are Allah's Shadow on Earth—not Selim."

On the seventh day, Mihrishah officially entered the harem at Topkapi. The new Sultan awaited his mother at the Gate of Felicity. The Kapon Aga, Lord of the Gate, the Halberdiers and the Black Eunuch had been advised one day in advance. The procession of Mihrishah was the most lavish Selim could devise. Under a bright, warm April sun, the procession wended its way through the streets of Istanbul from the Eski Serai to the imperial palace, along a route lined with forty thousand Janissaries standing at attention, shoulder to shoulder, in their yellow and red uniforms. Heading the cortege were the Sergeants of the Divan carrying silver batons and wearing high gold-trimmed turbans that mingled with the sea of green silk flags of Islam carried by pages. The Sergeants rode the waves of green on Persian Horses whose tails had been plaited and dipped in henna. The Valide's Lieutenant, Yusuf Aga, followed wearing a new ermine coat and the high white turban denoting his recently acquired rank of Pasha. Behind him marched the Halberdiers, armed with four-sided swords and dressed in leopard skins and orange livery. Music from tambours, flutes and brass swept over both the procession and the noisy population massed behind the Janissaries. Leading the Valide's grilled carriage was the Kizlar Aga, wearing white ceremonial robes lined in fox as black and luminous as his implacable face. Inside the carriage, which was harnessed to six pure-white Persian horses, sat Mihrishah, mother to the realm, her chest scintillating with a diamond bib, her face unveiled as was her prerogative. On foot, surrounding her carriage, were three hundred bodyguards who passed out silver to the cheering crowd. The Valide's carriage was followed by one hundred vehicles transporting her slaves, her furniture and her personal belongings. When the two-hour procession passed the Sublime Porte, just behind the golden dome of Aya Sofya, Selim, mounted on his favorite thoroughbred covered with steel and gold, rode forward to greet her. He was followed by his own cortege of 40 Agas, followed by 160 pages.

"Mother."

"Majesty."

Selim embraced his mother and kissed her hand. Then, dropping back, he saluted her before leading her into her private realm, the imperial harem.

"You are the renegade Kadine," said the Christian Valide.

The new Queen Mother's azure-blue eyes met Naksh-i-dil's green

ones like the meeting of sky and sea. This time, there was neither friend-
liness nor hostility in Mihrishah's gaze. She had a task to fulfill, which
was to rid the harem of Abdulhamid's wives and make room for those
of her son, and she intended to get on with it. Looking at Naksh-i-dil,
she remembered how Abdulhamid's mother's flick of the wrist had
confined her to the Eski Serai.

Naksh-i-dil swallowed painfully. It would do no good to deny her
conversion to Islam. She realized now that a Christian Valide was her
condemnation.

The long years of waiting had not visibly marked Mihrishah. Her
long blond hair was still silken and luxurious, her blue eyes clear, intelligent and frank, her smile both enigmatic and generous. She had spent
fifteen years as the First Kadine of Mustafa III and fifteen in exile.

"Our Lady," murmured Naksh-i-dil.

"Why did you do it?" asked Mihrishah, not without interest.

"For Prince Mahmud," answered Naksh-i-dil.

Mihrishah looked down at the male child swathed in brocades and
silks, standing beside his mother. Naksh-i-dil pressed Mahmud against
her knees protectively, then picked him up in her arms.

"Ah, yes, our little Prince. A pretty boy. A Prince needs his mother
as long as he is able . . . which is not very long, to keep her beside
him," Mihrishah said wistfully.

"Inshallah," whispered Naksh-i-dil. Now was not the time to equivo-
cate. She was a Moslem. She would defend her new Faith and her son,
for whom she had sacrificed her God, to the death. Her eyes, pleading
at the same time, searched those of Mihrishah. Suddenly the Valide
kissed Mahmud, and his mother found herself on her knees, her head
bent and her hands clasped before her. It was not the attitude of a
Moslem, but of a Christian. It was not lost on Mihrishah. Would her
first act as Valide be as vindictive as Selim's first act as Sultan? she asked
herself.

"Inshallah," whispered Naksh-i-dil, waiting.

"What you are really saying, my child, is as God Almighty and His
Son Jesus so will . . ." replied Mihrishah sternly. She extended her
hand and lifted the trembling girl to her feet. "How old are you?"

"Twenty-three," replied Naksh-i-dil.

An eternity to live, thought Mihrishah Valide. "Love and protect
your son as I have mine. And may the Lord have mercy on your soul.
You may stay."

Naksh-i-dil felt the blue and white tiled hall swim around her, and

Hadidge Sultane suddenly appeared at her side, like a capricious guardian angel.

"I understand," said the Valide, "that your language is very pretty and that you speak also French and you read and write. You may serve my court as my personal dragoman. . . . Does this satisfy you, daughter?"

"May you live to be a hundred, Mihrishah Sultane," replied Hadidge.

"Never mind that, daughter. That I have survived my forty-third year, and have lived to see my son Sultan, is quite enough for me."

The Valide's eyes clouded suddenly, as if the beating wings of one of the "damned souls" of the Bosphorus had blurred their incredible blueness. Mihrishah swayed slightly and the pleats of her heavy jeweled robes, encrusted with precious stones and pearls, struck each other like the click of a rosary. "You and little Mahmud may keep your apartments," she added.

She and Mahmud were safe, thought Naksh-i-dil. For now. And by grace of the caprice of Hadidge . . .

Hadidge had decided to claim the reward she knew was due, and she knew that Naksh-i-dil would not deny her, yet she was strangely subdued. This quiet, stubborn, unhappy American fascinated and troubled her. Hadidge was moved as she took the soft cool hand of the Kadine, leading her through the galleries and gardens to her apartments. Neither woman spoke until they had crossed the favorite's courtyard where they stopped and faced each other. Naksh-i-dil spoke first, her voice low and extenuated.

"When I came to this place, it was forbidden for me to allow another woman to touch me or I her . . . except . . . except for the Kiaya . . . long ago. Her name was Hurrum."

"Naksh-i-dil, you know what goes on in the harem . . . between women . . ."

"I wanted to be Kadine. I wanted nothing to spoil that. I wanted Mahmud. I made no friendships, Hadidge . . . though many were offered. . . . Could it be that you love me?" Instead of answering, Hadidge began to speak softly.

The sun plunges into the baths because you enter them. That which should by nature extinguish flames, kindles my fire when you are there. Alas! Is it possible that you grant to persons other than your own sex, who are other you's, the delectation of the

stupendous beauty which surrounds you? Flee men's embraces
who have only contempt for women. They only love those who
resemble themselves. Fulfill your ownself with us, of the content-
ment men don't deserve.

The Princess Hadidge moistened her lips. Should she tell Naksh-i-dil
the truth? That she *wanted* to possess her? Love had so many faces, she
thought. And most of them were just the other side of desperation and
loneliness—at least in the harem. How could this Kadine not know
that? That love between women was exactly the same as love between
men and women; a mixture of need and power, lust and loneliness. She
loved only her brother, Selim. It was of Selim that she dreamed. It was
Selim who laid claim to that residue of tenderness left by her atrophied
female organs. She loved him. Why should she love anyone else. Loving
another woman was merely narcissism, loving another man was dangerous. By taking Naksh-i-dil, not only did she not betray Selim who was
after all a man . . . she made Mahmud a little bit hers. . . .

The light played on the two beautiful faces. The shade shaping first
one perfection, then the other. The rustle of leaves and the scent of
jasmine dared to intrude on the singular silence. Naksh-i-dil knew that
as the weaker and the younger of the two women she would have to
appear the stronger. If she were not to become a slave to Hadidge, she
would have to become her master. She had had enough of masters for a
lifetime.

"If we are to love one another," said Naksh-i-dil, "then let us not be
coy about what we are to each other. You consider me your slave. But I
consider myself your equal—I can make you happy, Hadidge. I can also
make you suffer."

"I believe you could, Naksh-i-dil Kadine," lied Hadidge (no one
could make her suffer). "But there is your debt . . ."

"You know why?" interrupted Naksh-i-dil without listening.

"I know why women suffer," said Hadidge, "and why they
love. . . ."

"Because even without knowing you or ever having touched you, I
know things about you no man can ever know."

It was Naksh-i-dil who raised Hadidge's face to hers and kissed her
lightly on the mouth. It was Naksh-i-dil whose hand slid under
Hadidge's elaborate dolma and into the slit in her trousers. Hadidge
gasped but, out of pride and anger, didn't move. Instead she returned
Naksh-i-dil's kiss, forcing her head back. But Naksh-i-dil still held her

prisoner with her hand. Naksh-i-dil felt the heat of her own excitement, agitating her perfume, suffusing the thin gauze that separated her body from that of Hadidge. Naksh-i-dil released her and merely pressed the sides of her waist with both hands. Their breasts were still touching. The Kadine let her hand drop onto the Sultana's shoulder, for a fleeting second, then they heard someone or something behind them—a fleeting shadow or branches stirring or only their imaginations.

Then they were alone in Hadidge's rooms, Hadidge's bare feet placed on those of Naksh-i-dil as she held her with force, moving against her, their undone hair, bright red and white gold, almost covering the voluptuousness of their lovemaking. Hadidge forced Naksh-i-dil to her knees, pressing her head against her immaculate smooth dome of flesh, then, shaken, found herself kneeling in response to Naksh-i-dil's mouth. Hadidge cried out once, twice, then flung Naksh-i-dil on her back. She opened her thighs, exposing the faultless, painted lips as red as her mouth, determined to bring to the reclining, expectant, ravished body the pleasure the Kadine had surprised in her. Hadidge brought the Kadine to the edge, then over it so that Naksh-i-dil sobbed that ugly sound she had kept in her deepest consciousness. Naksh-i-dil moved upon Hadidge like a man, pounding, forcing her thighs wider and wider, until the never-forgotten sound broke loose again and again from her.

Hadidge had planned her seduction carefully, but she had not counted on the instincts and sense of strategy of a harem Kadine. She had no defenses left as she abandoned herself voluptuously to Naksh-i-dil's expertise. Naksh-i-dil had realized her as a woman.

"Stay here," she said. "I'm going to get Mahmud."

When she returned with the small child and his nurse, both women clutched the tiny Prince at once, smothering him in a cocoon of velvet and silk.

"What, what is that, Maman, what is that?" he kept repeating in a tiny voice that wavered over the hum of a hundred exclamations of grief. But Hadidge took Mahmud into her arms, covering him with kisses.

Naksh-i-dil had planned it. Now she was sure. Mahmud had now two mothers. Hadidge had become part of Mahmud's survival.

CHAPTER THREE

IṢHAK BEY 1789

Constantinople, July 4, 1789

To Selim III, Successor of the most celebrated Sultans, Noble of Khans, the most renowned for his goodness, distinguished by the favor of Kings, the Pillar of Islam, that your glory as Sultan augment from day to day, most honorable and very magnificent Emperor, Allah's Shadow on Earth, Defender of the Faith, have the good grace to accept my homage, and most profound and prostrate respects,

Three of four days ago, Ismail Bey arrived on behalf of Your Highness to ask the whereabouts of Iṣhak Bey, and why he has postponed his return to Constantinople for so long. Ever since Iṣhak Bey went to France on behalf of Your Highness, he has received all the proofs of respect and considerations which are his due.

I have hastened to announce to my court, the happy accession of Your Highness to the throne of the Ottoman Empire and in the supposition that you have given an imperial order for the return of Iṣhak Bey, I have written to my court.

The very humble servant of Your Highness,
Choiseul-Gouffier
Ambassador of His Most Christian Majesty
Louis XVI

Topkapi, October 15, 1789

At the arrival of this sublime message,

Very honorable Ambassador of France. I was very pleased with the tobacco box and the clock you sent me. Write to our very honored friend, the King of France, the glory of the most august Princes of the religion of Jesus, column of the great who recognize the Messiah, conciliator of the public affairs of the Christian people of France, who trails the train-bearer of authority and splendor, and who reunites in his person proof of glory and splendor, to send my servant Ishak Bey here. I am surprised and astonished that our friend, the King of France, defender of the Christian Faith, etc., etc., has not given, up to now, any proof of his attachment, his zeal and his fidelity.

You have asked us several times for an answer on the subject of peace. Our Empire, thank God, is not put off by war and our ardor has not lessened. We have not the desire for peace. If the inviolable conditions we want are met, perhaps we will consent. But be pleased to remember that peace or war is all the same to us.

Do not lose our friendship.

Selim III

"Oh, shit!" exclaimed the archangel Gabriel, Ishak, in the sun-flooded gold and white salon of his mansion near Versailles. He was *commanded* home.

The news of Abdulhamid's death had reached Ishak Bey more than two months ago, but he had yet to hear from his archangel, Selim. Until he did, thought Ishak, he had no intentions of sailing for Istanbul. There were too many dangers from too many sides. He thought of the old Ottoman saying: "Rising like the mist at dawn to the greatest degree of honor benignly by the hand of the Sultan, evaporating before nightfall."

The archangel Michael was finally in power, but the archangel Gabriel would wait for word from him before budging, even to take his rightful place in power, fortune and glory beside the Sultan. One must rise slowly, Ishak thought, like Montgolfier's balloon, with a great deal of hot air, and stay aloft in order to succeed. Besides, there was a great deal to do before leaving. He had to close his house at Versailles. He had to dismiss his staff, pack his belongings and send a message to the Minister of Foreign Affairs, Vergennes. He wanted a last audience with Louis XVI, and the privilege of taking a letter from him back to Selim. This was very important to him. This, and to supervise the gifts of Louis XVI to the court of Selim. He had to visit a certain Marquis de T . . . take leave of his charming compatriot Madame de Witte from St. Petersburg, now a Polish princess. Ishak felt in an exuberant mood. Doubts about his reception at Topkapi, despite Selim's silence, faded at the prospect of setting eyes on Istanbul.

Ishak was homesick. Neither Russia nor England had agreed with him. He was tired of France as well. And it was harder and harder to get more money out of the French foreign minister, Vergennes. He had been reduced to becoming a Freemason and accepting money for passage to the Crimea from his fellow Freemasons' lodge in Brussels. . . . In France he would leave numerous souvenirs especially for his creditors. . . .

• CHAPTER FOUR •

HADIDGE SULTANE 1789

There are four pleasures in life: the pleasure of an hour, which is sexual union; the pleasure of a day, which is the baths; the pleasure of a week, which is the depilatory; and the pleasure of a year: that of marrying a virgin.

—The Tradition of the Prophet
Mohammed, A.D. 632

In the back of the Jewish merchant's shop, the young woman lifted her veils and then dropped the copious brocaded cashmere cloak that covered her. The surprised youth started at the pair of perfect breasts, the thin waist and the high, white shaved mons veneris that could fill the hand of a man and glistened in the darkened room like a half-moon. The young man, whose name was Haroun, had no idea who she was, this woman, except that she was rich, noble and of such high rank that just the thought of her distinguished husband or father chilled his quickening blood. He guessed that she was about twenty years old. Her language had already betrayed her, for it was the language spoken by Ottoman nobles and hardly intelligible to the common inhabitants of Istanbul. He was also certain he would never know who she was, nor would he even be likely to see her again after this hour. An eighteenth-century Turkish noblewoman knew the advantages of the veil even if her European counterpart did not. For if the veil hid one's face from other men and from the world in general, it also hid it from a jealous husband, father or lover. A woman was not meant to be seen by any man outside the harem. Her veil and cloak were as sacred as its doors.

Not one husband in a thousand would recognize his veiled wife or dare to touch her if he passed her on the street. And the lover, never having seen the face of his best friend's wife, could hardly be expected to know that it was indeed her to whom he was making love. As the cloak dropped to the floor, the youth, trembling, reached out for the offered flesh. Falling to his knees, he placed his lips on the immaculate mons.

The woman lowered herself to the floor and onto her cloak lined in sable and silk, and opened her legs. Without preamble, she said:

I am the perfect woman deemed one
of those of whom kings dream
I live to be taken
A wide-hipped reservoir

Cursed be thou if thou profit
from a liaison that is not thy fate
Lift your parts high
Lay your parts low

That your serpent follows
the longest road
Enlarge my bearing
and labor swiftly in my slit

Abide until morning
So as not to finish but at that moment
If not, there exists no stroke of luck
But only a hasty quickening before it's time.

The woman watched as the boy, a Serbian of about sixteen, undressed, weighing his beauty against others she had already known, her green eyes clouded with celandine. The young woman resembled the spread wings of a wounded bird as the boy lifted the white thighs onto his shoulders and entered her. Her hand, in which there was a gold-embroidered handkerchief to stifle her cries, flew to her mouth.

She turned her head from one side to the other, the moist crumpled square of silk stuffed in her mouth. The Sultana and her choice coupled with a fervor born of expertise and the violence of the very young.

The two young people made love far into the evening. And when the youth had taken her for the last time, the woman rose and pulled her ferigee around her. She picked up her cloak. Out of an inner pocket she drew a small jeweled dagger called a candgiar with which both Turkish men and women armed themselves, and pressed it between the legs of the drowsing boy. The diamond and ruby head of the dagger was worth a fortune. The Serbian and his family would be comfortable for life.

The woman drew two veils down over her, one that covered her face except for the eyes, and the other, her entire head to the waist. Her cazeta covered her from head to foot and to the tips of her fingers. She was as unrecognizable as a kitchen slave unless she opened her mouth to speak.

Hadidge Sultane, now ranking Princess of the Empire, stepped out of the back door of the Jewish shop, trailing the scent of musk and jasmine. She was twenty-four years old, today was her birthday and she had just been unfaithful to Naksh-i-dil. Her dark eyes searched the filthy, half-lit, deserted street before she turned into the somber shadows in the Jewish quarter's narrow streets in Balata, and almost bumped into a tall Jew who had crossed her path. He stopped and watched curiously as she entered the European-style carriage that awaited her, as if he recognized it. But Hadidge was deep in thought. She decided to go to her cousin's new palace on the other side of the Bosphorus. She directed the carriage toward her caïque waiting at anchor. She and Beyhan Sultane would dine together, quietly gossiping. Hadidge felt bruised and used after her afternoon of lovemaking. She needed her bath and she needed company. Beyhan Sultane was her half-sister. As was the custom, she lived alone. She was caring for twelve-year-old Esma, who Selim had decided to marry to his former page, Huseyin Kuchuk. Esma was Selim's gift to Kuchuk to thank him for his sister's having saved Selim during the Halil Hamid conspiracy. She was Kuchuk's oblivion of slavery, his badge of nobility. Esma had undergone the customary treatment to render her sterile and unable to produce a male who would be a relative of the Sultan. In Beyhan's magnificent coral, alabaster and Persian marble baths, Hadidge would be steamed and massaged. Then, cleaned and perfumed, she would fall asleep under soft eiderdown and satin, a Turkish delight still melting in her mouth . . . and she could comfort little Esma and try to reconcile her to her childless fate.

Hadidge was long, lean and blond like her brother, Selim, with jade-yellow eyes and dark eyebrows and lashes. Her tall epicene body seemed actually to sway in the wind like the black cypresses of Topkapi. She towered over most other Turkish women, and her trademark was the comforting aroma of musk, cinnamon and ambergris, a perfume of her own invention. Hadidge had a square face and square hands that were constantly in motion, as if they too, like the Topkapi cypresses, were being buffeted by breezes and sudden gusts of wind. It seemed to her that to still them would be to take less from life than she felt entitled to, and she felt entitled to everything. In the time since Naksh-i-dil's arrival, greed and luxury had become Hadidge's habits. Always favored by her brother, Selim, she did what she pleased with her life and with her money. Turkish noblewomen depended upon neither father, husband nor brother for their wealth. Like everyone in the Empire, they depended only upon the Sultan. Women of high birth were free to invest, to loan, to borrow, to speculate and to spend their money without the consent of any male. And already Hadidge's spending was legendary.

A sensation of desolation flooded over her. The nameless boy's fresh body was already fading from memory and she had had so many memories, she thought. She always passed three or four months of a love affair in complete incognito. There was nothing to fear from an indiscretion by her lover, for his life was in danger. The punishment for adultery was either death by starvation or bowstring strangulation. Adultery with a Giaour was even worse; the lovers were bound together back to back in a leather sack and thrown into the Bosphorus or off a cliff. And she *was,* after all, married.

Hadidge Sultane stepped into her black and gold hooded caïque, which slid silently off its mooring onto the slick waveless waters of the gulf. Her rowers sprang to attention, and the Sultana closed the heavy black curtains of the enclosure around her. Her pilot lit the torches, which cast long shadows on the rowers, accentuating their silent movements and reflecting the ripples made by the movement of the slaves' oars.

Hadidge arrived at Beyhan's palace. She swept by the stupefied eunuchs, guards with drawn sabers, soldiers and Janissaries, and made straight for the baths. There, she dropped her cloak at the door, startling the Nubian slave who rushed to pick it up and give her a silk gomlek. Hadidge refused the fine muslin smock, but accepted the nalins and, placing her feet onto the eight-inch, raised-platform pattens of rosewood studded with silver nails and inlaid with mother-of-pearl, which protected her feet from the hot moist floor, she marched into the steam, disappearing like an apparition. She paused for one moment on the marble steps leading down to the circular alabaster pool, as warm and as smooth as the young nameless male skin she had so recently touched. Hadidge was silent as she began her ablutions.

The Sultana looked down at her fine, white flesh. She was old, married and as dry and barren as the distant steppes of Bursa. Her sterilization had taken place at the onset of her first menses. The daughters and sisters of Ottoman Sultans were by law forbidden to give birth to male children. A male child was suffocated the instant it saw light by the same hand that had delivered him. Sterilization was the alternative to male infanticide, in the interest of the succession to the throne. Of what use, thought Hadidge, to give birth to daughters who, although they lived, would never be considered Sultanas but merely Hanum, the title of all noble Turkish women? A Sultana's children were no better than the general population, denuded of all paternal and sentimental ties to the Sultan. Even as a child she had known what they had done to her. She would never forget the horrified look on Naksh-i-dil's face when she told her of it. The pride she had taken in her birth had far outweighed the necessity of the act. What could console this poor body now? wondered the Princess.

Shah Sultane, Selim's other sister, also lived her life far away from Topkapi and the harem. Shah Sultane, out of favor with Abdulhamid for years, lived in a palace in a suburb of Istanbul called Eyup. Her husband, who had had no title and no function, had not been admitted at court. Now that her brother was Sultan, she could come officially to Topkapi. Her husband had been covered with honors, revenues and functions. Beyhan Sultane was a widow who contented herself in building palaces on the Bosphorus and taking lovers. She lived in Istanbul itself, and in a lavish summer palace along the canal of the Black Sea near Bechik-Tash. Only Hadidge remained in the sanctuary of the harem, coming and going as she pleased. But her undisciplined fornications brought her restless nature neither peace nor comfort. What if she had caused men's deaths? thought Hadidge. What was one death more or less, when she carried death in her womb everywhere she went, and forever? Hadidge leaned back and let the expert hands of the bath slaves knead and massage her youthful body out of its bitterness and into the cynical lethargy that passed for her existence. Slowly the pain dissolved in the heat and mist and the caressing hands. Soon, soon she would be ready to show her face to the world.

Hadidge, accompanied by a black eunuch, entered Beyhan's reception room. The black eunuch retired, sword drawn, and Hadidge approached her half-sister. A balustrade of pillars ran across the width of the room, leaving a passage in the center ascended by steps so that the upper end of the room, where Beyhan now sat, was raised like a dais. This portion of the wall was covered with gilding, the walls pierced by various niches and circular recesses ornamented with pendant woodwork like icicles. Decidedly, thought Hadidge, Beyhan has gone too far in her lust for decoration. The effect was more like the gilding on a coffin than anything else. The wall panels were decorated with embossed festoons, glittering with burnished gold. The ceiling was enclosed in an octagonal molding with a central motif from which issued radiating decorations; the background was azure blue studded with gilded stars. There was no furniture, only a divan which occupied the whole length of the wall facing her, flanked with marble columns and covered in pale blue velvet embroidered with silver. Beyhan sat crosslegged smoking a chiboque, whose long tube extended yards onto the cushions below where it was received into a gilded vase.

Hadidge's bare feet (for she had removed her pattens) caressed the layers of silk rugs piled one upon the other at times eight or nine high, each more beautiful, more delicate, more embossed with gold or silver than the next. There were fifty or sixty covering the space between the two Princesses. In the dim lantern light, Beyhan scintillated in silver filigree, her long hair hanging loose and unornamented.

Beyhan didn't approve of Hadidge's conduct with men, especially Christian men, but being profoundly indifferent to everything, she didn't hold it against her favorite relative. Hadidge's offenses against Mohammed and Jesus did not concern her.

Esma Sultane was reclining, pale and wan, on a divan next to Beyhan, attended by the nurses and a slave. Hadidge's throat constricted in anguish. Where were those happy days with Naksh-i-dil in the harem now? Esma would be a married woman in a few months. Young as she was, thought Hadidge, Esma already had the seven cardinal attributes of Ottoman beauty: white skin, straight black eyebrows that met over huge, almond-shaped eyes, thick heavy eyelashes, a straight nose, a fine waist, long luxurious hair, and ample hips and thighs. Her hennaed hands were delicate and sculptured, the nails white and burnished. Her mouth, which was reputed to be the smallest in the Empire, turned up at each corner, winglike, as if she were always half expecting to burst into laughter. And her raucous laughter had become famous in the harem with its full-throated roughness and high timbre that both startled and provoked. What a waste! thought Hadidge. Esma's beauty would remain celebrated for years to come.

Esma's sterilization had been supervised by the Kiaya Roxanne and the Kizlar Aga himself. Shrouded in secrecy and mystery, it consisted of a delicate operation which left no mark on a Sultana's body, combined with pastes, drugs and herbs, both applied and taken orally, which slowly atrophied the barely developed fallopian tubes of the victim. There was no hemorrhaging and no trace. Esma could receive (if she chose) her husband completely intact.

"Hadidge!" cried Esma, raising herself on one elbow. "Oh, Hadidge!"

Hadidge laughed and ran to embrace Esma. It had been a long time, yet Esma didn't seem in the least surprised to see her.

Beyhan picked up a Chinese perfume bottle and scented Hadidge, caressing her neck and shoulders, pressing her closely. Wrapped in a handkerchief at her side, as was the custom, was a gift for her cousin. It was an exact replica of a carnation in beaten gold with a glass stem and a leaf. Hadidge caught her breath in surprise. She had rarely seen anything so beautiful. Beyhan must have taken it from her own jewels. Why?

"Boof, no news, my darling," replied Hadidge. "I am in love with Naksh-i-dil Kadine . . . I asked Mother to save her from the Eski Serai. She has been made a Kiaya."

"Because she's a Frank?" Beyhan placed her fork, which had pierced a piece of fruit, beside her plate. Beyhan was a Francophile, so that the trays laid out before the three women were set with knives and forks made of gold encrusted with diamonds, and the linen was of the most exquisite lace embroidered with gold thread and silk.

"No, Naksh-i-dil reneged after Abdulhamid's death, didn't you know? She is very beautiful . . ." said Hadidge Sultane in sign language, kissing the five points of her united fingertips and then opening them.

"Bravo," said Esma.

The three Princesses ate slowly and frugally, turning away more than half of the thirty or so dishes the silent slaves and eunuchs served them. At the end of dinner, sherbet was served in Chinese porcelain bowls, and the Princesses prepared to take their coffee and smoke their pipes. The supper had lasted slightly over four hours, and now they seemed talked out. But silence was as natural to them as speech. Silence had been the rule of their lives for as long as they could remember. Silence had ruled the Seraglio and the harem.

Beyhan's salon was lit softly with wax candles and multicolored lanterns which made patterns on the blue-tiled walls. Esma Sultane turned her perfect profile with its aquiline nose and exquisitely angled forehead toward Hadidge. Lying on her silken pillows and gently puffing on her pipe of tobacco, she listened to Hadidge, but her mind was on her marriage.

Esma's wedding was the only break in the monotony of harem life in Topkapi that year. Esma, installed in a specially rented Yali on the Bosphorus that served as her residence, received the official congratulations of the Empire seated on a throne. First came the other Princesses, Hadidge, Beyhan, Durrushevar and Shah. Esma's brother, Mustafa, imprisoned in the Cage, would not be allowed to attend the marriage of his sister. Esma then received the visits of the wives and daughters of Selim's ministers and viziers who kissed the pavement before rising to greet the twelve-year-old Sultana. The men were installed in the Selamlik, divided from the women's quarters as in all Ottoman houses. The noblewomen were presented by name, one by one, by the first wife of the Grand Vizier.

The Yali that Selim had rented was huge, comprising four large reception halls and forty or so rooms. Other guests' quarters had been built in the gardens, but even these didn't suffice to house the enormous crowd of dignitaries who would attend the Sultana's wedding. Special rooms had been prepared for each Princess, but it had been impossible to lodge each noblewoman separately, and so they ended up two or three or a whole family to a room. The vestibules and halls of the ground floor were so crowded it gave Esma the impression of the Last Judgment rather than a wedding.

Meals were served separately in the rooms assigned to those persons of the first rank. Those of second or third rank were served at communal tables. Esma dined alone in her room, as was the custom, on a small, low folding table of silver, its surface and legs covered with white linen, a silver tray placed upon it. On the tray lay a silver spoon for the soup and the pilau, and a spoon made of coral for the dessert. Two damp perfumed napkins rested on the tray beside the golden plate, surrounded by small bread rolls, olives, caviar and a carafe of water. But Esma was not hungry. Tears ran between her fingers onto the golden plate.

Princess Hadidge was also dining alone in her room. But when her mouth was not full of food, it was full of solitary laughter at the day's incident. She wiped her tears of laughter away with her napkin.

The wife of Vassif Pasha and the daughter of Hasan Aga had found themselves in the reception chambers in identical outfits: the same material, cut, fringe, color, decorations, up to the last detail. Even their hairdos had been identical. It had been one of the most comic, pathetic, hysterical scenes possible. Not, thought Hadidge, because of the exaggerated affectation, but because identical toilettes were considered an exterior sign of a reciprocal sympathy between two women that exceeded the admissible and moral limits of pure and innocent friendship . . . which was not at all the case. She, Hadidge, had gone to considerable trouble to bribe the two pompous ladies' dressmakers, hairdressers and silk merchants in order to replay in coin the remark they had made concerning her excursions into the Jewish ghetto!

The feast would last three days. A fourteen-cannon salute commemorated the event and Constantinople was decked out and lighted and festooned with flowers. The scarlet flags of the Ottoman Empire and the green flags of Islam flew at full mast. Thousands of lanterns lit the processions led by the heralds and the saluting, cheering crowds. The streets of the capital overflowed. There were hot loaves of bread and olives for rich and poor alike. There was a banquet of great splendor with fifty courses served by two hundred attendants in red silk and gold cloth who formed a solid line from the kitchen to the tables, looking like figures of wood as they stood next to the silver tables, the carpets and cloth of gold, the hundreds of gifts, the iced sherbets packed in snow from Mount Olympus. Presents had been sent from all over the Empire, and had followed the couple's procession of 200 mules loaded with carpets, furniture, gold and silver vases, accompanied by 160 magnificently dressed eunuchs, half of them black and half white. But his Sultan, Selim, had already shown his colors at the Arsenal—hysteria and the shadow of melancholy and depression, a presentiment of the misfortunes to come.

Naksh-i-dil watched the tall, black-bearded Sultan, surrounded by his black eunuchs, make his way slowly across the vast hall in total silence. He was dressed in a white pelisse trimmed in sable. His green turban was draped with coils of muslin that fell in voluminous folds around his cheeks, the whole held at the top with a diamond brooch in the shape of a branch with leaves from which shot the spray of a heron feather. With his elegant frame and his height accentuated by the two-foot turban, Naksh-i-dil had to admit that he made a much more imposing figure than Abdulhamid ever had. The handle of a pearl-encrusted dagger, symbol of absolute power, which was half revealed in his white sash, the black eunuchs' scimitars and his mother's gold dagger were the only arms in the entire harem. In the silence, Selim's enormous brown eyes, edged in black, swept the company almost timidly, a slight smile hovering around a sensitive but humorless mouth almost hidden by his beard. He greeted his mother, then Hadidge and his other blood sister, Shah, before turning to the Kadines, Ikbals and Kiayas. Naksh-i-dil got a whiff of his perfume and lifted her eyes to his for a split second. In them she saw desperation. Then, with an imperturbable nod, Selim gave the signal for the feast to begin. Mihrishah Valide, according to custom, had consulted the royal astrologer, the astronomers, the magicians, the Ulemas and her own confessor to find a date acceptable to all for the feast. Selim had then accompanied Esma into a private apartment, where they had remained cloistered for more than an hour.

Esma had resembled a porcelain doll, in a caftan of pale green bordered with gold and pearls. She wore a diamond coronet and an egg-sized diamond her husband had given her the day before, as was also the custom. The bridegroom's gift was called the yus gueurumluk, Hadidge had whispered, or "the gift to look upon the face."

As the music continued, the Kiaya Roxanne stood before a silk sheet held by two young slaves, and taking handfuls of gold and silver coins, flung them down the stairway onto the ground-floor vestibule. The vestibule took on the aspect of a wheatfield, thought Naksh-i-dil, standing close to Hadidge, as the guests bent and rose like cornstalks swaying in the wind as with billowing silk veils, jeweled hands and hennaed feet they rushed to gather the carpet of gleaming coins. The noise was such that it covered the sound of the music.

The next day the official public procession wound through the streets of Istanbul for more than four hours. The city danced; the streets were hung with lanterns, flowers and wooden triumphal arches. Eunuchs sprayed pitch to clear the way for the procession, and Janissaries threw coins into the crowd. That night the guns of Topkapi roared. Only the faint rumblings of the celebrations reached the Kadines and Ikbals back in the harem who stood in the gardens to listen to the boom of cannons and watch the lights of the fireworks. After the wedding, Hadidge took a new lover.

"On Taraf! On Taraf!" Hadidge Sultane urged her black Persian charger across the arid and sunbaked steppes of Cappadocia. Here she felt free and safe from the eternal intrigues of the Seraglio, the incessant demands of her brother, his obsessive vengeance. Here she felt the all-embracing security of the Ottomans, the continuity of their history and the rise of their glory. She breathed deeply. Two great armies had come together here in 1071, where one of the most momentous battles in history had taken place and the Turkomans under Alp Arslan had taken the day, founding the greatest Empire of all times. She was in love.

The man, a European, and Hadidge Sultane had stopped at Sivas, the ancient capital of Bayazid's Empire. The fortress was in such contrast with the palace she was building on the Bosphorus that she laughed out loud, her teeth flashing through the transparent veil she used as a shield against the dust rather than as a disguise. What would Bayazid think of such a place? She smiled. Hadidge looked around at the imposing and timeless landscape. Russia, the war, were very, very far away. This was the land where she wanted to bring her only love. This was the real heart of the greatest Empire. What was Istanbul except a capital? This was the land of the Hittites—long before Alexander the Great. To live here, one needed not a palace but a tent like Genghis Khan's, a tent large enough for fifty women. Nature like this was dominated only when one was mounted on a Persian charger. How could Catherine hope to dominate such a landscape with her fat ass, her galleys and orchestras, an old, ugly, mean provincial German Princess, no matter how many airs and titles she gave herself.

She, Hadidge, was the true European, the true aristocrat with centuries of incomparable monuments and imperial cities in her blood. The emotion she felt here in this place transcended everything. Here met the Khans, the Turkomans, the Romans, the Byzantines. . . . Hadidge Sultane's blood was racing with the emotion of the moment and the Christian man she was with. She had kept her liaison with Tabib Lorenzo Noccioli secret even from Selim.

Hadidge rode astride like all Turkish women, but she rode bareback, disguised in a Janissary uniform, her hair hidden by an immense white-cotton turban, to which was attached her veil. Hadidge reined in to wait for Lorenzo. The long expedition had excited her and the warm flesh of the Persian charger quivered under her in exhaustion. Her thighs ached and she was out of breath. Here she was safe, surrounded by her ancestors, her landscape, her freedom. She looked around in satisfaction as Lorenzo joined her. Her passion for Lorenzo came closest to what ordinary people would call love.

Dr. Lorenzo Noccioli shaded his gray eyes from the bright sun, savoring the presence of the Princess beside him. Cynic that he was, he had been as surprised as Hadidge at their genuine mutual passion.

Hadidge was twenty-four and he was forty-eight years old, hardly an age for the griefs and riches of adolescent love. Yet here they were, informer and Christian, reigning Princess and Moslem, with no past to speak of and no future to dream of, happier than they had ever been in their lives. Everything had been burned out of their memories by this vast, unrelenting landscape. For Lorenzo it was like nothing he had ever seen before, filled with endless conical shapes like pyramids and volcanic craters like open graves. They started up again as the last rays of sun touched the fantastical, otherworldly landscape.

Hadidge and Lorenzo's splendid horses, thick in the neck, small in the head, solid in the barrel with long silky tails set high and standing off straight in the pureblood Arab fashion, had stopped short at full speed, flung themselves back upon their haunches, and now stood like horses of stone. Both horses looked wonderfully picturesque with their gold-embroidered saddle cloths under peaked saddles covered with crimson, green and black velvet, their long shover-stirrups and their tasseled headgear. The furious gallop had excited the two riders, and Hadidge's thighs and hips ached with effort and sexual excitement. She had been known to ride for hours in this state since she was a girl, her excitement, her body burning her, ebbing and flowing, rising and climaxing in the solitary gallops. But this time Lorenzo was beside her. She could hear him breathing. She had only to turn her head to study his handsome profile crowned with wavy blond hair, untied and etched into the hazy light as if with a stylo. Yet she stared straight ahead. She sensed that Lorenzo too wanted to savor the moment. She moved her stallion closer to his so that their knees touched. Lorenzo's mare brought her head down as if in compliance as Lorenzo dismounted and held up his arms to Hadidge. Hadidge descended. She would have preferred the tent, the silken pillows, the slow, leisurely comfortable exploration . . . but they would have that too, she thought, as Lorenzo took his pleasure swiftly, brutally, Hadidge submitting to his rough caresses. There was something both stoic and pathetic, thought Lorenzo, in their coupling in this overwhelming landscape.

Hadidge was silent beneath him, almost subdued, as if even her willfulness could not break nature's oppressive silence. Lorenzo also made not a sound, for fear of penetrating the wilderness surrounding Hadidge's contorting form. Lorenzo thought suddenly of music, the Venetian intertwining lines of melody both sharp and curved. His head made a movement not unlike that of his spirited mount, whose rich saddlecloth lay under the prone body of Hadidge Sultane.

• CHAPTER FIVE •

LORENZO 1790

> My love is your happiness?
> It is possible for you to buy this happiness
> Listen—I can establish equality between us . . .
> Who amongst you will buy with your life,
> One of my nights?
> —ALEXANDER PUSHKIN, *Egyptian Nights,* 1837

It had been months since Ishak Bey's arrival in Istanbul and still Selim refused to receive him. He went from old friend to old friend, trying to find a reason why he, of all the pages who had spent their youth with Selim in the Cage, was being ignored.

The gentle Kuchuk Huseyin was now Vice Admiral to Hasan Gazi. Kuchuk's eyes seemed actually to will Ishak Bey out of Istanbul.

"What with King Louis practically a prisoner," Kuchuk said, "and Selim suspicious of everything and everyone, even his loyal Grand Vizier. It doesn't seem a propitious moment, Ishak . . . for your return. I'm sorry . . ."

"But my letters from the King of France . . . my presents!"

But even as Ishak said it, he realized how stupid it was. Who the devil wanted a letter from a deposed King? Who would be stupid and unlucky enough to bring such letters except someone called Ishak Bey? Why, he thought, was it every time he washed up on the shores of the Bosphorus, he was swept out to sea by fate, or should he say Hasan Gazi?

"Gazi never forgave you for once being forgiven by him, having taken advantage of his pardon to escape to France with letters from Selim while Abdulhamid was still alive. . . . It is not so much Selim but Gazi. If you insist on staying, at least lie low and for heaven's sake, keep your nose clean. . . ."

All Ishak Bey could do was wait. Or go. He waited. That was how he came to renew his relationship with Lorenzo Noccioli.

"Perhaps you can persuade Selim to see me. Why has he turned away from me? I don't understand." Lorenzo really wasn't listening to Ishak. He was thinking of Hadidge. Vaguely Lorenzo, in his jovial, expansive mood, promised to intervene for Ishak with Selim; however, he had no intentions of speaking to Selim. Ishak was France's man. He, Lorenzo, had changed camps. He was now working for the Austrians.

Ishak's brother Ismail at the Admiralty was even more emphatic. "It's the war. We have virtually lost the war on our eastern front," he told Ishak as he in turn complained bitterly at Selim's silence and refusal to see anyone.

"Selim has come to the throne bent on revenge, the recovery of the Crimea, Ochakov, and everything Catherine has taken from us. To get the money for a new campaign, Selim has publicly sent his own gold and silverplate to the imperial mint to be melted down. He has ordered all the notables of the Empire to do likewise. It is forbidden to use gold or silverplate on houses, horses or persons. All male subjects between fifteen and sixty are on standby orders to serve in the army.

"The Empire is on the brink of disaster," Ismail continued. "Selim has recalled the old Algerian veteran corsair Hasan from his post on the Black Sea to become Grand Vizier and commander-in-chief of the army. But Hasan is unable to administer the government and the army at the same time, and both are falling apart. The Grand Vizier's attempt to recover control of the Bug and Dnieper rivers has been thwarted by Potemkin and a Russian general of genius, Suvorov. He and the Austrians have smashed the Danube defenses. Both are ready to drive into the heart of the Empire if something doesn't happen. . . ."

"And what could possibly happen?" asked Ishak, shaking his head.

"Well," continued Ismail, "Selim wants to continue the war through another summer so that both his enemies will at least return what they have taken in exchange for peace. He has issued an ultimatum: Alliance or Peace. . . . And the whole of Europe *needs* peace. The seditious ideas of the French Revolution are spreading across the entire Continent, causing internal unrest everywhere. Austria is especially weakened by troubles within. One victory for us," mused Ismail, "and we, the

Swedes and the Poles, with the tacit agreement of the English and the Prussians, could dictate peace to Austria and Russia, by force if necessary."

"Dictate peace by force." Ishak smiled. "What a novel idea. So . . . Oriental . . ."

Selim's first military action was a surprise attack on the banks of the river Rimnik. It was three days before he knew that three hours after sunrise, of his 100,000 men, there were 57,000 dead, 27,000 wounded, 10,000 prisoners taken and 6,000 deserters abandoning tents, cannons and artillery, straggling toward the Danube. The Russian general Suvorov had marched through the Balkans in April to meet up with the Austrians at Rimnik, reaching them just at the moment when Hasan, Selim's Grand Vizier, had thrown 100,000 men into battle in hopes of reestablishing the honor of the Moslem army. For his victory Catherine gave her General the surname of Rimniski, "river filled with cadavers." She had more than a hero, she had the first General of Europe for the next eighteen years.

The Algerian Grand Vizier, Hasan, retreated across the Danube, where he saved his own honor by committing suicide.

The Admirals Hannibal and Vshukov had crushed the Ottoman navy in the Black Sea and their fleets approached Constantinople. Another fleet, under the command of the Neapolitan pirate José de Ribas, had blocked the mouth of the Danube, fending off every Turkish galley that attempted passage. Kilin had been taken, followed by Tulcha and Izakchi. Prince Coburg had entered Valachie and was advancing toward Bucharest. Laudon was bombarding Belgrade, and soon all of Serbia would be at the mercy of the Austrians. Selim had already lost Bender, Akerman, Ochakov, Moldavia and Bessarabia, and Galatz had been reduced to ashes.

One of the bloodiest battles in history was about to begin.

Izmail.

"Little Mother," wrote the General Suvorov to the Empress Catherine II at the end of July, 1790. "Izmail is at your feet."

Selim recalled Hasan Gazi the Victorious as Grand Vizier to lead again the armies on land and sea and settle his old score with Russia's Suvorov. . . .

For Gazi, there remained only one question. How had Suvorov found out the plans for the Battle of the Rimnik River?

Selim, who had always expected to be betrayed, who had lived with

betrayal, bowed his head. There was only one person to whom he had
confided his plans . . . breaking the sacred rule that a Sultan never
confided in anyone. Hadidge. He had told Hadidge Sultane . . . his
sister.

"Who did you tell of my plans?"

"No one."

"You're lying, Hadidge. It was my mistake to have confided in you
but I command the truth from you."

"Lorenzo."

"My Lorenzo?" asked Selim in disbelief.

"My Lorenzo," said Hadidge, her eyes blazing, "but never. . . ."

Lorenzo. This confidant, doctor, teacher. He's a . . . traitor. Of
course, thought Selim. For if Lorenzo had betrayed *one* Sultan,
Abdulhamid, for him, he had betrayed *all* Sultans. A traitor of a Sultan
was always a traitor of a Sultan.

"But you can't be sure it was him!" cried Hadidge. "There must have
been others besides us who knew! The Divan!"

"I have interrogated the entire Divan. There is no traitor
there. . . ."

"How can you be sure. . . ?" cried Hadidge.

"Hadidge, why did Lorenzo have over fifty thousand piastres with
the Jew Calmin? Why is he on the payroll of both the Austrian and the
French embassies? Why did he need more money when I gave him more
than enough. . . ? I'll tell you why. To leave here rich. To return to
Italy a rich man. Hadidge, he has a fortune and part of it is probably
yours. . . ."

"No."

"You gave him money!"

"No! No!"

"To leave you, my sister. For that was his plan. We even found his
passport and his paid passage . . . leaving here in three days."

"No," said Hadidge. But it was not a protestation. "You don't want
to kill him!"

"No, I don't want to kill him, God knows."

The Meadow of the Dead dominated the most beautiful view of the
Bosphorus and Asia. It was a forest thick with cypress, acacia and
sycamore trees, and from a distance the white tombstones gave it the air
of immense temple ruins. Since the Ottomans had been born of Asia,
they turned toward Asia in death. The dead from all regions were bur-

ied there, except Jews, and Greeks, Armenians and Franks could be found walking along the serpentine alleys of the cemetery. Lorenzo Noccioli decided to cut through the cemetery on his way to the Arsenal, where he had been summoned. There was such shade and such peace, he thought, one had the impression of entering a great half-illuminated cathedral. Each stone, laid horizontally, was covered with regular and elegant inscriptions in Armenian or Greek, and most of them had a sculptured symbol of the deceased's profession: hammer and scythe, pens, feathers, necklaces; a banker was represented by a scale, a priest by a miter, a barber by a basin, a surgeon by a scalpel. Lorenzo passed a stone on which was carved a head separated from its trunk—the grave of someone assassinated or beheaded.

Darkness was falling, but Lorenzo knew that if it was possible to get lost in the winding streets of Istanbul, it was impossible to lose one's way here. From the smaller lanes, one entered the larger roads and the courtyards like little cells, encumbered with barely visible boxes and bundles, and one returned by other smaller courtyards lit by lanterns. One mounted toward the daylight, or walked, head lowered, along the long corridors under the humid vaults between black walls that led to tiny secret doors. But there were always people present and voices could be heard from behind hedges; couples picnicked close to family graves and lovers made furtive appointments. One would suddenly encounter black objects whose nature was mysterious until the play of light revealed either an old man smoking a pipe or a veiled woman cleaning a gravestone.

Dr. Lorenzo realized he had made a mistake to walk through the Meadow of the Dead. It would have been quicker if he and his servant had taken the normal route to the Arsenal. He was going to be late. Lorenzo stopped abruptly, his hair prickling on his head. He felt the bowstring around his neck even before he heard the footsteps or the grunt and thud of his servant, who had fallen dead behind him. Lorenzo slipped his hand between his throat and the cutting edge of the bowstring, which immediately severed it to the bone, causing blood to gush up the open sleeve of his robe. Lorenzo's life flashed before his eyes. He was young. He didn't want to die. True, he had lived dangerously, but it was the times, not the man, who had chosen danger. Lorenzo remembered the night he had stayed at Selim's side. The night Selim had seized his hand and said: "You are my friend, yes, my friend, for I am not a man like any other man, this I know. They want to deceive me, but you, you will reveal the truth to me. I asked it in the name of my father, Mustafa, who was so good to you." Lorenzo struggled with his assassins, his body twisting toward the setting sun, his face illuminated by it, his eyes wide with the search for oxygen. The horizon was covered by puffs of clouds grouped in picturesque formations. The inflamed globe before him seemed to augment in size as it descended while all the shadowed creatures pursued their dance of death. The clouds took on the most brilliant colors as the sun plunged into their thickness, offering the image of an immense fire. Little by little the globe disappeared and the flames slowly diminished, passing through all the imperceptible degrees of paleness, until all was extinguished.

During his stay in Naples as a young man, Lorenzo had always regretted not seeing an eruption of Vesuvius, thinking that it must be the greatest, most imposing phenomenon that nature could offer to a man's eyes. Dr. Lorenzo consoled himself that except for the terror which faraway danger always inspired, the most beautiful eruption of Vesuvius, overflowing its thousand-meter circumference with its explosions, smoke, rain of ashes and rivers of red lava, could never match a sunset in Constantinople with all the magnificent conflagrations that accompanied it; the dark azure of the firmament, the purity of the air, the burning tint of the Orient, spreading its dye over the least of nature's phenomena. "Hadidge," he whispered. His own death, thought Lorenzo, as he heard the crack of his neck being broken, the death of a man in the flower of his forty-eighth year in the mortuary field of Istanbul, had an end, a perfection, a charm unknown anywhere else. . . .

In the depths of the citadel of Bursa in Anatolia, Hadidge touched her forehead to her prayer rug: "God is great," she whispered.

The Austrian Consul refused all comment when the bodies of Dr. Lorenzo and his servant were found strangled in the cemetery, their money purses intact. As a Florentine, Lorenzo was technically under the protection of the Austrian delegation, but his close relations with the Seraglio, Selim and the Princess made him, well, "almost a Turk," said the Ambassador. And, he added meaningfully, "a Turk accused of high treason." At any rate, the report presented by the Austrian delegation verified that none of Dr. Lorenzo's effects had been touched, which indicated, along with the manner of death and the absence of all pillage, the powerful and mysterious hand of the Sultan. . . . The Austrians made no official protest. No note was taken of the splendor of the Oriental sunset or the eruption of Vesuvius. Or the death of a spy.

*   *   *

Naksh-i-dil had expected to see Hadidge destroyed by grief. Instead a cold fatalistic anger had gripped her. "What could I do, Naksh-i-dil? Selim was adamant," she said. "Selim asked me point-blank who, besides he and I, had secret information concerning the invasion. I had to say that there had been only one other person—Lorenzo."

"And you don't hate Selim for it?" Naksh-i-dil asked.

"Hate Selim? What right have I to hate my sovereign, my brother. . . ?"

"You mean Lorenzo deserved death?"

"How should I know?" Hadidge screamed. "How can I tell? How can I judge? I have never been taught the difference between right and wrong!"

Naksh-i-dil's mouth opened in astonishment. Hadidge's brother had executed her lover and this was all she had to say! Yet it was so long since she herself had thought about right and wrong in this shoreless, anchorless, amoral dream of real life that she was at a loss to answer Hadidge. Treason. Betrayal. Should Hadidge have protected Lorenzo with her life, or have betrayed him to her sovereign brother to whom she had sworn fidelity? Should Selim have condemned Lorenzo without a hearing, or did Hadidge also furnish the evidence and become the jury? If Hadidge had loved Lorenzo, then she was a monster. If she had not, then she was a fool. What did that make her, Naksh-i-dil? Did her slavery remove responsibility for her acts? Responsibility for her soul was still hers, thought Naksh-i-dil. Or had she bartered it away to Allah for Mahmud's life and her own safety? For one second of indescribable terror, the fear of God seized her, then released her like a small animal in the jaws of a hound.

"It was Hasan Gazi," sulked Hadidge, "who demanded Lorenzo's head. Selim was against it. He *told* me he didn't want Lorenzo's death."

"And you believe him?"

"It was his kismet," said Hadidge. "I had sworn Lorenzo to secrecy. I pleaded for Lorenzo's life . . . I almost succeeded, but in vain. He had beem compromised too many times. He . . . he was a triple agent. I even warned him. But *he* didn't believe me. He thought that once again, he could escape . . . that Selim owed him too much . . ."

But Naksh-i-dil knew as well as Hadidge that in a Sultanate there *was* no useful warning once a man was condemned!

"It was his *kismet,*" repeated Hadidge stubbornly.

"You loved him, didn't you?"

"I no longer cared if he loved me or not. Or if I was only useful to him. And I never really knew if he loved me. . . . Occidentals and their ways . . . the ways of *men* are still, after all these years, a mystery to me. . . . I am not even sure he was a *doctor.* I am not even sure he was *Florentine.* I never bothered to inquire. If only I could be sure he loved me . . . even if he used me . . ."

"You loved him, didn't you?"

"I loved the wrong man."

Hadidge Sultane did not have the moral force necessary to support either loss or love. She had been brought up that way. . . .

Izmail was on the Danube, its garrison had 35,000 men with 265 guns. The advancing Russians had 31,000 men and 600 guns as well as their fleet. The Russians laid siege to the fortress, but the three Russian generals quarreled and decided to withdraw. Suvorov, on his way to take over, met the retreating troops and ordered them straight back.

With the words "My brothers, no quarter: provisions are scarce," Suvorov launched his night assault. Suvorov forced the walls of the fortress. The Ottomans fought for every street, every house until, on the seventh day, the fortress fell with 33,000 killed, 9,000 taken prisoner and 265 guns seized. Ten thousand houses had been smashed by cannon, 15,000 bodies of women and children were found burned, looting went on for three days and amounted to some 2 million rubles in addition to the value of the slaves taken.

On the last day of the year, the sole survivor of the siege of Izmail appeared before Selim, like a specter from its common grave.

And for the first time in the midst of total disaster, Naksh-i-dil found the courage to love the Empire of the Ottomans.

At that moment Catherine II had been playing with her two-year-old grandson, Alexander. She had reached an age that few lawful despots ever achieved. And her goal was at hand: Selim would sue for peace. She would keep all that she had gained by the Treaty of Kuchuk, and more. She would have the Crimea. . . . Only one dream remained. She looked into the clear blue eyes of the child she wished to succeed her. Not her son Paul, but her grandson Alexander would prevail over the Ottomans.

"Solvogod," the Empress whispered in the ear of her grandson Alexander. He squirmed in her arms, his tiny black boots rustling in the folds of her satin skirt.

"That tickles," he said.

"Solvogod," repeated Catherine, laughing. "Remember, because it tickles!" she joked.

Solvogod was the old Russian name for Constantinople.

• CHAPTER SIX •

ISHAK BEY 1792

In the midst of the war, the old Lion, Hasan Gazi, died, attended by his one wife and his grief-stricken overfed lion. The last order of Hasan Gazi had been the assassination of Ishak Bey.

In his obsession with chasing traitors and the unmitigated defeats of the Empire, the unwinnable war, Hasan Gazi had associated Ishak Bey with the Lorenzo affair. Without asking the permission of Sultan Selim, he sent Ishak Bey to the island of Lemnos on a false mission, accompanied by two tchiaoux, guards from the Admiralty, to dispatch him.

Ishak Bey's destiny seemed fixed: his errant and agitated life, settled once and for all, as it had been lived, under a great misunderstanding. It seemed to say: Ishak, you have gone too far this time, made too many mistakes, made too many enemies. This time, your beauty, your intelligence, your charm, your luck won't save you. You have been compromised too many times, taken too many chances to live in a place where a man's life and fortune is at the mercy of the whim of an absolute despot. You have dealt with duplicity, scandal and treason in every degree, color, religion, race and nationality. You have loved and been loved in every imaginable intensity by both sexes. You have trafficked in power and let it slip through your fingers as Zorich had his great fortune. The Ottomans accused you of working for the French, the French for the English, the English for the Russians, the Russians for the Ottomans! Yet in your own way, you have been a loyal and faithful servant, a Moslem, a lover, a man who has never counted the cost or the consequence of an action if the action seemed a good idea at the time. . . . Your fatalism, if that's what it is, stems from your belief in kismet, that

mere man can change nothing—yet you have tried to change everything. Even beauty seems to curse you, tripping you up in squalid,
ridiculous or sublime circumstances, making it impossible for anything
ordinary to happen to you: family, home, wives, children, fortune, position. Yet you are an *ordinary* man. You have simply risked your life in
so many places, in so many different languages, that of all the titles you
held, from Reis to asshole (that was what his brother, Ismail, had called
him), the only title that really matters to you now is *"son of your
mother"* (may Heaven repose beneath her feet).

Bitterness shadowed the fabulous beauty which had been both his
blessing and his curse. For how, he asked himself, had it served him?
Love, yes, the envy of his peers, the isolation and solitude of a freak. For
uncommon beauty as any uncommonness—a dwarf, eunuch, deaf-mute
or blind man—separated one forever from the race of ordinary men.
What happened, he mused, in the life of a Sultan who was never Sultan,
of an Osmanli too energetic for the Turks and too lazy for the Europeans? In a way, he thought, his life had been as empty as that of a
sterilized Sultana: unfruitful, frustrated, dreamlike, anonymous, almost
as if he, like they, would never engender.

By the time the boat upon which Ishak was prisoner stopped in the
Dardanelles, Hasan Gazi was dead, but his order still stood. Two Jewish dragomen who had just spoken to the tchiaoux warned Ishak of the
fate in store for him at Lemnos.

"You still have friends," said the two Jews. "Jump ship. There is an
Algerian corsair anchored in the Dardanelles. We have asked the young
Reis to kidnap you. He has agreed for the sum of five thousand pias-
tres."

"But I don't have five thousand piastres," wailed Ishak.

"The Reis in question offers you credit," said the dragoman, "when
he realized you were the famous Ishak Bey, the friend of Suleiman Aga
of Tunis, the favorite of Sultan Selim . . . the . . ."

"Stop!" cried Ishak.

That night he jumped ship, escaping his guards, and was rowed out
in a small boat to meet Reis Hamidou for the first time.

"Well, I agree to give you credit," said Hamidou.

When Ishak Bey was discovered to be a naval expert, a passionate
and dedicated sailor, a distinguished mathematician and a Reis,
Hamidou begged him to return with him to Algiers. After all, where
was he to go now? London? Paris? The Algerian navy could teach Ishak
Bey a great deal . . . especially about piracy on the high seas. . . .

*   *   *

Hamidou began to curse softly. His squadron had lost the Danes and they were nearing the Strait of Gibraltar. His rage at losing the tempting capture made him decide to do something no Algerian corsair had ever dared to do, pass the strait into the Atlantic for prey. Profiting by night and a brisk breeze, Reis Hamidou broke out of the Strait of Gibraltar into the Atlantic with his fleet: his own *Americana,* the *Portuguese,* a frigate carrying forty-four cannons commanded by the Reis Al Rarnaout, a frigate, also of forty-four cannons, commanded by the Reis Ahmed Zmerli, and a brig of twenty cannons, commanded by the Reis Mustafa, the Maltese.

For a few days, the Algerian division navigated in the Atlantic Ocean, whose horizons were so much more vast than those of the Mediterranean Sea; then it was time to start for Istanbul. As he came within sight of the mouth of the strait where it was about eight miles across, narrow enough that land was visible on each side, the tip of the Kingdom of Morocco glistening on the southern shore, and the steep walls of the jabal tariq rising up to the left on the Spanish coast, Hamidou found his course blocked by a tall ship, flying no flag but armed with forty-four cannons. As their flag was slowly raised, he saw that farther on there were three more ships, all forty-four-gun frigates. They were Portuguese. And they all barred his way home to Istanbul. What a fool, he thought, to have taken such a chance!

Hamidou had two choices: to flee back into the Atlantic or to call the Portuguese's bluff. The Reis gave the order to the station-crier, whose megaphone transmitted his order. The three Algerian frigates closed ranks and, with all sails unfurled, advanced on the enemy ships, bowsprit on stern.

"If the Portuguese ships of war attack," shouted Hamidou, "board them all at the same time. . . ."

The Algerians advanced as if there were not seventeen thousand tons of Portuguese maritime ahead of them.

Just as the Algerian frigates were on the point of ramming the vessels, the ships veered and turned right, taking another tack. It was at this moment that Hamidou entered the legends of Algerian piracy.

In an act of sublime bravado, Hamidou struck sails.

The astounded crowd, assembled on the farther shore to witness the spectacle of the naval battle, had broken into applause at Hamidou's cheeky maneuver. If the Portuguese wanted a fight, he had struck sails to accommodate them. After waiting long enough to have made his point that no fleet on earth could force him to flee, the great Reis loosened sails and proceeded through the strait always bowsprit to stern. The hurrahs of the Gibraltarians resounded across the narrow strait. Hamidou, his white teeth flashing, his laughter rising as high as the shrouds, saluted his admirers as his division placed itself into position to sail home to Algiers. His most famous battle, as he would recount later, had not taken place. Or rather had taken place with his corsairs down, showing his ass to the Strait of Gibraltar and to any ship who dared cross him in the Mediterranean.

"Mary, Mother of God, why hast thou cast me out?"
He walked into his chamber and laid his face upon his bed with his feet on the floor. It was July 8, 1792. He was forty-five years old, childless, friendless and penniless. And around him swirled the French Revolution.

The serving girl, Marie-Louise, wasn't sure what she saw when she opened the door of the tiny rented rooms near the Bastille on Rue St. Martin. At first she thought there was no one in the room. Then she saw what seemed to be a motionless shadow standing, yet leaning threateningly across the bed. She saw it was a man, immobile, his head laid on the side of the bed, his feet firmly planted on the floor. The shutters were closed and the room had a peculiar odor. Something she had never smelled before. It was not altogether unpleasant. It was the smell of something dried—like dried figs or dried hay mingled with an animal smell, or that of threshed wheat. Marie-Louise was from the country.

"Monsieur Jones," whispered the maid. She approached the dark shadow. The man's legs were braced apart as if on the decks of a rolling ship, his two arms grasping the wooden bed column as if it were a mast. The malfunctioning shutters let in a slit of light that outlined the man's contours in a halo of radiant white.

"Monsieur Jones," Marie-Louise repeated. Then she realized that the standing man was dead but not yet cold; an Admiral dead of dropsy, jaundice, poverty, mischance, broken dreams and unbearable disappointments.

A letter waited for him at the American Legation in the Hôtel de Langeac on the Champs-Élysées.

GEORGE WASHINGTON, PRESIDENT OF THE UNITED STATES OF
AMERICA TO ALL TO WHOM THESE PRESENTS SHALL COME
GREETINGS

Know ye that reposing special trust and confidence in the integrity, prudence and abilities of John Paul Jones, a citizen of the United States, I have nominated and appointed him, the said JOHN PAUL JONES, a Commissioner for the United States, giving him full power and authority, for and in the name of the United States of America to confer, treat and negotiate with the DEY and GOVERNMENT of Algiers concerning the ransom of all citizens of the United States of America in captivity with the same Dey . . . and to conclude and sign a convention thereupon transmitting the same to the President of the United States for his final ratification by and with the advice and consent of the Senate of the United States. . . . Given under my hand at the city of Philadelphia the first day of June in the year one thousand seven hundred and ninety-two and of the Independence of the United States, the sixteenth.

George Washington
by the President and the Secretary of State
Thomas Jefferson

John Paul Jones had been appointed American Consul for Algiers. He had been authorized to pay $27,000 to redeem the thirteen American slaves still alive—$25,000 for a treaty, his salary and $1,000 to clothe the freedmen and to send them home . . .

• CHAPTER SEVEN •

COSIMA 1793

Ishak's life at sea cleansed him of Gazi's betrayal and Selim's condemnation without a hearing. It reinforced his own innocence and his own determination to start again. And at Smyrna he made his way down the gangplank and was received by the French Consul, Amoureaux, a man he knew from his old days in Versailles. He looked into the eyes of the Consul's daughter, Cosima, and knew, like his dead enemy Gazi, that he too would love only one woman. He left Reis Hamidou for good.

Smyrna, the queen of the cities of Anatolia, was on the western coast of Asia Minor on the shores of a gulf that bore her name. The city was the largest commercial center in the Levant, formed of a population of Jews, Franks and Greeks in which French was the official language. Raked since the beginning of time by fire, earthquakes and plagues, ten times destroyed and ten times raised again, Smyrna's central position in the Mediterranean and the perfection of its harbor attracted goods from the whole Empire, by sea and by caravan: silks, camel's hair, cotton, gold- and silver-embroidered muslin, Moroccan leather, wool wax, resins, grapes, nuts, hashish, sugar, coffee, iron nails, porcelain, arms, indigo and opium; amber, musk, lapis lazuli, rubber, rugs, pearls, diamonds, emeralds and rubies. Smyrna counted 120,000 inhabitants, of which 16,000 were slaves.

Mount Pagus looked down lovingly on the city's narrow twisting streets and alleys and white-washed houses and terraces with their sudden bursts of rhododendrons or morning glory. The city's pride was its roses, which grew both wild and cultivated and spread their perfume and blossoms like clouds of woven silk into shade and sunshine, light and darkness. As a colony Smyrna had belonged to many nations. It had fallen to the Ottomans in 1322.

Ishak Bey felt very much at ease and happy in the house of Cosima's father: a good and jovial man, erudite, disgusted and bored with the world, who passed his days in bed, where he pursued his diplomatic duties. Amoureaux's comfortable house stood on a knoll overlooking the gulf, the only habitation allowed to fly a national flag. The Consul was a widower and a longtime friend and political ally of Choiseul-Gouffier. Cosima had fallen in love with Ishak. It was so different from anything Ishak had experienced or imagined before that, for him at least, it was a kind of resurrection. He realized he was too jealous of Cosima to seduce her; the only solution was to marry her. He would have only one wife. Renouncing Islam for the sake of Cosima seemed a mere detail, becoming a Christian convert, a painless, utterly unedifying experience.

"I have only one faith and one country," he had told them all. Could he reasonably claim either now? thought Ishak.

He married Cosima.

Cosima asked a million questions about Ishak's past life, the court, the Seraglio, Sultan Selim, Reis Hamidou, the eunuchs . . . but always she returned to the harem. It drew her like a magnet. One man who had seven official wives and countless others? One man who had the power of life and death over them all? And the veil? Like a convent, was it not? All that luxury and all that terror, she exclaimed, in one place! Cosima never tired of hearing about the riches of Topkapi, the myriad costumes, the jewels and furs. And the harem both repulsed and mesmerized her, thought Ishak. One day she arrived at dinner dressed as a Sultana, veil and all, her fair hair under a huge white-gauze turban. "The French Sultana," she exclaimed, pirouetting before him, opening her cashmere shawl. Imitating the Countess du Barry, she had had her dressmakers sew her a European version of a harem costume. It was ludicrous yet frightening, thought Ishak, seeing Cosima turned into an Odalisque . . . a slave. He imagined the large and lofty gate of Topkapi, the Bab-i-Humayun, closing in on Cosima forever. His heart beating faster, he took her in his arms.

"When the top layer of society is composed of slaves," asked Cosima, "what sense does it make to speak of slavery?"

But Ishak thought of it, and the injustice it had done him, constantly. He thought of the harem gate called the Yali Kiosk, where a suspected Vizier or a white eunuch or a dismissed favorite would be ordered to await his destiny. And when the door opened behind him, he would not know if it had been opened by the bearer of a bowstring or a sable pelisse and new honors. . . . That dark, dangerous, sordid world seemed far away from sunlit Smyrna and sunlit Cosima. Yet his unexplained death sentence haunted him. Ishak didn't want to worry Cosima and his happiness, but in his heart of hearts, he knew the reason.

The Ottomans had ruled slaves for four centuries in an intricate, complicated balance of terror, ideology, bakshish and caste. Terror was a weapon, but ideology was the true weapon of slavery. For one had to be *convinced* that one was a slave in order to be one. Everyone in the Ottoman Empire was a slave, and they *knew* themselves to be . . . but there were *slaves* of slaves, and *slaves* of *slaves* of slaves. What more ingenious way was there to preserve peace than to convince every slave he was one notch better than every other slave! The wearers of sable despised the wearers of leopard, the green turbans looked down on the red turbans, the long-sleeved had only contempt for the sleeveless. . . . And Islam itself, which enslaved only nonbelievers and in which one worshiped a Sultan who was the son of a slave woman and a slave himself! Ishak pulled Cosima closer. He was so happy to be where he was. Safe.

"Regicide," repeated Naksh-i-dil to the Valide Sultane. The news of the beheading of the French King and Queen reached Istanbul at the beginning of 1793.

Selim had been first amazed, then neutral, then benevolent toward the newly proclaimed French Republic. But Mihrishah and the Kiaya Naksh-i-dil were shocked and outraged as daily, then weekly, then monthly reports flowed in about the rising anarchy in France. "How is it possible to govern without a King chosen by God?" asked Mihrishah Valide. "And who looks after men who decide to govern themselves. . . ?" she asked, shaking her head in confusion. She could not conceive of a republic.

Naksh-i-dil was the most vehement. "It is not possible. Louis and Antoinette decapitated like common criminals. It is not possible that there is a France without a King." She turned to Mihrishah. "Why," she said in surprise, "I suppose they think they can look after themselves!"

*   *   *

"Regicide," repeated Cosima Amoureaux to her husband, Ishak. Cosima's father and Ishak Bey avoided each other's eyes. Already they had had news that Amoureaux's patron, Choiseul-Gouffier, had fled to Russia and the arms of Catherine. His flight had created an enormous scandal. The French Ambassador had fled to the enemy territory of Russia, sending in advance the collection of Greek antiques destined for the Louvre. To keep their own heads, thought Ishak, they would have to run and hide, but where? The grand exodus of royalists had begun in earnest. How could fate be so consistent? wondered Ishak Bey. Would his head never sit securely on his neck even in this paradise where he had found solace, family, love and one wife? But as usual, he thought, his kismet, which always seemed to correspond with historical events, had struck again. Amoureaux had now lost his job. Choiseul-Gouffier's flight had wiped out any chance of his friend Amoureaux changing camps. Ishak's old patron Vergennes had fled to Sweden. Now he, Ishak, the Beau Turque, had a family to protect. For once, he would have to depend upon himself. Of course, they could also take refuge in Russia—but his father-in-law had no personal fortune to establish them in St. Petersburg. Amoureaux didn't have a collection of art, only a price on his head. Ishak Bey smiled. He knew a great deal about prices on one's head. Or . . . they could return to Istanbul. Now that Gazi was dead. Would he have a chance at least to know what the charges had been against him and why?

Three years of unclouded happiness, thought Ishak Bey. What more could a man ask for? What matter that they were in danger? He had enough lives for them all. He had been an exile, an émigré for so long, why not home, since history had changed so drastically? It was the Jewish God who had saved his life and the Christian God who had given him Cosima, but it would be as a Moslem that he would return to Istanbul. He had no choice.

Ishak Bey arrived with his family. His only hope was the new Captain Pasha, commander of his new troops, the Lord Admiral Huseyin Pasha Kuchuk, the husband of Esma Sultane, the confidant of Selim. Kuchuk had convinced Selim that Ishak had had nothing to do with Lorenzo's plot and that his death sentence had been only the last vengeance of Hasan Gazi. Kuchuk took Ishak back into the Admiralty.

All the members of the old page clan were in power: Ebubekir, Ratib, Osman, Serri . . . Gratefully Ishak threw himself into serving Huseyin Pasha Kuchuk. Restored to all his old privileges and rank, Ishak fortified Huseyin's taste for Western arts, contributed to the reforms the Grand Admiral intended to introduce in the Ottoman navy. But more than that, the archangels Michael and Gabriel were reunited.

This time Ishak Bey knew Selim was not the frightened isolated Prince of nine years ago. Selim was Sultan. He was Sultan over an empire greater than that of Catherine's, with the power of life and death over them all: favorites, Generals, Viziers, Janissaries, commoners, Kadines. . . . He wondered what changes absolute power had wrought in his Prince.

The Sultan rose to greet Ishak as the White Eunuch executed a temennah and left them alone staring at one another. Ishak felt both power and weakness radiating from the Sultan, who after seven years on the throne had still not generated an heir to the Ottoman throne. He could almost hear the rustling and stirring of a hundred dissatisfied women, smell the bitter frustration of an unused harem filled with un-fecund Kadines. Like all of the Empire's subjects, he was the property of a despot to whom he owed total obedience. For one split second the image of Catherine rose up before him. Ishak approached the tall, slim figure who rose and seemed to grow larger and more imposing with each step. Selim's handsome pock-marked face shone in the penumbral light that accentuated its rough pits and furrows as if they had been a mountain landscape. Selim's kohled dark eyes had grown hard with the years, and unfathomable. They held something more now than affection, they held authority. His beard, which was too fair and had been dyed a deep black, covered his beautiful mouth, and his high, white-gauze turban, held by a spray of rubies, rose around his head like smoke. His eyes had fine lines of age and melancholy around them, although Selim was only thirty-four. And there was something wild, even maniacal, about the dilating nostrils. Yet his smile was as endearing as ever.

"Our archangel Gabriel!"

"My Sovereign Lord Sultan," said Ishak, but he did not prostrate himself; he remained standing. There were a thousand questions on his lips, but he remained silent. Selim also remained silent. However, Ishak's gesture had not been lost on him. Instead of speaking, he pulled Ishak close and held him, his head resting on the other man's shoulder.

"How I've missed you all these years. . . ."

"And I, you," lied Ishak.

He felt the pressure of Selim's strong hands on the nape of his neck, forcing his face toward him. Ishak's first reaction was resistance, then slowly he brought his face level with Selim's and the two men's eyes locked, then their lips brushed lightly.

Ishak knew the power he had over Selim was intact. Nothing had changed. Yet everything had changed. He had married Cosima.

They spoke far into the night, Selim and Ishak, all the old affection rekindled. Slowly it dawned on Ishak that whatever power he *retained* over Selim must also *come* from Selim. Ishak was no more than he had been to Catherine. The same ruthless, sentimental, autocratic greed which made fools of Kings also made slaves of those they loved. Ishak's heart sank. That kind of power over Selim would never get him what he wanted: independence. He was, and always would be, Selim's page . . . Selim's slave.

Ishak felt his neck muscles loosening under the pressure of Selim's seductive fingers. In time it was Ishak who lowered his eyes, strangely subdued yet aroused. He felt Selim stir beneath his silken robes against his own hardness, flat on his belly. He felt weak. He imagined how often a woman had reacted to him in exactly the same manner.

But there were two things Ishak could reveal to no one. Especially to Selim: that he had a wife, and that he was a Christian.

Princess Hadidge glanced down at a European leather-bound book, Catherine II's *Instructions,* which was partly covered by a prayer rug next to Naksh-i-dil's divan. The Empress's Nakaz was Naksh-i-dil's obsession. The Princess smiled. What could be going on in Naksh-i-dil's head? she mused. Vengeance was something the Osmans did very well. But Naksh-i-dil was not Osman. She was simply one of Abdulhamid's wives who had escaped the Eski Serai by the grace of Allah. A Kadine whose power resided only in the fact that she was the mother of a royal Prince. Hadidge knew that Naksh-i-dil spent most of her time in Abdulhamid's library with French and English books that the Black Eunuch provided for her. It was of no importance. Personally she saw nothing wrong with Naksh-i-dil's obsession. She simply considered it a waste of time better spent on scents or sweets or sex. She lay down on Naksh-i-dil's couch to wait. She pulled her girdle open and undid her turban and lit a cigarette. The thin gauze of the headdress had fallen in swirls around her neck and shoulders and breasts. Her hennaed hands fidgeted nervously with her golden-blond plaits and her lit but unsmoked cigarette, an unreasoning jealousy of the half-hidden books preventing her from peeking at the copy of the Nakaz.

*   *   *

"What do you do with all the books I get for you?" asked the Lazarist. "Who wanted Catherine's Nakaz in French? Not you, I suppose?"

The Black Eunuch was evasive. "There is an American Kadine in Mihrishah Valide's court who is literate in Arabic and French. She devours everything you send her. . . ." He hesitated. "I don't believe it is a good thing—knowledge in a Kadine—but she believes her son will someday reign. Therefore, I believe it is like serving a future Sultan. . . ."

"And you believe this Prince will reign?"

"Yes."

"Why?"

The Black Eunuch was silent. He really didn't know why he believed in Mahmud's star. Not only was Selim young and robust, but there was Sineprever's Mustafa, a virile, nasty little boy who was next in line.

"Call it kismet," said the Black Eunuch carefully.

"You know I don't believe in kismet," said the Lazarist.

"This Kadine told me a strange story," began the Black Eunuch, "of three little girls in the islands of America, of shooting stars, of the predictions of an Obeah, predictions confirmed by *her* Golia, Hitabetullah. . . . This woman, this insignificant little Kadine, actually dreams of avenging her Sultan whom she believes the Russians destroyed. Actually wants revenge against the Russians. The imprisonment of Mahmud obsesses her. His ignorance of the outside world. She believes it is her duty to instruct herself so that she can instruct him when the time comes."

"She has seen him then."

"She sees him all the time. He still lives in the harem. He has not yet been circumcised."

"She is, you might say, your protégée," remarked Father Delleda.

"She is also Princess Hadidge's protégée," said the Black Eunuch unsmilingly. He knew about that as well. But he was helpless to stop it even if he wanted to. Princess Hadidge was too powerful. And besides, on what grounds except moral ones could he object? Illicit love in the harem was an everyday fact of life, much as he fought against it. He was too old to combat the ingenuity of scores of young, frustrated women. Selim neglected his harem to the point of treason to the throne, thought the Kizlar Aga. Had he been rendered sterile years ago as he claimed? Or did his *nature* refuse the normality of fatherhood?

The Lazarist thought of the voluptuousness of the baths. "Illicit love among locked-up women is almost inevitable."

"As it is in your convents and monasteries," said the Black Eunuch, not without hoping to shock the Lazarist.

"A convent is not a harem," said Father Delleda. But he was remembering love between a priest and a woman. Not between two men or two women.

"But a harem," said the Black Eunuch, "is a convent. It was meant to be so."

"It is against the laws of nature."

"Against the laws of nature!" exploded the Black Eunuch. "Man is naturally polygamous. It is your Christian laws that are against the laws of nature, not ours. Celibacy, enforced or voluntary, is against nature and God."

"And slavery?" asked the Lazarist. "Don't you include slavery in the crimes against nature and man?"

"It depends if the slavery is based on war or on crime," said the Black Eunuch.

"And there is a difference?" asked the Lazarist. "War is not a crime? And your slavery, which is not based on war, is not a crime?"

The Black Eunuch smiled. "After all my lessons, you still believe in your 'free will.' My slavery was my kismet. I could no more change it than the stars. . . ."

The Lazarist was silent. Such a seductive explanation for everything, he thought. Sleep, slavery, kismet, the stars, obedience, submission, God's will, all so seductive. Like the baths, where his own personal torment was assuaged each day for an hour or so . . .

"What have you for me today?" asked the Black Eunuch.

"The newest pamphlet of Voltaire."

"How much do I owe you?"

"The book is new. It cost me three piastres."

The Black Eunuch took his purse out of his sash and handed the money to the Lazarist. Father Delleda hesitated a second and then said:

"Ishak Bey is leading a double life."

The Black Eunuch was so astonished, he dropped his purse, which fell with a thud at the Lazarist's feet.

"He is married to a Frenchwoman, a Catholic, whom he hides in the Jewish Quarter with his father-in-law and her brother. Her name is Cosima Amoureaux."

"A double life," repeated the Black Eunuch.

"Yes, and a very happy one, from what I suspect."

The Lazarist observed the Black Eunuch carefully. He knew the value of his information; he also knew the impeccable truth of it. Sooner or later it would be repaid in kind by the Kizlar Aga, of this he was sure. Moreover, it bound the Black Eunuch to him in a way that only knowledge in a world of slaves and spies could do. Would he use it? he wondered. Now or later? Would he sell it or hoard it, barter it or deliver it to the man he considered his master, Selim? The Lazarist didn't like Ishak Bey—a renegade and a fool who had put the soul of his wife in mortal danger. Yet even as he thought the words, he wondered if he were betraying the soul of the husband, Ishak, the wife, Cosima, or the priest Delleda?

The Black Eunuch knew that the information the Lazarist had so gratuitously (or not) dropped into his lap was worth a fortune. He had no doubt that the Lazarist was telling the truth. He had enough money, thought the Kizlar Aga, but only one life. Only hoarded information might save his one day. Or Ishak Bey's.

The Kizlar Aga left Naksh-i-dil's book at her door before he entered his own rooms. He called for his writing materials and started a new poem for Tityi with the calm deliberation of fathomless, endless love.

Gira   *Esking-ilen oldum ghira*
Match   I burn, I burn, my flame consumes me

CHAPTER EIGHT

CATHERINE 1796

Les cinq frères Orlov	17,000,000 rubles
Vysotski (comparse non recensé)	300,000
Vassiltchikov	1,110,000
Potemkine	50,000,000
Zavadovski	1,380,000
Zoritch	1,420,000
Rimsky-Korsakov	920,000
Lanskoi	7,260,000
Ermolov	550,000
Mamonov	880,000
Les frères Zubov	3,500,000
Dépenses courantes des favoris depuis le début du règne	8,500,000
Total	92,820,000 rubles

—The Accounts of Czar Paul I, 1796

"**H**ail Mary, Mother of God . . ." The Metropolitan Patriarch droned over the moribund body of Catherine II of Russia who was dying on a mattress on her bedroom floor at the Tsarskoy Selo in St. Petersburg. The Patriarch anointed her eyelids lightly, then her ears, nostrils, mouth, hands, feet and breast, each unction accompanied by a prayer. The day before, the Empress had been overtaken by a massive stroke in her privy. Her servants had forced open the door of the water closet, and because she was too heavy to lift, they had placed the Empress on a mattress on the floor of her chambers. She was still alive, breathing heavily and fiercely, and a multitude of intrigues had sprung up around her prone body. Who was to succeed her? Her adored grandson Alexander, or her despised son Paul? Courtiers wavered between pledging allegiance to one or the other, too late or too soon.

The aged and agonizing Empress struggled to proclaim her last wish and official act—the disinheritance of Paul in favor of Alexander. She clung stubbornly to life for another thirty-six hours, dying at 9:45 P.M. on November 17, 1796, without being able to pronounce the name Alexander as the next Czar. She had followed her beloved Potemkin by four years, and left behind her disorder, dissension and an unfinished war with Turkey.

The first official act of the new Czar, Paul I, was to choose a father.

The Empress's funeral was a double one. Paul had his father's body exhumed from its resting place in the convent of St. Alexander and placed beside Catherine, the woman who had murdered him thirty-four years before. Side by side they lay in state, united forever; the still-fresh cadaver of an old woman and the mummified remains of a young man were lit by the same thousand candles, which reflected on the same thousand gold icons, serenaded by the same sweet Oriental chants, gazed upon by the same mammoth procession of the population of St. Petersburg, and buried in the same tomb. Thus Paul revenged himself on the army of Catherine's favorites, his parentage no longer in doubt: If he was not his mother's son, he was the son of Peter III, and if Peter had not been his father, so much the better. He had chosen. He had obliterated his mother's adultery while assuring his direct descent from the only Peter who counted—Peter the Great. In cash, serfs, land, palaces, jewels, porcelain and pensions, his mother's adultery had cost the Empire—92,820,000 rubles.

In Topkapi the end of Catherine II's reign coincided with the circumcision of Prince Mahmud.

The elaborate ceremonies following the circumcision lasted for seven days and the celebrations in the city, three. Istanbul was festooned and illuminated. Mahmud was now placed in the Prince's Cage along with his half-brother Mustafa. Naksh-i-dil knew it might be decades before she would see her only son.

The friends, pages and Princes of the blood, all gathered outside the hall, dressed in costume, wearing paper hats and carrying wooden swords and shields, and shouting: "Hail Moslem, thou who wast an Unbeliever."

* * *

That same year, a young Corsican officer, recently named General, married in a civil ceremony in Paris a Creole whom he had found amongst the girls at Madame Tallien's. Her name was Joséphine Tascher de la Pagerie, widow of the Marquis de Beauharnais. She wore a dress of white mousseline trimmed in red, white and blue flowers, and at her waist was a tricolor wreath. The new General's name was Napoleon Bonaparte. Just the year before, he had been the artillery commander ordered to head a mission to Constantinople as a punishment for his political leanings.

◆ CHAPTER NINE ◆

SULTAN EL KABIR 1798

It was by becoming Catholic that I ended the war in Vendée. By becoming Moslem that I conquered Egypt. By becoming Ultramontane that I conquered the hearts of the Italians. If I ruled a nation of Jews, I would restore Solomon's Temple. . . .

—NAPOLEON BONAPARTE, 1799

Winter in Istanbul was long and rainy; but at last, near the middle of April, mild temperatures, accompanied by frequent light rains, brought forth new life. The banks of the Bosphorus were covered in tender greenery; little by little, the majestic plane trees donned their thick foliage and spring arrived.

In the first days of July, the Bay of Yeni-Kapi, a meeting place for all the small boats bringing fruit to Istanbul from the opposite Asian shore, hardly sufficed to contain them all. It was the time of eggplants, cucumbers and watermelons in the harem. . . .

The women had already moved to the summer harem two months earlier, by Mihrishah's orders. The tramontana, the north wind, which dissipates the sirocco, the humid south wind, suddenly stopped after having blown constantly for three months. The change occurred in the middle of the night. Naksh-i-dil had been awakened by the low monotonous cry of a wood owl perched on one of the neighboring cypress trees. Her sleep, normally light and calm, had been disturbed. Her blankets, which had made the coolness of the nights and the north breeze agreeable, had suddenly become irksome. Perspiration that before had evaporated easily now covered her body. She felt heavy and discouraged, a weakness in her limbs. The Kiaya opened the curtains of her kiosk, which gave onto the Marmara Sea, but instead of seeing its vast expanse, flat as a mirror, reflecting the rays of the rising sun, she saw nothing but a thick, dirty fog.

The fire broke out, as they did regularly in Istanbul, devastating a crowded quarter of the city. Selim, as Sultan, was obliged to leave the harem and ride out to console the population, according to tradition.

The people of Istanbul during great political crises, above all those that concerned their beliefs, deliberately set fires, manifesting in their own way their preoccupations. Because the Sultan had the obligation to be present at a fire, the fires of Istanbul had become its traditional petitions.

Through the smoldering crossbeams and unextinguished flames, an anonymous female voice rang out ominously:

"Mecca is taken, it has fallen to infidels. Sultan! What are you waiting for?"

The woman's voice rang out again: "Cinsi sapik! My house is in ashes, but so is your Empire!"

Sultan Selim knew the voice referred to Napoleon's invasion of Egypt.

The English Lord Admiral Horatio Nelson had given the now master of Europe, Napoleon, a lesson in admiralty. He had proven that Napoleon was as stupid as a Reis and he, Nelson, *May Allah grant that his soul rest in peace,* was brilliant. At the Bay of Aboukir, the Admiral Nelson had found and destroyed that entire French fleet, cutting off Napoleon's 55,000 men, 1,000 cannons and 32 Generals, and leaving only one boat for Napoleon to escape back to France in. It had been of no importance to the Algerian Reis that Napoleon had invaded Egypt, proclaimed Ottoman rule at an end, declaring himself "Sultan El Kabir." Egypt was only nominally a part of the Ottoman Empire and Napoleon had been after the English, not the Egyptians or the Ottomans. What had caused all the trouble was that his minister Talleyrand had never bothered to make the 1,400-mile journey from Paris to Istanbul to sign a treaty with Selim III, the Sultan, *before* he invaded Egypt. At the Pyramids, Napoleon had destroyed the Mameluks, panicking the 16,000 Egyptian foot soldiers who had never even seen heavy guns and had desperately tried to swim the Nile. . . . Napoleon had even proclaimed himself a true Moslem who was destined by Allah—yes, he had even taken God's name in his infidel mouth—to drive the Ottomans out of their province of Egypt. "Cadis, Sheykhs, Imams," he had said, "tell the people that we too are true Moslems. Are we not the men who have destroyed the Pope, who preached eternal war against the Moslems? Are we not those who have destroyed the Knights of Malta because those madmen believed that they should constantly make war on your Faith?"

Sultan Selim shook with rage. What this new General *did* do was to shoot four thousand Turkish prisoners of war in cold blood so as not to have to feed them. . . . Selim's Empire was embroiled now in the wars of the French Revolution.

Twenty-four hours later, another fire broke out in the city. And then another. And then another. To these hieroglyphics in flames, all in less than seventy-two hours, the humiliated Sultan was forced to respond. On his return from the fires, his Grand Vizier, Mehemet Pasha, was condemned to exile and replaced. But the decision of the rupture with the French was not yet made. He clung pathetically to the dictates of his weakness: that he could escape the inevitable.

The Sultan ordered the regencies of Algiers, Tunis and Tripoli, all Ottoman provinces, to chase after the French and mistreat them in every way:

"You know the grave events that have taken place. You know that the accursed French have established themselves in Egypt through treason, and the people of Mohammed, victims of this felony, are bent under the tyranny and the fist of oppression. . . . The Sublime Porte invites the three regencies of Algiers, Tunis and Tripoli to pursue the French and trap them, imprison them, pursue their ships, and capture them and sink them . . . these are my orders. . . ." "Your ships are called on to combat the enemy of the Faith, impious double-dealers destined for destruction. Carry on, thus, the holy war for the love of God who will accord victory to your ardor! Blockade them . . . capture them . . . burn them. . . ."

The news of Admiral Nelson's victory at Aboukir had given the indecisive Selim the courage to match his fury. He finally entered into war along with the English against the French. A fetva, a declaration of war, was issued. In Istanbul the pro-French ministers were arrested by Selim, and the entire male French community was arrested and thrown into the prison of the Castle of the Seven Towers and their property confiscated. A joint English and Ottoman naval squadron sailed for Syria with Selim's new troops under the command of the Captain Pasha Huseyin Kuchuk and his second, Ishak Bey.

An ominous silence fell over Istanbul.

That week two deaths from the plague were officially admitted by the
Grand Vizier, and in a week the deaths had climbed to five hundred.
The Black Death was upon Istanbul.

The Black Death came near the end of the day or during the
course of the night. It almost always sneaked up on one; a
slight shiver, a terrible migraine, a kind of hoarseness, an affliction, more or less, of the stomach, a general despondency of the
soul. The glands swelled. The eyes became brilliant and the
gaze fixed like someone affected by rabies, bringing a swift and
unwanted change to the features of the face. . . . The buboes
most frequently appeared in the groin, under the arms or
around those parts. The form was round and elongated and
resembled nothing more than an eggplant in color, shape and
size. It could be soft or hard, and it could keep the color of
flesh or turn a deep black purple. Sometimes there was one,
sometimes two, three or four. . . .
The season it struck was that of the eggplants and water-
melon. . . .
The Black Death depended on the state of the air and the
heavens. It was produced by a putrid miasma that formed its
essential element and resulted in an inflammation of the internal organs or viscera which sometimes gave way to the formation of buboes in the groin. Some advised bleeding by leeches.
. . . The dangerous miasmas were aggravated by bad treat-
ments. The plague was fought with opium, alkali, volatile oils,
musk and ether in small doses repeated often and combined
with coffee, quinine and lemon to cause vomiting. . . . But
the best treatment was flight. Flight to the north, high up in the
mountains, isolated above the winds. . . . And the most severe cleanliness of one's body and every object one touched.
Besides, one had to avoid crowds, public places, laxatives, alcohol, overtiredness, sadness, passion, violent emotions, nostal-
gia, despair and excesses of all kinds. . . . As remedies there
were the fumes of vinegar, the tutsu, the smoke that rose from
the burning of ironbark. There was raki, alcohol, and there
were amulets. . . . Some carried a feather stem, filled with
mercury and sealed at both ends, in the crease of their stom-
achs. Greeks, Armenians and Jews carried a closed triangle
containing saffron, camphor, garlic and aromatic herbs. Mos-

lems carried a scrap of paper under their tongues with a verse
from the Koran.

Processions and any public congregating had been banned. The baths
remained open, but the first crude signs had begun to appear on the
courtyard doors of infected houses: the sign for Allah and the yellow
crescent. Doors would remain locked for months while those imprisoned inside fought for their lives and buried their dead. Each infected
house became a sort of harem.

The insupportable suffering and terror of the Black Death, which
neither the conjunction of the planets, miasma nor God's anger could
explain, marched on Napoleon's army faster than Selim's troops.

Three times in three centuries the plague had been unleashed from its
prehistoric cradle in the high plains of Asia Minor. The first, Justin's
Plague, originated in Constantinople in the seventh century and for two
centuries it scoured the Mediterranean from Egypt to the Bosphorus.
Then in 1347 the Genovese occupied the Counting House in Jaffa in the
Crimea and the great army of the Khan, ancestor of the Ottomans, laid
siege to that city. But the Genovese repulsed the Khan's army so violently that the Khan surrendered, but his army, struck by the plague,
catapulted the cadavers of the plague victims over the walls of the city.
Immediately the Genovese understood the diabolical weapon unleashed
against them and they fled, but too late; they carried with them the
Black Death, disseminating it at every outpost: Constantinople, Mes-
sina, Cyprus, Venice, Naples and finally Genoa. The Black Death gave
the Khan a victory he had never dreamed of.

Thus, in Syria Napoleon's army began to die by the hundreds. The
Black Death stopped the French General's dream of marching on Damascus.

In Syria a bubo was much more common than a carbuncle, and it
occurred most frequently in the groin, in the armpit and in the soft
tissue near these parts. The form was round if found in a gland, and
elongated if in the slack flesh around it. Buboes were hard to the touch
and purple-black in color. Sometimes buboes appeared all of a sudden,
without any pain, and then disappeared without causing harm. At other
times they would appear and with them, sudden death would occur.
More often they announced themselves by radiating pain, developing
regularly and slowly before turning into an abscess, suppurating and
finally healing. Others remained for a long time, soft and immovable,
and were reabsorbed into the body, sometimes without danger.

"I will enlarge my army as I go," Bonaparte raged to his horrified stepson Eugéne Beauharnais, "with revolutionaries. I will announce to the people the abolition of slavery and the tyrannical governments of the Pashas. I will arrive at Constantinople with my armies massed. I will overthrow Selim and the Ottoman Empire. I will found a new and great empire in the Orient which will assure my place in posterity and perhaps I will return to Paris by Andrianople or by Vienna after having annihilated the House of Austria!"

And Beauharnais didn't know whether to believe him or call the army doctor.

When Huseyin Kuchuk Pasha's fleet of thirty ships arrived with Sultan Selim's troops, Napoleon had overrun Gaza and Jaffa, but Acre was holding against him. Acre had the most formidable defense system in the Orient: a castle built by the Crusaders, known as St. Jean d'Acre, defended by a ditch, ramparts and 250 guns. The siege was in its sixth week. In bloody assaults, the French would force their way in only to be driven out, captured or instantly beheaded. Selim's Nizam-i-jedid under the command of Huseyin Kuchuk and Ishak Bey, fought their way into Acre and relieved the embattled defending Pasha, Ahmet Cezzar. In their baptismal fire the Nizam-i-jedid had turned the tide against Napoleon. For Kuchuk it was a triumph that earned him the name "Gazi." Napoleon failed to take Acre. In Jaffa, Bonaparte regrouped all his soldiers who could march back to Egypt. He poisoned those who had the plague with overdoses of opium. When the English arrived in Jaffa, there were only five Frenchmen alive.

In the march back to Egypt, the army continued to abandon the plague-ridden to the mercy of the inhabitants. The army carried torches to incinerate the villages, towns and fields that fell across their path. The dying were left by the side of the road with their feeble cries of "I don't have the plague! I'm only a wounded man!" The desertion of the costly siege of St. Jean d'Acre planted rebellion within the ranks. "We farted in a pile of shit at St. Jean d'Acre" was the consensus of the army, who couldn't know that this retreat under the merciless sun and sand was only a rehearsal for a far more terrible one under ice and snow.

Forty-five thousand men had debarked fourteen months before at Alexandria. Only twenty-two thousand remained. "The Plain of Nazareth is the end of the career of the so-called Sultan El Kabir," said the Captain Pasha Kuchuk.

Napoleon Bonaparte sailed back to France in the only ship Admiral

Nelson had left him undamaged: the *Muiron*. He was named First Consul before the news of the disastrous campaign of Egypt reached Paris. His General Kléber was to continue the war. General Kléber sued for peace. Huseyin Kuchuk and Ishak Bey were in Alexandria to start the peace parley when the news reached them that Simon Zorich was dead.

Simon Gavrilovitch Zorich had lived on quietly in Shklov. The exfavorite had been named honorary Colonel in a regiment of imperial cavalry, giving him access to the court and its privileges. The cadet school he had founded with Ishak Bey was famous. The cream of Russian nobility sent their sons there. It was the only thing Zorich had left to be proud of. He still slept in the replica of the bedroom he had shared with Catherine.

Looking out the window one night, he wondered why the northern white night framed by his window had suddenly turned orange. Then he realized that the light was fire rising from the boys' barracks. Zorich was into his breeches and out of his palace before he heard the first screams of children and horses. The thin cries of adolescents washed over him like waves of terrible orchestrated music, as if his ball musicians had gone mad with their instruments. It was three in the morning. He ran, hoping to rouse three hundred sleeping children from their beds. Everything vibrated in the roar of flames and light. Zorich rushed into the blaze. The silhouette of figures, horses, their manes on fire, and crashing timber were outlined in red, in gold. Servants, soldiers and instructors fought to enter the raging inferno. The three hundred boys of Zorich's cadet school all burned to death in their beds.

Count General Zorich didn't perish in the fire, although he had prayed for death. He had died of a broken heart.

Ishak Bey and Kuchuk conducted the peace parley halfway between Cairo and Syria at Al-Aris. Kléber wanted peace. The Grand Vizier wanted peace. The English representative, Sydney Smith, was undecided. But the Russian emissary, Vassili Tamara, wanted war. Czar Paul I had decided to protect the Knights of Malta after Napoleon captured the island. Using all his charm, finding always the right word or the right phrase in four different languages, lying to some, evading others, praising, flattering, amusing, cajoling, Ishak Bey, to the amazement of the Grand Vizier, managed to negotiate an armistice. Success had come to Ishak. Before Kléber fell under the knife of a fanatic he had signed a convention accepting the evacuation of the Upper Nile.

The final absurdity of the war was the repatriation of the Sultan El

Kabir's troops on Lord Admiral Nelson's ships. Selim's tenuous hold on the Empire was strengthened. Selim and Kuchuk now wanted to erase every trace of the war.

The plague was over.

• CHAPTER TEN •

THE LORD ADMIRAL, 1803

The frigate of Our Lord Reis Hamidou has captured 282 Christians; 2 of these infidels were given to the first mate who was the first to mount on board and Our Lord Pasha sanctions this custom. Another infidel was given to Sidi Abderrahman and after these donations, there were left 279 Christians: Friday, 28th of May, 1802.

The AMERICANA has brought to Algiers 65 Christians: March 1804. The proceeds were 11,340 francs or 354 francs per Christian.
—The *Khodjet-el-r'enaim* [The Book of Prizes of the Algerian Navy]

The Arsenal of the Turkish Admiralty was built on the heights of a knoll that dominated the port of Istanbul, and along its rise, the buildings, shipyards and hangars necessary to the various stages of shipbuilding were situated in such a way that the Grand Admiral Kuchuk could follow the progress of construction with his own eyes. The palace, which from the port side offered a panoramic view of the Bosphorus and the seven hills of Istanbul with its thousands of gold minarets and domes, occupied a large courtyard consisting of the main building flanked by two slightly projecting pavilions. The walls were whitewashed with fillets and delicate ceramic decorations in pale blue. The architecture was the architecture of many Turkish palaces: the windows were grilled in cane and shuttered from the sun with wooden doors that opened outward and downward. The roof was a half-balloon shape, low and crowned with copper-plated lead domes, each topped with a soaring golden arrow. One arrived at the palace by a steep approach ramp carved into the flank of the hillock. The other ramps were situated and designed in such a way as to be part of the architectural plan of the palace, and they gave it an air of severe grandeur as the deepening sun struck the golden domes.

Inside the reception hall, Esma Sultane, Hadidge Sultane and Kiaya Naksh-i-dil sat behind the fretted wooden screens that hid them from the hundreds of Ottoman nobles, Ambassadors, foreigners, diplomats, musicians and ushers gathered in the Lord Admiral's newly finished palace on the opposite shore from Topkapi. A ball was being held in honor of the peace treaty concluded with the French. The halls, decorated by Mihrishah Valide in the European style, began to fill with gesticulating, conversing, agitated guests, their rich costumes blending into a cashmere shawl of color, gold and silver. Chandeliers and torches lit the room. Mihrishah had supervised the decorations herself with the help of Esma and Naksh-i-dil. Now Naksh-i-dil looked through the screen, relegated to invisibility by the laws of the harem. Only Mihrishah Valide sat on a raised platform flanked by the Grand Admiral, ironically known as Gazi for his victory at Acre, the Grand Vizier and the Grand Master of Ceremonies. Hovering above them like a black cloud was the Kizlar Aga, and surrounding him like little puffs of black smoke was his army of eunuchs dressed for the occasion in livery.

Naksh-i-dil kept her eyes on the resplendent General Horace Sebastiani, the emissary of Napoleon, and Ishak Bey, and scanned the crowds of guests waiting, she knew in vain, for the appearance of Selim. When Ishak Bey and Sebastiani disappeared, they would be on their way to meet in secret with the Sultan. The much glorified peace was not popular with everyone and the various palace factions were unceasingly at war, pulling the weak-willed Selim first one way and then another. It was one thing to make peace, thought Naksh-i-dil, and another to keep it. The handsome Sebastiani was here to seduce Selim.

But Napoleon had set in motion a series of events that would sweep up both the weak and the strong. No sooner had one enemy disappeared, thought Naksh-i-dil, than another, even more formidable, one arose. Catherine was dead, but Alexander I, her grandson and spiritual heir, now reigned. The abominable Republic of France was in the hands of a dictator: the ex-Corporal Napoleon. Russia and England were again allies, and the French were desperately trying to prevent Selim from renewing his treaties with them. Napoleon wanted Selim as an ally in the wars to come, but so did England, Austria and Russia.

Once again the throne of Russia was occupied by a Czar who considered Constantinople his.

Naksh-i-dil saw Sebastiani, Ishak Bey and Huseyin Kuchuk slip away from the ball.

The secret meeting took place at the kiosk called Ainali Kavak. The Sultan arrived incognito by caïque.

Dressed in his brilliant uniform of an infantry General with a plumed helmet but unsabered, flanked by the Captain Pasha Huseyin Kuchuk and Ishak Bey, Sebastiani presented himself to the Sultan. Executing three low reverences, his helmet sweeping the ground, he held in his other hand the envelope of gold lamé which contained the dispatch from the First Consul:

Most August Majesty and Khan, Emperor of the Ottomans, the First Consul Bonaparte has charged me to deliver to Your Imperial Majesty this letter, proof of his friendly dispositions and high consideration for Your August Person. . . .

Ishak Bey cleared his throat and began translating:

The First Consul is extremely sensitive to the interests of Your Imperial Majesty. He desires to reestablish relations between the two greatest nations of the universe [the Russians and the English would be happy to hear that, mused Ishak].

He continued:

Their prosperity and their happiness will be the fruit of the friendship of their invincible rulers. My wish is for the long duration of this, this happy union, my arm and my blood for the defense and the glory of His Imperial Majesty.

Ishak Bey thought that Sebastiani was overdoing it a bit, but then that was his job, he thought: Seduce Selim. Selim, on the other hand, was impressed and happy. Sebastiani then bowed again three times and, flanked by his two escorts, retired, leaving a forlorn Selim alone in his caïque, his cloak of white camel's hair pulled tightly about him.

Ishak scrutinized the high-strung former priest Sebastiani. He knew how sentimental Napoleon was with his friends. He had even carried back to Paris with him the embalmed heart of one of his officers. What part of the murdered General Kléber would he want? Ishak wondered. What manner of man was Napoleon? he had once asked Sebastiani, already afraid of Sebastiani's penchant for rhetoric.

Horace Sebastiani had been admirably chosen: a favorite of Napoleon, the twenty-six-year-old Sebastiani, whose articles in the Paris *Gazette* on Napoleon's "victory" in Egypt had made Napoleon First Consul and made the French think they had won the war. Sebastiani was young, handsome, blond and ambitious, brave as a soldier; an unfrocked priest, he was shrewd and cynical as a negotiator. He had the audacity, suppleness and energy that Ishak Bey envied and had always lacked. Sebastiani had been one of the architects of Napoleon's peace in Cairo and been made a Colonel for the occasion. He mixed the adventurous spirit of a Corsican with the grace of a Frenchman and the finesse of an Italian, thought Ishak Bey in admiration. Sebastiani decided immediately on a course of action that would compromise neither himself nor protocol. The Ambassador had his instructions: to profit from all favorable circumstances and to employ all seductive means at his disposal to induce a treaty between Selim and Napoleon, to drag the Porte and the Sultan into another war with Russia and England. Kléber's assassination must not be used against the Ottomans, but rather to separate them from Mehmed Ali Dey of Egypt and keep him fighting the English. He must not forget the ninety-nine French citizens languishing both in the Castle of the Seven Towers prison in Constantinople and throughout the Empire, where they had been thrown at the onset of war.

Sebastiani, Ishak remembered, had for example been quite appalled by Napoleon's decision to reestablish slavery in order to finance his costly wars. Napoleon had revoked the abolition of slavery proclaimed by the Republic, and as First Consul had just sent an expeditionary force to Guadeloupe to reinstitute slavery in the French islands of America.

"I'm for whites," Napoleon had said, "because I'm white! I have only that reason to give and it is a good one. . . ." "If you," he had said to a Republican politician, "had come to Egypt preaching liberty to blacks and Arabs, we would have lynched you from a minaret. . . ." And Sebastiani threw back his head and laughed. "Marvelous, no? The logic of genius!"

What an adversary for poor Selim, thought Ishak Bey. A man in possession of an embalmed heart, who had written pathetic letters out of *A Thousand and One Nights* . . . then Nelson had captured a

French ship carrying Napoleon's letter complaining to his brother Joseph about the infidelities of his wife in great and tormented detail and had it published in the most famous newspaper in London. Before the year was out, Napoleon had been the laughingstock of Paris, London and the Barbary Coast. Ever since his victory at Marengo, Ishak had taken to praying for Napoleon. When he had heard of that famous battle, he had remarked to Kuchuk, "God keep Bonaparte. As long as the Europeans have to deal with him, they'll suffer so many defeats, they'll have no time to bother about us." For despite Selim's arrangements with Napoleon, his fear and admiration for him, and Napoleon's overtures of peace, peace didn't reign in Selim's regencies. Unable to depend upon the protection of the Sultan, they had become autonomous and no longer looked on the Sultan as their leader or protector . . . from God only knew what new enemies, thought Ishak.

Naksh-i-dil sat enclosed in her cabinet of fan tracery, suspended in time. The dancers twirled, the world turned, but the harem remained as static and immobile as the stone of a crypt. The women seated behind the screens had no desire any longer to reach out and touch the world beyond the elaborate geometrical, pierced, arabesqued carved woodwork diverging like the folds of a fan. Each had her own reasons.

By the end of the year, Esma Sultane was a widow. The Grand Admiral Kuchuk was found slumped over his maps in the Admiralty, already cold.

Without Kuchuk, thought Naksh-i-dil, who would protect Selim's Empire?

The next year, 1804, a most unexpected and unknown enemy attacked the fringes of Selim's Empire.

The frigate *Constitution* with forty-four guns, the brig *Argus* with eighteen guns, the brig *Siren* with eighteen guns, the schooner *Vixen* with sixteen guns, the schooner *Nautilus* with sixteen guns and the *Enterprise* with fourteen guns lined up in formation facing the white-fringed shores of the Bay of Algiers like polite children at a Fourth of July parade.

Reis Hamidou couldn't believe his eyes. The goddamned Americans had found themselves a bloody navy and were showing their ass in the Bay of Algiers, 6,666 miles east of the capital of Columbia, Washington, just as he had shown *his* ass in the Strait of Gibraltar.

Commander William Easton's squadron stood with its back to the wind, facing a total of 115 Algerian guns, 55 of which were heavy brass cannon and the others, eighteen- and twenty-pounders. Nineteen gun-boats, each with a brass twenty-four-pounder on the bow and two how-itzers abaft, two schooners with 8 guns, a brig of 10 guns and two galleys with 4 guns each, defended the entrance to the harbor. In addition to the regular Turkish garrison stationed on the ramparts and the 3,000-man crew of the ships, the Dey, Mustafa Pasha, had called 23,000 Arabs to the defense of the city.

Algiers, the houses appearing one above the other in resplendent whiteness, made a gorgeous appearance from the sea. There were five gates to the city. The housetops were all flat and the inhabitants walked on them in the evenings, just as the Dey and Reis Hamidou were doing at this moment. Covered with earth, the roofs served as the gardens of the city, which contained 160,000 Moslems, 25,000 Jews and 6,000 Christian slaves, including 102 Americans.

Hamidou followed the American commander's maneuvers with interest, even attachment. The wind now veered eastward, allowing the squadron to gain sea room without carrying so great a press of sail.

"They really mean business, these sons of bitches."

"They are merchants and slavers, not warriors," said the Dey.

"Oh, really?" answered Reis Hamidou.

Thirty thousand dollars, yearly tribute from the Americans, was three years in arrears. Thomas Jefferson had sent one year's tribute in cash, another year's in goods, and finally, in rage, the American fleet. The Americans captured a Tripolitan cruiser, but because they had not officially declared war on Tripoli, the American Congress ordered the Captain to release it.

In 1803 Commodore Prebles, cruising the Mediterranean with the forty-four-cannon *Constitution* and the thirty-eight-cannon *Philadelphia,* lost the latter. Disaster had befallen the *Philadelphia* when she ran aground under the guns of the fort of Tripoli and was forced to surrender. Captain Bainbridge and three hundred members of his crew were made captives and set to hard labor as slaves. But a daring commando group sneaked boldly into the harbor at night, under the very noses of the Tripolitans, drove the occupying crew overboard and burned the *Philadelphia* to the waterline. Jefferson rushed to send a mightier squadron to rescue the American slaves "and beat their town about their ears."

"Sons of bitches," muttered Reis Hamidou.

Fifteen minutes later, the Americans began shelling Algiers and the Algerians returned their fire with no less than 204 guns and 2 mortars, firepower that was promptly returned by the entire American fleet now within musket shot of the main batteries.

The undeclared war against the piracy of the Barbary States had burst around Reis Hamidou's head; the incessant rounds of cannon fire, columns of smoke and the promiscuous hissing of grapeshot and shells made the Reis throw back his head and laugh in exultation.

Lieutenant Stephen Decatur's squadron rushed into the center of nine Algerian gunboats, keeping up an incessant fire, and had managed to engage the Algerians in hand-to-hand combat with bayonet, spear, saber, sword and tomahawk. Decatur had boarded one of the Algerian ships and five sailors had fallen upon him with scimitars. The American parried the blows with so much address that he received no injury until a blow from the Damascus blade of an Algerian Reis cleaved his sword. Decatur scuffled with the Reis but, overpowered, fell under him across the ship's gunwale. Hamidou held his breath as he waited for the coup de grâce, but while the Reis was trying to dispatch him with his tō-gun, Decatur managed to draw his side pistol and shoot the Reis through the kidneys. At the same time, a Lieutenant Sergeant, armed with a fixed bayonet, and a sailor, armed with a cutlass and a tomahawk, had come to their Captain's rescue, dispatching the four other assailants on the spot. By this time other members of the crew had gotten the better of the Algerians, and the ship's colors were hauled down. Decatur had leaped aboard another vessel.

"Al-Dârr!" muttered the Dey. The American Lieutenant had taken two prizes in ten minutes, taken twenty-seven Algerian prisoners and killed thirty-three men.

The bomb ketches kept up a steady mortar fire and battered the town. The deadly fire of the *Constitution* created havoc, not only on board the Algerian squadrons but on shore. She laid her broadside to the powerful shore batteries and, as often as not, reduced them to profound silence. But the American squadron, exhausted by two and a half hours of incessant fire and by the pounding of the Algerian batteries on shore, lifted anchor. The Algerians had suffered heavy losses. The three captured boats had been manned by a crew of 103, and three other ships lay crippled in the bay.

Mustafa Pasha stood at his palace window, carelessly surveying the withdrawing American squadrons.

"Those fellows should be careful to keep their safe distance for tacking. They are a species of Jew! No nation of fighters at all."

Reis Hamidou looked at the Dey. They had just lost 3 ships, 105 sailors and 1,000 civilians and soldiers. The Americans had butted their asses good. Yet, as he looked around, all the terraces of Algiers were covered with spectators watching the battle, amused by coups regardless of who got or who gave. The Dey was ready to negotiate. He sent word to the French Consul that he was ready to treat on the basis of a reasonable ransom for the Americans.

Meanwhile, Admiral Easton was on his way from the Cape of Virginia with Captain Bainbridge to join Commodore Prebles at Tripoli. The shores of Tripoli were next. Thomas Jefferson was determined to recapture the American hostages held in slavery by the Bey of Tripoli. The new American squadron under Prebles had left Philadelphia on July 15. He had crossed the Atlantic in fifteen days, but having endured forty-one days of head winds and calms, it took fifty days to arrive at the rendezvous.

A flag of truce flew under Tripolitan colors from the French Embassy as a sign that the Bey was ready to treat. Commodore Prebles and Easton sent a boat ashore with letters from the families of the captive Americans. The boat was not permitted to land, but returned in the afternoon with a letter from the Bey stating that he would accept $500 for each American slave and terminate the war without any consideration of peace and without tribute from the Americans. But the American Commodores were adamant.

"They were asking five hundred thousand dollars exclusive of peace, presents and annuities before we arrived," Easton said, shaking his head in amazement. Even the intervention of the Ottoman Sultan Selim couldn't bring down the price. Now the Bey seemed to solicit rather than demand only about $150,000 for the ransoms and peace.

"At least," said Prebles, who had been bloodied, "we got the damned price down by almost one thousand percent!"

But Easton was not convinced. Thomas Jefferson would never accept even this tribute. The President's words resounded in his head: "The people of the United States have resolved that national honor is to be redeemed not by gold, but by steel!"

Ten days later, on the twenty-eighth of July, in a pleasant easterly breeze, the American Admirals weighed in and stood for an attack on Tripoli. The gunboats, accompanied by the *Siren,* the *Argus,* the *Vixen,* the *Nautilus* and the *Enterprise,* advanced to their stations. At three in the morning, anchored within pistol shot of the enemy's lines, the Americans began to bombard the shipping, the town batteries and the Bey's castle. The frigates remained with the gunboats to assist in boarding if the Tripolitan fleet ventured out of the harbor. But the Tripolitan ships remained anchored. It was Commodore Prebles who weighed in, slanting under the direct fire of the guns of the Fort English, and those of the Bey's castle. When the Commodore arrived within a sure distance, he opened fire with round and grapeshot on the thirteen gunboats and galleys that were in the harbor, sinking one, disabling two and putting the others to flight. He then hove to and fired three hundred round shot, and grapeshot and canisters, into the Bey's castle. The town smoldered under the barrage, sailors fell off the moored galleys and gunboats like flies. A Tunisian galley sank slowly and majestically in the mall, a Spanish frigate exploded spectacularly. The American brigs and schooners continued to maul the boats in harbor. Two bomb ketches were almost sunk by direct fire from the castle, and Prebles gave the signal to the small ships, ketches and gunboats to retire from action while he covered their retreat with firepower from the *Constitution.* The *Constitution* had all her shrouds shot away.

The Commodore decided to send a fire ship into Tripoli's harbor to ignite the Bey's entire fleet and project a column of shells onto Tripoli with the same explosion. The *Intrepid,* commanded by Captain Somers, was fitted out with 100 barrels of powder and 150 fixed shells rigged in her hold so as to be fired without endangering Captain Somers's retreat.

On the evening of September 4, the Captain chose two fast rowboats, his own, manned by four seamen from the *Nautilus.* At eight P.M. the *Intrepid* parted from the squadron now at anchor about three miles from Tripoli, convoyed by the *Argus,* the *Vixen* and the *Nautilus.* The *Intrepid* had gained the inner harbor, but a Tripolitan squadron was hard upon her and, near her point of destination, boarded her.

Captain Somers had one choice apart from captivity and slavery. He seized a match and, before the Tripolitan sailors could reach him, touched the train of gunpowder that lit the mined ship and instantly the sky was yellow and orange with the explosion of the *Intrepid.* Moslems and Christians, believers and infidels, all blew up in one giant flash of light, heat and thunder to their respective eternal rewards.

But a sea battle won or lost by two sets of pirates was much less impressive to the Pasha than the surprise occupation by land of his city of Derna by a tiny expeditionary force of Americans led by the American Consul at Tunis, to the great fortune of the American slave hostages.

◆ CHAPTER ELEVEN ◆

THE EMPRESS 1804

16 Pluviôse, Year II,

The National Convention declares that black slavery is abolished in all the colonies: in consequence, it decrees that all men, without distinction of color, living in the colonies are French citizens and are entitled to all rights guaranteed by the Constitution.

—Decree abolishing black slavery in the French colonies, February 4, 1794

30 Floreal, Year X,

In the colonies resituated to France by the Treaty of Amiens, slavery is re-established in conformity with the [slave] laws anterior to 1789.

—FIRST CONSUL NAPOLEON BONAPARTE, decree reestablishing slavery in the French colonies, May 20, 1802

"Mother." Mahmud flung himself into the arms of his mother. It was one of Naksh-i-dil's rare visits from Mahmud and she flushed deeply when Mihrishah Valide remarked that Mahmud had kept his dagger in his belt in the presence of Selim who stood beside her. Mahmud, dark red and trembling with humiliation, handed his dagger over to Mihrishah while his half-brother Mustafa snickered.

Prince Mahmud had grown into a young man of medium height, dark, with Naksh-i-dil's green eyes and a smile that was as brilliant as it was rare. His mother hadn't seen him for more than a year, and now her eyes devoured him. She would have only this to last until their next meeting, which might be another year away. If only she and Mahmud could have some time together alone without his Lala, the Sultan, Mustafa, Ishak Bey or Mihrishah. But it seemed impossible. Naksh-i-dil reached over and touched the boy's dark auburn hair; it crackled under her fingers. To him, thought Naksh-i-dil, she was a stranger and yet a mother, the most sacred of symbols. For eighteen years now, she had cultivated this image. Somehow she had left an everlasting impression on Mahmud. She knew not how. His life as well as her own was regulated to the minutest detail. How could she meet with him outside the Cage? How could she communicate with him? Educate him? Form him? Cherish him? Love him? Yet, she had done so. Now they spoke quietly, happily, under the surveillance of Mihrishah, Selim and Mahmud's Lala, Tayyar Aga.

Fifteen years had passed since Selim had ascended the throne and still he had produced no heir. Mustafa, it seemed, would one day rule, but Selim, in his early thirties, handsome and healthy, seemed a likely prospect for a long reign.

Naksh-i-dil's face was as devoid of grief as it was of compassion. Hers was an empty countenance, secret and marked with disillusion. But the eyes still blazed with ambition, the nostrils flared with an instinct for survival, and the features were alive with love for Mahmud, now a man who belonged to the Osmanlis. If she had no family, his was a thousand years old.

The now opulent Mihrishah eyed Naksh-i-dil enviously. She had never had the pleasure of seeing her son grow up as had Naksh-i-dil. For nineteen years she had not set eyes on Selim. Not until he had greeted her at the door of the harem as Valide. Not one glimpse of Selim had been offered her. Naksh-i-dil had no idea how lucky she was—how generous Selim had been. Selim. Her son of no heirs. Didn't he realize that he could be legally disposed of for not having engendered an heir in the first seven years of his reign?

Why didn't she have grandchildren? thought Mihrishah, watching Naksh-i-dil speaking with Mahmud. How could she make him a father? Why did he refuse? How, most of all, could she make him prefer women when he preferred men. . . ?

Selim was full of attentions and affection for Mahmud, but his kindness did not include education. Naksh-i-dil could not bear the idea of her son's learning to read and write according to the rules of the Kafes, only through the Koran and its commentaries. What about science,

mathematics, history, geography? She despaired of Mahmud's ignorance.

The shadow over the harem during these years of uneasy, humiliating
peace with Russia was the frustration of Selim's Kadines and Mihrishah. Sineprever and Naksh-i-dil watched the fierce and virile Valide
slowly crumble under her son's impotence, which had become her impotence as well.

Naksh-i-dil's feelings for Selim were almost maternal. She seemed
always to see this august descendant of the Osmans as a midget on an
equestrian statue, proportioned to the height of his illustrious father,
Mustafa III. Selim's inclinations were exaggerated in foreign diplomatic
circles. And with a moral point of view, which was strictly Occidental,
they were considered the cause of his weakness, his indecision, his
procrastinations. Yet his hysteria pointed more to a man on the verge of
desperation or, worse, madness.

Little by little Naksh-i-dil became convinced that Selim *was* going
mad. The enthusiasm that had followed the succession of the young
archangel, Selim, after her decrepit husband, Abdulhamid, changed to
consternation as Selim's behavior became more and more erratic, his
mistrust of everyone more and more pronounced, the power of the
Janissaries more and more evident. Then the Captain Pasha Kuchuk
died, slumped over his maps at the Admiralty. Kuchuk, his childhood
page, had been the last man he had trusted. Everything and everyone
trembled in the capital, from ministers to favorites. Sometimes Selim
would escape the harem disguised as a policeman. His disguise fooled
no one, and his summary justice made his subjects flee before him as
from the plague. If Selim could not inflict vengeance on the Hapsburgs,
the Triple Alliance or Russia, he could inflict the vengeance of the lone
vigilante on his own population. Once, furious at being recognized, he
had had the offender whipped by the officers of his suite, themselves
disguised, which meant that no one dared lift his eyes from the ground
as the Sultan passed. One day, in the guise of a naval Lieutenant and
accompanied by officers disguised as sailors, he saw a woman being
mistreated by a Janissary.

"Brothers of my Faith, defend me!"

Selim cut the Janissary down with his saber, slicing him down the
middle, with the ferocious strength he had reinforced by his violent
military exercises.

For the Janissaries, it was an act of violation. Janissaries recognized
chastisement of another Janissary only by their own justice in Execu-

tion Square. Not even the Sultan could play the judicatory. The arbitrary executions only added to what the Divan and Mihrishah considered reckless: reforms that went against the national grain, the national character and the national religion, Islam.

The Black Eunuch had heard Selim shout at the Divan: "It is I who make the customs!" But Naksh-i-dil realized it was not so easy. People did not obey orders when they insulted age-old customs and ingrained opinions. Naksh-i-dil realized Selim was primed for a fall.

Mustafa and his mother, Sineprever, were mounting a coup against Selim. The Janissaries' contempt and hatred for the Sultan had been building slowly for the past ten years.

Naksh-i-dil had listened carefully. The Janissaries inspired terror in the Seraglio and suspicion in the nation. Since they received a bonus at the investiture of every new Sultan, they had an interest in deposing the Emperors as often as possible and did so regularly. Each year of any Sultan's reign was bought with gold and favors for the Janissaries, whose salaries impoverished the realm. Their protection, thought Naksh-i-dil, had cost Abdulhamid the accumulated treasure of the government destined for the defense and administration of the Empire. Their abandonment, she knew, would cost Selim his throne. And if ever Mahmud ruled, the destruction of the Corps should be his goal.

"You have news, Kizlar Aga?" asked Mihrishah Valide, bringing Naksh-i-dil back from her thoughts, and the alert eyes of Mahmud toward Edris Aga.

"Our Ambassador in Paris reports that Napoleon has crowned himself Emperor of the French and his Creole wife, Empress."

"Creole?" exclaimed Naksh-i-dil, her heart racing.

You will be more than Queen.

"Oh, Lord Edris, find out her name! It is the most important thing in my life!"

"Return with the name of this . . . this so-called Empress," Mihrishah Valide ordered the Black Eunuch.

"Joséphine. Joséphine Tascher de la Pagerie, widow of the Marquis de Beauharnais," said the Kizlar Aga when he returned.

". . . your stars promise you two marriages . . . the first of your husbands was born in Martinique, a noble, but lives in France . . . the Kingdom of France will know revolution and great troubles, and he will perish tragically . . . your second husband will be very dark, of European origin and without fortune or name . . . he will become famous

and fill the world with his glory . . . you shall be famous and cele-brated, more than a Queen . . ."

At twelve o'clock, Napoleon and Joséphine with their cortege entered the cathedral of Notre Dame, where eight thousand people awaited them. The cathedral was draped in blue satin embroidered with golden bees as large as birds. They walked slowly to the nave while a military band played the Coronation March. Napoleon was dressed in purple velvet embroidered with a laurel branch surrounding the letter *N*. Joséphine was dressed in white satin with a white-velvet cape embroidered in gold and lined in ermine.

The ceremony started with the recitation of litanies. The Pope anointed Napoleon then Joséphine. Placing his fingers in the baby oil, he anointed head, breast, between both shoulders, on each shoulder, the arm socket and the bend of the arm. Joséphine broke into tears. Then Napoleon walked up the steps to the altar, took the golden laurel crown from the Pope with both hands and placed it on his head.

"Vivat Imperator in Aeternum," chanted the choir as Joséphine came forward and bent at the foot of the altar steps, her cape flowing out behind her, tears of emotion dropping onto her clasped hands. Napoleon lifted her crown high above her head and then, after a dramatic pause, lowered it carefully onto the curly dark head. The three-hour ceremony began: the removing and replacing of miters, incense into thuribles, washing of hands, kissing of rings and hems of garments, and the mass entered its last stages. Then the herald at arms announced:

"The most glorious and most august Napoleon, Emperor of the French, is consecrated and enthroned."

At eleven o'clock, the night of the coronation, a bouquet of fireworks burst into a thousand starry lights in the sky and a colossal hot-air balloon lifted into the air. . . . The balloon rose slowly . . . majestically attached to a replica of Napoleon's crown decorated with three thousand multicolored rhinestones. It was a magnificent spectacle . . . but no one could imagine how far this gorgeous balloon was going, by what route, and the sensation it would end up making. . . . The next morning, at daybreak, the inhabitants of Rome saw on the horizon a radiant globe. . . .

First it hovered over the dome of St. Peter's and the Vatican like a celestial coronation. Continuing its course, posing here and there, the balloon finally lifted the golden crown for the last time, swept over and then landed askew on the tomb of the infamous Roman Emperor Nero.

Traced in gold letters on its vast circumference to amuse all Italy was the following:

PARIS, 25 FRIMAIRE, YEAR 13, CORONATION OF THE
EMPEROR NAPOLEON I BY HIS HOLINESS PIUS VII

• CHAPTER TWELVE •

ESKI SERAI 1805

Mihrishah Valide was dying. The Sultana had been in a coma for more than forty-eight hours and the rumors in the city were that she was dead even before she actually breathed her last. Crowds gathered in front of the mausoleum in Eyup that she had been building for almost three years. In Istanbul crowds always gave an impression of hostility even in their grief.

It was the night of October 15, 1805. Father Delleda was summoned from his prayers by the Kizlar Aga and escorted to Topkapi. The winds off the North and Black seas had stirred up the storms and gray fog of the bad season. The Lazarist was rowed from his monastery in Galata on the other side of the Bosphorus. He found Mihrishah unconscious on a bed of white silk, the only furniture. The burning braziers had heated the room to an almost unbearable intensity. In the corner of the Queen's chamber stood the shadowed bulk of Selim, bent under the weight of his forty years, unraveling his turban in grief.

"Mother, here is the priest of the religion of your fathers."

Delleda began his incantations, trembling for his own Faith. With the Oil of the Infirm, the Lazarist anointed the five organs of the senses: the eyes, the ears, the nostrils, the hands and the mouth of the Valide.

"I absolve your sins committed by sight . . . I absolve your sins committed by hearing . . . I absolve your sins committed by smell . . . I absolve your sins committed by touch . . . I absolve your sins committed by word." The Valide died the next morning at ten o'clock.

Naksh-i-dil mourned the Christian Valide, yet was relieved to be out from under her censorious eye. Mihrishah had loved her without liking her, always hoping that she could convince Naksh-i-dil to return to the religion of her childhood. But under her tutorship, Naksh-i-dil had learned the last finesses of the harem and its power. She had learned how to direct and control the passions, the irrationality and the implacable scenarios of female slavery. The harem taught her the hidden motive, the obscure explanation, the obsequious excuse, the astute detour. The ever-changing surfaces of deceit, of light and shadow, forgery and decomposition ate away at penitential lives like water ate away the stone that lapped the ramparts outside, thought Naksh-i-dil. Each woman finally found her niche by harvesting some privileges, a few jewels, a small fortune, a little power, a platonic friendship. As the noble harems across the Empire, what went on here formed a system unto itself. Women interacted with each other, helped or competed against one another, stood together vis-à-vis the men's world, and not infrequently influenced the course of events, not only in their own small world but in politics, in affairs of State, in war. Mihrishah had been right, thought Naksh-i-dil, to have substituted her virility for Selim's impotence. His pederasty was only a viceroy to the sovereignty of cowardice.

As was the custom, Mihrishah Valide's funeral took place four hours after her death. Her son commanded that a bath, a mosque and a fountain be erected in her honor. For eighty-seven days and nights Selim wept at her tomb.

With Mihrishah dead, Yusuf Aga was revoked as Grand Vizier by Selim in a pique of rage. He left Topkapi to make the required pilgrimage to Mecca. Ishak Bey became secretary to the new Grand Vizier.

Selim, in his delusions of persecution and mistrust of everyone, especially his mother's favorites, made a cruel mistake.

"Naksh-i-dil, you are banished to Eski Serai," said Husni-Mah, Selim's First Kadine.

Naksh-i-dil bowed her head, but a smile played around her lips. She had learned well from Mihrishah. *If* one was mother of a hereditary Prince, it was easier to use political influence from the Eski Serai than here. She had learned every act of political intrigue, manipulation, assassination, corruption and bribery in the Empire. She had stayed in contact with the West, had an immense fortune placed in real estate in order to keep Mahmud alive. And even if Mahmud was not ready to rule, she was. Hitabetullah had predicted that Mustafa would not last out the year. For this prediction, Naksh-i-dil had given her slave the diamond necklace from around her neck, an estate in Syria and her freedom. Hitabetullah was a free woman. She had served her for twenty years, and if she followed her to the Eski Serai, she did so of her own free will.

As for Sineprever, they, too, would meet in the Eski Serai.

"I would like to see Mahmud," said Naksh-i-dil.

"Of course," said Husni-Mah. "For the last time," she added.

Mother and son spent the night together, talking into the early dawn. Mahmud wept in his mother's arms, while Naksh-i-dil tried in the last hours to impart to him all the urgent dreams and plans of a lifetime.

"Don't forget me," she whispered. "And remember Selim is our only chance. Selim is Sultan and master. Stay close to him, invest whatever money or presents he gives you with the banker of Zuzuh. This is not forever. Mother has prepared for this moment both in spirit and in capital. I won't fail you. I have vowed to survive. I promise you, Mahmud, I will live to see you Sultan of this Empire."

At dawn the Kizlar Aga conducted Naksh-i-dil and her slave to the Eski Serai in a small curtained caïque that left from an iron door carved into the four-foot ramparts of Topkapi. The women carried with them all their trunks of clothes, their boxes of jewels, but this did not assure that either Naksh-i-dil or Hitabetullah would ever reach the Eski Serai. Too many Kadines had disappeared into the iridescent and still waters for the two women to expect anything but the worst. Hitabetullah, who had hidden a dagger in her sack, had already decided she would go down fighting. Naksh-i-dil thought of the strange route that had brought her here to the middle of the Golden Horn on this morning of the last day in May, about to give up a life she had never lived. For years the Eski Serai had loomed in her mind, she thought, tormenting her imagination in the middle of the most banal and unrelated conversations. To Naksh-i-dil it was a confusion of beautiful and terrible enigmas written or spoken about in legends: vague innuendoes and contradictions, hundreds of years of fabulous life, dreams, images, senseless prejudices and unquenchable mystery.

Behind the Aya Sofya, which occupied the center of her eye, all lacelike and drenched with the filtered golden light, the three-hundred-year-old Eski Serai shimmered with its magnificent past. That incomparable thing, she thought, rose up, jetting out of the acropolis of Istanbul, backed by the thousands of minarets, lead and gilded domes and dark green cypresses of the city. All this was barely outlined in tints of blue eaten away by the sun, just recognizable under a veil of luminous dust. Behind the beautiful mosque in the foreground, Istanbul's houses and

Istanbul's palaces huddled together, into which the Eski Serai intruded its bulk, making everything else very, very small, like a Persian miniature.

She was now a part of this arsenal of females. A prison of ceremonies, massacres, madness, poison, conspiracy and revolt. The fortress that had haunted Europe for three centuries, defied Asia and defeated Africa . . .

Overhead flocks of "damned souls" shadowed the deepening rose of the sky, against which were silhouetted the Black Eunuch and his guards. Over the slap of the oars of the galley, the hawking of seagulls and the alcedos overhead, Naksh-i-dil recalled the voice of the Greek dragoman who had brought her to this place:

"No one I have ever spoken to has ever heard the sound of their wings . . ."

Naksh-i-dil pulled back the curtain and began to talk rapidly and obsessively to the Kizlar Aga in a vain attempt to stop time, to stop the fatal advance of the boat toward her purgatory. She went down the list of her bankers and moneylenders, the places where she had invested, hidden or loaned her fortune. She knew she would need every penny of it to stay alive. She promised the Black Eunuch 40,000 piastres for keeping her informed daily of Mahmud's health and safety, for hiring assassins in Topkapi in case immediate retribution was necessary. She gave him her final instructions concerning Sineprever and Mustafa. If Mahmud died, Mustafa, Selim and Husni-Mah should not see the light of another day. One hundred thousand piastres was invested with the banker Alfair. For her own safety, the eunuchs and the Kizlar Aga of the Eski Serai were to be bribed, corrupted or eliminated. "And let it be known, Kizlar Aga, that it is easier for me, prices being what they are, to pay a Bazam-dil-siz than to pay an excessive bribe." Naksh-i-dil passed messages via the Lebanese merchants, Hussein Aga and Mahmud Aga, who supplied both the Eski Serai and Topkapi. Each day the manner in which information was passed would be changed by previous agreement. Naksh-i-dil was in despair. No matter what preparations, what resolutions she had construed against this day, nothing had prepared her for her rising panic and dread.

A sheen of perspiration broke out on her upper lip and forehead. Hitabetullah stiffened as the Chief Black Eunuch moved toward them, blocking out the rising sun. But he only wanted to exit first from the boat in preparation for docking. They had arrived at the Eski Serai by the long passageway that connected it to the sea, and another iron door

awaited them. Naksh-i-dil and her slave entered into the old harem by
this door. The enormity of the key, the groan it made turning in the
lock, the sharp click of steel on steel made Naksh-i-dil's knees turn to
water. Two black eunuchs held her on either side as they faced still
another door, this time of wood, about twelve paces from the first.

"No!" screamed Naksh-i-dil suddenly. She balked. Twisting and
turning in the iron grip of the eunuchs who held her. "No! No! No!"
But her screams were muffled by the closing of the steel-hinged iron
door behind her and the opening of the bronze-bolted wooden door in
front of her.

"Courage, my lady," whispered Edris Aga.

The slaves' quarters on the first floor consisted of a vast gallery, some
three hundred feet long and fifty feet wide, pierced on both sides with a
multitude of niches, each separated by a window and divided down the
middle by a double row of wardrobes, making two distinct corridors.
Near the windows in the niches were small spaces filled with rolled-up
bedding where the slaves and Odalisques slept in groups of fifteen. Between the bedding and sofas and the wardrobes was a passage of about
six feet, which permitted circulation. Some of the painted blue, red and
white wardrobes were open, and Naksh-i-dil could see their miserable
contents: pieces of cheap cloth, trinkets and beads of no value and sweet
tobacco. She calculated that the visible compartments could provide
sleeping room for three hundred women. She thought of the noxious
quality of air which filled this space, though the decks rose up some
twenty feet. Naksh-i-dil examined everything, all the details of a slave's
unbearable life that she had never seen in Topkapi; the paucity of furniture and objects, the lack of light and air, the macabre darkness where
candles burned at daybreak. A few yellow wax candles here and there
and high chandeliers cast lugubrious shadows but did nothing to dissipate the darkness of a crypt. At both ends of the double gallery were
two staircases which closed by trapdoors above and fastened with iron
bolts.

The Chief Black Eunuch led Naksh-i-dil and Hitabetullah through
this door, which led to the courtyard of the harem. With silent gestures,
he quickly rushed them through flowering gardens, as if even this freedom of light and air was to be denied them as soon as possible. They
found themselves in the Kadines' apartments. Giving onto a large
square, one side of which measured about 260 feet, the rooms were
hidden behind a colonnade of columns providing a shade-giving gallery
around the four sides of the square. Naksh-i-dil thought of the slave-

market square in Algiers. She grasped Hitabetullah's hand. She looked up. The columns of white Paros marble were beautiful, fifteen feet apart, their slender and elegant proportions topped with Ionic cornices and fan traces placed on circular bronze gold-leafed pedestals. Between the columns were small delicate lanterns, not large enough to illuminate the gallery at night but giving just enough light for the eunuchs and slaves to survey and serve the interior. In that part of the harem which gave onto the sea from the heights of the hill, stood a dozen small isolated kiosks that made up an ensemble where Naksh-i-dil imagined only rank or jealousy established the limits of each frontier. On the farther side were the kitchens and slaves' quarters, and in the high wall was an iron door which led to the Court of the Black Eunuchs and the Kizlar Aga of the Eski Serai. It was into his hands that the Kizlar Aga of Topkapi handed over Naksh-i-dil Kadine and her slave. Naksh-i-dil's apartments had already been selected, and she passed a lone weeping willow in the second courtyard on her way to being locked into one of the isolated kiosks. This was to be her home, and Hitabetullah's perhaps, forever.

Naksh-i-dil could see the minaret of the harem mosque from her small grilled window as Hitabetullah placed her possessions in the painted wood closets that lined the kiosk. She could also see the sky and a courtyard with a cypress from her window. "What luck," commented Hitabetullah. Naksh-i-dil broke down, weeping, but Hitabetullah threw back her head and laughed.

"Mistress," she said, "before a thousand days pass, you will be Empress of this cursed, bloody land."

"If I live."

"Yes," said Hitabetullah. "I will see to that. As you must for Mahmud. For Mahmud lives . . . of that you can be sure. Spies and bakshish will tell you the rest, even from this tomb."

Galata, October 16, 1805
Superior General Father Brzozowski
The Company of Jesus
St. Petersburg

Most Reverend Father,
   The Lord have mercy on my soul. Amen.

The Christian Valide Mihrishah is dead.

She came to me in a dream at the baths . . . and conducted me across the Bosphorus to the Seraglio . . . where . . . I entered, at last, the Door of Felicity of the harem of Topkapi. . . . I performed the last sacraments in Latin to a Christian God, while in the corner Selim wept and prayed to Allah in Osmanli, our prayers mingled, interweaving in one lamentation as in a piece of music. But who was the soloist and who was the chorus? Which contained the real melody and which only the accompaniment? Who was the organ of God? In the corner, the Black Eunuch I have spoken to you about also fingered his tespi, but in silence as if weighing the delirium of our duet, the lunacy of our music, the incoherence of the universe . . . ELI, ELI, LAMA SABACHTHANI?

His blackness struck me for the first time as demoniacal. . . .

Suddenly Father Delleda heard a great flapping of wings by his temples. His last conversation with the Black Eunuch swirled in his head. He knew he wasn't the true fanatic the Black Eunuch insisted he was. The fanatic was the Black Eunuch. The fanatic killed for an idea just as much as he *allowed* himself to be killed for the same idea. Murder and martyr were equal. . . .

"I am much more dangerous," the Black Eunuch had said to him, "than one who suffers for a belief. Take the Prophet Jesus (the blessings and grace of Allah be upon him). Evil comes from a conviction of truth. Fanaticism gives a man the taste for efficiency, prophecy and terror, and yet without a *conception,* man has only his caprices, his interests, his familiar vices, his harem. . . ."

"No. It is the transformation of this *conviction* into God that produces the fanatic who kills in the name of that God, or his forgeries; that is, nations, classes, races . . ." Delleda had argued.

"It is true," the Black Eunuch had said after a long pause, "that evil pales beside one who *thinks* he disposes of the truth. . . . When a man loses his faculty for *indifference,* he always becomes a potential assassin."

Then the Black Eunuch had looked at him oddly with his dark eyes, the whites of which were as yellow as the palms of his hands. But he had said nothing.

"Mohammedanism teaches nothing, has no idea except to obey to the letter without discussion or comprehension a Sultan!" Delleda had said.

"Fanaticism is necessary," the Black Eunuch had continued. "It is

true that evil pales beside the man who thinks he disposes of the truth
. . . when a man loses his faculty for indifference, he always becomes a
potential assassin. You have taken a vow of obedience. Would you really
hesitate to kill me if the General of the Society of Jesus commanded it
of you?"

"But I am a Lazarist," he had cried.

"Oh, come now, you are a Jesuit in hiding and everybody knows it.
You are also a spy. Are we so different one from the other, you and I?
Two old eunuchs. Two old, old eunuchs . . . All I do is offer the
Master the possibility of loving himself through me."

"In a world where some have nothing or are nothing, when the Other
is everything and possesses all, *flattery* is the gift of life, the spontaneous
form the lust for love takes. It is the gift of an image that gives the
despot *more* than he has but which supposes in exchange that he ac-
cepts *not* to be everything. If I do nothing, the Sultan is displeased
because I don't conform to the function of the Black Eunuch and so I
risk my head. But if I act, I also risk my head because I am liable to
displease the Sultan. An impossible situation. Death is the only exit," he
had said.

Delleda had not protested at this strange idea. There had been too
many confusing revelations in what the Black Eunuch had said.

"You, Delleda, are an idol worshiper by instinct, therefore not apt for
religion, since you insist on converting the unconditional into the object
of your dreams. . . . For even when religion is eliminated, man ex-
hausts himself forging counterfeits of God."

He had answered that man's power to adore was responsible for all
crimes. Crime! He had actually said the fanaticization of his soul was
criminal. More than criminal; what he had implied was that it was
useless! That beliefs in any case were interchangeable.

"In itself," the Black Eunuch had said, "all idea is neutral or should
be; but man animates and projects his passion and his madness; impure,
transformed into belief. Thus are born ideology, doctrine and bloody
farce. . . ."

"It is you who dream of a pilgrimage to Mecca!"

"That is merely a doctrinal obligation on my part," said the Black
Eunuch. "Like your confession. It implies neither salvation nor fanaticism. You don't actually believe you can give *absolution,* do you? That
you personally can absolve a crime?"

"In the name of Jesus Christ, yes."

"So can the Sultan," said Edris.

"Satan!" the Lazarist had cried.

"I said, *Sultan,*" the Black Eunuch had answered.

"Is the sacrament you gave to Mihrishah Valide," he continued, "sufficient when she is lying face down on Moslem soil in her mausoleum, mourned as Empress of the Veiled Heads?"

"Yes, such is the power of Christ."

"Well," said the Black Eunuch, "such is the will of Allah. Why don't you come to Mecca with me?"

"Me!"

"Afraid? There is nothing to fear except your own fear."

And now the Lazarist knew he was afraid. More afraid than he had ever been in his entire existence. Satan. He had said Satan . . .

The Lazarist reread the letter to his General. Would he survive all the contradictions of his life? he wondered. The solitude of his existence? Now only the Black Eunuch remained, for God had grown away from him in spirit and in thought. And the Black Eunuch was taking him back to the Orient, back into Asia. Only the Bible sustained him now, and he held tenaciously to that one link.

For Father Geronimo Delleda found Islam more and more seductive. Mohammed, like Jesus in his earliest preachings, stressed the same four points: the sole sovereignty of God/Allah, the sinfulness of idolatry, the certainty of resurrection with the rewards of heaven and the damnation of hell; and his own divine vocation as prophet. . . .

The Lazarist shifted the Koran and the Bible, both of which he held in his hands. Mohammed had been rejected by the Meccans, but he had also been rejected by the Jews and Christians of the neighboring city of Medina, where he had settled in 622. Mohammed accused the Jews of misrepresenting the Old Testament, of turning the universalistic religion of Abraham, destined to conquer the entire world, into an exclusive, nationalistic and racist theology; and of rejecting the virgin-born Prophet Jesus, who had been sent by God to show the Jews where they had gone wrong. As for Christians, Mohammed accused them of reverting from monotheism to idolatry, adapting the doctrine of the Trinity; of blasphemy against God by saying that His Prophet Jesus had been defeated in the humiliation of the Crucifixion when he had really not died at all, but had escaped to Kashmir and lived.

Father Delleda closed his eyes. . . . The monastery had long lost all utility in Istanbul. He and Father Alby Jean were only two old priests roaming its deserted corridors in search of souls that had long escaped them. They were two eunuchs against the hordes, two against the Buddhists, the Confucians, the pantheists, Jews, the Moslems, the Freemasons, the secularists, the atheists, the rationalists . . . the Protestants, the renegades, the Wahabi rebels who had taken the holy cities of Mecca and Medina from Selim's weak hands.

"*O Al-Azîz,*" cried out Delleda. He tended more and more to use a Moslem word for God. "What is happening to me?" He put his head in his hands. The baths were closed. Perhaps it was only his own fear. Only sweet, sweet transpiration could steam out the demons tormenting him. Satan. Perhaps it was only solitude. He wished he could speak with someone other than Father Alby Jean, who only heard his confessions and prayed for his soul. There was nothing wrong with his soul! It was his head! He needed the Black Eunuch.

The Lazarist looked out of his window. The small diamond in his left ear glistened. Eternal flames of another Constantinople fire rose high into the sky across the waters like a giant burning hand. A serious fire, it stretched a mile along the opposite shore.

To the Lazarist the sound of flames was as if a thousand chariots beat upon stones. The drums rolled and the cry of *"Yanghinvar!"* rang out. It seemed too loud to him to be so far away. . . .

The Lazarist peered out into the empty corridors of the deserted monastery. The heavy flapping of birds' wings seemed closer now than ever, and Delleda shuffled his Koran and Bible one upon the other in a ceaseless scraping of leather as if he were shuffling a deck of cards. He had vowed to explore the depths of Islam at the peril of his soul. . . . And now his soul flew about his room in a wild battering of wings that pierced his skull and smashed into his brain. One wing buffeted him to one side of the corridor, while the other sent him reeling in the opposite direction like a drunken man. He staggered forward.

Father Alby Jean heard someone sobbing as he neared Delleda's study. Peeking around the corner, he spied the Lazarist, his head touching a tiny prayer rug given him by the Black Eunuch, repeating the ninety-nine names of Allah. The second Lazarist stared in horror. Delleda was praying like a Moslem, but then Father Alby Jean noticed, not without a certain satisfaction, that Delleda was facing the wrong direction.

Father Alby Jean wrestled Delleda onto his back, binding his arms and legs. He and his servant dragged the Lazarist back to his cell, which had long been devoid of all furniture except a bed, and of every sharp instrument except a crucifix. Delleda heard the enormous key turn in the lock behind his back as he clutched, back to back, his Koran and his Bible.

Father Geronimo Delleda had lost his mind. Father Alby Jean took him to Santorini. To die in his own country.

As Moslems considered madness a divine gift, the Kadines who had fallen into lunacy were especially revered in the Eski Serai. Within its seven-foot walls resided the debris of the celebrated beauties of Topkapi. Those who had not had the chance to escape into marriage with a rich Pasha or Officer of the Empire (the women of the Sultan's harem were much prized) were forgotten behind its walls. The Eski Serai was the spectral afterimage of the real Topkapi, for everything—the hours, the rituals, the organization, the baths, the architecture—was exactly the same except for one thing: there was no Sultan. The openings of the windows seemed smaller to Naksh-i-dil, the doors narrower, the light dimmer, the eunuchs more terrible. It was a world in which the voice of the master, the Sultan, its reason for existence, was only a memory. Naksh-i-dil noticed that the voices of all the women, no matter what their age, had the pitch and timbre of very young girls. The same voices as those of the convent of St. Cyre. It was common in Catholic convents. As if the gift of the women's bodies to Christ included also their voices, which remained as unchanging as their chastity. In the harem the sound gave the singing and the conversations of the inmates a beautiful, unearthly lightness, a childlike purity. The faces, too, seemed cleansed of the passing of time. Everything was one shade paler than real life except for two things: the harem was suffused with the heaviest and most lavishly poignant perfumes imaginable; as if their scent could pierce the walls of the Old Palace and let the outside world in. Sound was also magnified beyond reality. The clank of a door, the turn of a key, a scream, the chant of a bird, the tuning of a kemangeh, were all abnormally loud and harsh.

One of the first inmates Naksh-i-dil encountered was Ayşe Sineprever. She had become the Kiaya Kadine, the Mother Superior of the Eski Serai. She was dressed in a black caftan drawn in at the waist by a cashmere shawl, and on her head rested a red bonnet. The light descended from the high sightless windows illuminating her face, which was the color of wax. Naksh-i-dil was stunned into silence. Other ghosts appeared in the days that followed: Abdulhamid's Kadine Mehtap was there. Binnaz and Hatice had remarried. Seda and Leyla Saz, old women who had been Kadines of Mustafa III, were still alive. There was the mad Ikbal Pervizifelek who told fortunes, had visions and spoke in tongues. There was even a ninety-nine-year-old doyenne of the harem, Nur Banu, the last wife of Ahmed III, Mustafa's father and Muhmud's great-grandfather, who had died in 1730. Being the last and youngest of his Ikbals, she had not had sufficient time to amass the dowry necessary to attract a husband after his death. Nur Banu, her blue sightless eyes with white-rimmed irises, sat for hours immobile, and spoke in parables in her adolescent voice that spanned a century. "Ah," she would say, "the famous veil. Invented to protect men and is nothing if not protection for women. We put on a transparent one in order to excite our caprices and a heavy one in order to satisfy them. . . ." The baths became once again Naksh-i-dil's refuge. Only there did she have an impression of reality. The obese, oleaginous flesh of aged bodies, polished, moist and made transparent by constant ablutions, became intensely vivid in the vaporous underworld of the baths, where the absence of color and the echo of hollow sound seemed normal and everyday-like. The atmosphere of voluptuous and terrible poetry was ten times more powerful than in Topkapi with its chattering narcissism. Here, one saw things the human voice could not describe. For here was the world made for the Other who was permanently absent. The same religion, thought Naksh-i-dil, that defended the harem of Topkapi violated the penitents of the Eski Serai. For a harem without a Sultan was a convent without a God: the Shadow of Allah which now made no shadow, only oblivion and darkness.

Naksh-i-dil began by investing a considerable fortune in bakshish. She established herself as the Valide-in-waiting, the mother of a Prince, the equal of Sineprever. Everyone from the kitchens to the ramparts was bribed. Hitabetullah established her position by curing several Odalisques and killing several others. Once this was done, Naksh-i-dil sought out Sineprever who, although officially living in the Eski Serai, passed much of her time in the palace of her daughter, Esma Sultane. Sineprever was frank, even friendly, now that they were both in exile.

"Be careful of what you do, Naksh-i-dil. I am neither blind nor crazy. And I am freer to act than you. We both have sons to protect and I don't want your life or that of Mahmud or I would have already had both. Which is, I suppose, why Selim sent you here. So that *I* could kill you. Well, I'm not playing his game. Now I can tell you this: Yusuf Pasha counseled me long ago to have you killed, but I refused and today I am glad I did. The enemy of my enemy is my friend. Protect me out of self-interest and I will protect you."

Sineprever's dark eyes blazed. "Remember that, Naksh-i-dil. And leave me *my* life."

Naksh-i-dil remembered. She thought of all the murders these walls had seen. The Viziers, the eunuchs, the favorites, the Generals, felled by a thousand blades, in ten thousand episodes, in a hundred thousand different ways, for a million different reasons. . . . Murad III had delivered up Mehmed his son; Osman, his Kizlar Aga; Ghaznefer, his White Eunuch. Murad IV had executed Hafiz, his Grand Vizier. Abdulhamid had condemned Halil Hamid to the bowstring.

Over the "Palace of Tears" full of its amplified sounds and omnipresent perfume, lay another odor: opium.

"Beware of the poppy tree, my lady," warned Hitabetullah. "It is very low but he who falls, breaks his back."

Naksh-i-dil had never been attracted to narcotics, even at Topkapi, although she had no idea what Hitabetullah put into her mysterious potions. And now, though she craved only forgetfulness, she fought the impulse. The gardens and disordered maze of the bizarre architecture and courtyards of the Eski Serai were full of women who roamed them in a stupor of addiction.

But there was one drug she couldn't resist: Nur Banu. Nur Banu who, with her blind eyes, her weighed words, preceded by the most furtive movements of face and hands, handed down, accentuated by splendid silences, the history of the Eski Serai. She always began the same way:

"It was the caresses of Roxelana that tightened the bowstring around the necks of the Grand Viziers Ahmed and Ibrahim. It was the kisses of Safiye the Venetian who maintained the network of espionage between the Porte and Venice. It was the seven Kadines of Murad III who governed the Empire from 1580 to 1600. It was Makpeiker, the Kadine of two thousand shawls, who reigned over two seas and two continents for twenty years. It was Rebiz Gulnuz, the Odalisque of a hundred silver carriages, who governed the Divan from 1650 to 1660. It was Sekerbuli the Greek who led Ibrahim the Mad a merry chase between Istanbul and Andrianople. . . . The Eski Serai has burned three times. . . ."

Fire, thought Naksh-i-dil, always fire . . . ? "It was the third fire in Eski Serai in the time of Suleiman that allowed Suleiman's favorite Khurren to move the entire harem to the Great Seraglio of Topkapi. She took her possessions, a hundred ladies-in-waiting, her dressmaker, her purveyor and his thirty slaves, and moved them all. Of course, women had sometimes been permitted to sleep in Topkapi, but Khurren stayed for the rest of her life, and in time a new harem was built within the Third Court of Topkapi to take the place of this one. Thus began the ascendancy of the women of the harem known as the 'Sultanate of the Women . . .' In seven years another favorite, Roxelana, had gained supremacy over Suleiman and had married her daughter by him to the Grand Vizier, and established a dynasty of Grand Viziers and a Sultanate that would last fifty years. Now Suleiman wanted his firstborn son, Mustafa, to be his successor. But Roxelana had borne him three sons, and she was determined that one of them succeed to the throne instead of Mustafa. Roxelana made Suleiman believe that Mustafa had designs on the Sultanate and was ready to dispose of him like Suleiman's father had disposed of his grandfather. Mustafa was exiled and Roxelana achieved the succession to the throne of her eldest son, who ruled as Selim II. He was succeeded by his son, Murad III. Four women, called by the people 'The Four Pillars of the Empire,' ruled Murad's life: his mother, the Valide Roxelana; his favorite, a Venetian beauty called Safiye, or Baffo after her family; Janfeda, who, was the Kiaya of the harem; and his sister. Safiye became the mother of Murad's eldest son. Janfeda never shared the Sultan's couch, but her role was to fill it with others. Of the four, the most powerful was Safiye, who influenced foreign affairs, dissuading the Sultan Murad from making war on her native Venice during his reign, and continued her influence over her son, Mehmed III, in the next generation. It was Mehmed III who strangled his nineteen brothers and twenty sisters upon his ascension to the throne. But it was the Valide Baffo who held the affairs of State in her hands. When Mehmed III died, his son Ahmed I succeeded him. Ahmed didn't kill his only brother, Mustafa, because he was a lunatic, and Mohammed teaches us that madness is a sacred gift. But Janissary revolts put Mustafa on the throne twice; the second time Valide Baffo formed a government in the name of Mustafa and killed his still-living predecessor, Osman. The reins of the government of the Empire were held by a woman.

"Osman's son, Murad IV, succeeded Mustafa as a child. His mother, Kosem Valide, ruled throughout the whole minority of her son, but Murad IV, once emancipated from the regency of his mother, began a reign of terror which only ended with his death at twenty-seven. Kosem saved the life of Murad's last living brother, Ibrahim, who Murad had condemned to death. Kosem would live to regret it. Ibrahim plunged the dynasty into unheard-of depths of depravity and became known as

Ibrahim the Crazy. With his craze for women, love of sex automats, jewels and scents, he taxed his Empire into still another revolt led by the Janissaries. Ibrahim was finally murdered by his Black Eunuch when he tried to copulate with a Kadine giving birth. It was Kosem who placed the turban on her own grandson Mehmed's head. Thus, for a second time, a child was on the throne under the regency of a Valide. For eight years, two Valide Sultanes, Mehmed's mother, Turhan, and his powerful grandmother, Kosem, vied for power. Turhan finally murdered Kosem. With the death of Turhan Valide and the ascension of Mehmed's son, Mustafa II, the Sultanate of the women ended . . ."

Nur Banu's blind eyes darted back and forth in their whiteness.

"I spent six years in the harem of Sultan Ahmed and the sixth year, the year of his death, I was Gozde. I had just begun my ascension. I remember many other women . . . I am the last. Nothing is left, not a strand of hair, not a thread of veil, not a graffito on the wall nor the light to read by it. It all ends here, in the Eski Serai."

Again and again Naksh-i-dil was drawn to the accelerated murmur of Nur Banu's chronicle of the Eski Serai. And in Nur Banu's voice, their biographies flowed into one long dirge of femininity and slavery.

Naksh-i-dil began peering more closely into the faces she saw every day. Some were still young, even adolescent. Some were old women with white hair, most were thirty or forty locked-up women without men; there were timid faces, bold faces, stoic faces, nude faces, ravished faces, serene faces, drugged faces: favorites of a night, a day, a week, a year, a lifetime.

Women who had had children and lost them, who had been beautiful and were no longer, who had been young and were now old, women who had been someone and who now were no one, women who had been loved and now were nothing but dust in a wren's nest of kiosks and dry courtyards, women who had been women and were now only pale imitations. Second-, third-, even fourth-generation creatures who would have children, grandchildren, great-grandchildren. They passed, all mute and light as phantoms. An immense pity wrung Naksh-i-dil's heart. She was reminded once more of God's convent, of nuns and abbesses, of ecstasies and flagellations, of prayers flung out of hearts purified by solitude, of girlish voices that never aged endlessly rising and falling.

Then Hadidge Sultane appeared, it seemed to Naksh-i-dil, a long time after her imprisonment unannounced, unexpected and unexplained.

"Mahmud?" asked Naksh-i-dil. Her voice creaked. She was hardly able to pronounce Mahmud's name.

"Mahmud is well treated by Selim. He is well protected by your bribes and your spies. He is a man," said Hadidge.

Naksh-i-dil's eyes brimmed with unshed tears.

"I couldn't save you," Hadidge said simply. Naksh-i-dil knew this was true. Husni-Mah had had every right according to the laws of the harem to banish her to the Eski Serai. Those who could had already escaped into marriage with the Officers and Pashas of the Empire, and so many of Abdulhamid's harem were gone. The others survived on sugar, opium and those peculiar friendships that flourished in places where one of the sexes was locked up only with its own kind. The love affair of Fekti-Seza and Aynisah had ended in tragedy only days ago . . . Aynisah was dead.

"A harem without a Sultan is like a convent without God," said Naksh-i-dil as she led Hadidge toward the baths. Hadidge glanced at Naksh-i-dil. Was she suffering the torments of the renegade? she wondered.

"What," she said, laughing, "does a harem have to do with a convent?"

"A lot of things, I've found, Hadidge. . . . Worship, obedience, protocol, prayer, fanaticism and ignorance—not only personal ignorance, but ignorance about the outside world . . . here is a world apart . . . and then there is tyranny and fear. . . . It is fear most of all that prevails here . . . and fear is always the same, whether it be of hell and damnation or merely the damnation of living death. Either way, it is hell: of knowing that tomorrow which was just like yesterday will be just like today, only worse."

"I came to offer you love," said Hadidge, smiling.

"The need for love," said Naksh-i-dil, flushing, "goes with a certain vision of life that doesn't exist here. I have books and news of the outside world. I have the Koran. I have my will. I have Mahmud. I don't need more. The women here"—she paused—"take care of themselves and of each other . . . they have no choice. But we are different. . . . For a brief moment we found ourselves in ourselves. But this was not our destiny. We are men-lovers. What we brought each other in joy once, we can never recapture here in prison. Love demands freedom. Love exists only in freedom—not only of choice, but place, gender, race.

"I pray four times a day and retire at nightfall without a candle, for

my fear of fire is as great as ever. I eat a little lamb and rice, just enough
to sustain life, and I drink only water. I take light tea without sugar and
smoke judiciously. I guard my silence. I am happy with everything.
Happy even to be without you. Try to understand. I have learned contentment in the abnegation of false needs."

"Our love?" asked Hadidge.

"Our complicity as women," answered Naksh-i-dil.

Hope burned out, thought Hadidge Sultane, and took the soul with it
. . . or perhaps Naksh-i-dil was too much of a woman to see the world
in any other way except that of a woman. . . .

"As a slave, Hadidge, your love is odious to me. Try to understand,
my darling. I found in you those durable qualities which grace *men* full
of power, beauty, enjoyment, reserve, strength. Let us leave it thus. We
must leave it thus. . . . War unending has crept into the Empire and
caused its downfall. Yet each year, nature's elements declare war on
each other. The strife of every winter for a new spring is infinitely more
terrible than any *human* war. More life is destroyed in one winter's day
than in all the human wars put together. I must free myself from *all*
slavery. If incertitude has slid into my spirit, which I had the conceit to
find so lucid, so quick, it is the fatigue of yearning, the routine of
illusion, the necessity for survival. Forget me and I shall bless you.
Forget me and I shall kiss your hands. Forget me without remorse, and
I will love you forever. . . ."

"Naksh-i-dil, there is no real ending in words," said Hadidge.
"Wherever life meets, even centuries from now, I shall love you. . . ."

*"I swear by Allah, Shahrazad, that you were already pardoned before
the coming of these children. I loved you because I found you chaste,
tender, wise and eloquent. May Allah bless you, and bless your descendants, O Shahrazad, this thousand and first night is brighter for us than
the day!"* whispered Naksh-i-dil.

Naksh-i-dil watched as the forlorn mummylike form swathed in veils
that was Hadidge leave. *"Al-Alî,"* said Naksh-i-dil.

Naksh-i-dil had been in the Eski Serai for two years, one month,
fourteen days and twelve hours when something so unexpected had
happened that neither her spies nor Hadidge had been able to forewarn
her.

Naksh-i-dil heard the far-off boom of artillery.

It was the morning of the twenty-ninth of May, 1807.

• CHAPTER THIRTEEN •

MUSTAFA IV 1807

A new Chief Black Eunuch Naksh-i-dil had never seen before, dressed in his elaborate ceremonial robes, came to escort Sineprever from the Eski Serai.

"My name is Merdjan Aga. Long live Mustafa Khan!" Naksh-i-dil felt the very earth move from under her and the familiar sensation of the scent of fire engulfed her. Mustafa was Sultan.

A few weeks before a group of young Janissary recruits, called Yamaks, who guarded the Bosphorus forts at Buyukdere assassinated a Nizam-i-jedid after he tried to force them to wear new uniforms. A riot broke out and Selim's envoy was killed trying to escape. Once the news of the riot and the death of the envoy reached every battery along the Bosphorus, fighting broke out everywhere between the Yamaks and the Nizam-i-jedids. If the bellicose Mihrishah had been alive, Selim might have had the stomach to stifle the revolt, but the Ata-Ullah, so much stronger than the weak-willed Sultan, convinced him to negotiate and conciliate, which only convinced the Yamaks of Selim's incapacity.

The Nizam-i-jedid were ordered to remain in their barracks as a sign of good faith. A negotiator was sent to the rebels, but they refused to negotiate and began marching on Istanbul and were joined by thousands of Janissaries, Ulemas, religious students, housewives, vagabonds and sightseers. When they reached the palace, Selim again tried to appease the rebels by officially disbanding the Nizam-i-jedid. The terrified Sultan sacrificed his entire Divan.

Eleven reformers were handed over to the mob. Selim's private secretary, Ahmed Efendi, was torn to pieces by them. The Sultan saved two of his other ministers from this horrible death by dispatching them within the confines of the palace and sending their heads out to the rebels. The two-faced Ata-Ullah joined the rebels, issuing a fetva supporting all their demands and sent it to Selim. He recommended that the Sultan agree at once to everything in order to save himself. No one wanted to depose Selim, the Ata-Ullah assured the Sultan, only his evil ministers and reformers. The Sultan sent his acceptance, but tried to save his friends Ibrahim and Raif Efendi by allowing them to escape through the Door of the Dead. Yusuf Aga was in exile in Bursa and so escaped, temporarily, assassination.

"There has been a coup d'état," said Hadidge when she arrived two days later. "Selim has been deposed by the Aga of the Janissaries, the Grand Vizier and the Grand Mufti." She paused. "It was bloodless. Selim is still alive. He has been placed in the Cage . . . Prince Mahmud is with him."

Hadidge saw Naksh-i-dil sway and then right herself.

"Edris Aga escaped. He has not returned from his pilgrimage to Mecca. Ishak Bey has disappeared completely. There is a death warrant on his head. Selim delivered up his entire Divan in hopes of saving himself, then he retired behind the doors of the harem.

"I have been with him until now," continued Hadidge. "It was the only thing to do. I was the only one he loved, trusted—the only one left." Hadidge's eyes glistened with tears.

"I found my brother huddled in the corner of the sofa that ran around the four sides of the immense marbled and tiled space. The Ata-Ullah, the Sheykh-ul-Islam, presented himself and advanced slowly toward him, traversing the thousand or so yards between them, feigning grief with his affected shivering and lowered eyes. Selim watched him approach quietly, his gaze that of someone who wanted to wrest from the features of the religious leader of the Empire the words his lips had still not uttered. . . .

" 'Oh, my Lord and master,' he said, 'I must accomplish a painful mission, accepted in order to prevent an enraged multitude from violating this sacred sanctuary. . . . The Janissaries have proclaimed Mustafa Sultan. All resistance is useless and dangerous and can only serve to spill uselessly the blood of your faithful servants. This sad event was written in the book of destinies. What can we do, weak mortals that we are, against the will of God? It remains to us only to learn to humble ourselves before him and to worship his eternal decrees.'

Selim answered:

Kendi élimlé yaré kessib verdighim calem,
The pen formed by my hand and offered to the beloved,

Fétvaï houni na hakémi yazdi ibtida.
Has signed above all the arrest of my innocent death.

"My brother abdicated. Mustafa now rules," Hadidge said.

"But how can that be if Selim lives?" asked Naksh-i-dil.

"Mustafa is a usurper. Selim is still Sultan. . . ," shouted Hadidge. "There is an army now grouping under the command of the Pasha of Ruschuk to restore him to power. But Mahmud is alive, Naksh-i-dil. Don't cry. He is alive, I tell you. Imprisoned with Selim . . . I give you my word! You thought I would abandon you?" Hadidge smiled.

"Perhaps."

"I love you, Naksh-i-dil."

"Mustafa swore his religious vows in the Chamber of the Sacred Tunic and fastened the Osman sword at his side in the mosque of Eyup," continued Hadidge. "The cannons you heard were salutes from the palace, from the batteries of the foundry, from the Arsenal, from the warships anchored in the harbor, announcing to the capital and to the world that there was a new Sultan. The Janissaries and the Yamaks have acclaimed their new Sultan. The Ulemas and the Ata-Ullah don't bother to hide their satisfaction. For the masses outside, the coup d'état is a popular one. Selim's regime was always unpopular. The Ulemas claim that Selim's reforms were the cause of high taxes; the inflation imposed by the war has turned into a catastrophe. Selim and his blind attachment to Napoleon exasperated the Empire. His lack of children meant the extinction of the dynasty." Hadidge shook her head, thankful it was still on her shoulders. "I have taken refuge with Esma, who is, after all, Mustafa's sister.

"Mustafa is a twenty-nine-year-old, solid, simple-minded, not very handsome, fanatical Moslem. What else would a people want in a Sultan?" said Hadidge. "The people see in the magnitude of his belly the symbol of his manliness. The Sheykh-ul-Islam, the one they call The Limp, remains the religious head of the Empire. . . .

"Decapitated heads are rolling off the meat block. Only two people on the entire list of proscription have been pardoned: the Grand Vizier, Tchelebi Mustafa Efendi, went on his own to the Execution Place, but his white beard and his noble silence were so awe-inspiring that no one dared to touch that venerable head. On the other hand, Yusuf Aga tried to buy his life by sending three million piastres to the Janissaries, assuring them that was all he had. He was exiled to Bursa, but a few days ago the execution orders arrived from Mustafa; his fortune had been found to be thirty-six million piastres—fifteen million in cash deposited with Chaptchi, your Jewish banker. Yusuf Aga's head now decorates the imperial gate of Topkapi. Bakshish and Esma bought my life.

"Sineprever has officially commenced her reign as Valide. The apartments are emptied and swept clean. There were the usual screams, cries and suicides," Hadidge said nonchalantly, with a gesture of her hand.

Naksh-i-dil uttered sympathetic cries and exclamations, but strangely enough, Hadidge's tale of woe invigorated her. She began to feel a determined courage: one down.

"Courage, my love. Mahmud needs you," said Hadidge.

"Can you get a message to him?"

Hadidge hesitated a second, but only a second, and then she said: "Yes."

"How much, Hadidge?"

"However much it takes."

"I have no more fortune."

"It doesn't matter. I still do."

"Are you afraid of dying, Hadidge?"

"No, Naksh-i-dil. It would be such a rest from the tiresomeness of living . . . even if one has wonderful things yet to do . . . a ball for example. There you are, all dressed in beautiful robes and jewels, and finally . . . finally you lie, still all dressed up, across your bed and sleep . . . bored with the ball. . . ."

Hadidge was silent. How could she admit even to Naksh-i-dil that Selim had delivered up everyone except Yusuf and Edris and herself. She knew Selim well enough to know that he would sacrifice Mahmud to save himself just as she would gladly deliver up Mahmud to save Selim.

"What have you done with your fortune?" asked Hadidge.

"I've bought Mahmud's life—until now."

"I will do my best," said Hadidge. "I may not be alive much longer myself."

"I seem destined always to ask of you something you can't accomplish . . ."

Hadidge and Naksh-i-dil stood face to face while a thousand miles away a provincial Pasha called Mustafa Bayrakdar, the "Flag Bearer," was already on the move to restore Selim to the throne.

• CHAPTER FOURTEEN •

SELIM 1808

The reason of the strongest is always the best.
—CATHERINE THE GREAT

Naksh-i-dil had heard rumors for months that Bayrakdar was on the march. The tomb of Eski Serai had taken its toll. Naksh-i-dil was forty-two years old. Outwardly she was still a beautiful woman, the golden hair streaked with silver was even more beautiful than ever, and Naksh-i-dil knew that solitude hadn't broken her spirit, but had diminished her strength.

Selim had been imprisoned in the Cage for eleven months when Mustafa Bayrakdar's armies, thirty-thousand strong, arrived at the outskirts of the city from Bosnia. Bayrakdar's province of Ruschuk had become, little by little, the most important military center in Turkey. And Bayrakdar was determined to restore Selim to the throne. For Naksh-i-dil, it was a matter of indifference. Selim had left her in the Eski Serai and Mustafa had not released her. All her fears centered upon Mahmud.

Mustafa Bayrakdar Pasha was a peasant born in Albania. No one was quite sure when, but his birthday was placed somewhere in the middle of the previous century. At ten he had run away from home and gone into the horse-trading business. He soon enrolled under the flag of the Pasha of his province and quickly distinguished himself by his ferocious courage, earning the name Bayrakdar, Flag Bearer, for having retaken their captured flag singlehandedly from the enemy. From that time on he did not quit the side of the Pasha of Ruschuk, and finally, he had succeeded him. When the Russians invaded Moldavia in 1806, Bayrakdar had engaged the Russians several times, sending sacks of ears to Istanbul as trophies of his victories. He was rude, rustic, religious, unlettered, ambitious, simple and superstitious, but he had the innate intelligence of a savage animal combined with the ruse and conservatism of an Albanian peasant. Mustafa Bayrakdar had expected to be appointed Grand Vizier and commander of the new army as a reward for his success against the Russians. But the Ata-Ullah managed to obtain the Grand Vizierate for Chelik Mustafa Pasha, one of his own men. Bayrakdar was so furious that he bent his steel-plated copper shield with his bare hands. Then he and his men departed for Ruschuk, taking with them all supporters of Selim and reformers who wanted to go.

The authority of Mustafa had diminished in the past year. Bayrakdar wanted to prevent the Sultan from ratifying a new treaty imposed by Russia and France, which would mutilate the Empire of some of its richest provinces: Bosnia was joined to Dalmatia, Morea was given to the Kingdom of Italy, Serbia to Austria, Moldavia and Walachia to Russia.

In June, with the excuse of making a tour of inspection, Bayrakdar marched on Istanbul and camped some twelve miles outside the city.

Bayrakdar wrote to the Pasha of Andrianople: "When you read this letter, either Selim will be dead, or he will again taste the délices of the throne."

On the twenty-fifth of July, the alarm was launched in the capital. At sundown Bayrakdar's army approached the city holding high the unfurled Sacred Banner of Islam. In Istanbul Mustafa could count on no one to defend the gates of the city.

Half of Selim's friends wanted Bayrakdar to arrest Mustafa at once, in the midst of the Sacred Banner ceremony, and to direct his troops toward the palace to rescue Selim. But Bayrakdar was a simple man and no expert in deception, which he found disagreeable. He found it indecent and a violation of every secular custom to arrest a Sultan during a sacred ceremony. He decided to wait until the next séance of the Divan. Three days later at dawn Bayrakdar made his procession to the Porte.

After ordering guards to seal off all the exits and entrances to the Porte, Bayrakdar went straight to the office of the Grand Vizier, Chelik Mustafa. He asked for the imperial seal, and when the Grand Vizier hesitated, he snatched the seal from around his neck. He then sent for the Sheykh-ul-Islam, who in respect for tradition had to consecrate the substitution of the Sultan with a fetva. Arif Efendi Arab Zadé was old and cowardly. When he, too, hesitated, Bayrakdar, indignant at his refusal to go with him, lifted him off his feet with one hand.

"And you," he said, "son of an Arab [translating his name into popular Turkish]. Move your ass!"

Bayrakdar then unfurled the Banner of the Prophet and the immense cortege left from the Porte in the direction of Topkapi. Bayrakdar was at the head; following him were fifteen thousand cavalry and infantrymen and the clerical and secular dignitaries of Istanbul. The first gate, Soguk Cesme Kapi, the Door of the Cold Fountain, was open and the cortege passed. The second gate, the Bab-el Salam, the middle door, was closed, but it was opened immediately, and the cortege arrived before the gate of Bab-i-Sa'adet.

Bayrakdar demanded the Chief Black Eunuch, Merdjan Aga. There was no answer. The Pasha repeated his demand to open the door to the Sheykh-ul-Islam, who in turn, demanded to see the Padishah. There was still no answer. Just then, a secret side door, the Door of the White Eunuchs, the Akagalar Kapisi, opened a crack in order to let the Sheykh-ul-Islam, Arif Efendi, pass, then slammed shut.

The whole palace was in a panic. The Sultan received Arif Efendi who was trembling as Mustafa remarked, "Like a canary in the eye of a hawk." Once again a Sheykh-ul-Islam was charged with informing a Sultan of his deposition. Arif Efendi told Mustafa about Bayrakdar's intention to substitute Selim as Sultan.

"So, you are one of the conspirators!" said Mustafa. "I'm going to kill you . . . lying whore! Leave here and convince the Pasha Bayrakdar to depart. If you don't, you'll be in the Execution Place tomorrow." The courtiers took Arif Efendi by the scruff of his neck and threw him out of the Door of the White Eunuchs. The wretched Arif Efendi stuttered out the Sultan's order to Bayrakdar to disperse his troops.

"Stop fidgeting like a dog between two villages, ignoble cheat! Go and do what you are supposed to do. Get in there!" And Bayrakdar pushed Arif Efendi back through the Door of the White Eunuchs with the top of his saber.

This time, the Sheykh-ul-Islam found no one in back of the Door of Felicity. In relief, he hid behind a magnificent cedar tree to wait it out.

Mustafa, seeing that Arif Efendi had not come back with an answer from Bayrakdar, turned to Sineprever and said:

"Now what?"

"If Selim and Mahmud are dead, you are the last Osmanli," Sineprever replied to her son.

The Chief Black Eunuch, Merdjan Aga, the real master of the harem, hid in his room, giving free rein to the executioners. The Sultan's treasurer, the Black Eunuch Nezir, his intendant, Ebé Selim, the renegade Serb, Abd ul-Fettah, the White Eunuch, Cevher, the one-eyed Mirahurkor, and the chief of the Bostanjis started through the narrow passages and stairs of the palace to Selim's apartments in the harem.

On entering the harem, the group of assassins was completely lost. It was the first time in two hundred years that the harem doors had been forced. Wandering about in the confusion was one of Selim's wives, Peykidil, who approached and said: "Come, follow me."

Selim was praying in his auditorium. He was wearing a robe of green silk, his turban was unwound. With him were his Fourth Kadine, Refet, and two slaves, Nesrine and Pakize. For days Refet had been having nightmares. . . . Selim had tried to calm her. But now they heard noises in the harem. Nesrine rushed in.

"The Bostanji."

"Selim!" cried Refet. "They're in front of the door!" Instinctively the three women covered their heads with their prayer rugs to veil themselves.

It was Selim who called out: "You are the Bostanji?"

It was the White Eunuch Cevher who answered: "You are the cause of disorder in the Empire." Then he said to the others: "Kill him! What are you waiting for?"

At this moment, Pakize threw herself in front of Selim. "Don't touch my master."

Nesrine fainted from terror, but Pakize's two hands were sliced off as she tried to fend off the first blows. One of the Bostanji took her by the hair and flung her across the room. Refet smashed out with her fists but was thrown back against the sofa. Selim, defenseless, received a saber blow on his right jaw which sliced off part of his beard. Selim seized one of his assailants' weapons and defended himself with rage and with more courage than he had defended his ideas. The diamond ring on Selim's fist slashed the face of Nezir to the bone. Selim was strong and his women fought to tear the sabers out of the hands of the eunuchs and murderers who assailed him, but the White Eunuch Cevher, felled by a violent blow, found himself between the Sultan's legs, and if anyone knew the most vulnerable parts of the male anatomy, it was a white eunuch deprived of such parts. Cevher seized them and squeezed with such rage and tenacity that Selim, with a horrible hollow inhalation of breath as if to smother the terrible pain, fell insensible. The bowstring went around his neck, and a dozen saber blows struck him down. He had long ceased to live.

Refet gained consciousness and, finding her Sultan dead, she fell over his body, screaming: "I will never forget that among the murderers, there was a *woman.*" A woman. A woman. A woman. A woman. A woman. The sound echoed through the silenced harem like a dirge and a curse. Refet's curse would be carried to her grave sixty-two years from this hour.

Selim's body was transported from the harem and placed on a white stone bench before the Door of Felicity in the very place where Mustafa had received the Sheykh-ul-Islam. The assassins then made their way to Mahmud's apartments.

Naksh-i-dil could think of only one thing as she rushed through the streets of Istanbul, her veils billowing behind her, a manic energy propelling her onward: Where was Mahmud? She had to save him. By this time, she had been found and was being escorted to the Porte by a contingent of Bayrakdar's Albanians and Edris Aga, who had joined the Pasha of Ruschuk.

But Mahmud's former Lala, Tayyar Aga Efendi, had already acted. Selim's fierce and prolonged resistance had given him time to assemble a small group of men, and when the assassins approached Mahmud's apartments, they fell upon them as one. At the top of the stairway leading to the baths, Tayyar and two black eunuchs with their sabers drawn barred the way to the Bostanji. The fight began. Ebé Selim threw a dagger through the open door at Mahmud, but only slightly wounded the Prince's hand. At that moment, an amazonian Albanian slave called Cervi seized a shovel of hot ash cinders from the baths and threw them in the eyes of the closest of Mahmud's pursuers. In the confusion that followed, Tayyar Aga slipped Mahmud out onto the roofs by way of the chimney, and from there, Mahmud and his small group raced over the lead domes and cupolas of the palace. Mahmud was forced to rescue Tayyar Aga several times as he threatened to slip off the slippery surface and crash into the gardens below. Using their laced belts as ropes, they finally descended from the roof into the gardens of the palace.

Bayrakdar waited in vain for the Sheykh-ul-Islam's return. At last he decided to violate the sanctity of the harem. At his signal, Bab-i-Sa'adet was forced, and in a few seconds, hundreds of Bayrakar's soldiers poured through the breached doors. Bayrakdar, his sword unsheathed, was the first to enter. They met dead silence. Every single person in the harem was hidden. Bayrakdar took several uncertain steps, not knowing how or where to search for Selim. Then he stumbled against the white bench and the body of his former sovereign, his splendid beard torn off along with his cheek, his leg broken, the bowstring still around his neck.

The crude soldier burst into tears of rage and fell to his knees, licking Selim's wounds in traditional Osmanli custom. His soldiers were silent and lowered their eyes, aghast at the spectacle of their commander-in-chief on his knees, weeping like a child. So many hopes were smashed. If he had had less respect for religion, his Padishah would still be alive. . . . He had lost precious time, and Selim's precious life, because of his respect for the traditions and sanctity of the imperial palace, sterile negotiations, and in the duplicity and cravenness of the Sheykh-ul-Islam.

"Vengeance," he screamed, his troops echoing his cry.

Naksh-i-dil heard the cry and knew that Selim and Mahmud were dead. Sineprever heard it and knew that Mustafa, if he still lived, was the last Osmanli on earth.

Bayrakdar was determined not to leave one living soul in the harem of Topkapi. He intended to kill Mustafa, annihilate all the courtiers and sack the palace. Bayrakdar's wrath and the menace of a general massacre terrified not only the palace of some twenty thousand souls but the friends of Selim as well. If Bayrakdar's orders were executed and a massacre followed, Mustafa would perish by the hand of the Albanians and Mahmud would be killed by those loyal to Mustafa, and the Osman dynasty would be extinguished.

At that precise moment Mahmud, covered in chimney soot, was standing flanked by Tayyar before Bayrakdar himself.

"Well," said Bayrakdar, irritated. "What is it now?"

"My lord, it is Our Sovereign the Sultan Mahmud," was the reply as the little group advanced toward Bayrakdar. "And it is to you, Pasha, upon whom resides the responsibility for his life and safety."

Bayrakdar looked up. "It was for Selim that I came, and it will be for Mahmud that I stay . . . but woe to the murderers! They will pay dearly!"

"Yes," said the Sultan Mahmud, "I will find them and I will deliver them to you."

"He was your adopted father, your friend, your cousin, your professor," said Bayrakdar. "His principles and his virtues relive in you. Live to defend the religion of the Prophet. Live to relaunch the force and the glory of the Osmanlis!

"Long live Sultan Mahmud Khan!"

One thousand men in the courts and gardens of the Seraglio, and soon a million voices along the sea and in the city, would repeat that acclamation.

For now Bayrakdar had to get his soldiers out of the harem and Mahmud to the Chamber of the Sacred Tunic, where as the new Sultan he would pronounce his first vows of fidelity. The exhausted and grief-stricken Pasha gave the order to his troops to evacuate the palace. He did not have the heart to accompany Mahmud and so stayed in the harem gardens, where he sat slumped over with his head in his hands and his sword unsheathed on his knees.

Almost at the same time, Naksh-i-dil appeared and said: "I am the Valide Sultane." Before Bayrakdar could rise in respect, the Valide, hysterical with fear and anxiety for Mahmud, flooded the astonished Pasha with coarse insults and curses he had heard only in army barracks. There is a gradation of abuse in the Turkish language that is applied according to the degree of offense. The first is Giaour, Christian; the next is chiffût, Jew; and the last is karadhan, black soul.

"Giaour, chiffût, karadhan! What are you doing sitting there? You have offended Islam! You have dared set foot in the 'sanctuary of sanctuaries.' You with your smelly soldiers! Giaour! Thousands of men have set foot in *my* harem . . . this sacred soil . . . I am the Valide! I must defend this place with my life and my honor. Chiffût, you have dishonored me! You sit there in a daze defiling the harem of the Sultan Mahmud II! Karadhan! Have you no shame! No respect! No honor! Karadhan! You are worse than a karadhan!"

The new Valide dissolved into tears of years of humiliations. She knew instinctively that this breach in the harem would never be repaired. Never. Naksh-i-dil's rage was not a caprice but a cry for a lost world—her world. The harem had been defiled like a violated woman.

Naksh-i-dil stood facing the man who had saved her son's life; the man who had made her the Empress of the Veiled Heads, Diadem of Moslem Women. The messenger of her destiny. Tears flowed down her cheeks. Bayrakdar had half risen from his seat, his eyes also wide with shock and brimming with tears, his beard trembling. He unsheathed his sword.

It was at this moment that he saw the deposed Mustafa for the last time. Without understanding anything, Mustafa was walking along the side of a pond, asking the palace servants: "Why have you let Mahmud escape?"

Hearing the innocuous voice, Bayrakdar exploded with rage. "Get that son of a bitch out of my sight immediately, or I will kill him without the permission of my Sultan. So help me God!"

"Get this . . . this Valide and this . . . Sultan out of my sight. Out! Out! Into the harem!" He resheathed his sword. His heart was black with rage and tears were still spilling onto his cheeks for his lost Sultan.

"Or, I swear by God, I'll kill everyone in this goddamned place! I'll start another massacre! And this time, everybody goes! I'll kill the whole bloody lot of you! The whole pitiful harem and every *kouss* in it! Including the Valide!"

Bayrakdar paused for breath.

"Jesus (the Blessings and salutations of Allah be upon Him)," he whispered, "and this is the woman called 'embroidered tongue' . . ."

• CHAPTER FIFTEEN •

MAHMUD 1808

So many faces have pressed the dust in these palace halls, they might be a portrait gallery.

—KHA GANI, XII Century

It was not only Bairam, it was Taklidi-seif, the coronation of Mahmud II. A magnificent procession left the Seraglio at daybreak for Aya Sofya, led by Mahmud's new Grand Admiral on horseback wearing a green satin pelisse lined in ermine and his ceremonial turban. Marching before him on foot were his officers wearing the wide trousers and loose shirts of the corsairs and with daggers and pistols in their belts. Between the Grand Admiral, his escorts and the next dignitary was a ceremonially dressed Janissary, his back to the spectators. Then came the new Grand Vizier, Bayrakdar, on horseback. His pelisse was of white satin lined in lynx, and he wore the same ceremonial turban as the Grand Admiral. To his left were *his* officers carrying sabers and wearing copper cummerbunds. To his right were his valets. The Minister of Foreign Affairs and the Aga of the Janissaries followed. A riderless horse, richly harnessed in silver and gold and covered with a heavily embroidered horsecloth and a parade shield, led by a Hasa, preceded the escort of the new Sultan. The crowds that lined the streets strained to get a glimpse of the new faces of government and to make note of who of the old faces had disappeared, along with their heads, on the block in Execution Place. But Mahmud had refused to execute Mustafa, whom he held in the Prince's Cage.

Two rows of Janissaries lined the route on both sides, armed only with long sticks that struck the blue of the sky like a defoliated forest. Following the lead horse came the Sultan's stablemaster on horseback surrounded by his grooms. Mahmud himself was escorted by his imperial bodyguards wearing gold-plated copper helmets crowned by black panaches. Between each bodyguard was a Hatchet Carrier dressed in red and blue silk, a high, cone-shaped bonnet made of white felt, and carrying a cane. The second rank surrounding the Sultan were the Capidji-Bachis whose felt casques were topped by the highest and largest panaches, which almost entirely obscured the view of the monarch from the crowd. Then came those closest to the Sultan: his pages, richly dressed in gold lamé and gauze turbans, unarmed. Behind the Sultan and mounted on horseback was the Sultan's Sword Carrier who wore a yellow pelisse lined in black fox and studded with diamonds. He was followed by an officer who carried the Sultan's parade turban, and another officer who carried the brocaded stool he used to mount his horse. After these officers came the Hazinedar Aga, the Palace Treasurer, who threw silver coins into the crowd. Finally, mounted on a white stallion, came the Kizlar Aga Edris, returned from Mecca and reinstated in his functions.

The Kizlar Aga held his silver reins loosely in his hands. Mahmud was not quite twenty-three, he calculated. The new Sultan was of medium height, had all the suppleness and nervous energy, the force and sweetness of his American mother. The ceremonial turban, topped with a single diamond cut in the shape of a crescent holding a heron feather, hid his dark hair. His beard did not darken his high color nor his laughing dark gray eyes with the green irises, thought the Kizlar Aga. His high arched eyebrows, the sign of his race, formed a classic arc over a gaze that was penetrating and smoldering, mobile, marred slightly by the secret illness only he, Naksh-i-dil and Mahmud's doctors knew: mild epilepsy.

Perhaps he saw Mahmud with the force of love, thought the Black Eunuch, but what of it? Castration of testicles and penis had never once defied that power. Never had he felt such pride in a Prince before. And now that his pilgrimage to Mecca was accomplished, he was ready to die for him.

The last column of Janissaries performed military homage to the Sultan, which consisted of bowing deeply and bringing their heads over to their left shoulders. Mahmud then entered the royal mosque of Aya Sofya, the former great Christian church of the Byzantine Empire: built by Constantine, shattered by earthquakes, consumed by fire, yet still intact. The vast hemispherical dome of blue light with smaller domes swelling from each angle of the square foundations had represented for the Byzantines "the wounds of Christ," but for Mahmud it was simply the most perfect of mosques. Every part of it, except the thick wooden doors, was covered with millions of sapphire-blue glazed mosaics and tiles. Mahmud had not entered this mosque since childhood. The great dome hovered over him not like a roof, but like a giant cupped blue hand. From the smallest domes, spotlights of white light struck the shimmering pavement piled with lush silk prayer rugs. Truly, thought Mahmud, this was a greater temple of Mohammedanism, the proud golden crescent of Mohammed rising from its center, than it had ever been of Christianity. Mahmud II, the youngest of Abdulhamid's fifteen sons, knelt and kissed the ground.

In seven days Naksh-i-dil would make her ceremonial procession from the Eski Serai to the harem. But Mustafa's harem had to be removed first.

The time for this was sunrise, so that the women could pass through the streets when no one was abroad. One morning, before dawn, the women issued in covered wagons from the gate of the Seraglio, but instead of turning toward the city and the Eski Serai, they turned toward the sea. Here they were received on board the waiting caïques, and rowed out across the Sea of Marmara for a distance of about thirteen or fourteen miles. There they were thrown into the depths. Most submitted to their inevitable destiny without a struggle. But the four Kadines who it was suspected were pregnant, resisted, their shrieks heard distinctly on the surrounding islands even at this early hour. Thus the whole or greater part of Mustafa's female establishment had been disposed of. They had all been charged with treason; having been accessories to the murder of Selim, having been in the presence of the eunuchs who murdered Selim, it was assumed, as a proof of their guilt, that they did not prevent it. The real cause, Naksh-i-dil knew, was to prevent any chance that a child of the brother of her son existed.

What was the death of a few dozen women? In one day one Sultan had been murdered, another had been deposed, and a third had ascended to the throne.

The screams of one condemned Kadine provoked the screams of the neighboring Kadine as cubicle after cubicle exploded. Naksh-i-dil stuffed her ears with her veils to shut out the echo of scores of lamentations which reverberated across the Bosphorus into Europe.

The Kizlar Aga Merdjan, who did not defend the harem, was the first to die. Afterward, ten young women slaves of Mustafa, among them the handless Pakize, were put into a caïque, taken to the tower of Leandre, and strangled, their bodies jettisoned. Refet hid in the house of a friend and dreamed of escaping to Serbia, but there was no escape. She was found and beheaded. On the day of Selim's funeral, thirty heads fell. Bayrakdar had respected the dignity of the Osmanlis by placing the Chief Black Eunuch's head on a silver platter as befitting his rank.

Sultan Mahmud returned Mustafa to the Prince's Cage, and Mustafa's mother, Sineprever, remained at Topkapi despite Hitabetullah's violent objections.

"I would not send even my murderer to the Eski Serai," murmured Naksh-i-dil. "Inshallah. You will protect me from Sineprever."

Hitabetullah took her mistress's admonishment to heart, for one day Naksh-i-dil came upon her conjuring over a closed glass jar which contained a scorpion, repeating the incantations seven times over.

"Aryush, shar hush: He is God so great that there is none beside Him. Bartima, maltima, azrian. Understand what I say, O scorpion, born of a scorpion: otherwise will I give the fire power over thee. Tariush, lahush bamkush darkianush—by the glory of God and the light of His countenance, go to Sineprever and sting her in the left shoulder."

She was about to release the scorpion when Naksh-i-dil screamed: "No! Hitabetullah. I forbid it."

"She would have done it to you."

"I am weary of murder. It has become a banality like trees, water, light. We are bathed in murder. I want no more of it."

"You will have a great deal of it if you consider war murder."

"Do you?"

"Yes, Mistress."

Naksh-i-dil saw something in Hitabetullah's eyes she had never seen before—compassion. Hitabetullah shrugged. Naksh-i-dil would have to deal eventually with Sineprever and Mustafa, who were plotting against Mahmud. Now, or later, they must die. For her it made no difference. It would be Naksh-i-dil, who hated murder, who would decide, thought Hitabetullah. Events would overtake her in more than one realm, and Naksh-i-dil's heart, both burdened and shattered by the Eski Serai, would be torn as never before.

The terrible death of Selim, which Hadidge had contemplated so calmly so long ago, had had a devastating effect upon her as a witness. Hadidge had flung herself over her brother's mutilated body laid out upon the stone couch in the harem, and had echoed the broken-hearted sobs of Bayrakdar. The funeral Mahmud had given Selim was the most royal and lavish in the memory of Istanbul; the cortege, stretching for miles, had taken from sunup to sunset to wind through the city, the mourners' cries thundering over the Bosphorus. Hadidge had rent her clothes and torn out her golden hair by the handfuls. Then slowly she had succumbed to mania. She closed herself up in her newly built palace and began to give balls for the Europeans of Pera, as if literally dancing on Selim's grave. Her parties, her caprices, her adventures defied even the lascivious storytellers of the bazaars. She fought bitterly with Naksh-i-dil. Her grief for the only person she had ever loved unconditionally was bottomless and hopeless. She ran wild in the streets like the savage, ownerless dogs that roamed the canine district of Istanbul scavenging. She could be seen at all hours of the day and night, swathed from head to foot in gray mourning veils, roaming the bazaars, the cafés, the cemeteries in search of adventure, solace or fantasy. The "Demon" Sultana became more and more notorious. Selim's death had released in Hadidge the last restraints. And there was no way to stop her. Neither the Valide Naksh-i-dil nor Esma Sultane could or would control the inconsolable Princess.

Esma was married to Mustafa Bayrakdar. Naksh-i-dil had urged it and Mahmud had consented. Bayrakdar, he agreed, needed the legitimacy of a royal Princess as a wife. Besides, Bayrakdar had ceded to the State, for the expenses of military reform, fifteen million piastres, Esma's bride money.

• CHAPTER SIXTEEN •

BAYRAKDAR 1808

The trouble, Naksh-i-dil knew, had begun with the coronation. There was a tradition that on feast days, a show of arms was to be avoided, and the Janissaries, the artillery, the imperial guard and the Yamaks carried only white painted sticks. But Bayrakdar had appeared in the cortege with a bodyguard of three hundred Albanians, armed to the teeth, instead of the brilliant entourage of a Grand Vizier. The people of Istanbul had been greatly shocked. This had been no way to begin a reign as Grand Vizier. But Bayrakdar held himself responsible for Selim's death, and his procrastination before the doors of the harem haunted him. Touchy and unhappy, he considered Mahmud too young and inexperienced to rule, and his mother, too virile to cohabit with. Bayrakdar's easy victory had also influenced his attitude toward Mahmud, still shaken by the death of Selim and the bloodiness of his succession to the throne. Bayrakdar believed he could make or break Mahmud as he had Mustafa, but Bayrakdar didn't know Naksh-i-dil Valide. Nor did he realize that he was underestimating Mahmud. After all, Mahmud had married Esma Sultane to Bayrakdar for a reason: to legitimize a stubborn, ignorant peasant with pretensions to power. The Pashas, jealous of Bayrakdar's rise to power, had already expressed their disdain for his arrogance and refused to obey him, and it was not long before Esma followed suit. She neither lived nor slept with her husband. Every Ottoman Princess had the right of refusal to her couch, and Esma exercised this right. Nor was it her business to point his errors out to him.

Bayrakdar's speeches before the notables were brilliant, his projects of reform laudable, his proposals intelligent, his attitude full of common sense. His projects were unanimously approved by all.

Naksh-i-dil knew she could not oppose Bayrakdar alone. But she knew her son was crushed by the authority of his Grand Vizier. Esma, on the other hand, pleaded with her husband to leave Istanbul with Mahmud and his prisoner, Mustafa, and retire to Adrianople until he could recall his now disbanded army and march once more in force on Istanbul: The Janissaries were spoiling for a fight and spreading antigovernment propaganda among the population. For once, Esma Sultane was truly sincere, but Bayrakdar, knowing her contempt for him, thought her advice a ruse and did just the opposite of what she begged of him. In a moment of weakness Esma had tried to save her husband—now, she left him to his fate, withdrawing to her palace on the other side of the Bosphorus. Bayrakdar constructed himself a fortified residence in Istanbul, and with his harem, his eunuchs, his favorite slave, Moonlight, moved in and affected even more arrogance, audacity and self-confidence in a city seething with counterrestoration.

Esma told Naksh-i-dil: "His answer to sedition is insolence."

And so Esma washed her hands of him.

"We are all adventurers, my Lady," Bayrakdar had brazenly replied to Naksh-i-dil. "You were a slave, now you are an Empress. By what right, except the caprices of despotism? I am an ignorant peasant, despised by my aristocratic wife but military commander of thirty million Moslem souls. By what right, except the will of Allah? But you, Madame, *chose* Allah as an expedient for your own rise to power, whereas *Allah* chose me!"

Istanbul began to regret Selim's death. Public criers embroidered on the circumstances of Selim's murder in the cafés and squares near the mosques. Naksh-i-dil had her first lesson in the fickleness of the masses: quick to forget the past, disdainful of the future, living only in the present. In no time at all, Selim was rehabilitated. Forgotten were his weaknesses, the humiliations at the hands of the European powers, the territorial losses, the unequal treaties.

But Naksh-i-dil had learned well. Catherine, thought the Valide, gifted with intelligence, born with powerful passions, raised in hardship, had learned to obey before she commanded. Selim in his splendid isolation had been a victim of his education, and had had no idea of the outside world except for the glimpses smuggled in to him by an Ishak Bey or a Lorenzo. Catherine's activity, her unshakable firmness, her sober and carefully thought-out values, her fighting qualities, her choice of men regardless of rank or birth, her liberalism might be beyond even Mahmud's imagination, but not hers, she thought. Even Catherine's cruelty was not beyond her capabilities. Mahmud, raised in harem captivity, had never led an army into battle, had not the slightest idea of men's passions, thought Naksh-i-dil. Mahmud was susceptible, sensitive, even noble, but he was incapable of imagining real danger or dealing with it in cold blood. He pardoned when he should have punished, gaining only insolence from his enemies. Too sweet to inspire terror, too weak to inspire esteem, too timid to act alone. He needed her.

As for Bayrakdar, she thought, his devotion to Mahmud had never had the ardor or finesse that Selim had inspired. Oh, he was loyal in his heavy-handed, barely literate way, but he had become much too powerful with his distribution of favors and bribes, and his Byzantine mode of living, which the military class despised.

But Bayrakdar had made his name known and revered. No Grand Vizier had ever had both the complete influence over and gratefulness from a Sultan as he had from his child-master, Mahmud, nor enjoyed more fanatical devotion from his army, more authority over the Divan and over the capital. He had no rivals to fear except the excess of his own power and being dazzled by his ascendancy. But he had learned one thing: To be a reformer, one had to be either a saint or a soldier, and Bayrakdar was a soldier. He was determined to protect young Mahmud's reign with a forest of sabers. Even Mahmud's coronation, a religious affair, had had the aspect of a military ceremony. In a country of conquerors, it was the strapping on of the sacred sword of Mahmud which represented the coronation for Bayrakdar; not the crown on the forehead, but the sword in the hand.

It was during the thirty days of Ramadan. Naksh-i-dil and Mahmud roamed the streets of Istanbul incognito, hearing orators preach the downfall of Bayrakdar. Each evening they made their way secretly back to the safety of the harem. Fasting, nervous activity, predictions and divinations predisposed the city to riots, uprisings and insurrection. Since it was forbidden to eat between sunup and sundown, night replaced day. They saw people meeting in the courtyards of mosques, in the cemeteries, in the Meadow of Death, in squares and cafés to listen to traveling orators and public storytellers recount the Oriental equivalent of the newspaper. Naksh-i-dil and Mahmud exchanged glances and their eyes, like the orator, spoke volumes. Opinion ran high against the Pasha of Ruschuk, Bayrakdar.

It was Kadir Ghedjessi, the Night of Predestination, the night according to tradition on which the Prophet Mohammed had received the Koran, the last week of Ramadan. Istanbul justified its name "The Beauty of the Orient." Summer still reigned along the banks of the Bosphorus, despite it being the month of November. The superb weather, the rays of the sun giving off summer heat, the scent of the cypresses and umbrella pine trees, which grew everywhere, impregnated the air. All the gardens of Istanbul were in full bloom, and fruit still ripened on the trees. Mahmud and Naksh-i-dil were again in the streets, their gray hooded cashmere cloaks bluish in the deepening twilight.

But that night both nature and men changed. A chilling northeast wind blew in from the Asiatic strait. Suddenly it was cold. Crowds of irritable Janissaries roamed the shadows of the badly lit streets. The solemn Iftar Ghedjessi, the feast that was held, according to tradition, in honor of the Janissaries, had turned into a riot, and bloody fighting broke out as the terrified Mahmud and Naksh-i-dil made their way back to the palace. They saw the Grand Vizier's soldiers open a passage for him unceremoniously with the lashes and butts of their hippopotamus-skin whips. The mounted Albanians pushed the crowd back with their horses and the flat side of their sabers. The crowd dispersed before the Pasha's horsemen, taking refuge in the bazaars and cafés nearby. Suddenly someone in the crowd cried out: "This is what you merit, you Janissaries who have abandoned us! A vile frontier pirate and brigand, a Giaour with infidel blood, becomes the master of Sultan Mahmud and the executioner of the Osmanlis!"

Mahmud began to tremble violently. It was only the strong hand of Naksh-i-dil on his shoulder that calmed him. Her mind was racing. There was not much time, she thought. Bayrakdar's moment of truth had arrived. Thank God, she thought, she and Mahmud had gone out and were not shut up behind the harem doors! Now, they must get back to the safety of the palace and make plans—even plans for escape. For if Bayrakdar fell, thought Naksh-i-dil calmly, she and Mahmud must stand on their own.

By the time Mahmud and Naksh-i-dil reached the palace, it was a besieged fortress, and in a few minutes the lighted torches carried by the milling crowds and soldiers created a sea of flames that engulfed the whole quarter, which was built of wood-planked barracks. Bayrakdar was trapped inside where he lived as Grand Vizier. Outside, rumors of the Grand Vizier's decision to suppress the Janissary Corps totally at the end of Bairam, the feast that followed Ramadan, had the effect of a match to a powder keg. The drunken Pasha had retired to his harem and was with his favorite Kamertab, Moonlight. He was awakened by a wall of flames engulfing his palace. The flux of fire, the noise of crumbling walls, the desperate cries of burning men and women and the immense agitation of the mob had blocked the entire quarter. The bucking and whinnying of two hundred horses, abandoned by their riders and running to escape the flames, tore into the night. Bayrakdar announced a fight to the death. A thousand Janissaries had fired a warehouse full of wood and the barracks of Bayrakdar's bodyguards. A strong breeze whipped the flames into a blazing cyclone which reached the Porte. The dreaded cry of *"Yanghinvar!* Fire! Fire!"* resounded throughout the city. The dazed and drunken Bayrakdar tried to come to his senses. He had no doubt that he would be rescued after the fire by his troops, so he concentrated on fighting the flames.

Esma Sultane watched the flames from her palace on the opposite shore, understanding nothing.

At one end of Bayrakdar's wooden palace stood a stone tower destined to serve as a refuge in case of fire for the Vizier, his family and his treasure. The tower communicated with the palace by means of a stone vault and had several iron doors that flames could not destroy and bullets could not penetrate. Only artillery could open a passage in this walled block of granite. The Pasha of Ruschuk was to hold out for three days in this tower, accompanied by his favorite and his black eunuch, his jewels, his arms and food, confident that his master, Mahmud, would come to his rescue. Meanwhile, once again Istanbul burned.

Mahmud and his mother were also watching from the terraces of the harem, their troops in flight and their capital consumed by fire. The palace no longer returned the fire of the Janissaries' muskets and cannons. Mahmud issued an imperial decree ordering the Aga to stop fighting and put out the fire destroying Istanbul. Houses were torn down, trenches dug; but the fire overwhelmed the square before the Seraglio, while the mob screamed curses against Bayrakdar, the Grand Admiral, the Bostanjis, the Capidji-Bachis, the pages, the Sultan himself. The voices heard above the tumult all cried the same thing:

Long life Mustafa Khan!
Long live Mustafa Khan!

Why did it always have to be *fire,* thought Naksh-i-dil, drawing close to Mahmud as she too heard the single voice, then the chorus. Naksh-i-dil thought of only one thing: that Mahmud would never be safe while

Mustafa lived. Wasn't it the Koran itself which sanctioned fratricide between Princes. . . ?

If there are two Caifs, kill one.

"Kill him," Naksh-i-dil whispered. "Kill him and no one will dare touch you. You will be the last male Osmanli. Sacred. Kill, kill, kill him, Mahmud."

"No!" Mahmud turned on his mother, horrified. "Mustafa spared me when he could have killed me!"

"He asked Bayrakdar why he had let you get away."

"What?"

"I heard him myself. . . . And Mustafa killed Selim!"

"No! No! No!" Mahmud put his hands to his ears to shut out the pleas of his mother. But Naksh-i-dil had learned her lessons too well. Politics had no morals and the métier of the despot was first of all to survive. His mother was one of the most cold-blooded Valides, thought Mahmud. Her facsimile of Oriental fatalism had an Occidental sense of requisition. A dangerous combination. There was no way his mother could reconcile the philosophers with the Koran, a firman with a constitution . . . the East with the West.

For two days Mahmud resisted the entreaties of his mother. On the third day, Naksh-i-dil returned to the harem where, without speaking a word, she dropped the emerald ring she was wearing into the sash of the Black Eunuch. She held out her two hands in front of her. The palm of one hand faced downward, its extended fingers touched the base of the other hand, held vertically, which descended swiftly in a falling movement upon the first. Then her delicate white right hand went to her own white throat, seized it and squeezed tightly. Finally her forefinger slashed a line from ear to ear across her own fine neck. Mustafa IV had been condemned in the language of the Bazam-dil-siz.

The next morning at daybreak, the Janissaries opened their offensive against Mahmud's palace. In the ranks sounded the traditional call for a change of Sultans:

Sultan Mustafa Efendi nizi isteruz!
We want our Lord, the Sultan Mustafa!

They took their positions before the imperial gate of Topkapi and placed their marksmen in the minarets of the mosque of Aya Sofya, from which point they could fire on the courts of the palace. Then they cut off the palace's water supply. That night thousands of Janissaries, Ulemas and dervishes spread out along the streets of Istanbul.

He who is not with us, his wife is a whore and he is a Giaour-lover

The Valide and the Sultan went on the offensive. The imperial gate of Topkapi suddenly opened and four thousand Seymens behind four cannons counterattacked. The Janissaries fled in all directions pursued by Mahmud's troops, who divided into three columns, their destination the Hippodrome. At the same time, on the orders of Naksh-i-dil, the bombardment commenced. Naksh-i-dil and Mahmud had decided to bombard their own city. With a ship of the line, a frigate and a corvette anchored in the Golden Horn, their Captain Pasha opened fire on the Janissaries' barracks, and on the dispersing troops wherever they could find them. The bombardment was imprecise but continuous, and the effect terrifying. The wooden houses smashed and caught fire. Women and children took to the streets. Panic spread. This time it was the Janissaries who were accused. The population demanded that they surrender to the Sultan as soon as possible. A delegation of Ulemas went to Topkapi as a testimonial of their submission to the Sultan on condition that he stop bombarding Istanbul and return his troops to the palace. Mahmud consented to receive the deputation. His first words to them were uttered with epic serenity. He announced the death of Mustafa. He said:

Birader de efat kyledi
And our brother has passed away

Then Mahmud made the speech his mother had prepared. The one everyone would remember:

Ah people! What infidelity you deliver yourselves up to! It is not enough that because of you perished the light of my eyes, my brother Selim, you continued under my reign to cause such a violation of the people of Mahmud. Today to top it off, you have said to me, "Our Lord, come to the palace," and after that with what intentions did you invade my palace? If you don't want me anymore, I will drink on the spot a poisoned sherbet and after that, make Sultan whoever you want.

Mahmud threatened to commit suicide in front of the army, which would not have hesitated to chop him into pieces the day before. The delegation of Ulemas sent to stop the bombardments suddenly realized that whatever the circumstances of Mustafa's undoubtedly unnatural death, Mahmud was left as the unique and last representative of the Osman dynasty. Henceforth, his person was inviolable whatever the success of the Janissaries. No one in the Empire could conceive of anything other than a Sultanate, or of any other dynasty except the Osman. The fear of being left with no Sultan at all was greater than anything. And Mahmud was the last Osman.

The next morning was a Friday. Mahmud II had left the palace, as usual, for the mosque of Aya Sofya. His guards were Janissaries. The town crier announced to the city that order had been established. Order and dynasty and religion triumphed. Everything returned to the ancestral millennium.

Naksh-i-dil had made her son sacred, sovereign, safe and suicidal.

BOOK VI

TATCH-UL-MESTOURAT
·1808·

❖ CHAPTER ONE ❖

ALI EFENDI 1808

Neither the favor of the Sultan nor the advantage of being rich, nor to be somebody after having been nobody, nor the return after exile, nor security after want and fear, has the same power over the soul, nor procures the same felicity over the being as love.

—IBN HAZM, XIV century

When Naksh-i-dil first set eyes on Ali Efendi, he was already Mahmud's Lieutenant. The son of an Albanian horse merchant and a Venetian Christian from Corfu, he had been sent along with a contingent of Albanian stallions by his father as their trainer. Selim had been Sultan, and he, Ali, had been eighteen at the time. Thus he found himself, ten years later, in the service of Mahmud's cavalry. Mahmud had noticed his Lieutenant one day when he was a simple Janissary in the midst of military maneuvers, and Mahmud's own horse, frightened by the sudden flash of a saber, had reared out of control. Ali had leaped from his mount to the ground and in a swift movement had secured the reins of the Sultan's charger, struggling against the beast. Mahmud had bent down to thank the soldier. His eyes had met Ali's in an intensity of emotion that occurs only once or twice in a man's life and had never before occurred in the lives of either young man.

The Janissary stood quietly on the open wind-swept plain behind the village of St. Demetri, also called Ocmeiden, controlling the still-frightened mount as Mahmud descended. The guard lowered his head and eyes in deference to his Sultan, but lifted them when Mahmud touched his shoulder. For Ali, all the dreams and ambitions of a young soldier's lifetime were reflected in the eyes of his sovereign. He had never been so close to power before and he knew that in the realm, one glance was enough to change or end a life.

"Your name, Janissary?" asked Mahmud.

"Ali, son of Esau, Sire," replied the soldier.

"Ali Efendi," said Mahmud, speaking in the florid formal language of the court, which Ali barely understood.

"Could it be that Allah set you in my path for a reason?"

"It could be so, Master," Ali, now Efendi, replied softly.

Mahmud looked steadily at the man who had just spoken to him in the vernacular but with a simplicity and honesty that touched him. They held each other's eyes for so long, it provoked excited murmuring. It was as if the simple Janissary were passing judgment upon his Sultan just as the Sultan had passed judgment upon him. By dusk, Ali Efendi was a Lieutenant in Mahmud's personal guard.

Despite the Lieutenant Ali Efendi's great efforts to appear the perfect Ottoman Janissary, he was the opposite of a stocky, dark, well-muscled corpsman. He was tall, blond, with kohl-lined eyes so incredibly and piercingly gray-blue that even to a casual passerby they seemed beacons of pure sky. Their luminosity bewildered rather than attracted, as if some other-worldly creature had passed by. For they were set in a face of classic proportions and faultless beauty. He wore neither beard nor moustache. His face had something of the feline about it now that his head was not covered by his bonnet, and a mass of curls had fallen to his shoulders. His straight mouth was full-lipped and shaped with a hint of femininity. His narrow face was intelligent, his expression one of tender candor. His face pleased men because of its strength without violence and women because of its vulnerability without innocence. His young body was slim but had given proof of remarkable physical endurance. His small waist and hips were only accentuated by the plaits of the wide corsair pantaloons that stirred with every motion. The flawlessness of Ali Efendi was hardly found in reality, thought Naksh-i-dil, staring at the Janissary. Mahmud's new Lieutenant's profession was riding master, but he had also been trained as a musician and zithermaker. It was said in the barracks that when he sang, dogs listened and birds fell silent; and when he danced the world stopped turning. His hands were long, wide and strong, and used to controlling thoroughbreds. It was for this reason that each of his movements was graceful and that despite his looks and youth, his bearing was unmistakably male. The Valide had the impression that all nature's gifts had culminated in the absolute masculine beauty of the man kneeling before her.

Before the Lieutenant sat the most magnificent, opulent, terrifying creature he had ever beheld. Unveiled, the Valide's heart-shaped face seemed more luminous despite its paleness, softer despite the heavy powder. Her gaze was penetrating but infinitely sad. He would have given up his new post, thought Ali Efendi, to have the power to make that mouth smile. . . . Her features had more delicacy than regularity, and the almost imperceptible marks of age contracted his heart. The azure-green upturned eyes, which had been elongated to the edges of her elaborate turban, had the brilliance of a young girl's, but the eyelids, darkened with surmuh, spoiled their expression. Her eyebrows were darkened and drawn to blend together. He had no idea what could be the color of her hair, for her head was completely covered by a turban of white embroidered muslin, draped with strands of diamonds and pearls, topped with a red calohe and studded with jewels in the shape of flowers. Her gaze was severe and her mouth seemed betrayed by disappointment, for in fact it was a childish mouth, small, highly colored and flanked by two dimples. Although her complexion was fresh, her cheeks were covered with powder and one carried a mouche in the shape of a star. At the slightest movement the jeweled drapery scintillated around the extraordinary face. So covered was she with jewels, chains, ropes of pearls, veils, shawls that it was impossible to discern any form beneath. But if he took into consideration her perfect immobility and purity of expression, and the glacial seriousness of her features, he would have said that she resembled one of those sculptured Madonnas his Venetian mother had told him Christians dressed up as on their feast days, and whose image they worshiped. . . .

The glance that had passed between Naksh-i-dil and Ali Efendi was not that of an Empress eyeing her son's new man, nor was it the scrutiny by the Queen Mother of a new Lieutenant of the Sultan's guards. It was more a longtime recognition, as if the Valide had found in Ali Efendi's eyes all the surprised yearning of a solitary life. Ali knelt and kissed the hem of Naksh-i-dil's skirt, murmuring, "Tatch-ul-Mestourat," Queen of the Veiled Heads. Naksh-i-dil had an almost uncontrollable impulse to unravel the turban, now level with her waist, and run her fingers through the hair she dreamed would be thick and undulating, soft and dry to the touch. The new Lieutenant rose, making the classic shalam, heart, lips, forehead, accompanied by the sacred words

"Mother of us all, the living." But the gesture was charged, almost insolent in its intensity, and Naksh-i-dil noticed he was trembling visibly. It could be from fear, she thought. No one knew better than she that in her Empire, the art of pleasing one's master counted for one's life. But the intelligence she saw in the Lieutenant's eyes, the audacity in the curve of his cheek, the sweetness in the indentation of his mouth, the Valide had already decided could lead him to *anything* he wanted from Mahmud or from her, including love.

This one, thought the Valide, glints, like the edge of a saber . . .

"Our Lady," Mahmud said proudly, "Ali Efendi wishes to renew his vow of obedience to our Queen, Mother of the Janissaries."

"Thou may so do it," replied Naksh-i-dil, her voice strangely uncertain to her ears.

"I hereby do it," said Ali Efendi. It was the twelfth of March, 1808.

They rented a small kiosk on the European shore of the Bosphorus, accessible only by boat. The Valide had risen, undone her girdle and let her cloak fall. She rushed toward her Lieutenant with all the desperate velocity of nineteen years of longing. His kisses burned away those of Hadidge, his rough hands erased the expert caress of Hadidge's soft ones. O Cure. O Resurrector. O Penetrator. The Lieutenant found nothing to reproach in the perfection of the ardent, lavish, forlorn body he pressed to his. The whiteness and shape of Naksh-i-dil's thighs surprised him. As he knelt and pressed his lips to them he saw all the animation leave her face as if she were on the edge of unconsciousness. Instead of lifting her, Ali Efendi laid himself down on the sofa in the position of a woman receiving a man. That so surprised Naksh-i-dil that she knelt before him and took him between her palms, astonished at the size, strength and firmness of the flesh she held. Her hair released from its turban fell to the floor, as it had so many years ago, only now it was luminous with gray.

"I never saw a more beautiful one," she said.

"Then take it, Lady." Ali trembled. This was not the taverns of Pera. Or the orchestra of Greek boys dressed as women . . .

Naksh-i-dil lifted herself upon him and gave herself up to him, breaking twenty years of continence.

The Valide rose and fell again and again against the strong body beneath her. Ali Efendi touched the magnificent shoulders, the full breasts that stood like hyacinths, the vaulted belly. At the moment of her pleasure, an "Oh" issued from Naksh-i-dil, and her neck moved to one side like that of a surprised falcon. Her lips opened, thought Ali, forming an *O* like a ring, as fresh and red as a bloody saber. . . . And her eyebrows, Ethiopian-black over green slits, resembled the rounded flourish of a skillful calligrapher tracing the letter *N*. His left hand touched the *N* above her eyes and the *O* of her lips in desire. He turned her and met her again immediately, quickly and violently. Mounted, he slowed, then went on and on until the woman beneath him pleaded for mercy, her voice a stammer of desire, her full, wide forehead slicked with perspiration, her eyes trancelike. Ali kissed the Valide's mouth to smother her cries while he held her waist firmly and tightly against his strokes, shaking her gently, thrilling her breasts. She cried out. He kissed the smooth purple-centered vulva while Naksh-i-dil moved neither hand nor foot. A spiral of perfect happiness filled her as she felt Ali's lips upon her breast, her neck, her lips. She moaned softly. Her Lieutenant's hands moved over the still beautiful and firm bosom and torso, opening her gomlek, his own heart beating wildly, unable to utter the words dearest to him, that he truly loved this strange European woman who had rescued him from obscurity and elevated him to power. But power counted for nothing now. Only their two bodies, in silent and tense conjunction, mattered. This time Ali placed his right hand under her neck and drew her closer while his left hand bore her up like a musical instrument. He placed himself against her entrance, and as soon as she felt him touch her, her whole body convulsed with astonished yearning. Slowly and deliberately, Ali took her with such violent pressure that her hair shook loose. It flowed out, a wide serpentine red river across the pillows. Leisurely he stroked her back, her stomach, her sides. Naksh-i-dil clung to him, rotating in his arms, as supple as a corpse. Every part of her body received her lover's kisses, and when he saw she was ready, he came quickly to her again and again, opening her thighs with determined thrusts, stroking her breasts, while he stayed in constant, splendid motion.

"Receive my seed," he whispered.

"Ah, give it, beloved."

Ali Efendi drew back to admire her. Her kouss was magnificent, its purple center setting off its whiteness. It was round and without imperfection, projecting like a graceful curved dome over her body. Seeing her in such rapture, trembling and defenseless, Ali was filled with anguished and violent tenderness.

He made a strong thrust and lodged completely in her, which made her cry out, but a moment later, she moved with greater fury than before, as if her life and his depended upon those same movements.

They moved in each other alternately, their legs interlaced, their muscles unbent, until the crisis came upon them once more simultaneously.

Then Ali rose from their couch and spreading his arms outward, his caftan falling open, began to turn slowly, gracefully and rhythmically, his face turned upward, gleaming in the penumbral light. Naksh-i-dil sat up in surprise. "I come from a country where only men or slaves dance," said Ali as his body wove slowly in the fretted light, the slap of his bare feet on the tiles, the snap of his fingers his only music. His body, framed by the brilliant folds of his caftan, was as charged as lightning in a darkening sky. Naksh-i-dil felt her blood quicken as his caftan slipped from his body, and, nude, he turned, his poses changing in the bluish light like the friezes on a Greek vase. He began to hum under his breath the Albanian love song to which he was dancing, and Naksh-i-dil thought she heard tambourines. The strong disciplined warrior's body twirled and swayed, the smooth shadowed face was transformed, the eyes were closed, a faint beatific smile played at the corners of his mouth. The man danced. For a woman. The virile hands hung delicately in space, the soft melody and the delicate snapping of his fingers, the only sounds in the room except Naksh-i-dil's fascinated breathing.

She watched, caught up in the harmonious flow of his movements, the play of smooth muscles, the blaze of his eyes, which, though he turned, never left hers. She felt as if her heart would stop cold, caught as it was in the clamor and revolution of an impossible love.

"The first time was for you," whispered Ali Efendi. "The second time was for me. The third is for Allah."

The ancient Kizlar Aga watched the small oilcloth-hooded boat dock and the two cloaked figures leave the shadow of its sinister shape. Two children playing hide-and-seek, he thought. How could they imagine for a moment that their love could be kept secret for more than one night? In days the whole court would know and then the whole Empire. For the moment only he and the Sultan knew, but even with Naksh-i-dil's strict control over the harem, her absence was sure to be noted. The only way to ensure respectability was to name Ali Efendi the Valide's intendant as quickly as possible, thought the Chief Black Eunuch. A renegade after all, he thought, deserved another renegade. . . .

It was the Black Eunuch who explained to Lieutenant Ali his new position.

"The Valide, Our Mother and Lady, has bestowed on you the greatest gift as Valide she can bestow except for her own person. For she will make it known that you are in her favor: her intermediary . . . and bakshish will fall upon you like rain. She has given you not one gift but the *gift* of gifts. Your intervention on behalf of others. . . . She has made you a rich man if you are a loyal one . . ."

"I am loyal because I love her," said the Lieutenant.

"I believe you," said Edris Aga, "and believe me, it will cost you dearly."

"I am ready to pay the price even though you speak only of gifts."

"It is because the price of the Valide's love for you is so high," said Edris. For he knew that the Valide had made Ali not a lover, because this was impossible, but a eunuch, like him. . . . For she had extracted her Lieutenant's undying fidelity. The ghost of all power, he thought, was fidelity. The reward of a despot was not courage, love, or honor, it was fidelity, the one thing that couldn't be bought. Intelligence, talent, adoration, even passion could be bought. Fidelity, he knew, could not be . . . it was the dream and the drama of everyone's life. . . .

The next day, the venerable sixty-seven-year-old Kizlar Aga kept his eyes lowered as he came before Naksh-i-dil.

Then Edris Aga's eyes met those of the Empress. How many years had passed since that first day on the quay? How many years did he have left on this earth? he wondered. *"Your intendant,* Our Lady. I assume Ali Efendi had taken . . . or you had appointed him the functions of your intendant. The Valide is of course well aware that a Valide always has need of an intendant."

Naksh-i-dil smiled. So he knew already . . . was it written in kohl on her forehead?

"This is so?"

"Absolutely. I would say not even a day's delay was wise, Our Lady. Our Sultan Mahmud insists. He is very happy with the idea. He believes you are *safe* with Major General Ali Efendi. I am too old to guard you. Too old . . ."

"Major General Ali Efendi! Mahmud knows!"

The Kizlar Aga smiled.

"Oh, Edris Aga, we are both old. *Old* . . ."

"No, Our Lady is young, a very young girl. You know now what love is. . . ."

"It means the end of . . ." She stopped short. "Perhaps the Kizlar Aga has another suggestion . . . or my son?"

"There is no other possible suggestion, Empress." And he, too, had the same look in his eyes, thought Naksh-i-dil, that Hitabetullah had had: compassion.

The Valide turned away abruptly. Ali. Favorite. Ali was *her* favorite. For all to know. Even in this, she had imitated her old mentor/enemy Catherine. The heavily veiled woman stumbled. Slavery and all its prerogatives had ruled her life ever since she had been born, and now, as sure as Allah had written it, it was her doom. She could lift her finger and Ali would live or die. She had enslaved the one man she wanted free. Unbidden, anguished tears rolled down her cheeks behind the opaque veils. The longer she kept him, the more cruel her love for him became. Naksh-i-dil's lips formed an exclamation of pain, but overwhelming fatigue prevented the sound from escaping. She was tired of playing slave, of being the slave, of owning the slave, of ruling the slave. She wanted only the peace she had found in the Major General's arms. From favorite she had achieved the power to choose favorites, from slave she had become absolute master, from prisoner she had become jailer, from property she had become a landlord Queen. Her head began to burn. It was such a strange feeling, this sense of fatality. She could not complain that it made her sad. It simply would never make her happy. It was. That was all. The force of slavery was too great, its all-encompassing power too brutal, its impediments too fatal, its omnipresence like God himself. Oh, she could escape in war, in drugs, in dreams, in sex, in sickness, in solitude, in the harem itself—her house—despite the grand palace she was building for herself on the opposite shore of the Bosphorus facing Topkapi. But she would never be free, never be free enough to love Ali. How could she love a slave? And how could Ali love a master?

"Don't tire me with your regrets, my Lady. What came to pass was what was meant to come to pass. On the opening of each woman's vulva is inscribed the name of the man who is to enter it, in love or in hate," said Hitabetullah.

"Just as each man has his destiny written on his forehead," said Naksh-i-dil.

Then the Valide smiled. "Why, beloved Hitabetullah, are not the destinies of men and women at least written on the same spot?"

"Who says that a man's forehead is not a woman's vulva?" her slave had said.

• CHAPTER TWO •

MAHMUD 1810

Clearly people who neglect all the fine arts and lock up women, deserve to be exterminated.
—VOLTAIRE to Catherine the Great

Who doesn't know the dangers the great and the distinguished expose themselves to under a despotic government? The Sultan whose hand dispenses favors, destroys with one breath, the man whom he had elevated and covered with favors; . . . the essence of despotism is to wither everything and to use promptly Nature itself.
—FRANÇOIS POCQUEVILLE, *La Turquie,* 1805

The Osmans and the Levantines had never seen anything like it. A huge crowd had gathered on the slopes of the valley. Under the shade of great plane trees had been raised gigantic four-cornered tents painted green, before which stood five thousand men of the newly renamed Nizam-attick, the regular troops, in their new uniforms. Mahmud had changed their name from "new" troops, Nizam-i-jedid, to "old" troops, Nizam-attick. Twelve pieces of light artillery flanked the assembled men. And perched on the inclines of the valley were several thousand Turkish women seated Oriental style with their yachmacks and their obligatory veils. Spread out over the whole surface of the western hill were the Franks and the raia. Beyond, the multitude crowned the heights, and thousands of caïques bobbed upon the transparent water of the Bosphorus, bringing the curious from the villages on the two shores, as the ships from the Black Sea descended the canal and the warships at anchor raised their flags and colorful pennants in salute. The weather was beautiful. The intense heat, mitigated on the heights by the light breeze of the tramontana, was almost unbearable in the depths of the valley where the men stood. The Moslem women circulated the air incessantly with fans made of dried goose wings that swept the green valley like soundless applause.

Halfway up the eastern slope stood the kiosk of Naksh-i-dil. Beside it, Mahmud was mounted on a gray bay harnessed in silver. His saber and dagger glistened as he too pushed the hot air to and fro with a fan of peacock feathers. Then Mahmud wheeled his charger to the left, and joined his Lieutenant. He faced the vast dead silent valley of Dolmabahce. It was the first review of his new Turkish corps, and four regiments of five thousand men stood massed before him.

Mahmud's narrow silhouette cut into the distant view of the landscape of Scutari on the farther shore like a crescent. Heavy-shouldered, narrow-waisted, with a short tunic reinforced at the sleeve junction with strips of ermine under gold gallets, the Sultan wore a long robe of green damask embroidered in silver, under which billowed the wide pants of a Turkish officer and short pointed yellow boots. Little by little he would change his Sultan's caftans, adding more and more European touches until nothing Oriental was left. Mahmud was a handsome man, dark with gray-green–irised eyes as opaque as a stagnant pool. He had strong small teeth, and his short black beard glistened against the silver brocade of his robe and the high white silk turban fixed with the traditional peacock feather held with a diamond brooch. The turban enhanced both his paleness and his medium height. His face was refined, almost banal in the regularity and idealness of his features. Only his eyes, roaming restlessly across the horizon, betrayed something fundamentally amiss in his constitution: the epilepsy of his childhood. He was tough and he was young, and he would soon no longer be childless.

His First Kadine, Besma, would soon present him with a child. He was sure it would be a son, as if in her great love for him, she had only sons in her to give. No more would half-brothers and cousins and uncles be imprisoned in the Cage. The age of fratricide was over. The execution of Mustafa weighed upon him like a stone, even now. The Janissaries had even tried to spread the rumor that Mustafa had had a son who still lived. But he had stamped out this lie before it had taken hold of the volatile population of Istanbul. His father, Abdulhamid, had failed. Selim III had failed. He, Mahmud II, would not. Yet he awoke in the night almost as if he could feel the bowstring of the Bazam-dil-siz

around his own fine neck. He swallowed hard. He turned his eyes restlessly on the golden landscape dotted with cypress, olive and vineyards
on the other shore.

Mahmud had chosen the profession of calligrapher when he became
Sultan, just as Selim had chosen lace-making, and Abulhamid, arrow-
making. Now his eyes followed the lines and curves of his massed men
as though with a fine-haired brush, changing them into a swirl of black
lines on white parchment, his brush, smooth and expert, interlacing the
arabesques and convolutions into sumptuously beautiful calligrams. He
wondered if he liked best the filling of space with line or the line with
space of a poem . . . for he was also a poet, not unknown in the capital, who wrote under the pseudonym of Adli.

But his mind was far from calligraphy and poetry. He was lost in the
maze of arabesques and convolutions of his Empire, which resembled
more a confederation of anarchists than an Empire. In Albania the
Pasha was founding a rival Empire and flirting with the Russians. In
Algiers, Tunis and Tripoli the Deys were squabbling among themselves
and against him, daggers drawn. In Syria the Pasha of St. Jean d'Acre
obeyed only his caprices, and in Lebanon the Druses and the Maronite
Christians allowed their army of mountaineers to raid the plains of
Beirut and the valley of Damascus to fight the Moslem Pashas. Finally,
in Arabia the Wahabi fanatics still held the two holy cities of Mecca and
Medina. Even as his mother was preparing his gift as reconqueror of
Mecca, Mohammed Ali of Egypt, who had promised to regain the cities
for him, had used this as an excuse to massacre his Circassian
Mameluks, the Egyptian Janissaries' sister corps, and end their long
reign of terror over the country. Mohammed Ali, an ambiguous, ambitious man, was also founding a rival Empire on the Nile. He had lured
the Mameluks and their chiefs into the citadel of Cairo and had slaugh-
tered all of them in a matter of hours . . . only twenty had escaped.
Mohammed Ali, too useful to be denied, too obsequious to be alienated,
too powerful to be punished, had turned into a dangerous ally, if not an
outright rebel. But his objective was straightforward: to rule, destroy
the Janissaries. . . .

As Sultan, Mahmud was also a Janissary, first but equal to the last.
At rollcall, he answered to his name, "Mahmud!"—and received his
pay.

"Mahmud! Mahmud! Mahmud!"

With a shiver of pleasure, Mahmud luxuriated in the sound of twenty
thousand male voices joined as one, accompanied by the thud, like

cannon thunder, of twenty thousand clenched fists striking twenty-thousand brightly uniformed leather breasts.

The military exercises started with the artillery firing; then the war games began, and Mahmud could hear through the musket shots, the ominous detonation of cannon fire that echoed from one slope of the valley to the other in spiraling repetition, while military music, like counterpoint, sounded in the intervals between each explosion. The whole valley filled with sound and the haze of gunpowder, through which appeared a legion of flapping goose-wing fans. Mahmud knew the parade would not end before evening, more than six hours from now.

Naksh-i-dil agitated her peacock-feather fan excitedly as she watched the maneuvers from behind the kiosk's grilled windows. It was Mahmud's first real triumph, the gauntlet thrown at the Janissaries' feet. Moslems and Christians were amazed at the new army's elegant uniforms, the discipline and the precision of their maneuvers. Everyone assembled here would return home stirred by the spectacle they had witnessed. And this was just the beginning, thought Naksh-i-dil, as she glanced at the broad-shouldered, ornamented back of Ali Efendi next to Mahmud. The blood rushed to her face. Love was so different, she thought, from what she had imagined, or even dreamed. Love was not the romantic schoolgirl dreams of Joséphine and her lonely childhood, nor the half-witted manipulations of the harem. . . . Love was the heaviness in the heart and in the loins, the fear for the loved one's safety, his comfort, the very air he breathed, the giddiness of expectation of seeing him, not only in private but even now; the unreasonable pride in him, the rage against the years wasted, the caresses and embraces never to be consummated, the years of her greatest beauty never to be a gift to him. . . .

Naksh-i-dil bent over her swaying, pearl-handled fan. Only her green eyes were visible as she devoured the high-seated mounted figure, half hidden now by her son's strong wide back as he changed places to be closer to Ali. The backs of the two men touched, the rich brocades of their tunics glistened in the intermittent sun. The sound and clamor of the new corps and the cannon fire seeped through her skin.

"Mahmud! Mahmud! Mahmud!" The terrifying sound washed over them like the ocean.

Ali Efendi, on the small rise, contemplated the population of Istanbul swarming over the slopes of the valley, and the neat identical rows of white, green and red which formed his Nizam-attick.

The Law said: "Don't borrow anything from the infidel, you are their superior, if you frequent them, they will pervert you," he thought. And the Moslems remained moored in their superstitions, stationary in their vision of the world. One verse more in the Koran, pondered the Lieutenant, one verse that would have allowed the Moslems to have appropriated progress and enslaved that Europe now deliberating their dismemberment.

Ali Efendi felt Naksh-i-dil's eyes boring into his back. He felt none of the enthusiasm that she and Mahmud felt for the magnificent sight before him; the massed white and green of the population clinging to the sides of the valley, the colorful and endless files of the Nizam-attick, the gleaming artillery, the detonation lifting small puffs of smoke into the azure sky, and the war cry of twenty thousand strong voices: "Mahmud! Mahmud! Mahmud!" did nothing to assuage his premonition of disaster.

The Koran had lost none of its sacred authority. Yet Mahmud had begun to introduce infidel tactics into his army and had called upon infidels to help him. Naksh-i-dil had pushed him even further. The Sultan had established a school of medicine that permitted the dissection of cadavers, which was expressly forbidden by the Koran. He had, under the urgings of his mother, started a postal system, ordered new roads built, created a national guard, and little by little, beginning with the elimination of the turban, had begun to modify the very clothing worn by the Ottomans. The Koran, thus violated by the religious head of Islam, God's Shadow on Earth, would soon be violated in more of its precepts. The Moslem, shaken in his Faith, would soon scorn and ridicule it. Ali Efendi looked up into the sun. Yet he believed, as did Mahmud, that the influence of a progressive civilization should be able to replace the precepts of Islam with the severest of moral principles. But such a rapid upheaval would never permit this. It was probable, thought Ali Efendi somberly, that the Ottoman was destined to offer to Europe very soon the example of a decaying nation before it had even achieved its reforms. . . .

Ali Efendi gazed beyond the valley to Asia. The Great Meadow of the Dead was situated on the Asian shore as if the Osmans were convinced, as he was, that one day they would be forced to retreat into Asia from whence they had come. The field was called for that reason Meit-Iskelli, "the Ladder of Death."

Behind the white stone barracks, he could see scintillating in the distance a small elegant mosque. Selim had begun clearing the valley between the barracks and the mosque in order to use the space for military exercises. His death had interrupted the work, and the field remained a wasteland of rutted earth, uprooted trees, desolation. The gulf between the Moslem world of the mosque and the European world of the Nizam-attick barracks would never be filled in, leveled, made smooth and accessible. The gulf would remain forever. Just as the Bosphorus and beyond, not more than 1,800 meters away, Asia.

Ali Efendi felt Naksh-i-dil's presence behind him. He felt the low-lying insupportable heat like a cashmere shawl clinging to his shoulders; he felt the grotesqueness of the spectacle before him, the birth of a bloody fiasco. In itself, all progress was neutral, or should be, but man animated it with his follies, which transformed it into belief, which made itself into an event; the passage from logic to lunacy.

"Mahmud! Mahmud! Mahmud!"

Ali Efendi turned in his saddle to look back at the grilled windows of Naksh-i-dil's kiosk. He knew her triumph. Her sense of accomplishment. Her pride in Mahmud. Naksh-i-dil observed Ali.

According to Islamic custom the female partner of a man should be half his age plus eight. She smiled. Ali was now thirty-two, which meant that she should be twenty-four years old. . . . The light struck her ageless features. She trusted Ali with her life. But she didn't trust life. He would weary of her, leave her either for another war or for another woman. He and Mahmud formed a set of twin wills to power. It was so evident that they had inherited the famous nicknames of the dead Ishak Bey and the dead Selim III: the archangels Gabriel and Michael. Could not at least the two religions have different names for their angels? thought Naksh-i-dil. She wondered casually what Ali's fortune was these days. Surely he was a very rich man, for she, Naksh-i-dil, was a very, very rich woman. . . . God had smiled on her, or had He?

◆ CHAPTER THREE ◆

TATCH-UL-MESTOURAT
1812

> Constantinople. Constantinople. Never.
> Constantinople is the Empire of the World!
> —NAPOLEON BONAPARTE (to himself)

The black veil swirled around the laboring women like the black-ink calligraphy of Mahmud. Bent over a quarter of an acre of silk cloth were two hundred women, all holding gold thread in one hand or in their laps and stitching minutely, while other Odalisques ran to and fro, moving and stretching the material as Naksh-i-dil carefully inspected the work being done, stitch by stitch. Her eyes glistened and her cheeks were flushed. This must be a work of perfection. She would tolerate not one mistake if her women had to sew and unsew a million times . . . until their fingers bled. And it took years. Allah would give Mecca back to Mahmud, and this would be his gift of thanks to the holy mosque. A veil that would cover the entire Kaaba, which itself englobed the cornerstone of the house of Abraham . . . the black stone. She let the silk slip through her fingers. It was so fine it was like touching clouds or wind, or like Ali's dancing. . . .

This one is for Allah. . . .

"Mother!" The Odalisques of Mahmud and the ladies of Naksh-i-dil's court scattered like a flock of disturbed pigeons, cooing and chirping. Naksh-i-dil clapped her hands and she and her son found themselves alone.

"My son," said Naksh-i-dil. "Master of Two Continents and Two

Seas, faithful servant of two holy cities, Sultan Mahmud III, may your
reign be eternal, your mother greets you."

They were silent. War had commenced again with the Russians. They
had occupied the north of Bulgaria and the Dobruja. That summer
Mahmud's armies had stopped their advance but only with heavy
losses. On the twenty-seventh of September, Ruschuk, Bayrakdar's old
province, had been taken by the Russians and they were advancing
toward Serbia. Their only hope was that Bonaparte would declare their
war on Russia. With the victory over the Austrians at Wagram, thought
Naksh-i-dil, Napoleon was the undisputed master of Europe.

Sooner or later, they both knew Bonaparte was going to invade the
frontiers of the Empire, just as he had done in Egypt thirteen years
before. . . . All the world wanted Istanbul as the jewel of his con-
quests.

"I look across the waters at the Castle of the Seven Towers," Naksh-
i-dil said to Mahmud. "It marks the line of separation that sets the
Ottomans apart from the rest of Europe. It stands at an angle made by
the wall which bounds the land and seacoasts of Istanbul. Nothing
marks the assumptions of Moslem pride over every European people
than this. Yet the Christian nations submit because the injury or degra-
dation of one is always the object of triumph to the other. The English
and Russians against the French, the Austrians against the Russians,
and all of them against us. *That* is the reason no one will ever have
Istanbul, for no one wishes another to have it, so none will. . . .

"There will be no winner: only two losers," continued Naksh-i-dil.
"Both our enemies. It is the greatest battle we can win without losing a
man. For when Napoleon and Alexander count their dead, only the
Osmanlis will rise from those cadavers victorious! It is of no importance
to me *who* wins, the Czar or the Emperor. And the 'winner' will be the
one with the least dead . . . let them massacre and destroy each other.
It is a very economical war, Mahmud."

Naksh-i-dil thought of Catherine. Her revenge would be cheap if
Napoleon prevailed over Czar Alexander, or she would use Catherine's
own grandson as a means to her own ends if Alexander prevailed over
Napoleon. The thirty thousand men of Ochakov would be a pinprick
compared with the Danube of blood that would flow because of the
presumptions of the French and the arrogance of the Russians.

She gathered strength from the strong muscled arms supporting her.
Was it possible, she thought, that she had carried this august, imperious, arrogant Sultan in her womb, had nursed him, crushed him in her

arms, dried his tears, swung him in the air? She gazed up into his green-gray eyes, his rich beard cut short, European style, the square heavy shoulders under the half-European, half-Oriental uniform, the short jacket draped over one shoulder, Austrian fashion, which he had designed himself and which became him so well. She would not let up.

"Napoleon will refuse to believe an alliance between you and Czar Alexander of Russia, but that . . . that is what he is going to get," said Naksh-i-dil with a smile. "Napoleon's first defeat was on the plains of Nazareth, on Ottoman soil. . . . Let the coup de grâce fall upon him because of the Ottomans! Napoleon will never resist the temptation to invade Russia; it is a matter of time. The Treaty of Tilsit was just a ploy. . . ."

"Another peace treaty with the Russians! It is unthinkable in our weakened military position. We have no right! They are the enemy! It is too much, Our Lady. The people would never accept. The Janissaries would revolt," said Mahmud.

"Let them, we will kill them all," said Naksh-i-dil to Mahmud.

"All forty thousand of them?"

"So what? With the best terms we will ever be able to get from the Czar," she added. "Either that, or Alexander will have a war on two fronts."

"Peace with Russia! It is madness!" said Mahmud.

"The Black Death is upon us, Mahmud. It has always been the precursor of disaster for Napoleon. Remember Egypt!"

"Russia is not Egypt."

"We can get terms we can never win, if we do this! That is why the treaty with Alexander is necessary. And it must be signed before winter. Napoleon, according to our Ambassador, is *ready* to invade Russia. Napoleon will never share the Empire of the Osmanlis with Alexander. He believes the Empire is his. If he marches across Russia he will keep marching all the way to Istanbul. He has staked it as his domain, for it is the Eastern Empire of Constantine and Alexander the Great. He will never renounce it while he has breath in his body . . . and he will never have it while I have breath in mine—if I have to lead the armies myself!"

"You might just be capable of doing that, Our Lady."

"And what's wrong with that?" asked Naksh-i-dil.

"You, Tatch-ul-Mestourat, want to be Emperor of the East."

Naksh-i-dil threw back her heavy turbaned head, and laughed.

Mahmud regarded his mother in consternation. She was escaping into her own world more and more, leaving those who needed her, leaving *him* who needed her, falling into a haze of vague superstitions, the predictions of Hitabetullah, or the evocations of the Koran, or, worse still, a mixture of precepts from the Christian Bible *and* the Koran. Couldn't she make up her mind? he asked himself. Was she a confirmed Christian or a converted Moslem?

Naksh-i-dil noticed the deep furrow between Mahmud's eyes. She knew what he was thinking. He thought she was going mad. Well, was she? The fainting spells, her depressions, her lapses of memory, her confusion. . . . "The wars of Napoleon are about to knock at the doors of Istanbul!"

Mahmud was silent. His mother wouldn't let up.

"Napoleon *needs* Istanbul," Naksh-i-dil argued. "Only then will he be *The Emperor,* not simply an emperor. He wants Russia thrown back into Asia. Goddamn him. . . !"

At four A.M. on June 14, 1812, at Kovno, Napoleon watched the leading regiments of the Grande Armée cross the river Niemen where five years before, on a tent raft, he had first embraced the Czar Alexander and secretly divided the Ottoman Empire between them. There were Italians, Poles, Portuguese, Spaniards, Bavarians, Croats, Dalmatians, Dutch, Neapolitans, North Germans, Saxons and Swiss. In all, twenty nations and 600,000 soldiers, only one third French.

"He can try either to conquer and detach certain territory or secure from Russia as a whole the terms which he desires. Whoever wins is our mortal enemy. Whoever makes peace is our mortal enemy. Only if they war are they our friends," said Naksh-i-dil.

Mahmud had no liking for his negotiations with Alexander II in Bucharest. But mesmerized by the force of his mother's passion, he acceded. The Russians were afraid.

The Czar, despite Mahmud's military weakness, made peace with the Ottomans on Ottoman terms. Alexander returned Moldavia and Walachia to the Sultan, leaving only Bessarabia to Russia. He also returned all his gains north of the Black Sea and in the Caucasus. Serbia was rendered autonomous. Alexander could now withdraw more than 100,000 men, a fourth of his army, from the banks of the Danube and the frontiers of their empire to throw against Napoleon's approaching Grande Armée. Naksh-i-dil had won the first part of her gamble. Would she win the second? Mahmud wondered. She was not the first Valide to cause war or peace, or to ruin or cause an empire to prosper, thought

Mahmud. What did she want, he mused, this Valide who starved her body and sold her soul?

"He can strike at the feet, Kiev, the head, Saint Petersburg, or the heart, Moscow," said Naksh-i-dil Valide as she opened her gammon table and faced Mahmud.

One month after he had crossed the Niemen, Napoleon looked down with stupefaction at the document in his hand. Either Mahmud was a fool or a madman. No sane sovereign would reject the terms he had offered that bloody Sultan. No sane despot, no matter how Oriental or devious, would deliberately put his Empire in such peril when there was a way out! Mahmud *couldn't* have made a treaty with the Russians! It wasn't strategic. It was lunatic! It didn't suit his plans for the Ottoman Empire at all! That Russian son of a bitch, Alexander! That Oriental Tartar! He *needed* Mahmud. Were not the French the *traditional* allies of the Ottomans? Wasn't that bastard's whore of a mother French?

Alexander needed 300,000 men for the Turkish frontier alone, and now he was free to withdraw his troops from the Danube and throw them against him. He deliberated. He paced up and down, turned in circles in all directions. He asked for the time, threw himself down on his cot, got up again. He hummed, he swung his hands, he reckoned the time, and then completely absorbed he stopped short, hummed with a preoccupied air, then started pacing up and down again. . . .

"Scratch a Russian and you find a Turk," said Napoleon Bonaparte.

Each of Napoleon's divisions was followed by a six-mile column of food supplies: cattle, wagons of wheat, masons to build ovens and bakers to turn the wheat into bread. There were twenty-eight million bottles of wine and two million bottles of brandy. There were 1,000 guns and 3,000 ammunition wagons. There were ambulances, stretchers and field dressings; there was equipment for building bridges and portable forges. Every senior officer had his own carriage and a wagon to carry his bedding, books and maps. A special covered wagon, protected by the imperial guard, contained the Emperor's crown, coronation robe and scepter. Wagons and carts totaled 30,000; horses, excluding cavalry, 150,000. . . . Some officers believed they would end up in India. Others dreamed of Constantinople. . . .

In Constantinople, Naksh-i-dil Valide continued her increasing game of gammon with Mahmud.

"Napoleon hopes Moscow will end in peace and alliance with Czar Alexander," said Mahmud to her. "He even has his coronation display

with him! But Alexander will never crown Napoleon. The Czar has said
he would rather let his beard grow and eat potatoes in Siberia. But I
don't see how he can avoid it. . . . Napoleon must get face to face with
the main Russian army on a given field of battle, defeat it decisively
and, above all things, cut it from its communication. The Czar is drawing Napoleon farther and farther into Russia without giving battle."

The main Russian army of some 120,000 men with 600 guns, acting
on the orders of the Czar, refused to fight and drew Napoleon deeper
and deeper into Russian territory. They abandoned Vilna, they escaped
from Vitebsk and they burned Smolensk. For seven weeks Napoleon
marched onward, and all he conquered was empty space. The farther he
penetrated into Russia, the more he and his men became aware of the
emptiness and the silence. Napoleon gave the order to march to Moscow.

"The Russians will fight before Moscow," said Naksh-i-dil.

Alexander drew up his defending forces south of the village of Boro-
dino, on a ridge intersected with ravines on the Kolotcha River which
flowed through Moscow, seventy-two miles east.

In Istanbul, Naksh-i-dil's forehead touched her prayer rug in unison
with Mahmud, separated by the walls of the harem. For two months she
and Mahmud had met every day to read the dispatches together and
continue their gammon games.

"The slaughter has begun. Let's see whose stomach turns first," she
said.

Napoleon and his stepson looked down on Moscow, sitting on a vast
plain in the middle of which were situated its ancient walls, thousands
of gilded belltowers and golden domes reflecting the rays of the sun like
prisms. The city was a conglomeration of wood cabins, rich brick mansions and magnificent palaces of an aristocracy as numerous as it was
proud. And at the heart of the city stood the Czar's red brick Kremlin,
around which swarmed the Muscovites, a population of opposites—the
eighteenth century mingling with the nineteenth, the civilized with the
barbaric, the European with the Oriental.

Out of 250,000 inhabitants, only 15,000 remained: foreigners, beggars, and criminals released from the city prisons. There was only space
and silence. That night sporadic fires broke out in the city. The French
could find no hoses or pumps.

The next day more houses caught fire, and the French finally realized that the Governor of Moscow had armed a thousand convicts with muskets and gunpowder and told them to burn Moscow to the ground. In the Kremlin Palace, Napoleon descended the great staircase between blazing walls. For the next four days Napoleon watched as 8,500 houses, 300 churches and four fifths of the beautiful city burned. Napoleon's emissaries were turned back before reaching their destination.

"Moscow is burning," said Mahmud excitedly. "The Russians have burned their own city to the ground. It is . . . an inferno like the hell Jesus (may the blessings of Allah be upon him) imagined for his believers!"

Naksh-i-dil began to laugh, her head thrown back, her round white neck throbbing, her green eyes blazing. She clutched Mahmud's hand so tightly he flinched. Moscow destroyed as a bonus. "How wonderful," she sneered. "Perhaps the Czar himself will decide to burn Kiev and Saint Petersburg as well."

At two P.M. on the afternoon of October 19, the first units of the Grande Armée left Moscow after a stay of thirty-five days. The soldiers wore sheepskin jackets, fur bonnets and lined boots; they carried sugar, brandy and jeweled icons in their knapsacks, while their wagons were filled with Chinese silk, sables, gold ingots and suits of armor. Altogether there were 90,000 infantrymen, 15,000 cavalrymen, 569 cannons and 10,000 wagons containing food for twenty days, but less than a week's supply of horse fodder. In the chain of steel and muscle, the horses were the weak link, dependent on what their riders could forage. Three inches of snow had already fallen. The snowflakes were so large, the soldiers lost sight of the sky and the men in front of them. Lips cracked, noses became frostbitten, eyes were blinded by the glare. The men who wandered off the route were killed by peasants who had been told by their masters what to do.

Russian Cossacks harassed the fringes of the retreating troops constantly, felling dozens of the blinded men at a time.

When Napoleon's remaining troops reached the Berezina River, instead of being frozen solid, it was a raging torrent three hundred yards wide. The bridge had been burned in three different places and was under fire from Russian guns on the far bank. Napoleon had 49,000 men fit enough to fight and 250 guns. Three Russian Generals were moving in on him.

The French decided to make the crossing nine miles upriver at a ford that was only one hundred yards wide and six feet deep. Four hundred men built two bridges in twenty-four hours and perished from the icy water. Three days later, the troops crossed the Berezina River. All day and all night, weary men and battered material crossed. Men had to clamber over hundreds of dead horses and wrecked wagons. The dense mass of troops fought to get to the river, trampling any who stumbled and fell. Only forty thousand men had crossed the river.

To the sound of bugles and the neighing of panicked horses, the pale daylight broke over the sad white plains of Poland. The long cold night had been one long cry of the dying of the day and the wounded of yesterday. The snow was so tinted with blood that it would remain red until spring.

Czar Alexander II had won the war. The war had cost 400,000 dead for the French and 700,000 dead for the Russians.

Mahmud gazed at his mother sitting impassively in front of him. The barrier between them grew higher and higher every day. He despised himself for having agreed on an alliance with their most hated enemy, Russia. It was not the glorious military victory over the Russians he needed. But he could not express this to his mother. It was not a rational or a political or a self-serving motive. He was not the French renegade coolly savoring her victory, having gambled the entire Empire on the defeat of one enemy by another. He had renounced the only victory the Ottomans could have claimed over the Russians since his grandfather's reign. Osmanli history meant nothing to her. What, thought Mahmud, did they do now . . . with the Russians? His mother had been right in strategy. But she didn't have the mentality to deal with his Oriental Empire. Only military victory could hold the Empire together. Because only military victory had created it, and the terror, which was the brick and mortar of what was still the greatest Empire in the world. His mother had been intelligent, but she had not *frightened* anyone. Not the Greeks, not the Albanians, not the Algerians, not the Egyptians . . . not the Tripolitans. . . .

She had changed the history of Europe perhaps—but she hadn't changed the history of the Ottoman Empire.

Nevertheless, Mahmud said: "Mother of the Veiled Heads, you have won."

◆ CHAPTER FOUR ◆

HITABETULLAH 1813

The Sultan transported into our camp the Christian relics found hidden in the walls of Santa Sophia: the column of the flagellation, straps, rods, the scarlet robe, the crown of thorns, a fragment of the true cross, the nails, the hair and the head of Saint John the Baptist.
    —Memoirs of Marshal Maurice de Saxe
        on the taking of Belgrade, 1717

Hitabetullah drew a circle in the fine white sand in front of the Valide's kiosk and placed the tooth of a crocodile, the vertebrae of the Isqanqoûr bird, the skin of a chameleon, three hairs of the tail of an ass, the dried powder of a hyena's genitals, a handful of sesame seeds in a baboon skull. For half of her life, the sun had set upon her and Istanbul at the same time. Thirty years had passed since the Festival of the Negress when she had entered into the service of Naksh-i-dil. And she was tired. She had been her slave all that time. She had followed her mistress into the Eski Serai with a light heart. She regretted nothing, neither slavery nor prison, for what were they after all but the appendices of womanhood? She regretted not even the pleasure she had never known. Her children had been taken from her at such a young age that even their small thin voices no longer reached her heart or her ears. She was alone. Her eyes widened when she saw what she had conjured in the feathers and bones strewn around the circle. She took out her amulet and bound it to her right arm. Her poisons, her conjuring instruments, her medicines and her cash were wrapped in a silk coverlet, tightly bound.

Hitabetullah began a moan, which rose like the wind rose over the Bosphorus, and it seemed to billow out her robes until she stood like a tall black mast and sail on the steps of Naksh-i-dil's sanctuary.

She knew now what she should do with her freedom after all these years.

"Hitabetullah," her mistress and ruler's voice rang out behind her. "What in heaven's name are you doing out here, sitting in the dark all alone?"

"I was thinking of Africa and my children. Don't you, my Lady, ever think of your island or your family?"

"No," lied the Valide. "Never. It never pays to look backward. Mahmud knows who I am. That is sufficient. I am no longer that person, if I ever was. I am no more the daughter of my father than I am a child of the Prophet . . ." continued Naksh-i-dil. "How amazing the lives, the beliefs, the emotions one sheds with the years . . . as if the preparation for death was only the shedding of one veil of emotion after the other until nothing is left but silence, solitude and indifference to this world . . ."

"Your Majesty is not indifferent . . ."

"True, Hitabetullah, I am not indifferent."

Hitabetullah looked down upon the face of her mistress. The face was lined, rouged, weary. She knew that under the turban the knee-length red-gold hair was streaked with gray. She had cared for her mistress for thirty years—years that had dissolved into nothingness. Naksh-i-dil was an aging woman in love with a young man. A mother in love with her son. A despot in love with her Empire. Naksh-i-dil had no love for her, thought Hitabetullah. She depended upon her protection, her magic. She thought that she, Hitabetullah, could save her from the Great Judiciary, death. But that was not in even her power. And she, Hitabetullah, was tired. She had served and served and now she could serve no longer. Her term of service was over. Naksh-i-dil, having taken on the traits of a tyrant, would think she had something against *her*. Because the essence of tyranny was ungratefulness. The master saw the world only from one point of view. Naksh-i-dil was a master. It was her duty to rule, but she, Hitabetullah, in her sixtieth year, was not obliged to serve . . . even the Valide. There was no absolute tyranny, just as there was no absolute slavery. Neither could absolve the other . . . there were reciprocal duties. If a tyrant cut off heads capriciously, he would lose his own. There was circumstantial tyranny just as there was circumstantial slavery. Thus, power took on the form of a masquerade and

Hitabetullah was tired of pretending. She was tired of promising the Valide that she would never die. . . . The fragility of masters had always amazed Hitabetullah. It seemed as if they couldn't exist *without* their slaves; that *their* only function would be extinguished without *them* . . . without *her* and without *her* slavehood. Faced with such a contradiction between fiction and reality, thought Hitabetullah, no wonder all the Sultans were deranged. Hitabetullah knew that the Eski Serai engendered passionate desires that made nature shiver. . . . The women of the Eski Serai had perfected love between themselves to a fine art and burning passions. Naksh-i-dil burned for Hadidge, though she remained chaste for love of Ali. Her mistress also burned with the fear of Satan. This, not her childhood memories, was her real fear of fire. The renegade Christians *never* forgot their original God, no matter how hard they tried. . . . Hitabetullah fingered the amulet on her upper arm.

"No, Modest Lady, you are *not* indifferent . . ."

"There is so much to be done . . ."

"You will do it, my Lady."

"And you will protect me, Hitabetullah? From everything?" asked the Queen of the Veiled Heads. "Everything?"

"Of course," answered Hitabetullah. Why was it, she thought, that the master always demanded more of a slave than they did, verily, of a lover, of being unable to imagine any independent thoughts of another human being?

She reached out and touched the Valide's head. A hand which grasped and held hers . . . a fine slim white hand which Hitabetullah had so often obeyed. What good, she thought, were all these criminal passions? Demanding of life what it was not. Of power what it could never be. Of slavery the one thing it could never provide: love.

Hitabetullah began to chant:

Pape Satan . . . Pape Satan . . . Hitabetullah lay at the crossroads at sunup, her face in the gray earth, her arms outstretched, her ear cocked, her body straining.

> *Thee, I invoke, the Bornless One*
> *Thee that didst create the Earth and the Heavens*
> *Thee that didst create the Night and the Day*
> *Thee that didst create the Darkness and the Light . . .*

Not one flake of snow fell on Istanbul. The winter was unreasonably warm. Warm enough for Naksh-i-dil to walk in the harem gardens.

Suddenly it was the season of watermelons and of eggplants. The Bostanji worked day and night in the gardens lush with fruit trees and orchards of ripe cherries hanging so low that the Valide's veil caught on the low, hanging clusters. The Valide Naksh-i-dil smiled to herself. But Czar Alexander, who had begun to feel mystical leanings, announced that God had destined him to be the "liberator of Europe" and crossed the Niemen River. In March Paris had surrendered to Alexander and Talleyrand deposed Napoleon Bonaparte.

It began the same month. Eight years had passed since the last plague in Istanbul when in the Greek Quarter of Phanar, a young girl dropped dead. The epidemic made no progress during April and May, and the city began to doubt that the sickness in truth existed. But in September the Black Death took hold. As each victim was reported, the city guards would lock forty houses, and forty more if a new case occurred. The desperate, often demented screams of grief-stricken parents mingled with the cries of their terrified and dying children and servants, echoed through the silence along the narrow blue and white streets and alleyways.

The plague did not start in one place or spread by degree, but fell upon several places in the city and suburbs like rain. Soon all roads out of Istanbul, lying in every direction like the spokes of a great wheel, were thick with fleeing traffic, moving slowly, with creaking carts, camels and shouting, sweating eunuchs. Poor families, their children on their backs, beggars and people, already ill, who fell sick or dying by the wayside clogged the roads. Those who fell were pushed to one side to die or recover, but were never robbed, their valuables safe in the circle of Black Death and the admonitions of Mohammed. The narrow gates of the city were blocked with carts trying to leave Istanbul. Overloaded carts became locked together. Terrified horses leaped up, kicking and foaming at the mouth. Axles broke under wagons pulled by oxen laboring under three times the weight they usually carried. Thieves and wild orphaned children slashed ropes and thongs that held the baggage, looting and robbing as household goods and food fell to the ground. And five times a day, in the midst of the gravest physical danger, the rich and poor, the sick and well, thieves and beggars, the young, the old, the strong, the weak, the beautiful and the ugly, all knelt with their foreheads to the ground to face Mecca and pray for deliverance.

One day Hitabetullah left the Seraglio, unaccompanied and unannounced, to attend the Feast of the Negress despite the banning of such gatherings. Naksh-i-dil waited a day for her servant to return, and at nightfall of the second day, she gathered her taffeta cloak around her, veiled her face, put on the amulet Hitabetullah had invented to ward off the plague and went out to find her, accompanied only by Ali Efendi in an oilcloth-covered cart.

Crazed victims, driven mad by pain, roamed the streets, some bashing their heads against walls, shouting with the urgency of the insane, shouts that mingled with the groans and screams of the dying.

The Valide saw dead rats in the middle of the streets, a sure sign that the Black Death was master in the largest city in the world.

Scene after horrible scene passed before their eyes. Nude bodies were piled everywhere. Carts and wagons transported the sick and the dying to hospitals. Deserted children, women and old men wandered aimlessly in the streets. Cremation fires burned continuously, casting shadows and dreadful stench everywhere. Naksh-i-dil clutched her amulet, murmuring the ninety-nine names of Allah as she passed a house from which the corpulent and nude body of a dead woman, her hair floating behind her, was flung out a window.

The infected staggered like drunken men until they fell dead under a cluster of greedy black flies. Others, too ill to move, lay face down in a coma on the cobblestones or in the doorways, or crawled around on their hands and knees vomiting as if they had drunk poison. Shrouds, improvised from sheets and blankets, covering the bodies were soaked in sweat, vomit and feces. Piles of fifteen or twenty naked corpses, eyes and mouths opened, were heaped together.

The field where the Negresses had held their feast was empty. Naksh-i-dil sent Ali and fifty torch-bearing black eunuchs to search every corner of the grove and field. Even the aging Kizlar Aga ventured out, and together he and Ali combed the flattened parade ground in fear and loathing, since in the space of three months the Black Death had swept away 22,000 Jews, Armenians, Franks and Greeks, and 140,000 Turks.

Hitabetullah, oh, Hitabetullah, had you prophesied this as well? wondered the desperate Naksh-i-dil as she buried her face in her hands. It was useless. One mass grave big enough to swallow two ships of the line had received two thousand bodies. One driver of a death cart was dead himself, the cart moving aimlessly at the whim of the horses.

Already dazed and wearied by the sight of so much misery, Naksh-i-dil and Ali took a caïque by dropping a sack of gold into the boatman's lap and crossed over the Bosphorus from Asia to Europe in search of her slave. In Pera Naksh-i-dil searched out the Armenian lazaretto of Don Courban and Don Giacomo. But the priests were of no help.

The pesthouse held thirteen thousand of the plague-ridden; its whole internal space was crammed with sheds, tents, carts and, in two endless colonnades with a pathway down the middle, the desperately sick and dying. Naksh-i-dil stood and looked out over more misery heaped together in one place than she had seen in the streets of Istanbul, or that she had ever imagined in her life. She stood there amazed and overwhelmed, whispering Hitabetullah's name. For here there was no harem —no separation of women from men. Here, in death, all were equal, men lying with women, the sick lying with the dead on bare straw. From the doorway the Valide saw Don Giacomo hurrying toward her. She saw the Armenians directing the pitiful operations of the lazaretto, cleaning, dragging things away, piling up filthy sheets and rags to be burned. She saw others come and go, stop, bend over patients, stoop or straighten up again, moving figures that could be convalescents, lunatics, attendants or priests. Together they made a movement like the undulation of a turbid pool of snakes over which rose a hum, a kind of primordial and steady musical sound made of coughs, lamentations, wailing, bleating, confused mutterings, groans, prayers, deliriums and screams, labored breathing and the absence of all breath. Naksh-i-dil went from pallet to pallet, looking searchingly into faces exhausted by suffering, contracted in agony, calm in death. But Hitabetullah's face was not among them. She went forward like a pilgrim, dazed by so many ghastly sights, until she sank under the oppression of a place destined for suffering and death, while hundreds made their final battle.

"Hitabetullah, my love, my cherished one, savior of my life and that of Mahmud. Hear me," whispered Naksh-i-dil. "Do not leave me and Mahmud. I beg of you."

But Naksh-i-dil never again set eyes upon either the dead body nor the live face of her manumitted slave.

The wind rushed through the empty streets and gusted over the rooftops of Istanbul, fanning the flames of the fire of purification to greater and greater fury. Men, women and children of all ages and all ranks, their backs loaded with their most precious belongings, stumbled through the streets, making anguished murmurs like the thrashings of thousands of hummingbirds. In some places entire streets were one flame that belched light and heat like a giant forge. Wooden structures folded together from the opposite windows, crumbling, uniting into one great river running the length of the street as blackened plank after blackened plank fell like dominoes. Houses snapped and broke in great musical crashes. The flames turned orange and rose high into the darkness, illuminating Constantinople's narrow and unlit streets as never before. The wind increased and clouds of billowing smoke and showers of sparks lifted high above the Sea of Marmara. Small boats scurried like busy water beetles to and fro across the strait to dump goods and refugees on the European side, colliding with each other because the dense smoke blocked their view like fog. The water that lapped the shores boiled in the intolerable heat. It reached even the harem and the Valide's apartments where Naksh-i-dil stood thinking that at least Hitabetullah's body, if she were dead, was not rotting somewhere in an unconsecrated mound of dirt but was being consumed by fire and dispersed over Istanbul like the red-hot cinders now rising in the air. The Valide's eyes were hard and tearless even as she heard the panicked screams and uproar of the population. She imagined the blindfolded horses and oxen rearing up, nostrils wide, terrified of the smell of burning. She saw the minarets and spires of the mosques shimmering in the heat and then crumbling like a deck of cards. Bewildered black-faced refugees camped outside the walls of the city in fields and meadows, which had received the plague victims' bodies, and which now were strewn with victims of the fire along with furniture, sofas, bundles, lanterns, torches, baskets, animals and unveiled women. From the harem the illumination could be seen for forty miles around. The great fire of 1812 which began that night raged for three days. The hundreds of lead domes of Istanbul melted, running lava-red down the sides of the mosques they had once crowned.

But Hitabetullah had known. She had known that the flames would reach the harem. She had known that the eunuchs with swords drawn would prevent the Janissaries from breaking the sacred doors of the harem to fight the fire. She had known that inside, Mahmud's two firstborn infants, Bayazid and Murat, would burn to death in their beds.

Once again fire had triumphed over everything Naksh-i-dil loved.

BOOK VII

VALIDE SULTANE
·1814·

◆ CHAPTER ONE ◆

THE BLACK EUNUCH
1814

Often a Black is white,
More than any Other,
By his soul's purity,
The body the color of musk,
By its candor, camphor becomes.
That darkness we presume,
Resembles the pupil of an eye,
Through which passes nothing other
than absolute Light.
—IBRAIM ABU ISHAK, 1783

To Mahmud II, successor of the most celebrated Sultans, Noble of Khans, the most renowned for his goodness, distinguished by the favor of Kings, the Pillar of Islam, may your glory as Sultan augment from day to day. Most honorable and very magnificent Emperor, Allah's Shadow on Earth, Defender of the Faith, have the good grace to accept my homage and most profound and prostrate tribute:

36 strands of pearls
80 branches of uncut coral, and the same number of strands
4 dromedaries
60 Arabian stallions outfitted with silver and bronze harnesses

1 live tiger
1 printing press made in Philadelphia
500 clusters of dates
1 large thermometer
1 dozen hunting dogs with collars and chains
1 ermine pelisse with a velvet lining and a diamond clasp
20 Christian slaves of which 6 are musicians, complete with instruments
16 Negroes, 4 Negresses, 10 baby Moors
1 magic lantern with glass and colored globes
1 service of Sèvres porcelain of 360 pieces
1 crystal ball with 12 goldfish
1 ton of Virginia tobacco
500 kilos of hashish
1 gold saber
2 bathtubs with 2 cylinders and 2 bath thermometers
10 tomahawks
1 Spanish rifle trimmed in silver by Provost
1 bronze cannon
A dagger in gold, scissors, mirrors, knives
A saber head in agate and diamonds
5 pairs of pistols, 3 pairs of gold spectacles
2 silver basins, of which one is in vermeil, a large soup bowl in gold-plated silver, twelve porcelain cups with saucers in gold-plated silver
500 repeating Winchester rifles with powder
6 measures of American cloth, 3 embossed in gold, 2 of velvet embroidered in silver
12 pieces of Holland linen
6 lions, 4 lion cubs and 40 lion skins
1 French coach by Allien Sellier and de Hache, harness-makers, on springs, lined in velvet with small blue bouquets, the paneling in dark lilac with its curtains, its tassels, its cockades, its mirrors and its harnesses from his most illustrious, most excellent and magnificent Omar Pasha, Dey of Algiers.

Without the voluminous turban, the hair on his head was dead white.

He laid down his pen, having finished checking the tardy, as usual, Algerian tribute. Edris Aga was tired. His thick heavy hands trembled with age as he stroked the white Persian cat in his lap and thought of the Kaaba. He believed that cats had souls, and so he spoke to his cat as a man. He told it of circling the sacred structure, in which was embedded the Black Stone, seven times, kissing it each time, then of walking to Jabal Arafat, twenty-five miles to the east, for a day of meditation. The lanterns glowed all night in the Kizlar Aga's apartments, for like all Egyptians he was afraid of the dark.

The light played around the sumptuous figure. A bit by malice, he coughed, he spat, he unfolded his embroidered handkerchief slowly, he blew his nose, he opened his tobacco pouch and fixed his pipe, waving away the young eunuch. And he heard his soul say between clenched teeth: *If history is short, the preliminaries are long. . . .*

He couldn't sleep. The world had changed for him.

And then he thought of something fascinating: that Man's power to adore was responsible for all crimes. The Black Eunuch thought of his own self-annihilation, the self-castration no one knew of. The *choice* of the act. He recognized it for what it was: a proselytism that revealed the beastly side of enthusiasm. He was a monster in the eyes of the world. And he would be a monster in *her* eyes, even if she knew of the choice. Just as he was a monster in all men's eyes—not only a fanatic, but a black fanatic.

The Black Eunuch stroked the softness of his cat's fur.

"O, Invisible One," whispered the Black Eunuch to the flickering lanterns, "how bloody are the hands that stroke one of Your creatures." How bloody with love, he thought. But love, he recalled, required genitals. And he had none. "O, Time!" he whispered, "of all the dwellers here below, only You elevate buffoons and fools or one whose mother was a whore, or whose anus was an inkstand, or who from his youth has been a procurer, or a eunuch who has no other work but to bring two sexes together! Oh, we Negroes have had our fill of women. We no longer fear their tricks, subtle as they be. Men confide to us what they cherish, but the truth is, oh you women, all, that you have no patience when it is the virile member you want! For in it resides your life and death, the end and all of your wishes, secret or open; your religion resides in your vulva and the phallus is your soul. . . .

"My cut body resides in the vestibule between men and women, the means of all rapport and the guarantee of its impossibility. I am the Other by which the two sexes define themselves. It is I who proceeds and announces, and I who recedes and recalls. And if castration is first, and the difference between the sexes second, then one becomes a man or a woman only in relation to me. One cannot say that a eunuch is neither a man nor a woman, no more than one can say that a eunuch *is* a man *and* a woman. A eunuch is simply the Other, the Invisible Man."

There had been many famous eunuchs in history, thought Edris. The shepherd Atys who castrated himself at the incitation of Cybele was his favorite. There was Hermotine, eunuch of Xerxes; Hermias, a disciple of Plato; Bagoa, the favorite of Alexander the Great; Halotus, the accomplice of Agrippina, mother of Nero, who poisoned her husband Claudius; Photius, preceptor of Ptolemy, Pharaoh of Egypt; Eutrope, the Emperor Theodosius's eunuch and preceptor for his son Arcadius, assassinated by the Empress Eudoxia. There had been Narses, General of Justinian, conqueror of Italy; Saint Germain Doroeus, Bishop of Antioch; Stavrakios, who blinded the son of Empress Irene on her orders and who cut out the tongues of four Caesars; Hassan, an Italian prisoner of war, who was castrated and converted to Islam and as Dey of Algiers defeated Charles V. There was the eunuch Ali, General of Sultan Suleiman II, who reconquered Hungary; and the theologian Abelard, castrated by the Canon of Notre Dame, as punishment for his passion for his niece Heloise. He, Edris Aga, was a zero of history.

The Kizlar Aga drew in a deep breath.

The Black Eunuch's journeys to Egypt and Mecca had given him a new perspective. His "reincarnation" as Kizlar Aga had caused a sort of fatalistic charisma to grow up around him in the palace. He used his power lightly now, his license to kill, judiciously. There was no God without virility and there was no virility without compassion. . . .

As long as man refused to admit the interchangeability of belief, blood would always flow.

And always in one direction, thought Edris Aga, from the weak toward the strong, like gravity.

His eunuchism he had chosen, nay embraced, with all the ardor and yearning of his love for Tityi. He could not say it made him happy, any more than he could say it made him sad. It was. That was all. It was his link to her. It was also his link to Faith and fanaticism. After all, he thought, wasn't "impossible love" the highest destiny? He imagined he heard the swift whispers of female voices, revealing by their questions and answers all the chronic intimacy of the Seraglio.

The Kaaba, its keys returned to Mahmud at last, still stood, but he, Edris Aga, had fallen. He had achieved the perfection he had always craved. He was *indifferent*. History, sex, religion had become for him a pack of false absolutes, a succession of counterfeit temples raised to false pretexts, a castration of the spirit confronted with the improbable. He was lost.

Tomorrow he would tell Mahmud and Naksh-i-dil that he no longer had the right to the keys of Mecca and Medina. That he had been rendered *impotent* by indifference. He wanted to go home to Egypt. He was tired. Weariness invaded even the rich folds of his silver-brocaded white pelisse that surrounded him like the peaks of white-capped mountains.

The Black Eunuch closed his eyes to sleep, intending to call out for Lily, his slave, but the fervor and bloody exploits of his heart had stopped its beating. He slumped forward, clutching at his turban to cover his head.

"O, Savior!" he cried out. "Have mercy on me!"

Of all the scandals the Black Eunuch had survived, there was one he could not escape: the scandal of death.

◆ CHAPTER TWO ◆

DIADEM OF THE VEILED HEADS 1814

Fortune is less blind than we imagine. It is largely the result of strong definite measures which pass unnoticed by the majority, which have gone before the event.

—CATHERINE II, *Publications*
de la société impériale
de l'histoire de Russie

The Valide put her hands over her face and wept. The tears escaped the prison of her gleaming fingers like the overflow of a bejeweled zarf. The death of Edris Aga had undone her. His loss had separated her from the life he had saved so often. The great, black empty space where there had been the Black Eunuch would never be filled in her heart.

If Euphemia David's prophecy had been the Table of Contents of her life, then she could now compile its Index: all the remnants of her fictional life, all the moral fetishes that haunted and obsessed her in her anonymous war against time. The burned hair of Bayazid, not yet cut and sent to Mecca. The pearl tespi of the strangled Halil Hamid. The amputated foot of Kiaya Kurrum. The proprietary soft hands of Hadidge. The foreskin of Mahmud on a silver platter. The bowstring slicing Mustafa's neck. Nezir Aga's hands around the jewels of Selim. The heel of Fatima's foot as it lifted itself in flight from the ramparts of Topkapi. The perfume of Ali Efendi's skin. The chorus of voci bianche of the Eski Serai. The scarred soul of Hitabetullah. The severed hands of Pakize. The hate-filled eyes of Angélique. The dry yellow palms of

Edris Aga. The mutilated body of Bayrakdar falling into a depthless well. Abdulhamid's overdose of aphrodisiacs. The soundless wings of the "damned souls." All annihilated by the roar, the snap, the boom, the rumble, the creak, the crash of Fires melting the myriad domes of Istanbul. . . .

Naksh-i-dil's fear of fire accepted no lanterns or candles burning at night in her rooms.

The darkness came, the stone-white face of Naksh-i-dil grayed under the fiery rouge, the magnificent green eyes became deranged. The trembling hands, the heat of her feverish breath, all transformed themselves into Belief: that Joséphine's death was the beginning of hers.

She had grown old having known only a capricious sojourn that had promised much but which, in the end, had given nothing in return except the vanity of Kings. Knowledge filled her now, a dark distinct knowledge of death, a preparation for death which removed all helplessness. She had lived forty lives and had lost Ali countless times. She had accumulated such experience of the heart, such experience of loss, of renouncement, of imprisonment, of solitude, of power, of murder, and of slavery, that nothing had any more sense now than the chorus of a Te Deum, or a monologue in a Greek tragedy, or a poem or a piece of music, or a yellow tile or a gilded dome, or a glass of pure water, or an illuminated Koran where the words clung together of themselves, unlike the Bible where each word was distinct, independent, isolated, immutable. The way God worked! The way he worked!

ELI, ELI LAMA SABACHTHANI!
O God, O God, why have you abandoned me!

She was the Mother of the State that had to be destroyed in order to be re-formed. She was the Mother of the Janissaries who must be destroyed in order for her to rule. She was the Mother of a God, Allah's Shadow on Earth, whose divinity Mahmud could no longer use as a hold on the people. She was the Mother of Moslem women and the harem which Mahmud no longer considered sacred. Mahmud had castrated the Valide . . . the *Matushka Gosudarynya.*

She was the Mother of no one.

◆ CHAPTER THREE ◆

ALI EFENDI 1814

Certainly the source of love is pure, but its Fanaticism is a monstrosity; it doesn't matter for what honorable motive someone has lost his reason; from this comes the dictate of Pythagoras: he who loves his wife with too much ardor resembles the adulterer . . . the impulse toward voluptuousness should not dominate him, nor should he precipitate head first towards copulation; nothing is more ignoble than to love a wife as one loves a mistress.

— ECCLESIASTICUS XX: 2–3

"**F**our hundred thousand French and seven hundred thousand Russians dead and not one Ottoman soldier lost makes you the greatest strategist in the Orient," Ali Efendi said to Naksh-i-dil, half jokingly.

"Oh, don't worry, my dearest. The English will get all the credit, not I or Mahmud. You see, they are the ones who write the history books. Every diplomat and statesman who puts pen to paper will each claim Mahmud's Treaty of Bucharest for himself."

She had turned to him. "You see, Ottomans, like women, don't write, let alone change, History. . . ."

Her voice had been bitter and resigned. "I not only do not write History, I do not have peace. . . ."

What more did she want from him? her Lieutenant asked himself. She was more Osmanli than the Osmanlis, more Islamic than the Prophet, more fanatical than the Grand Mufti, more in love than the object of her love. Yet there was neither pride in her Empire, Faith in her religion, nor love in her amorousness. And without this, Ali Efendi knew, she was doomed to unhappiness. For it was just this faith in Faith, this love of love, unthinking and unconscious and independent of one's own will, that bestowed true happiness. It was a fanaticism that produced joy. For it gave a kind of autosuggestion that one submitted to in spite of one's self and provoked that unreasonable passion to which one abandoned oneself. Fanaticism was one of the most dangerous, yet necessary, sentiments. But Naksh-i-dil was too Western to be a true fanatic . . . she would die for nothing of value, neither love nor Faith. If she renounced her Faith, then she could renounce her love. She deserved neither. And as much as he loved her, he was helpless to provide an impossible happiness from an impossible love.

Mustafa's murder and those of his wives had been a sickening mistake. She had saved Sineprever for that reason. One more life taken would have overflowed her cup.

"Why did you kill Mustafa when I saved Mahmud? You owe me the life of your son!" Sineprever had asked her.

"You never saved Mahmud, you simply failed to kill him. You killed Selim. You tried to kill Mahmud. That is the difference between you and me. I didn't fail," she had answered.

The Valide would never know that her logic and even her voice had been those of Czarina Catherine, Ali thought.

"What are you laughing at, Naksh-i-dil?" he asked. But she hadn't replied. . . .

The silent Ali Efendi walked respectfully beside Naksh-i-dil. He and Mahmud were united in one thing: the power of the Valide over the mind of one and the senses of the other.

It seemed like yesterday that she had looked into his eyes for the first time, thought Naksh-i-dil. But Ali was slipping away from her. He sided more and more with Mahmud against her. More and more, ambition ruled his days. His dazzling ascension was not unlike that of Bayrakdar. Like all young men, he didn't believe that death could come to him as she knew it would to her. And if ghosts roamed her bedroom at night, waked her with nightmares, he slept like a child, innocent of her grief, satiated with his power of love, while she burned.

"What are you laughing at Naksh-i-dil?" Ali asked again.

"Oh, nothing. Everything."

Ali Efendi watched the small silk-shod feet place themselves one before the other, heard the most beautiful voice in the Archipelago. Yet she was drawing away from him and everything he stood for: pleasure, joy, fulfillment. . . .

"That soon we will leave Topkapi behind us forever. That peace is made with Mecca. That Mahmud's black silk brocaded veil covers the Kaaba. That the keys to Mecca and Medina are once more in our possession. That our new Prince's curls have been cut and sent to that holy city. That my new palace is almost finished. That Dolmabahce will have real sofas and chairs, tables and silverware, balls and theater and receptions and musicians. . . . That it is 1814 and a new world is forming. . . . That I love thee more than I ever have. . . ."

His heart almost burst with pity, anger and passion for Naksh-i-dil. She still believed in magic when their only hope lay elsewhere. . . .

"Mother, Modest Lady, Crown of Noblewomen, Queen of Queens, Diadem of the Veiled Heads, to whom all happiness and honor are obedient, may your purity reign eternal!" whispered Ali.

They smiled conspiratorially, but they didn't embrace.

"Adieu, my Lady, it is time for prayers."

"Adieu, my love, do thy duty."

Then they had taken leave of each other.

The Molid-en-Nebi, which marked the end of Ramadan, always finished with a performance of the Doseh. Ali Efendi sat beside Mahmud in the lavish embroidered tent of the Sultan and witnessed the spectacle. The Saadiyeh dervishes, called whirling dervishes by the watching Europeans, were near the end of their ceremony. Drunk with opium, fasting and praying, rolling their heads and foaming at the mouth, they had begun to lie down upon the ground by the hundreds, packed close as paving stones, to be walked and ridden on by a holy procession. First came the standard bearers, then a priest reading the Koran aloud, then the Sheykh, their Aga, on a white Arabian horse led by barefoot priests. Ali Efendi watched as the Sheykh rode over the pavement of prostrate dervishes. He noticed that the beautiful horse trod with evident reluctance (horses, he knew, were notoriously unwilling to tread on living flesh), as lightly and as swiftly as possible on the human causeway under their hooves. The dervishes claimed that no one was ever injured or even bruised on this holy occasion, but Ali Efendi saw men carried away in convulsions who looked as if they would never walk again. He turned away, but at that moment Mahmud, who had been nervous and restless throughout the ceremony, stopped him from rising by grasping his shoulder.

"Ali," he began, "I have received a message for you from my mother
. . . I am told she has locked herself in her new palace for good, and
her eunuchs have drawn their swords . . ."

"What?"

"She has vowed never to come out again. Ali, I'm sorry. More than
you can know. . . . My mother . . . our mother is not well. You have
. . . *we* have known this for some time. *She* has known it."

Mahmud thought of the past years of illness and depression, of hysterical sieges and incomprehensible behavior, of the endless train of
doctors and medicines. He thought also of the devotion and passion of
the man she had chosen as her favorite. He had never understood her
cruelty to him. She had denied Ali his very nature in the arrogance and
passion of her love for him. Why?

"But she would never leave you, Mahmud!" Ali Efendi blurted.

"Ah, but she *has* left me, because she has left you . . . she has left
us both," said Mahmud bitterly. He would never, never forgive her.

Ali Efendi felt the world swirl around him as if he were one of the
dervishes now prostrate on the field before him. He imagined his head,
severed from his body, his wide, surprised eyes open, a skull nailed to
the Gate of Bab-i-humayun. He tried to utter a sound, but only a low
moan, half sob, half breath, shot out into the dense, rich atmosphere of
Mahmud's royal pavilion.

"You are free, Ali," said Mahmud.

"I will never be free," said Ali Efendi.

"She loved you, but she was unfair. She used her love like a tyrant
over us both. . . . She demanded the impossible . . ."

"You say loved, Lord," said Ali, shaken, "as if she were dead . . ."

But Mahmud wasn't finished.

"I shall keep you always by my side, Ali. I swear. For her sake, every
honor is yours—every gift is her giving. You will always be Naksh-i-
dil's favorite."

"But I don't want . . ."

Mahmud turned away so as not to see the other man's face. He
handed his Lieutenant General the letter from his mother.

My last word to you is folded lengthwise and knotted, neither
scented nor sealed, we are beyond that. We no longer exchange
gifts, our memories are too good. Our words are no longer the
language of love. We are clear of all courtesy and politeness. We
know only that whatever the hour, it is too late. Whatever the

place, it is too far. Whatever the need, it is not enough. Whatever the love, it is too great. For too much love like too much rain begets large and bloody puddles of discontent. My Winter is marked in your face. Whoever told you I was perfection?

Naksh-i-dil stood, her feet planted apart, clinging to the pillar of the canopy above her head as the sudden violent vertigo that seized her more and more often made the room swirl in a vortex of texture and color. Her whole body was braced as if the chaloup that had brought her to Topkapi was once again cutting through an angry, cyclonic sea. If she was going to die, she thought, she would die on her feet, not reclining on a harem sofa. The Valide resembled more a man than a woman, despite the livid color of her rouged cheeks, her hennaed hair, loose and streaming almost to the floor, her kohled, disordered eyes. One of her slaves held a cushion to her head, another under her feet, while two terrified eunuchs pulled the cords of the rectangular-shaped fan suspended over her.

"Oh, God, Nothing But What You Are! O Al-Mumît!" she cried out.

Even in her suffering, the Valide's brilliant will to live matched at least her will to die. The vortex swept past her like a giant brush over a decor of bright fabric, ermine coverlets, tapestries, brocades of silk, flowered curtains. Each detail was marvelously illuminated: The Queen's scarlet, fevered cheeks, the gold gauze of her dullimano, the cashmere scarfs and shawls thrown carelessly about, the sumptuous painted tiles. Yet it was her face that most truly reflected the cruel, autocratic, prideful, egocentric Queen she had become: a woman who refused to die.

The Valide's mind filled with images. She passed abandoned kiosks sad as graves, and gardens silent as death. She climbed and descended. Doors opened and closed without cease. She heard the swish of silk. She passed arches and small porches resounding with the sound of childish laughter. Something of her . . . all of her world lingered behind these walls, languishing forever in the air she breathed. She gazed upon women, shouted innumerable names, called them once, a hundred times, and heard some voice reply somewhere, far away.

She passed ten days and ten nights thus. She refused the medicines of her doctors. She refused to be led to bed or to lie down.

She sat now, with her beautiful Persian poses, her green eyes, veiled by their long silken eyelashes, fixed on the Marmara Sea, a ferocious jealousy shadowing her pale and melancholy face, resplendent in jewels, covered with wounds, moribund, transfigured by the long agony. She had left behind her only a long trail of withered flowers, tears and droplets of blood. Fire. The wooden tambours resounded under the blows of the alert, and shouts mingled with the thunder of drums. She had entered the last harem.

There remained only a passionate longing to erase everyone: her "people," who revered her as Empress, her Agas, Grand Viziers, Ulemas, Pashas, magistrates, priests, bankers, eunuchs, slaves, armorers, soldiers, Generals, even her son. . . . And Ali? She felt a forsakenness and a revolt beyond her passion for Ali. She had awakened from a grand dream which for thirty-five years had lifted her out of the world of her ancestors. But like the Basilica of Santa Sophia, which had been transformed into the mosque Aya Sofya, enduring its ornamental transformation without ever having changed its form or its foundations, her soul, that vast blue dome that had changed from cross to crescent, was still intact. The vertigo was nothing more than the foundations of her life shifting like sand because she had trod not on Absolute Faith but on Absolute Power, an empire of bondage that had become too small, its splendors, worthless, its grief bottomless. Ali had become the last intrusion of destiny in all its despotic meaninglessness. She had lived a moment of accomplished passion, where love verges on hatred and only the soul makes the decision between them.

The Queen had taken a great retinue with her into the palace, and they stood now in the huge hall, frozen in wonder at the Empress who refused to die. And she did not die for many years. But the doors of her palace remained closed to her son and to her favorite forever.

Often she sat in her old, deep window seat that framed the right angles of an endless sofa which encircled the entire light-drenched room, seated under a pale rose canopy that stirred in the airless room. Alone, she sat cross-legged, in the posture of the harem, rouged and jeweled and emaciated with fever, her water pipe leaning carefully against the low table, her gauze turban glistening with draped pearls; she backed into time and space as if washed up by the multilayered sea of shimmering Persian carpets that had flooded her into a corner.

From her lonely Sanctuary, like an invisible abbess, she stood vigil over the Empire she had renounced: solitary, serene, deranged, stupendous, superb. *Diadem of the Veiled Heads.*

She had lived a moment of accomplished passion in this strange Oriental world where love had verged on hatred and only the soul had made the decision between them.

She leaned her head against the marble wall, for it was warm. Beyond the fever or the month of August. Yonder to her left, through the barred window, another ship glided by. She turned her heavy turbaned head carefully to gaze after it.

In the Bosphorus new ships made ready, while others ran to harbor with shortened sails.

EPILOGUE

BAŞHOCA
· 1839 ·

The pictures used to seem exaggerations, they seemed too weird and fanciful for reality. But behold, they were not wild enough. They have not told half the story.

—MARK TWAIN, 1867

Report to the President
from
M. Shaler, Consul of the United States of America,
The War Department

The late war between the United States and the Barbary States

The people of the Coast of Barbary, even the Algerians, having committed great depredations upon the commerce of Columbia [The United States of America] and the Congress of the United States, declared war upon them in 1812.

Algiers stands where the river Euphrates emptied into the Gulf of Persia about 6,666 miles east of Washington, our capital of the United States of America. On May 15, 1815, I sailed from New York with a punitive expedition destined to back up peace talks between myself and the Dey of Algiers.

The fleet sent out as captained by Admiral Decatur and Captain Bainbridge, consisting of light ships, included the "Guerriere," commanded by Decatur, the "Macedonian," and the "Constellation." The first ship was named after a British ship, the "American Hull," which had burned; the "Macedonian" had been captured from the British by Admiral Decatur. The fleet, consisting of the brig the "Eperveer," the sloop the "Ontario," and completed by the schooners "Torch," "Chauncy," "Spitfire" and "Dallas," sailed from New York in May and arrived in thirty days. Admiral Decatur first fell in with and chased an Algerian corsair [the "Americana"]. In the space of a half hour, he took her with the five-hundred-man crew. Thirty of the Algerians were slain.

Admiral Decatur suffered no deaths. Four hundred prisoners were taken. The second day, Admiral Decatur captured another

Algerian fighting vessel, the "Massoda," killed twenty-three men and took four hundred prisoners.

Decatur sailed to Algiers. Decatur demanded the American hostages without ransom and ten thousand pieces of silver and gave the Dey three hours to answer. The Dey delivered up the American slaves, paid the money, signed the treaty.

Admiral Decatur made a present of the ship "Massoda" to the Dey. Decatur then sailed to Tunis and demanded of the Bey four thousand pieces of silver under threat of bombarding Tunis. From Tunis Decatur sailed to Tripoli, demanded of the Bashaw of Tripoli thirty thousand pieces of silver. The Bashaw at first refused, then after threats of bombardment paid almost the full price plus ten Christian slaves.

After Decatur came Bainbridge, who arrived after peace had been made and returned home after sailing around the coast. The British arrived in Algiers in April 1816 under Lord Exmouth and demanded the release of British slaves. The Dey demanded five hundred pieces of silver for every slave. Lord Exmouth paid the ransom for about five Christian slaves.

Affixed:
The seal of the United States
June 30, 1815
22 Redjeb, 1230

Decatur's Treaty
with
The Dey of Algiers
James Madison,
President of the United States

Treaty of peace and amity concluded between the U.S.A. and His Highness Omar Bashaw, Dey of Algiers.
James Monroe, Secretary of State   James Madison

Friday, December 26, 1815

Of the thirty Algerians slain, Reis Hamidou was among them.

August 15, 1837, Istanbul

"Oh, she must have come out. She must have: to supervise the building of her mausoleum which took two years; to see the doctors who could not cure her; to see her new grandson, the hereditary Prince; to stand between Europe and Asia, between the Occident and the Orient, between the Prophet Mohammed and the Prophet Jesus (the blessings of Allah be upon him), between two worlds, the East and the West, between despotism and bondage, between the power of love and the love of power; to watch the stars, to breathe the night-blooming jasmine, and listen to her failing heart as she stared out at the sea on which nothing can be seen without being seen and nothing is ever erased. . . .

"She must have," repeated the Başhoca, his eyes holding those of the young American Orientalist who had traveled so far to see him.

Başhoca Efendi was a Jew converted to Islam. He was the greatest scholar and mathematician the Ottoman Empire had yet produced. He was famous even in America. He spoke perfect Arabic, Persian, Russian and French. As the Başhoca, prefect of studies at the Mathematical School of Istanbul founded by Mahmud in 1816, he had written the greatest tract on modern mathematics in Osmanli. Yet the story he had just recounted to the astonished young American traveler had nothing to do with any science, unless, thought the young man, there was a science of slavery and passion.

"Nine years after her death, Naksh-i-dil had her revenge," the Başhoca said.

"The Janissaries, her spiritual sons, were exterminated to the last man on the night of the fourteenth of June, 1826, the Auspicious Event, the Vakayi Hayriye. . . . The Janissaries overturned their soup caldron in the sign of revolt. But this time, Mahmud was ready. Mahmud rejected the demands of the Corps and abolished them. The Prophet's Sacred Banner was unfurled, and a curse and sentence of eternal dissolution on the Janissaries was pronounced. A fetva was obtained from the Sheykh-ul-Islam giving his blessing, and the attack commenced by the Nizam-attick. The guns played terrible havoc in the narrow streets. Those who escaped the artillery or the sword were burned in their barracks. But even then Mahmud was not satisfied. The rest took refuge in the Cistern of the one thousand Columns, where a pitched battle in the dark took place. The fountains of Istanbul ran blood.

"The Bosphorus was strewn with thousands of them. Their white bonnets bobbed in the waves. The people in Istanbul had no water to drink, for the reservoir was clogged with cadavers."

"It was the beginning of modern Turkey," said the young American, "the work of Naksh-i-dil's son, Mahmud the Reformer."

The Başhoca was silent.

But Mahmud was also known as Mahmud the Bloody. In the end
Mahmud executed his longtime favorite, Ali Efendi, just before he himself died, like his mother, mad, solitary, refusing to see his family. Mahmud had killed Ali Efendi as if to erase the last remnant of love and
loyalty, for Ali had served Mahmud until the last, refusing to desert
him even in the face of his capricious, bloodthirsty behavior. Mahmud
had accused Ali of treason—of revealing the Sultan's epilepsy, which he
had learned of from Naksh-i-dil, thus betraying her last wishes, the
wishes of a Valide whose monuments, hospitals and mosques are everywhere.

The young man sitting cross-legged beside the tall Turk was silent.
The Başhoca's brilliant eyes gazed at him under lowered lids. He realized he had dropped off to sleep and wondered if the young man had
noticed or was simply being polite. The Başhoca was a splendid figure
of a man, seated on his cushioned podium. His once-black beard was
now an honorable white and reached to his waist; the green taffeta robes
he wore were peaked and folded like mountains and valleys. He clung
to his old-fashioned dress, including his pelisse and his gauze turbans,
even though Mahmud had declared that all functionaries should wear
the fez and trousers and frockcoat. He didn't dress like a Jew either, in
color or in cut, a detail rarely noticed, since all red costumes had been
abolished. He sat with one leg folded under him and the other bent in
front of his chest on which he rested his notebooks. One yellow papoosh
peeked from beneath his blue-striped skirts. He wore a sable pelisse, too
warm for the day and for the room, thought the journalist, but then the
professor was an old, old man.

The Başhoca, seated on the gracious yellow divan, was smoking now
a huge amber-headed pipe. He was thinking of a night long, long ago,
on the little frigate, when the archangel Michael, Kuchuk, Zorich,
Hamidou, Cosima . . . when everyone had still been alive. . . . Suddenly the Başhoca was startled from his motionless position by a noise
resembling that which precedes an earthquake. A dense cloud as black
as ink was rapidly approaching from the southwest, accompanied by
low, rumbling thunder and an indescribable rushing sound impossible
to identify. The young man and the old scholar rushed to the windows.
In the course of a few minutes, hailstones the size of melons had begun
to fall. The entire surface of the Bosphorus, as far as the eye could see,
resembled an army of decapitated heads splashing like a million fountains on the smooth surface of the water. From their position, they
could see the tiled roofs of Istanbul smash like glass. They heard hun-

dreds of panes of glass shatter into thousands of pieces in a few moments. The storm didn't exceed a half-mile in breadth, and it passed over Constantinople, Galata and Pera as if the angry hand of God had released a fistful of giant gaming pawns that smashed windows, unroofed domes, stripped trees and killed two men. Suddenly it was over.

"Who was Naksh-i-dil?" asked the young journalist.

Başhoca Ishak Bey, who had hidden for thirty years as a Jew, who had changed Faiths four times, who had been born in a country where family names didn't exist, turned to the young American and said:

"Names are the purest of all accidents."

But he wondered just the same which name Naksh-i-dil had whispered to the archangels?

Now praise and glory be to Him who
sits throned in eternity above the
shifts of time; who, changing all things
remains Himself unchanged . . . And blessings
and peace be upon His chosen Messenger,
the Prince of Apostles, our master
Mohammed, to whom we pray
for an auspicious
END